How To *Swindle* a Scoundrel

Hardback ISBN13:978-1-7338845-9-4

Paperback ISBN: 979-8-9904789-0-9

Ebook ISBN: 979-8-9904789-1-6

Library of Congress Control Number: 2024907549

Evil Goddess
— Press —

How To Swindle a Scoundrel

A Chaos Dragons Adventure

Dalila Caryn

For the woman with the triple rainbow smile.
I wasn't looking for you, but you inspired a vibrant new realm of adventure. This one gets gay!

Cast of characters:

Shiraz—(shee-RAHZ) sarcastic world traveler, thief, smuggler, avid reader, basically on her way to Ooloo'a.

Xinyi—(sin-yee) "perky, positive *princess*", orphan, war widow, mystery author of *Immortal Hunger.*

Makoa—(mah-KOH-ah) easygoing con-artist, thief, smuggler, cursed into shape shifting.

Golden Paw Gang:—monkey thieves

    Scabber —violent.

    Sweetums —sweet smile, fast hands.

    Screecher — all bark.

Nanghi— (naan-gee) "god of death" and namesake of the river, alligator body —very lazy.

Nuan—(nu-an) trickster "goddess" of friendship and mischief.

Feng—(f-uu-ng) trickster "god" of romance and irony.

Dao—(d-ow) commander of the elf kings royal guard, dry sense of humor.

Felicia—(fe-li-cia) demigoddess, abandonment and temper issues, dragon shifter.

Kookaburra —(koo-kuh-br-uh) skin slipping fey woman with a playful personality.

Euphemia Precocious Arrow—(yoo-fee-mee-uh) nudist witch of some centuries.

Candelaria Maidenhair Widget—(kahn-deh-lAH-ree-uh) *friendly* witch of less centuries.

Hua—(h-w-ah) ogre, chef, friend of Shiraz and Makoa.

Aiattaua —(EYE-ah-tao-ah) an elf prince, lover of all, spouse to fifteen.

The Immortal Elf King —self explanatory, giant slut though.

Daiyu—(dye-you) crown elf princess valiantly holding family together.

Pekoe —(pee-kow) an elf princess oft forgotten, wrestler in training.

Halimah—(ha-LEE-mah) an elf princess, creator of a bubble universe.

Larissa—(luh-rih-suh) short tempered, accountant for the city of Reyes, daughter of a witch.

Qiu—(chew) fearless five-year-old collects animals, daughter of Yinuo.

Yinuo—(yee- nuow) mother of Qiu, princess, daughter of deposed King Guo.

Mei— (may) war widow, community builder, sells *Immortal Hunger*.

Jian—(jhee-ahn) character from Xinyi's stories.

Kinmei—(kin-mei) character from Xinyi's story.

V—villain from Xinyi's story.

Varen—(vah-ren) character from the fairy tales of human folly.

Hikari —(hee-KAR-ee) friend of Makoa, a witch.

Miti —(me-tee) friend of Makoa, a fairy.

Aegis—(ee-juhs) child of the elf king, wrestler.

Riku—(ree-koo) an elf prince.

Uwizeye —(uwiz-eye) an elf prince.

Vui —(VUW-yi) an elf princess.

Zeynep —(z-AI-n-eh-p) an elf princess.

Morag —(MAOR-aeG) an elf princess.

Content warning:

The text lightly addresses such issues as abandonment, orphans, religious trauma, grief, near drowning, and murder.

Thriving, Albeit Illegally

At the moment Shiraz didn't look like the sort of woman who wore pink. Her blue tunic vest and green trousers were slightly dirty as she'd unloaded a shipment of manure and mulch early this morning before racing up the river to the market. And her sweaty hair was either clinging limply to her neck or frizzing chaotically. Since she tended to run hot, her arms were bare, showing off her muscles, a bruise, two scars and a tattoo. She was possibly the last person one would expect to be pining after a delicate finished jacket in pink silk with deep sheer sleeves embroidered with wicked birds and soft flowers. And that suited her purposes perfectly.

She didn't even look at it after the first glance. It was too large for her, but that had rarely stopped her; she would make something new of it. Maybe a loose vest, and the sleeves could become a sheer hood. She loved pink. It was bright and alive and reminded her of making moonflower crowns for herself and Tabby to wear, if only in secret.

Shiraz focused on some, also very pretty, blue silk, well aware that the proprietress of the fabric booth was tracking her hands, not in fear of theft, but of her grubby hands touching the lovely fabric. Rude.

Shiraz knew many women thrived in polite, ordered, *oppressive* societies. She liked a few. Loved one. But she had never managed to cultivate the same skills. Those women knew how to set someone like this at ease. They would smile, and apologize for their dirtiness, gush over her wears. And the proprietress would assist them happily.

But if they didn't have the funds, they would leave—*without the jacket*. Why set her at ease if you weren't going to get what you wanted? She could never figure it out.

A woman walked by the booth, carrying several bundles, *helpful*. Shiraz nudged a hooked pole, used to collect packages from the boats along the river. It fell to the ground between the woman's feet, tripping her. Shiraz jumped forward and caught her, but her packages scattered. The fabric vendor raced around her booth to help. The stranger and the vendor collected the packages, as Shiraz, after accepting the woman's thanks, quietly took her leave, wondering how long it would take the fabric vendor to miss the pink jacket currently rolled up in her bag.

She grinned, thinking of the women she'd grown up with. All of them taught that people like Shiraz suffered for their villainy. They would expect her to be a friendless, unhappy outcast, constantly punished for breaking societal rules. She doubted they would believe her if she told them there were women who thrived in chaotic, unordered, *unlawful* freedom. Thrived. She was thriving. This was exactly the life she'd always wanted.

She just—needed to move on. The charms of every new land wore off after a while.

Loqwan had held a special draw for her, but after five years waiting, through *a war,* her petition to enter the Great Library of Wehu had officially been rejected last month. The world's largest library really ought to be public, or at least be able to withstand a visit from *one* foreigner. Even if the dragon librarians couldn't "locate her background references" and they appeared "fictitious." If she'd known they would actually check references, she obviously would have used real ones. Joan Wilder, Regina Lampert, and Evelyn O'Connell just sounded like women she could have some fun with. Apparently the librarian dragons didn't feel the same.

But at least her boat was nearly perfect. A few more big scores and she could get her last spell to make the hull resistant to lava. Something she'd learned she needed the hard way; *azaqif, Felicia.* Once she had the spell, she could once again set sail for Ooloo'a and slip between the lava spouts surrounding the chain's three smallest islands. She'd been on her way to Ooloo'a and its Singing Hills basically her entire adult life. But something or other always got in her way. So this was it. One last spell. One last chance. She would go, and she *would* find the Singing Hills. Or she was done searching.

Anyway—she needed a new horizon, with new opportunities and challenges. She was bored of traveling the same route. Once a new government was established, people like her would be branded criminals. She should leave before that. But she needed that spell.

Shiraz paused her meandering path through the Nanghi River market, leaning over a flat boat to sniff a display of fruit. She had her hands behind her back, but a child rushed by carrying a mewling animal and knocked Shiraz forward. She struck the boat, shaking it. She threw her arms out with a gasp to stop a pile of sweet stone fruit from falling into the river. And, as was only fair, slipped two pieces of said fruit into the loose bag at her side without anyone the wiser.

With everything ordered again, she made to move away, but the proprietor, an elderly man with a mischievous smile, stopped her.

"For your trouble." He held out a fruit.

"I couldn't." Shiraz held up her hands in embarrassed refusal.

"I insist. It is *no more than you deserve.*" He winked.

"Oh, you are too kind." With a brow raised at the odd choice of words, Shiraz accepted the third free piece of fruit. It was the polite thing to do. This one she raised to her lips and bit into as she walked away. It was juicy and soft, perfect. It sprayed her face as she bit in. The tangy sweetness tickled her skin, pulling her mind into the past.

Varen dug his teeth eagerly into the fruit. When its juices raced down his face, he slipped out his tongue lapping up the sweetness so not a single drop could escape him.

The creature before him watched with wildly flashing eyes as the man sealed his own fate. When the last bit of sweet magic and wonder was swallowed, Varen felt the power rushing through him. It tingled from the tip of his tongue racing down his throat and from there into every edge of his being, delighting his senses with wonder. He felt warm. Wild. Alive as never before. Every vessel in his being alert.

Then came the pain.

Varen cried out in shock as a tiny prick of pain stabbed at his tongue. Then again he cried. And again. Pain raced through his entire being as the power had.

"Help!" Varen begged the hungry deity before him. But the creature only smiled. And smiled and smiled so wide that the rest of its familiar face disappeared and all that could be seen was a wide, glowing maw of teeth and the slick journey of a tongue across them.

Varen fell to the ground, groaning in agony. But his agony had only begun. The creature dived on him teeth first and devoured Varen, answering his wish: to be consumed by magic.

Shiraz laughed, recalling *Varen's Folly*. She'd loved the ghoulish tales best in her youth. Stories of humans so desperate for magic they caused themselves, and the world, terrible catastrophes trying to get it. That one came from a collection of tales written by fairies about foolish humans. Shiraz had wanted so badly for all of it to be true, even the ghoulish deaths. All of the wonder. Because when she met fairies, when one of them struck up a friendship with her and gave her that book, they seemed so...ordinary. Yes, their ears pointed at the tips, and a few had wings. But other than a few features that were unordinary on her island home, and some more open customs like varied clothing, and women allowed in trade, and magical stories! Other than that, they seemed like normal people. And most everyone she knew insisted that was so. But Shiraz wanted different, wanted adventure, wanted magic, and she was willing to trade every single thing she had in order to find it. Just like Varen.

"Even if magic is real. To go seeking it is to ask the world to crush you," Shiraz's last conversation with Tabby echoed in her thoughts. *"Asking it to show you how small you are. To offer you wonders and trick you into pain. That is what all of your stories are about."*

Shiraz tossed aside the inner seed from the fruit, ignoring the feeling that Tabby was partially right, with the thought that this fruit, unfortunately, held no magic wish. But she missed entirely the mischievous smile on the fruit boat proprietor's face and his own... perhaps...flashing eyes.

The pit rolled across the ground, tripping a local man with his arms full. He kicked the seed near to a tree dripping with vines as he tumbled into Shiraz. She kindly lightened his load, lifting his purse before setting him right and going on her way. Ha. The fruit seller was right; the fruit was what she deserved.

The Nanghi river market was hardly the most impressive market that Shiraz frequented, even within the region. The market at Bonma, facing the sea, was far larger and had a wider variety of products. The market in Lu was of a similar size to this one but held more intriguing and magical offerings. To the eyes of most travelers, the Nanghi River market was just another local "village" market. Its stalls mostly sold food or necessary items such as dishes, cloth, and tools. But to Shiraz, the market had four special draws:

One, the market was unique. Being held along the river, half the booths were large skiffs or even rafts moored at the river's edge, drifting from side to side with the current. Patrons would stand along the shore and shout to the proprietors, haggling over their goods. That was reason number two, the sheer volume of the market and that it had *its own particular music*. A music Shiraz had heard nowhere else in her nearly fifteen years of travel. She loved it. And that noise provided excellent cover for her secondary source of income.

Twirling around a pair of crisscrossing travelers, Shiraz happened to grab the gentleman's purse, slipping it secretly into her own bag with the sound covered by the volume of the market. He was well compensated for his coin, as Shiraz deposited the female traveler he'd been gawking at all day in his arms in exchange. The foreigners gazed at one another, wide eyed, hearts beating so hard their pulses could be seen at their throats, and Shiraz could easily imagine their thoughts: *this was fate*. Nothing but fate could have pushed them together.

Nonsense.

Shiraz managed to restrain the shout: *there is no such thing as fate.* Unless of course she was fate's hand. She did however, generously, offer a lesson in having more prudence, by stealing (some) money from the woman's purse. She hated to leave a woman without resources in a foreign land. Things could get dangerous for those foolish women who did not think ahead. Especially in a place this restless.

The nation of Loqwan was in a momentary armistice, but the civil war that gripped and divided them for five years was far from settled. This market being so near the newly established borders between northeast, northwest, and south Loqwan was reason C that drew Shiraz. It held a fair amount of trade for Shiraz's primary business: secret travel and delivery. Sometimes better known as smuggling.

Yes, it would amaze the girls she had grown up with to know all that Shiraz had accomplished, albeit illegally. They wouldn't believe a woman capable of such things. Even she would have doubted women could do all this. She'd learned a lot of things in fifteen years.

Her first thefts may have occurred before she left the island, and her first housebreaking, lawbreaking, and even the very first of her smuggling adventures. But she hadn't gotten good at any of it until she left. Now she had a reputation, a partner in crime and a life of her own making. Yes. She was thriving. That's what this bored, constantly annoyed, empty feeling was. Thriving.

Shiraz spotted her favorite market seller, reason number four that she loved this market: a flat blue boat with a canopy over the top and a painted screen depicting a woman emerging from the Nanghi river as a back wall. A woman worked diligently in the shade stringing the pages of the newest installment of *Immortal Hunger*. By far Shiraz's favorite thing she'd found in Loqwan. She raced forward with a smile to spend some of her recently acquired funds. She never stole from this boat; it wasn't worth risking not being welcomed back. Because this boat sold the greatest source of magic in the world. This boat sold stories!

The Proper Victim of a Bad Luck Curse

This was all Xinyi's fault.

Well, some of it was the fault of the thieves. But she should have expected something like this was coming. It was how her bad luck curse worked. Whenever she was comfortable, whenever she felt safe and loved, her fingers began to twitch with new ideas, stories formed in her mind rather than on her page, and disaster always followed.

Xinyi leaned into the fabric booth. She had neither the need nor spare funds to buy fabric. Most of the clothing she wore were salvaged from things left behind in the palace. That was why her gowns were overly ornate and somehow both too tight and too long.

Anyway, what Xinyi needed was information. She imagined herself as a spy, leaning in conspiratorially, and dropping her voice low and casual. "What a lovely boat that is." She indicated an unfamiliar vessel bobbing among other boats on the Nanghi river. "Are you familiar with it? Are they here often?"

The booth keeper was a local, but Hi'mau was not so small that Xinyi knew everyone. Not having bought fabric since before the war began, Xinyi only knew the woman by sight. The vendor observed Xinyi critically. Her hands rested heavily on her most expensive fabric and her tone was wary, perhaps even annoyed. "It is the first I have noticed it, princess."

She was being suspicious already, wasn't she? Xinyi rushed away. But she could do this. She just had to somehow avoid getting remarked upon, avoid seeing Mei and her children selling installments of *Immortal Hunger* near the end of the market. Find the smuggler, find—

Avoid!

Xinyi threw herself between two booths. One wobbled loudly as she slammed her right hip into it, hard. Why were they so close together? She peeked out at the man she was avoiding, her father in law. But it wasn't him.

Of course not. He never went to the market. He had servants for that. For all Xinyi knew, the whole family had gone north with other loyalists to the king and were in the newly established capitol. Anyway, there was no reason to hide; he would have refused to acknowledge her presence anyway.

Breathing out carefully, Xinyi peeked through her eyelashes. The booth proprietors on either side of her were staring in concern. *Focus,* she told herself. *You are a spy. You are stealthy. Focus on the mission.*

Find the smugglers. Find the thieves. Get your treasure back before evening. Breakfast at the latest. Then everything would be fine. She could be quiet, safe, sweet Xinyi, forever.

Turning sideways, Xinyi whispered her apologies and ventured forth. Stealthily. Alright she still shook the tables a bit as she squeezed out. How did anyone move between them gracefully? Perhaps when she had her treasure back, she would do as Yinuo suggested and participate in the combat training the princess gave to the other women. She could stand to be more agile. Xinyi hadn't thought it her thing; it looked sweaty, uncomfortable. Anyway, she hated wasting her time and she was unlikely ever to be involved in combat. She far preferred writing, creating fictional combat, where it was safe and required much less exertion.

In recent months, for the first time since Wei died, Xinyi had started to feel happy. Happy enough that she'd imagined adventures beyond the type she wrote for Jian. Fun adventures. Not just fighting and grief and momentary respites. Surely Jian would like a break.

So even though Xinyi knew she should have been working on Jian's next adventure, she hadn't been. She'd been doing something new. Something secret. And the universe took notice, stealing the thing she'd forgotten to cherish. Threatening every bit of peace she'd found.

Well, that was more melodramatic than accurate. But it would threaten her comfort. And her ability to work on her new project!

Yinuo's daughter Qiu ran by with what appeared to be a panther kitten in her arms headed towards the palace. Xinyi stifled a laugh and ducked, pretending to examine a display of copper pots. She didn't want the girl alerting her mother to what Xinyi was up to. But it was difficult not to stop her and ask about her new, dangerous pet.

Five-year-old Qiu was convinced that no animal liked to live outdoors, and she had a curious affinity to animals. A few had even protected her from kidnappers. So no one stopped her from rescuing her menagerie. The crumbling palace now held, in addition to several families, a few snakes, three birds, several lizards, a pair of monkeys and now a panther. It was getting crowded!

"May I help you, princess?" A man came around his booth, his tone implying clearly that she could not afford anything he sold.

He wasn't wrong. The locals called all the women in the palace princesses but it was not accurate. They were five war widows, their various children, and a few stragglers like Xinyi who lived together in the ruins of the deposed king's summer palace. Slowly restoring it so they no longer had to share one room per family. There was always a new family at the palace gates with nowhere else to go. And Yinuo, the true princess among them, promised shelter to them all.

Now Xinyi's greatest treasure was stolen. How was she to prove her worth among them? How was she to contribute? And help keep Qiu fed and protected? Qiu and her menagerie were half Xinyi's inspiration for her new project. But she wouldn't have the time or the funds to work on it without her treasure.

"All are welcome in our community. Just yourself, Xinyi, that is all we require," Yinuo insisted.

And she meant it. But things always changed. Space in the palace was dwindling. Xinyi had a full room to herself. She had been contributing by slowly selling her treasure in secret, but clearly someone had gotten wind of its true nature and size. It was her only contribution. She knew nothing of farming, nor rebuilding. She played with the children and provided what money she could.

Also—*selfishly*—Xinyi wanted her treasure back for herself. She made it. She collected it from the air, from her dreams and her life. It was her. Xinyi had new ideas, but that didn't mean she'd stopped loving the woman who led her out of her grief.

Xinyi stood once Qiu was far enough away. "I do not need a pot." She smiled hopefully at the man. "But might you have information about the River Serpent?"

"I do. He's a coldhearted smuggler. Knows all the secret ways through the new border, for a price. Zan might know more; he thinks the River Serpent brought the kidnappers who tried to take Princess Qiu." The man stretched out his hand after delivering the information.

Clasping his hand was too small a thanks. Xinyi hugged the man. "Thank you, you are helping me to preserve my family! Which is Zan?"

The man looked both startled and annoyed; perhaps he did not like hugs. But he pointed to a nearby boat laden with fish, and Xinyi rushed away. She could do this. She knew she could.

She had been asking about the thieves since they left with her treasure. No one knew who they were, but they knew who could get in and out of the now divided country without suspicion. The *River Serpent*. A proper villain name.

Zan did appear to know more, and the fish seller invested his story with more intrigue. She should speak to him again when all of this was over. "No two people describe the River Serpent alike. But…the Serpent is in Hi'mau every time one of Jian's adventures is released."

Why would a smuggler care about the release of a serialized romantic story?

"Perhaps he's the mystery author," Zan joked.

It was an unacceptable insult. Xinyi had to dig a finger into the bruise on her hip to keep from saying as much. Had to force a smile and play along or expose her secret. "Oh, how exciting." It left a sour taste in her mouth. How did anyone countenance lying?

What if the smuggler and the theft of her story were connected?

They would be if she were writing it. The smuggler might also be an information broker, who, having discovered Xinyi's secret, sold it to the thieves. *Or* the smuggler might *be* the thief! Either way he was her best chance at finding them. She would just have to put aside that he was a vile creature who'd assisted thieves and kidnappers. Helped someone sneak into her home and escape with her greatest treasure.

"What does his boat look like?" Xinyi inquired.

"No idea." The man shook his head. "The River Serpent finds you."

A surge raced tingling up Xinyi's spine. *The River Serpent finds you.* Oh yes, a proper villain. She thanked her neighbor with a hug like the last, though his hand as well was extended. She raced off to find the filthy, heartless smuggler. She was horrified, disgusted surely. She was.

She was! Such people made her blood boil—with anger.

Though apparently she hadn't been expressing it. Mei and Yinuo thought she was focusing too much on the loss of the story and not enough on the violation. They were worried it would make her "even more" frightened to leave the castle.

Xinyi wasn't sure where she'd gotten a cowardly reputation. She simply had all she needed in the palace and in her stories. She didn't need to leave. Well, she did, but only because of the theft. Only because others weren't taking her curse seriously. No one took it seriously.

"Xinyi, you do not have magical powers! You are an ordinary girl." Her adopted mother had sighed when Xinyi insisted for the fourth time that her mother abandoned her because she was cursed.

Naturally Xinyi did not believe she had magical powers. She merely believed that the universe had a perverse sense of humor and a mild hatred for her happiness. She didn't know exactly what she had imagined to make her mother abandon her at three years old, she barely remembered the woman. But it was likely more wealth. When one is abandoned in a basket of blossoms outside a wealthy man's home, one can assume they were born poor. But it was surely her own imaginings and the curse upon them that led to her abandonment.

Because whenever her imagination got the better of her, bad things happened in the most bizarre ways.

She'd made up a story of a wolf cub finding its lost mother, then saw a woman she was sure was her mother in a market, leading to fights and heartbreak when the woman swore she'd never had a child. At twelve, she'd invented a story about a girl who befriends a thief. A month later, Xinyi's adoptive family were robbed by Xinyi's only friend. Of course the family claimed not to blame her both times. Every time. There were a thousand little incidents like that over the years. But when she'd begun imagining a world with freedom for the impoverished citizens of Loqwan and a war broke out, then the family stopped reassuring her. And when Wei, her husband, died fighting against the king, his family, her family abandoned her. Leaving her entirely alone. Until Yinuo found her and invited her into the palace, telling her none of it was her fault. And what had happened? Xinyi got comfortable. She began imagining happier adventures, and someone stole her treasure and threatened the family she'd created.

Every time, someone told her she hadn't made any of it happen. That the universe didn't hate her happiness. That she wasn't cursed. She wasn't powerful. But at thirty-one years old, she was done accepting it. She had finally learned to say, *"Sometimes I am right and everyone else is wrong. I* am *cursed."*

Well—not *say*. She'd left a note.

Of course, it didn't *specifically* mention the curse. In that it mostly said not to worry and that she would be back by dinner. But it was there in spirit. And anyway she meant for today to be her last day as a cursed woman. She was going to make her bad luck curse work for her.

She was going to find those thieves and let her bad luck follow them. Her luck was exactly what these people deserved; men of low morals, despicable, greedy, and uncaring. They were the proper victims of a bad luck curse. It suited her poetic senses that the smuggler who caused her problems, and was her only hope of staying with the family she had *finally* found, would now suffer Xinyi's ill luck.

A Magnet for Dangerous Women

From the shadows of the dark green trees that hung over the river market, Makoa watched the patrons, watched the quiet chaos of bodies moving around one another, each vying for the things they needed. He imagined himself walking proudly into the light and waiting to see how long it took for someone to scream. How long it took for real chaos to erupt.

Wild panthers walking through markets had that effect. Or he could emerge as an Ogre, there probably wouldn't be any screams, but definitely some hasty exits. Even that giant lake dragon? Snake? Ancient monster thing he and Shiraz had smuggled into Loqwan for Aiattaua would shake things up.

He used to enjoy that sort of thing. When he was first cursed, it was a delight to shake people's comfort as his own had been shaken. But now, though the fantasy amused him, he also felt bad for having it. He watched them without jealousy any longer. Other people moved through the world unaware of the dangers. Or pretending to be unaware so they could move with confidence. While Makoa...knew.

A little girl ran through the market, bumping Shiraz, who intentionally stood in her way, and shoving her into the cart of fruit. Fruit, really! She didn't need to steal fruit. She needed to steal bigger things. She needed to get them another big score. But she did enjoy the game. Loved to practice the sleight of hand, the casual brush. Loved to improve her craft. Another day, another month, another market, he might not have cared. But she was not even trying to get big scores anymore because the last few had gone so poorly.

He saw his friend's eyes dart after the little girl but immediately look away. Shame and regret entered her gaze but were quickly disguised as she sunk her teeth into a piece of fruit. She would be better off if she did as Makoa had and accepted that they had made a mistake bringing those kidnappers to the village. A mistake. And they had fixed it, making sure they did not get away with what they were after. Everything was fine. But Shiraz was letting things eat at her.

Makoa blew out a cursed breath, transforming into a red panda. He ran into the market, snatching things off of tables, without causing the ruckus of a panther. Shiraz might benefit from his curse.

Transforming like this came with some very serious drawbacks: no one knew his true face. He had only glowing turquoise eyes, his own voice, and (if the form he took had ears) the shark tooth protruding through his left lobe as identifiers. It had caused some serious disappointments and uncertainties. But the curse also came with a great deal of fun. It led to him making all kinds of friends that he might not have otherwise, Shiraz for one. And led to the rare opportunity to be certain his mistakes were corrected, as he had already, earlier today.

"Then Ma drew a sword from the wall, and swished it at the man, and said he would die if he touched me. He ran screaming away, and the animals chased him, and bit him in the legs, and on the behind," the little girl giggled as she relayed the tale of her epic rescue from the bad men.

She had told Makoa the story three times now. And he had been there on the night in question, and thus needed no recitation. But he smiled and listened intently as her tale was embellished more and more, and her laughter filled the air, recounting the night when four men broke into her home and attempted to take the girl and her mother. It was good to know that she had escaped her ordeal relatively unscathed.

They had been thwarted by the girl's mother, a group of jungle animals, and Makoa. Only one had escaped, and Shiraz had dealt with him. But Makoa made a point whenever they returned to the village of finding this girl in a form she would be comfortable with and checking on her wellbeing.

She seemed far more resilient and well loved than he had been as a child. She was speaking to him as a panther for goodness sake and was completely certain of her safety. Some might find that worrying, but...there was something about this girl. Makoa was certain she would be safe.

"You are sure to be the bravest princess in all time," Makoa said encouragingly. "What have you planned for your next adventure?"

She giggled. "There is a new family come to live in our house," she said casually, referring to the palace of the deposed king, her grandfather. "And the little boy doesn't believe I can speak to animals. So I am going to show him!" She rubbed her hands together.

He grinned. "And what does that entail?" Makoa always befriended the most dangerous women.

"When he goes to his bed, my snakes will be inside it, and my monkeys will hang above him and screech, and he will be terrified and run away! But when his mother forces him back, I will be there petting my animals. They will cuddle me because they love me, and I am not afraid."

"An exquisite plan of vengeance. But don't you think you could perhaps befriend him and show him the animals love you in a gentle way?"

The princess thought carefully. She had a panther runt in her lap. Makoa had found it abandoned in the forest and was trying to feed it, though he knew he was unlikely to save it. Then the princess arrived. And though she was surrounded by a loving mother and so many aunts that she would eventually be too protected to have any hopes for an adventurous life, she was still looking for more things to love. Longing to give her love away.

She sat with the kitten in her lap, petting it, and slowly feeding it water by soaking a cloth and having the creature suck at it. A five year old, and she was rescuing this panther kitten.

He liked her. He wondered if this was what Aiattaua was like as a child. Makoa's bond mate was so full of love to give. He hated having anyone pass his way and feel unloved. So determined to be a safe harbor. But there was a loneliness to Aiattaua's behavior that this girl did not have.

"No," the girl answered finally. Makoa chuckled. If she said it could not be done gently, then it could not be; who was he to force friendliness upon her? "He'll learn my way. Then we can be friends."

Makoa chuckled. Now she sounded like someone else he knew.

"How do you know how to feed the kitten?" Makoa asked. He had not known the method; it seemed strange a five year old would.

"Ma taught me. We nursed the goats this way after the first bad men killed their mas. There are a lot of bad men."

"Yes. And you have met more than your fair share of them."

The princess bobbed her head from side to side.

"Ma says that too. She is teaching me to be a patient warrior, not a silent princess. A patient warrior is better, she says."

"And what do you say?"

"I can't be silent." She answered with words clearly pulled from those around her. "I'd like to be a warrior, but...I don't think patience is any fun."

"I didn't think it was either when I was your age."

"What do you think now you're old?"

Old was he? "I think...Patience is just a nice word for waiting, and everyone has to wait sometimes, whether they like it or not, so...you might as well try to like it," Makoa had said, speaking to himself as much as the girl.

This was not the sort of village where one found big scores. Nor, he was fairly certain, was this the place he would find someone to break his spell. They should move on. But Shiraz was rushing over to her favorite boat to *buy* a new chapter of someone else's story, and he knew that he needed to be a patient friend.

Whether he liked it or not. She wasn't working as fast as he wanted. But she was working, and though he was satisfied with the massive number of spells altering *The River Serpent* already, he knew this last one, to resist lava, was useful. If they'd had it during Shiraz's jailbreak, they would still have *The Island Rebel*. Of course it hadn't seemed nearly as necessary then, some thousand miles or so from the nearest volcano. But dangerous women were attracted to them.

Ducking between boats, Makoa edged closer to the gem trader. *Gem* was a bit of a stretch, as was trader. The man was a thief, and his wares were lower quality stones, but they were the products in the market of the highest resale value. So Makoa curled his feet paws around the edge of one boat, stretching out a hand paw towards the pole at the back of the gem boat. It held the highest value gems, lapis, turquoise, beryl and the like. He'd just closed his hand around it when a sweet looking woman on the shore shook the whole boat, causing Makoa to lose his hold and scramble wildly, taking the pole with him into the river.

"Hey, watch it," he had time to shout before he went under, getting a nose full of water and an annoying conk on the head.

He truly was a magnet for dangerous women.

Dirty, Rude, Deceitful Beings of No Morals

Xinyi's heart raced faster with every boat she eliminated, every step closer she grew to finding the smuggler. It was fear, *surely*... But she'd never done anything like this. Never thrown herself into danger of her own will. Never confronted thieves. Never sought out criminals. She rarely even went to the market alone. She liked company, safety and routine. It was time for her late morning tea. She took a break from writing at this hour every day and had a cup of tea in the garden.

But today Xinyi was on a mission. Surely it was alright that it was a little...*exhilarating.* She counted no less than ten unfamiliar boats, and one...well she wouldn't call that bit of scrap held together by ropes a boat, but it was tied off. Four of them were piloted by foreigners. Those seemed less likely to carry the smuggler. The River Serpent knew *every secret way* up the river. He must be a local. A mercenary who refused to take sides in the wars, not peacefully like Yinuo, but for his own profit. Xinyi should stop thinking of him in terms of morality and focus on her task. His lack of morals was to her benefit at the moment, even if ultimately to the world's detriment.

Xinyi's heart was louder than the racing waves of the river. Was Nanghi this loud in the north, where the thieves surely went? Were the trees along the banks as lush? Were there other river markets like

Hi'mau's, with boats for booths, and patrons yelling from shore? She had never left the shadow of this little jungle village. Was born here, grew up here, was married here and widowed here. She had imagined the rest of the world but had never left to see it. Surely her imagination was more wild and beautiful than the real world. In *her* mind, the river market wasn't just a market.

> The river market formed its own particular music. The water was a loud rushing blast like overzealous woodwinds. The boats bumping against rocks and each other served as playful percussion. In the trees, birds would sing in a dipping flowing pattern like strings. And monkeys and squirrels cried out at irregular intervals forming the sudden blast of trumpets. The voices of the patrons, rising and falling, arguing or conceding, gave the music a theatrical flare. A whole performance playing out before weary travelers or familiar neighbors whenever the river market gathered.

"Princess Xinyi, good morning! Looma blossoms for your table?" a merchant shouted as she walked by.

Xinyi nodded her greeting but refused the goods. Not all of the vendors were from Hi'mau; some traveled weekly from other small villages along the river. But she knew many by sight, and more knew her. But she needed the ones she didn't know.

Of the six most likely boats, three were piloted by women, so she eliminated them. Xinyi approached the nearest boat. It looked promising; there was an extravagance to it most of the others did not have. Opulence, she believed, was often displayed by criminals and despots. The pairing having in common a level of selfishness. There were jewels hanging from posts on the little flat boat, and two richly cushioned seats towards the front, as well as a seat for the pilot in the back. An older man leaned, half asleep, against one of the poles. His head lulled from side to side every few seconds and his eyes blinked heavily. There was an uncorked bottle that smelled, even from the shore, of strong spirits.

Very promising indeed.

Xinyi leaned as near to the boat as she could from the raised ledge of the bank. "Sir," she gently tried to wake the man.

"Er grrruh," the man grunted what sounded like they might have been words to his inebriated, half-conscious mind.

Emboldened by her earlier encounters, Xinyi reached out and shook the boat slightly, prepared to speak again.

"Hey, watch it," someone, not the pilot, yelped. Xinyi jerked her hand back, only shaking the boat more.

A lot of things happened at once. There was a loud splash, one pole or jewelry fell into the river, along with something very red. It went down, Xinyi tried to reach forward to help, but the drunk man woke with a knife in hand he waved at Xinyi.

"Stay back, thief."

"I am not a thief," Xinyi snapped, offended to her deepest core. "I was trying to—

"Back." The man waved the knife. "Where are my goods?"

"I didn't—" But Xinyi broke off, tilting her head to the side. She thought...but it wasn't possible. A few boats down, at perhaps the dingiest, least water worthy boat in the market, she thought she saw the pole of necklaces tossed onto its deck, and a red panda scramble on after it. It wasn't possible. It was her imagination, playing tricks.

"You'll pay, thief. What have you done with my necklaces?"

"I haven't taken a thing from you. Look," Xinyi said gently. She opened the embroidered wedding bag she had slung over her shoulder. All she'd taken with her was a single wrap, a journal, and five pencils. To have taken more would have alerted the other widows, and they would try to stop her. She didn't even have money.

"I have nowhere to have hidden it. I took nothing from you."

"Give me back my jewelry or give me the bag," he demanded.

"I...am sorry to have disturbed you." She backed away. "But I took nothing from—"

He stood, coming towards her, but lost his footing, falling backwards. Xinyi took the opportunity to race away before he could demand compensation again. People were beginning to look.

There was another vessel nearby that had seating along the interior and spaces of oarsmen on the outsides. It currently had only one occupant, the pilot probably. She approached this man more cautiously than the last, as he was already looking at her suspiciously.

"Excuse me." Xinyi put on her most charming smile. "I hoped you might have information about a group of thieves."

"Do I look like a thief?" he demanded, coming to his feet so quickly that Xinyi jumped backwards, nearly falling over a couple behind her who were heading to the boat. Oh dear, not an auspicious start.

"Oh, no. No!" Xinyi shook her head as the man advanced. "I...I only hoped you might know something."

"Why? What about me says criminal?" he shouted.

Xinyi squeaked in fear, stumbling around the people behind her. "I am sorry." She raced away.

The man didn't follow. She stopped between one of the booths on solid ground, tears rushing into her eyes. There was a large tree with low hanging vines, and she ducked into them to hide. Nectar blossoms poked out between vines. She liked to take a nectar blossom in her tea, sweetening it.

She loved safe. She loved quiet. She loved sweet.

But…she also loved the wild and adventurous, or she would not be in this situation. Xinyi might never have left home, might have *hidden* in a palace for the past few years. Might prefer not to be touched by immorality. But she understood it. She conquered it easily in her stories. But she couldn't expect that real life would be as simple. Real life criminals were dirty, rude, deceitful beings of no morals who threatened and abused any kindness. She needed to be prepared for that. She needed to remember that these were the sort of people who brought kidnappers to steal a five year old child. This was not an adventure; it was a dire mission.

Xinyi knew who could handle this situation. The woman who rode into battle beside her love. The woman who cast aside an entire way of life to explore something that intrigued her. The woman who was never afraid, never intimidated. She needed to be the girl she wrote to live out adventures. She needed to be Jian.

Xinyi stepped forward and immediately slipped on a large, poking stone beneath her slippers. She stumbled forward, catching herself on her knees. People rushed forward to help. *Of course.* She wasn't Jian. She was clumsy, helpless Xinyi, cursed with bad luck.

That ended today. Xinyi straightened, hot and red faced with embarrassment but determined. She was getting rid of this rotten luck and getting her treasure back. No matter what the curse threw at her.

Scoundrels Doing what Scoundrels Do

Jian dragged her bloody body towards the river. If she could get to the river, she would live. If she could get to the river, it would carry her home. Back to her love.

The pirates who held him hostage had no idea what force they had awakened. They should have killed her while they had the chance. Because she had it now—the seed of her power. The jewel she had sacrificed to be with her love. Her inhuman hunger, her brutal claws and teeth. Her rage made magic.

If she could get to the river—when she got to the riv—

"How can you read that maudlin drivel?" Makoa interrupted Shiraz's reading in his usual, dismissive, *let's do something else* voice.

"How can you slither along your belly one moment and fly away the next?" Shiraz responded equally snide. "We've all our own talents."

"Sitting around all pouty reading depressing romances wherein women are punished for disobeying tradition is not a talent," Makoa remarked. Of late he had a habit of calling out Shiraz's...lack of interest. It was growing annoying. "Half of the Jade Valley read that obsessively. And shape shifting is my curse. I've told you a thousand times I—

"*—was cursed by an old woman to never again take my own form unless I learned the meaning of true love and earned a true love's kiss—*" Shiraz managed to match both her friend's words and his dramatically pained cadence, saying the often-repeated words in perfect unison with him.

"I'm not falling for that story," Shiraz finished when Makoa's voice fell away.

Makoa smirked. At least she took the look for a smirk. He was currently in the form of a red panda, sitting behind Shiraz in a tree. His gaze held hers, two seconds, four, another few she didn't count.

"*Again,*" Shiraz hissed, giving in to Makoa's look. Her best friend and traveling companion got a good laugh, and Shiraz felt her skin heating in lingering embarrassment. The one incident of her falling for his tricks and kissing him had happened many years ago, when she was naive and hopeful. Desperately seeking magic and fate and wonder.

She was a very different person when Makoa, in the body of a green hook-eared elf lay *dying* on the ground and begged her to give him a true love's kiss to break his spell and save his life.

"I never thought I was your true love anyway," she muttered, facing forwards but aware her friend would hear. "I was just willing to try anything to save your life."

"And very sweetly too," he chuckled evilly. She had watched this rascal trick any number of people into kissing him. All she could tell that he had gained was the ability to take on their forms. If that? He'd certainly taken on nearly every form whose lips she'd ever seen him kiss, but she couldn't say that he hadn't done so prior to kissing them. Or if he had to kiss them in order to do so.

"You are an ordinary skin slipping fey creature and I will not be fooled by that romantic fate nonsense again."

"Unless it is in a story." Makoa's furry paw batted away the leaflet. Shiraz dove to the ground after it. This was priceless treasure.

To Makoa, *Immortal Hunger* was only a story, but to Shiraz, it was so much more. The small square leaflets of hand-written and strung pages, never more than ten pages long, detailed the ongoing adventures of Jian, a magical half-woman, half-river creature who fell in love with a human and entered the human world to be with him. The adventures had hand painted covers, and if you brought back your original pages, the woman who sold them would restring the book for you each time. Shiraz loved watching the adventures growing from the original ten-page leaflet to what she would have had today, near one-hundred-and-sixty pages of dramatic escapes and magical encounters. If only she hadn't left her copy behind at the Mushroom Grotto.

Azaqif, Aiattaua. The elf prince just had to make a huge show of swearing his **bond** to Makoa—when he was already **bonded** to fourteen other beings, and several of them were there. Fourteen others, like Makoa was just another face in the crowd. Shiraz nearly hit him. She wished she had. Then she'd have her copy of the story. And Aiattaua would have gotten a piece of her mind, and Makoa—would still be one of **fifteen** bonded spouses to the prince.

Shiraz lifted the leaflet from the ground, brushing water off the cover. "Why are you wet?"

"Run in with some woman." Makoa's answer drifted into Shiraz's ears, but she paid it barely any attention.

She slipped her story carefully into her book-holster in front of the extra copy of chapter seven she'd bought; it was her favorite. She tightened the strap gently to keep both safe. She didn't know why she hadn't thought of a book-holster sooner. She always wanted a book near. This way she wouldn't lose it again. She'd lost so many over the years.

Stories like these were what first drew her into the world. Far off lands, adventure, and always the mysterious understanding she only found in characters of fiction who, like herself, never fit in.

Shiraz had discovered the series by accident a few years ago. It caught her eye as she stole the bag of a particularly snarky client she was escorting up river—at very great risk to her person—who had the nerve to accuse her of taking an unnecessarily circuitous route. She took the book out of spite, and because the shimmery blue ink of the design called out to her.

She hadn't been able to tell that first night that the cover featured the long drooping hair of a woman with only her head and neck emerging from a river, this river, Nanghi. She'd only known it intrigued her, and it was right along side the leather satchel of coins she was lifting. But when she saw the book in the light she felt, fleetingly, that she must have been fated to pick it up.

Once in a blue moon, such childish urges crawled back over her, making her forget everything. Like that fate held no power in her life, nor anyone else's. And that magic, though real, was as mundane as anything else. Life was a series of disappointed hopes interspersed with fun escapes, pick pocketing, smuggling, and excellent food if one could afford, or steal, it. And also stories! Just because nothing they offered was real did not mean that Shiraz would ever abandon her first love.

She and Makoa were near the end of the market, by a cluster of trees. As soon as she'd bought this installment, Shiraz had to read it, and Makoa, who had been doing some pickpocketing of his own, had found her. He never had patience for her reading when there was anything else to do. But how could she wait?

Kinmei was being held by pirates, and Jian was in search of the power she had given up when she married Kinmei. The power he had made her promise never to use again, the power with which she'd killed his father and uncle.

Shiraz was on the edge of her seat. Yes, she was fairly certain Jian would find the power and rescue Kinmei. She usually did rescue him. Although, on some boring occasions, he did the saving. But...how would he deal with her having magic again? Would he apologize for ever asking her to give it up? Would he pout? Get angry? Fight with her? Get injured? *Die*?

While Shiraz loved Jian's adventures, she was not a fan of Kinmei. She hated that he had asked Jian to give up her power. Hated that he had benefited from her power, being saved from his abusive uncle and complicit father, and then called the power ugly, because he was afraid. But Shiraz was willing to be fair. He'd been new to the power at the time and afraid after years of abuse. If he saw the error of his ways in this moment and apologized, she would stop actively rooting for him to die. Though she longed for Jian to have adventures on her own or get together with the emperor's sorceress.

Shiraz loved that character. And the fact that she was nameless, called only *V*, not the letter, but the symbol for the Loqwanian word for power...Yeah, Shiraz loved that. It would be so much more fun if Kinmei died and Jian and V teamed up!

She smiled at the thought of the character's imminent death. She was certain that her own vision for the story would not be what she read in the next two pages, but a woman could hope. She moved to stand but had been crouched too long. A muscle cramped in her back, and the jerking pop in her left knee from an old injury kept her crouching. Ughhhh, she used to be able to crouch without aching.

A rich swath of violet silk shuddered in the air and caught Shiraz's attention. The woman wearing it raced away from the rivers edge and into the cover of vines beneath the nectar tree. She was strikingly lovely. How she ever thought to hide was beyond Shiraz. That was not a woman who could vanish. There was a radiance about her, so full of life that it was magnetic.

Shiraz watched her between the vines and blossoms. They fell around her, decorating her like a lovely watercolor painting. Her body stretched out against the trunk of the tree, softening in with her curvy form. Her head was tilted down, pulling her delicate threads of shoulder length black hair forward to frame her face. It was a mostly round face but for a playfully pointy chin. She was beautiful. And hers was the perfect pose for a painting of a woman in the blush of love. If not for her expression. She wore a frown as she chewed at her large bottom lip, fighting off some demon. Some fear.

Shiraz took in the area to see what had frightened her. The captain of the tourist boat was glaring at her. From the looks thrown his way by the locals, he wouldn't be welcome here long. But it also didn't seem like he'd touched her. People were drawn up in preparation for a fight, but no one was launching into one.

The woman marched out from between the vines with her shoulders back and a sharp smile on those lips she'd bitten bright red.

Shiraz grinned. That did not look like a very genuine smile, but she could tell from the little lines around the dimples in the woman's cushy cheeks that she smiled often. Shiraz liked that she had pulled herself together, ready to take on the world in her gorgeous, but overly fancy ground-length gown that was bound to—

He he. Shiraz chuckled as the woman tripped over her own hem just as Shiraz was thinking she would. She didn't fall to the ground, but it was a close thing. What a delightful bit of chaos she was. She caught herself on her knees and shoved up, venturing forth once more. Her cheeks turned bright red as many a local worried after her.

"Princess!" one woman shouted.

A princess was she? That explained the dress. And the richly embroidered bag she carried. It had luminous threads and gems. It must have cost a fortune. Not the sort of thing Shiraz would carry at a public market. There were pickpockets all around! Something fancy like that—it could be *stolen*.

Shiraz shoved to her feet, leaning into the aches. She could finish Jian's adventures later. She wanted to see what princesses carried when they went marketing.

"Bet you two gold rams she doesn't have a drop of gold in her bag," Makoa said, reminding Shiraz he was there. She'd forgotten, all caught up in the pretty pink princess. Apparently Makoa had noticed her too. That tended to happen. Rich looking marks were their noodles and tea.

But Shiraz was usually more aware of him there, ready to compete.

She grinned at him over her shoulder. "That's a princess, Makoa, of course she doesn't have money. People give princesses what they want. Let's make it an interesting bet."

"Alright," Makoa said in his deep tempting voice. "Bet I can get her to try and break my spell."

The woman had been frightened into hiding and tripped when she tried to be brave, not to mention the fact that her beautiful silk dress was dragging in the mud. She had every reason to be unpleasant. But she was smiling, making deep dimples in her cheeks and causing her eyes to all but vanish into lovely lines of joy.

Shiraz should not take Makoa's bet. There was no chance she would win. Also she shouldn't wish the same foolish feeling that lived inside her on anyone else. That looked like the sort of woman who would volunteer to kiss him if she only overheard his tale. Shiraz shouldn't take the bet. But she sort of wanted to.

She wanted to be flip and say 'bet I can get a kiss first.' They were on their way out of Loqwan, but at the moment it was on a low note. Nothing she'd done in the last few months felt impressive. But... swindling a farewell kiss from a princess...that would be special. That would be new at the very least.

The princess tripped again. This time landing in the arms of a near by boat captain. A slimy criminal if ever Shiraz laid eyes on one, just like herself and Makoa. Who knew how many curses that princess would get about breaking before Shiraz and Makoa even got near.

"No bet," Shiraz answered prudently. Princesses kissing scoundrels was the stuff of good stories. The stuff of her favorite stories.

In the Book of Anolani, Princess Omea had fallen for Anolani though the con artist had come to seduce and swindle her father. She even ran away with her. Shiraz adored that story. Adored their path to love, Anolani's sly wit, Omea's sweetness and generosity, and by the end—when they fled together seeking a world of their own—you could see deeper into both characters, learning Omea's wicked wit and determination, and Anolani's gentle heart. Shiraz loved it all.

If a story had characters of different worlds falling in love and changing one another, Shiraz fell for it every time. But she was world-wise enough not to go looking for it in reality any longer. Except for the Singing Hills—or even them. If she didn't find them this year. Shiraz shook off the morose thought and let her eyes drift back to reality and the pretty princess. Whether the hills were real or not, Shiraz was no

Anolani, and reality was scoundrels doing what scoundrels do, and princesses weeping over their stolen treasures.

"I don't take bets I can't win. She'd kiss you out of *pity*. How about this? Bet I can teach her not to trust strangers." Shiraz held up her hands like a question and walked backwards away from Makoa.

"Out of the goodness of your own heart?" he teased, racing down the tree after her, shaking off more of the river as he ran.

"Of course." Shiraz failed to conceal her sarcasm. "I am endlessly generous."

She'd never robbed a princess before! That would be new. Just what she needed. Yes, a life of freedom offered endless new opportunities. And this, this is what it felt like to thrive.

Never Count on a Gentle God

The man with his arms around Xinyi had yet to share his name. She leaned away, maintaining as friendly a smile as she could muster with his alcohol and onion scented breath right against her face and his hand rubbing at her lower back. Ugh, she hoped this wasn't the River Serpent, but she had a feeling he was. He would be in her novels. A slimy man, overly free with other people's bodies. Someone Jian would put in his place with a slap, or a kick, or a slamming of the head.

Why had she thought she could channel Jian? Jian didn't need combat lessons, because she knew how to fight. Jian was not afraid of anything.

"What are you after, sweet ball?"

What on earth did that mean? Was that meant to be a compliment? An insult? Was he comparing her to some sort of food? Commenting on her size? Xinyi had no idea, and was thus neither insulted nor complimented, merely...discomforted.

"I am steady now, thank you for catching me. But if you—"

"Princess Xinyi," a vaguely familiar elderly woman whose name escaped Xinyi interrupted. She peeled the man's hand off Xinyi's back forcefully. "I have your tea."

"Oh! Thank you, auntie!" With great relief, Xinyi leapt out of the man's arms. Her feet landed once more on her silk, but this time she dug her heels into the ground, soaking the silk in mud but keeping her footing. Other women walked in these dresses with such grace, you would think their feet never touched the ground. Why couldn't she? Well, this dress wasn't made for her. She really must learn to hem.

She followed the woman away quickly. Back towards the beginning of the market, where all the boats and stalls were familiar. She led Xinyi to a fruit boat and instructed her to sit on an upturned basket at the river's edge. Xinyi wasn't certain of its ability to hold her, but she sat, too shaken to do anything but obey. The exhilaration that had carried her this far was fading into shaky unease. Could she really do this? The basket sunk in as Xinyi settled but she was too disheartened to care. If it fell apart beneath her and she landed in the river, it couldn't be worse than being in the arms of that man.

Please, she begged the universe, *please do not let that be the River Serpent.* Anyone *is better.*

Oh, no! As soon as she was finished with her prayer, the words struck her and she covered her lips, though she had not said any of it aloud. But...she knew better. *Every* time Jian thought one thing was better than another, Xinyi made sure to prove her character wrong. And she knew the universe loved to test her. What would happen to her now? How much worse would the serpent be?

"What are you doing at the market alone in such fine garments and with your wedding bag?" the woman asked, with each word revealing how much she knew about Xinyi. Though Xinyi could not say she knew anything about her in return. It was shameful.

Xinyi did not know how to respond. She needed information, and perhaps these people might have it, but with as much as they knew of her, they might tell Yinuo or try to discourage her from retrieving her treasure.

Her rescuer was indeed preparing Xinyi a cup of tea, and the man on the fruit boat, a relative or husband most likely, took out a nectar fruit. He cut it in half at the center and pulled one half away from the seed, extending it to Xinyi. She took it and watched as he squeezed the second with both hands over an empty cup, using the seed inside it to draw out more juice.

That would be a delicious addition to tea that she had never thought of. She bit into the fruit and shut her eyes the better to take in the wonder.

"Ohh. This is perfect!" she said as the nectar bit at her tongue, making her feel more alert. "So sweet, and so tangy."

"Just something to rouse your fight." The old man winked.

What an odd thing to say. The pair observed Xinyi with matched smiles. Definitely siblings, she decided. "It was a bountiful year, and it is a genuine pleasure to share its beauty," the old woman remarked. "Come dear, tell us why you are about, so out of character. We rarely see you alone."

Xinyi finished chewing. The words were so familiar. Yinuo had been admonishing Xinyi for hiding in the palace recently. The week before Xinyi's treasure was stolen, she had encouraged Xinyi to do more. Almost as if she knew about her secret project, her secret desires.

"You never leave the palace alone. You do not speak to anyone outside our walls, or even vary your walks. Are you hiding?"

"Of course not. I know the walks I like, and the company. Have I hurt someone by not seeking them out?"

Yinuo shook her head as she lifted a steaming pot out of the fire and filled their waiting ceramic teapot, steeping the sharp leaves she preferred. Xinyi liked a sweeter tea, but she had adapted in the past years. She could ask, and Yinuo would provide a sweetener. Or different tea. But Xinyi hated being an imposition. Xinyi played with the steam, imagining a creature who was made of mist. A river creature, not of reality, but of her own invention. The pot depicted a maiden swimming beside a river dragon. She looked like a grown up Qiu.

Xinyi ran her finger along the heating back of the hairy serpent, feeling its fire, watching the paint react to temperature, turning the dragon's back a shimmering blue-green color where it had been gray before. Xinyi wanted to write a character like Qiu. Sweet and wild and unafraid of the world, having adventures of her own will, not because some force threatened her happiness.

Qiu's mother went on speaking, despite Xinyi's distraction. "Everywhere you go, you take a beacon of energy and goodness. But I worry that as the rest of us change and grow, you will remain exactly as you are. Your energy wants to grow."

"Not everyone needs to have children," Xinyi said slyly.

"I do not mean with a child. I mean with a life!" Yinuo poured green tinted water into their individual cups, setting one before Xinyi then herself. "You write such adventures. Don't you want adventure in your life?"

"Jian doesn't mind a broken bone, or bloody nose. I do. Jian does not mind missing a meal or sleep." Xinyi wrapped her hands around the cup, not quite touching, waiting for her skin to adapt to the temperature, waiting for the tea to cool. "Jian does not have an imagination; she is too busy running from thieves and sleeping on the ground with bugs! I will

keep my adventures on paper where they are safe and clean, and where they always end happily."

"Do they?" Yinuo asked with the sort of condescension elder women displayed when discussing Jian's adventures, as if the stories were very naive. "I begin to wonder if Jian hides inside of adventure because she is afraid that peace will never satiate the empty place where her power used to be. I wonder if hiding is what the pair of you have most in common."

Xinyi wasn't hiding. And she wanted something new, but only in her writing. Still, conversations like this were part of why so few people knew she was the author of Immortal Hunger. *Only Yinuo and Mei who, with her daughter's help, wrote out, bound, and sold the stories so the funds collected could contribute to their home. The more people who knew the more* talks *like this one she would have to enjoy.*

Xinyi loved Yinuo, dearly, but that did not mean she thought her every word was right. Yinuo was a princess raised. She had done what she was told all her life. Now widowed and separated from her father's power, she was free as never before. Yinuo didn't understand that for some women, the quiet that tamed her tongue was comfortable, it was safe.

Xinyi didn't want to lose what she had by wanting more. She was content. She was always content. No, more than that, she was grateful. *She was happy.*

Or she had been. Until the rest of her story was stolen. And her comfort was threatened, again. She had to get it back. She had to show the universe she was satisfied with what she had.

All her life she'd been just outside of families, asking where she belonged. When one has been found in a basket of blossoms next to a garden gate, it is only natural to ask where you belong and who you are. But surrounded by believers in fate and offered only platitudes and everyday growing annoyance to have to repeat the answers, one stops asking—aloud.

But the fear lived inside that any family found would be taken away. She wouldn't let that happen this time.

Xinyi sipped the sweetened, tangy tea. It slid down her throat, warming every bit of her body, soothing her tightened muscles and setting her more at ease. "This is the loveliest tea I've ever tasted, so sweet and comforting…invigorating!"

"A good reminder then that the world will often fail to meet our needs when *we fail to express them,*" the woman observed.

Xinyi smiled, until her lips closed on the rim of the cup and sipped again. "I was robbed," Xinyi confessed. She did not like to burden others with her concerns, but the tea was so perfectly what she needed. And the woman was so familiar, almost as if she walked out of Xinyi's mind. Speaking to this pair felt like speaking to the safest friend she had, her own thoughts.

"Ooooh, how exciting," the old woman said with a little giggle. "Hi'mau getting kidnappers and thieves in one month! We used to be such a staid community, now we're like one of Jian's adventures."

Hi'mau used to be staid. Before her. Before Xinyi imagined more.

"Not that my sister means to belittle your predicament." The man, apparently her brother, shook his head.

"Of course not." The auntie wore a conspiratorial smile as she nudged Xinyi. "But a little adventure makes life interesting, right? That's why we all gobble up those stories."

Xinyi smiled back at the woman shyly. She had been enjoying the adventure of sneaking around seeking the thieves. And it always brightened her heart to hear someone loved her stories. Any part of them.

"There is some fun to adventure," Xinyi admitted. "But there are also very real dangers. I am looking for men who stole from me, so I can bring back my greatest treasure. But in order to do that I must seek help from the lowest of scum. A man they call The River Serpent."

A crack of bitter laughter shook Xinyi's world like the violent winds of a winter storm. It was so exactly how she had imagined V's powerful and wicked amusement that she fell backwards off the basket, spilling the remnants of the tea down the front of her dress.

Jian climbed out of the river. She had made it far past the palace wall and around a bend where the guards from the tower could no longer see her. All she needed to do was get to the cliffs where her love would surely be waiting, and they could race away into the night. Safe. In each other's arms, they would always be safe.

"Hhhh hahahahaha ha," a twisted jangle of laughter shook the trees. Birds took to the air, crying out in fear and racing away on manic wings.

Jian spun around and watched her step forward. V. The emperor's sorceress. She dripped in luminous threads of jade. The train of her long cape tinkled musically across the forest floor. And the threads of her hood created enough illumination to hint at the woman's wicked grin and silver blade-like eyes.

All the air left Jian's body as she watched the sorceress walk forward through the dim. Mist rose off the river to roll before her feet like a royal carpet. And the moon shook off its curtain of clouds to send its light falling around her. Jian was as helpless as the forces of nature V commanded. All she could do was wait to meet her fate with her heart stabbed and tumbled by the rapids of her anxious anticipation.

Laying flat on her back beside the river, Xinyi looked into the angrily amused face of a foreign looking woman. She was dressed in loose leg coverings and a short tight vest that revealed a large swath of her torso. A bulging canvas bag hung from her shoulder. And her long, oily looking, jumble of curled brown hair was braided off of her ear on one side, revealing no less than four earrings, before falling down to her mid back. She wore several bracelets, a few necklaces, and had jewels and straps hanging off her pants. Few were the ways she resembled Xinyi's ultimate villain, the strikingly beautiful, incredibly precise V, but Xinyi felt her heart racing as Jian's had when faced with the sorceress. The woman's expression spoke of malice as she bent at the waist sweeping an arm behind her in an elaborate bow.

"The lowest of scum at your service, *Your Majesty,*" she said bitterly. Xinyi gasped and her face heated in shame.

The River Serpent finds you.

Oh dear. She had insulted the sorceress whose assistance she needed. This was bad. She knew she shouldn't have made that prayer. This was so much worse.

The Lowest of Scum at Your Service

"**B**ut unlike your kindly neighbors, scum like me requires *pay* in exchange for assistance," Shiraz bit the words out spitefully.

The tumbled princess had a stain running down her dress and her tidy hair was gathering twigs. But it did nothing to mar her beauty.

Shiraz had been imagining this puff of pink and bright smiles was someone sweet. But this just confirmed what Shiraz already knew. No wide-eyed, eager sunshine women for her. They judged people long before they met them. Calling Shiraz scum.

Sure, Shiraz had been lurking behind her with plans to rob the princess. And Shiraz knew what she was: a thief, and a smuggler. A woman without nation or family. She had worked hard to gain a reputation as the best smuggler on the continent, all without being known for her face or her name by any form of authority.

Shiraz supposed what annoyed her now was a combination of the insult of being thought a man and her shock at hearing herself described as *scum*. Otherwise, she never would have openly acknowledged the nickname she'd been given. Her boat's name. But it wasn't the name River Serpent that bothered her; it was the word *scum*.

Of course she was scum to this woman, with her lovely clothes and her safe village. Princesses often lacked a worldly view. Their lives and experience so limited, they thought of morality like a clean slip of paper; if it was not pristine, then it was immoral. When in truth morality was a window. It depended entirely on what side you lived as to what was moral and what was not. Who cared that Shiraz had smuggled in food to this very village during the war, or that she had helped people escape all the pointless murder? She took a fee, therefore she was evil. That's what *good* people thought.

They would have called that scum on Glen Harrow too. All the *good* people of the *steadfast island*. Of course then she would have taken it as a compliment. But...what had she done to earn the antipathy of this stranger?

The woman lay there, her mouth agape and bright red patches spreading across her face and down her neck. The red was so bright, it looked odd against the pink of her gown.

Shiraz heard the all too familiar gust of wind and felt something slither around her leg. Why couldn't Makoa change shape silently like other skin slippers? *Pain in the ngok.*

Shiraz bent towards her boot. The woman on the ground held out her hand as if Shiraz had been bending to help her. *The princess* expected her due. With a sneer Shiraz lifted Makoa off her leg and slung her, presently, snake skinned friend across her shoulders. Makoa hissed, but it sounded too human. He never could use the voices of the creatures whose forms he took.

"Serpent, ssss," he said and chuckled as the woman somehow fell over while on the ground already.

The elderly woman who'd given the princess tea had begun to pull the pretty pink princess up. So falling backwards was possible. But it did look a touch ridiculous to fall over while already on one's backside.

"Are you an animal spirit? Or a fairy? Or a river dragon?" The woman fired one question after another at Makoa, scrambling onto her side awkwardly, getting caught up in her gown and stumbling a few more times before she managed to get onto her knees, all the while looking at Makoa with bright, excited eyes.

Yep, it was a good thing Shiraz hadn't taken his bet. He could probably get this woman to kiss him within the hour.

"None of those. I am but a man who was cursed to never—"

"—*speak his name, nor take his own form until he learns the meaning of love, and earns a true love's kiss as well,*" Shiraz spoke with Makoa again, this time adding a sarcastic tone to counter his sincerity. Makoa had a few variations on the speech, and Shiraz knew them all.

He wound his snaky body around her neck more tightly, his tail flicking playfully at her throat. But before Shiraz could plan her retaliation the woman on the ground was clapping. *Clapping?*

"Oh, how marvelous!"

Shiraz blinked.

"That's a new response," Makoa remarked dryly. His body loosened from Shiraz's neck, apparently as taken aback as she was.

Marvelous? To be cursed? Shiraz might not accept Makoa's story, but...she didn't think being cursed should be viewed as a positive thing!

"Oh, I do not mean to diminish your curse. I am sure it is painfully disconcerting not to know yourself when you see your reflection. That must be terrible; it must devour your heart sometimes." Her eyes darkened, losing focus as she stared almost through Makoa. Her voice became dreamlike. "Some mornings you must question whether you would even know yourself if you were to find your old form again. Must question if you, the self you once knew, even exists any longer."

There were several awkward beats of silence as Makoa and Shiraz gawked at the woman, and her elderly friends grinned.

Then the princess snapped out of her reverie and smiled. And it was such a smile it seemed her joy alone was what moved the world. Shiraz was thrown again, breathless from that expression. The woman was…a lot. A lot of color. A lot of enthusiasm. A lot of beauty. But also a lot of judgement. Shiraz made sure to sneak the thought in when her mind was busy seeing only the complimentary.

"But there must also be *such wonder* in your experience," the woman effervesced. "You can know what it feels like to inhabit an entirely different form than that with which you were born. You will understand other creatures better. You must, by the nature of your punishment, have been equally gifted as you were cursed!"

Shiraz lifted a brow at that naive, yet fairly accurate, perspective on Makoa's curse. Magic tended to have a level of balance most people didn't see. But she did. Makoa blew out a puff of air and transformed again, this time into a muscular man with dark skin, a bald head, and a wide smile. A handsome young man he'd tricked a kiss from when they were in Maltuba. Shiraz tensed even further. He knew she did not like it when he took on this form.

To be fair, she had never said as much. But Makoa knew, he always knew.

Makoa bent, taking both of the princess's hands in his own, and lifted her to her feet as though she were nothing but a light bundle of wool. Shiraz rolled her eyes. The princess smiled in awe, examining this change of form with so much enthusiasm it was a wonder she didn't launch herself forward and kiss him then and there.

Tifit.

"How right you are. Thank you." Makoa set the woman on her feet.

"This, second piece of scum," Shiraz interjected snidely, "whose hands you're holding, is my friend Makoa."

Makoa threw her half a grin. Rubbing in that even though they hadn't made the bet, he was likely to win. There was nothing so unattractive as smugness in other people.

The princess jumped, taking her hands out of Makoa's. She looked between Makoa and Shiraz, chewing her lips again. "Oh, I am so sorry. To you both. I...I...I thought he..." She pointed behind herself.

Shiraz didn't bother looking. She knew what she would see. The man who'd tried to squeeze *a stranger's* rear and lick her throat.

The man who was currently without any funds as Shiraz had robbed him on her way over. And who was scratching furiously at his arms, legs and crotch because of the curse-lice she'd thrown into the bottom of his boat for revenge.

Shiraz did not dole out her precious sum of curse-lice lightly. She had *paid* for them, and rather a lot. Outside of her boat, she didn't think she'd ever made a better purchase. Curse-lice were the invention of a *particularly mischievous* jungle nymph. Denesh was tired of men touching her friends without permission, so she invented the curse. The invisible lice crawled *into* a person's skin under any hairy part of the body and bit whenever they tried to touch someone without permission, or thought about touching someone without permission, or if one had recently done so. They were awesome! And impossible to get rid of without another spell.

Shiraz met Danesh at a roadside inn deep in Reethurn's jungle years ago. They shared a meal, shared a drink, shared a good long laugh about the lice. Shiraz bought the lice, then struck around far longer than she'd intended enjoying a few adventures with the jungle nymph.

That was a good year. Maybe Shiraz should go back to Reethurn. Danesh could be a downer, but no one had called her scum. Nor compared her to handsy unwashed men. Shiraz sniffed. She supposed she hadn't bathed in a few days…but smuggling was not easy, and it wasn't like this jungle was full of inns and warm bathing huts.

Both Makoa and the princess were staring at Shiraz, waiting for her to accept the lackluster apology. They could go on waiting, but she was getting bored of the silence.

"For which of my scummy talents were you hoping to find me?"

"I…" The woman swallowed. "I need to find the men who robbed me a week ago. Someone suggested you might know where to find them."

Shiraz looked the princess over. She was somewhat dirty, having fallen in the mud and spilled tea down her front. But as soon as she'd stood, the leaves and twigs had abandoned her hair, leaving its fine dark strands neat, shiny even. She looked soft, and sweet, and helpless as the beached whale Shiraz had seen on Lig're.

"What do *you* hope to do with this information when I sell it to you?" Shiraz asked, intentionally snide.

"Find them." She lifted her chin. Her words turned passionate, if still naive. "They have stolen my greatest treasure!"

Shiraz snorted. "You must be at least thirty and you only now had your treasure stolen? Were you locked in a tower or something?" The woman didn't seem to catch onto the joke, so Shiraz went further. "You understand you cannot get that treasure back, right?"

"I certainly can." The woman entirely missed Shiraz's joke.

Makoa got it. He shook his head at her, and the elderly man on the boat snorted, the same man Shiraz had robbed of fruit earlier. His eyes seemed to flash as he laughed, but it was probably a trick of the light.

That or he was some sort of trickster spirit, fey creature, or informal god. That last was a phrase Shiraz had come up with to describe a phenomena of magically powerful and seemingly immortal beings who tricked or earned various forms of offerings from people. She'd heard of such creatures all over. The offerings ranged from money to feasts in their honor, but the beings did not seek out any sort of formal worship in exchange for their favors.

To her knowledge, Shiraz had never met an informal god, but she'd heard stories. By and large she thought they were made up, because their sole purpose in interfering appeared to be to help lovers meet, like the god characters Nuan and Feng had led Jian to Kenmei when they were both at their lowest and needed a friend. It was great in the story! Shiraz loved it. They were hilarious, and their actions were entirely self serving, as helping Jian thwarted another river god they hated. So it made perfect sense. But in reality, what would gods gain from helping lovers meet? And why would they do it if they gained nothing? Thus Shiraz doubted. But the princess's comment assured her that *the princess* believed in such gods.

"I can!" she insisted, having mistaken the cause of all the amusement. "I will."

The old woman, not amused but fully understanding Shiraz's joke, patted the princess's hands comfortingly.

"That was not what she meant." The woman lifted a reproving brow at Shiraz. "Princess Xinyi is a *widow*," she said with great emphasis. "And seeks to retrieve a tangible treasure. Not a nonsense one."

Shiraz winked at the woman. A *nonsense one* indeed.

The princess gasped as understanding dawned. Princess *Xinyi*, Shiraz liked the name; it sounded soft and sharp in one name. Rather like her softly inviting lips slicing her face now in a scowl. Oh, yes.

Shiraz liked that name very much. But she doubted she would like the woman it belonged to at all.

Princess Xinyi examined Shiraz like the scum she'd called her already. She drew up her shoulders and bit at the inside of her cheek, making one dimple visible though she did not smile. Shiraz loved it. The woman looked one tenth of the way to dangerous. Hmmm. Maybe four tenths. Still too sweet.

Xinyi tried for a forceful tone. "Will you take me to the thieves you assisted?"

You assisted, was it? Nope. Shiraz wasn't going to like this princess at all.

"First insults now accusations. And as yet no offer of payment," Shiraz pointed out dismissively. "Find your own way. Thieves have better manners."

What Would V Do?

It was difficult, but Xinyi managed to restrain the words *they would need them, when lacking so many other graces.* This was her own fault. She'd insulted the woman and her...she'd called him a friend but her tone when Xinyi held his hand sounded jealous. Perhaps he was a lover, or a secret love. Those, she had observed, frequently induced more jealousy than a spouse or lover. Less trust, she supposed.

She had to fix it. What would Jian do? How would she handle V? An angry, insulted, and jealous V? How would she get her on her side?

The trouble was Jian didn't know how to handle V. She avoided the sorceress when she could. The only reason Jian, without her magic, had survived any encounter with V was because the sorceress found her intriguing. The sorceress could not understand giving away power, so she was fascinated by Jian. Obsessively so. She did not want her dead. She wanted her tempted into taking her magic back. Jian had an advantage, well several, but in this moment a specific advantage that Xinyi did not. Jian's villain liked her. Xinyi's seemed to hate her.

The woman turned to walk away, and Xinyi felt the last bit of sweetness from her tea turning bitter in her mouth. She was going to fail. Her story would be gone forever, and she would become a burden to the women who had taken her in. Before long she would be without a home or a family—again.

Xinyi looked among the elderly pair and Makoa, who was absolutely fascinating. Xinyi wanted to travel with him, if only to learn more about his curse. It was a magic her mind had yet to invent. Not that she thought herself incapable of coming up with such a curse. She could have done it, but reality had beaten her to it. Wasn't that exciting! She couldn't let this opportunity slip away, but...how was she to stop them?

The old woman raised a brow. *The world will often fail to meet our needs when we fail to express them.*

"What about you, Makoa?" Xinyi bowed her head politely as the man had bowed to her when he set her on her feet. "Will you help me?"

"We work together," the woman snapped. Xinyi focused all of her attention on Makoa. Perhaps provoking the woman wasn't the way to go, but it was the best she could come up with in the moment.

"Does she control you?" Xinyi asked.

Makoa chuckled. His grin was so wide Xinyi took it to mean he was enjoying her method of getting the woman's help.

"She does not. But we tend to work together."

"But she does not make all of the decisions? You have a say in who to help?" Xinyi pressed.

"I do," he agreed. "Which means if indeed we helped them, I was a part of assisting your thieves."

"I understand." Xinyi nodded, steeling her spine. "I sought out the River Serpent because I was told they helped the thieves and might know where they are. But I should not have insulted you. I apologize. Please, will you help me? It is my greatest treasure. Without it...I do not know who I am."

From the corner of her eye, Xinyi noticed the other woman rolling her eyes at the remark. The drama of it, Xinyi supposed. But she could not possibly understand. Xinyi had only ever had *one thing* that belonged fully to her, her story. Many were those who thought they knew better how the story should go, or saw fault in the messages they perceived within it, but they read. She touched lives. And they in turn touched hers, giving her the means to support the family she had found during the war. Jian's adventures held her heart. She didn't know what she would do without them.

"Please," she begged Makoa, taking his hands in her own. "I...if you wish it, I will try to help you break your curse."

Makoa threw a superior expression to his companion before turning back to Xinyi. "Yes. I will escort you, sweet princess. It would be my honor."

"It is my boat," the angry sorceress snapped. She was advancing on Xinyi now. They were about the same height, this woman was perhaps a little taller, but not as wide, so Xinyi would use that as an advantage if she must to help her stand her ground. Because the woman's manner was *very* threatening, her presence gathering up all the ambient energy in her sphere and turning it volatile, as though she truly was the sorceress V come to life in tattered glory. "No one sails her without my permission."

"I have a boat," the fruit seller offered with a grin. He too seemed to know Xinyi's game and was happy to assist. The old woman put her hands on her hips and grinned at the River Serpent, who was beginning to go red, holding her breath with her hands fisted at her sides as she took in Xinyi's chorus of supporters.

Xinyi wondered why they called the woman a serpent. She didn't look at all serpent like. She had pronounced muscles and sharp facial features. A serpent's defining characteristic was its ability to bend, to squish, to slither through spaces that seemed too small. Its lack of a spine. This woman was *all* spine. A better moniker for her might be the armored tortoise.

"Fine," she bit between clenched teeth. "Good luck getting through the border." She turned away again, and Xinyi's heart sunk. Even this hadn't worked.

She couldn't play a convincing spy, nor channel her fearless character. But even when she'd spoken her needs like the old woman suggested, nothing worked.

"Shiraz," Makoa said softly. "She has offered to help me break my curse. Might I borrow the boat? Or perhaps have your help piloting it?"

"Oh, thank you!" Xinyi spoke too quickly. She was throwing her arms around the man in an enthusiastic hug when the woman, Shiraz, spun back and crowded into them.

Xinyi clung to Makoa for fear of falling. He gathered her close with a supportive arm at her waist.

"I don't believe it is a curse. And if she wanted to help you, she could kiss you now! But she'll call you scum and hold onto that kiss as extortion for your assistance. So no. You cannot have my boat."

"What would be the good of kissing him now? I have only just met him. I am very intrigued and honored to meet him, of course, but as yet I haven't any particular love for him," Xinyi defended herself. "I was not even offering a kiss! Merely that I would do all in my power to understand his curse and help him find a way to break it."

The woman opened her mouth. Clearly she had something to say, but it seemed to get stuck somewhere between her mind and her lips. All she could do was stare, open mouthed.

"I am no longer sorry for calling you scum," Xinyi said firmly. "Anyone who can call someone friend and not believe them when they say they were cursed is unfeeling. And *scummy*," Xinyi forced the insult out a second time.

The woman's mouth had not closed. She was blinking. Several times blinking. But her lips remained wide and no words emerged between them. It was hardly an attractive look, but Xinyi was having to fight herself not to smile at it. There was something pleasant about seeing this fearsome creature at a loss for words. She could almost taste the lovely tang of the nectar fruit again.

Just something to rouse your fight.

"Shiraz has tried to break my curse." Makoa patted Xinyi's hand in a brotherly fashion. "She claims not to believe me because it saddens her that she failed. But you should know that she is still here because, despite the insult, she is willing to help you."

"For a fee," Xinyi said with tart condescension.

That finally drew words from the smuggler's lips. "*Only a princess* would expect to be rendered a service without offering compensation. I need to eat, my boat requires attention to remain functional, all of that takes funds. You might be used to the world accommodating you, but outside of palaces, things are more base." Her words held a level of intensity Xinyi didn't think she'd earned, even with the insult. No, this woman was used to being disliked and had developed an angry streak in response. She was perhaps self-conscious, but it didn't stop her being bold, direct, even vain about her own abilities. "See me, I'm just a world traveler on her way to Ooloo'a, but I need food for the journey and funds to repair my boat when I pass through storms and means to defend myself from a dangerous world that tries very hard to crush any woman who dares to go out on her own. And that means sometimes," she leaned in, whispering with venomous drama, "disobeying laws and aligning yourself with the sort of scum who ask for money to help you, but don't try to force you to be something you're not."

Xinyi wasn't sure she was taking this lecture how the criminal wanted. Her mind tingled, her pulse raced, and her writing fingers twitched with ideas. Wouldn't it be fun to write an adventure from V's perspective? To show the reader why she was who she was?

"So yes," *Shiraz* continued. Her eyes drilled into Xinyi, stealing her ability to move or think. All she could do was breathe and listen. "I'll escort you upriver, past human patrols and magical impediments. I will lead you ways only I know, and you will get to your thieves safely so that you can...what? Nicely ask them for your treasure back?" She paused briefly, but Xinyi had no specific answer to give and the woman's smug look as she barreled on made it clear she knew it. "But I will *only* do it for a fee. Because it risks my life, my craft, and my freedom. That, princess, is how the world works."

Xinyi gulped air when the woman finally stepped back, looking cold and superior. Xinyi was sure she had fair points to make. But her mind had yet to start properly functioning again. So she was not prepared to argue.

"I...I do not have much. They stole my only means."

"How about the bag?" The woman pointed at Xinyi's wedding bag, the last thing she had left of her marriage. "Elvish thread, gems for beads. That's worth a fair amount."

Wei had given this to her on their wedding day. It depicted his aunt and uncle's home, and a nectar tree with blossoms falling into the basket where she was found. Xinyi's chest clenched as tight as her hands were around the bag.

"This is where you came into my life. Where our friendship was born, and our love. This is to remind you we are your fate. This was always meant to be your home and we were always meant to be your family."

Even after how things had ended, Xinyi needed this bag. She needed to be a part of his family still. His aunt and his uncle had been her parents, his brothers and sister, her cousins. If she let this go, it would make her an orphan again. It meant nearly as much to her as the story she was braving this base world to retrieve. This was a symbol of her old family, and the book a symbol of her new. She must defend it, but no words came out of her mouth.

She had nothing else. Nothing. But if she had nothing else, then she had nothing to offer this mercenary woman. No mercenary worked for free. How had Xinyi thought she could do this without means? She had always been without means, always, until Yinuo suggested selling the stories Xinyi told her daughter at night. Suggested taking power in her own life.

Selling those stories, letting Jian into the world, made Xinyi feel strong. But her strength had been stolen.

The silence stretched on such a long time. Xinyi couldn't understand why the woman had not left. The smuggler just stood there examining Xinyi's grip on the bag dispassionately.

She shrugged. "I'll take a share of your *greatest treasure* once we get that back. Forty percent to get you there and back," she offered.

She was thinking of treasure as gold or gems, not Xinyi's next thirteen written and edited installments of Jian's story. Xinyi ought to explain. She could offer the woman forty percent of the profits from the book sells, but that was not the immediate funds she would be expecting. Xinyi doubted the woman would stick around for steady, *honest* employment.

Xinyi also had no qualm over allowing the woman to read one hundred percent of the story without charge. But she doubted the River Serpent would accept such a payment. Xinyi ought to explain. The woman was clearly offering kindness, not forcing Xinyi to give up her last vestige of her former life in exchange for her assistance.

But there was no chance that the woman would help if she knew that she was going after pages of a manuscript, not silver and gold.

Xinyi had come out into the world planning to channel Jian. And Jian would be honest. She would confess all and beg assistance. And the world would honor her honesty. Or…the thief would kidnap her and Jian would fight her way to freedom. But always honestly. Xinyi should be equally honest. It was the right thing to do. The moral thing.

But…what would V do? How would V go forward faced with this dilemma and without the aid of her magic?

Xinyi stole a deep gulp of air, hardening her spine. She nodded her agreement, but her mouth opened to rush out one more request. "But only if you also help me to retrieve my treasure from the thieves."

Xinyi felt sick. Awful for lying. Every second terrified that this lie was as transparent as her earlier attempts to interrogate vendors. But she needed help. She would think of something, some way to pay them back. Or…maybe not. She had intended to inflict her bad luck on the criminals. Maybe this was how she did it. Maybe this, finally being willing to lie and manipulate and thrust her curse on others, was how she would keep a family she found.

The smuggler grinned. "That is the first prudent thing you've said, princess." She gave a mocking bow. "It would be my honor."

Princess Trouble in the Pink Dress

Makoa was having the hardest time not laughing. The hardest time. Never in their near thirteen years of working together had anyone manipulated Shiraz in just that way. He led Princess Xinyi towards the River Serpent, carrying one of the two baskets of food her friends pressed on them. Largely nectar fruit. Which was nice, of course, but hardly made for a meal. Still, free was free—mostly.

The woman who handed them to Makoa took his face between her hands and, looking deeply into him, said, "It's past time you used what you've been given and get to know others more deeply."

He didn't know what to make of it, so he'd just thanked the woman and took the offered fruit.

The princess was a nervous talker. She hadn't stopped talking even to breathe since they left her friends. An interesting contrast to Shiraz, who was fully silent, staring at the woman with a sour expression poorly masking her interest.

"So you see it's essential that I get my treasure back. I don't know what I would have done without the other widows. And if I cannot contribute…"

"We agreed to forty percent. I'm not altering our bargain because you are a widow," Shiraz muttered under her breath. It was low enough one might make the mistake of thinking she hadn't meant the princess to hear. But she had. "And neither is Makoa."

Makoa glanced back with a grin. Shiraz was trailing them and had gone from her recent bored attitude to just about the grouchiest he'd seen her in months.

The princess was going to be trouble. It remained to be seen if that trouble would be good or bad. But Makoa enjoyed a gamble. So he meant to make this as fun as possible.

"You were saying?" he prodded the princess. She was chewing on her lips with slightly narrowed eyes, restraining some snide remark. She shouldn't bother, but he imagined by the time they got her upriver, she would have figured that out for herself.

"All I was saying is that I need to contribute. I need the others to know how much I value them. We were small alone, just a bunch of widows and their children, fighting to survive a war. Then Mei suggested we would all be happier if we came together and—"

"I know I'm always happier with partners who at least try to *come together,*" Shiraz joked, chuckling even with the first word, very pleased with herself.

Makoa snorted softly. The princess picked up on this double entendre, but didn't seem to approve of it anymore than the first. Or… she was breathing so hard it was clear she was restraining something, but Makoa did see her lips twitching just a bit, and her eyes might just be sparkling under those drooping lids.

"Here we are, *the River Serpent,*" Makoa said, and gently nudged the princess.

She turned with her lips raised. "Oh, The River Serpent is the name of the boooooat?" But her expression froze, and her voice dropped off. And once she blinked, her expression became one of absolute horror. Oh yes. She was going to be a great deal of trouble.

"*That* is how you get upriver? Will it even hold one of the baskets of food?" The words were out of Xinyi's mouth before she had the good sense to restrain them. But...really? It was a tiny, flat skiff that looked like a bunch of boards held together by string! There was a long pole for steering, and she *supposed* it was large enough to hold all three of them, but she wasn't sure it would stay above water long enough for all of them to step on.

How did they get anywhere on that piece of junk? It couldn't possibly have brought thieves and kidnappers.

"The Serpent is sturdier than meets the eye, and very slippery," Makoa reassured, wrapping an arm around her as the captain growled and stepped forward, probably to kick Xinyi into the river.

Xinyi swallowed her words of doubt. For safety purposes, the boat didn't look safe. But its captain looked positively menacing.

Xinyi shouldn't have said anything. And she probably should have laughed at the woman's joke. It might have endeared her to her just a bit.

It was a little embarrassing having missed the smuggler's first sexual entendre. Alright it was *a lot* embarrassing. Not that she would have laughed, it wasn't funny. But...Xinyi was not some naive woman entirely unfamiliar with sexual innuendos. She just wasn't used to having them said to her. Or about her. And certainly not from strangers. Xinyi would never make a sexual joke on a first acquaintance, so she hadn't been expecting one. But she was perfectly capable of making such jokes, if she ever wanted to, which she rarely did. And she could certainly *understand* them.

The woman's second joke was actually funny. And, upon a very little reflection, Xinyi thought it likely that Mei actually meant the words exactly the way the smuggler did.

Yinuo had invited them all into the palace and offered them protection and food. But it was Mei who had made them a community, encouraging them all to take part in building their home and pursuing their passions and their personal bonds. Even if she hadn't meant the words that way originally, if Mei heard the joke, she would have laughed. She would have winked; she would have played along. Xinyi might have too, among friends. But she would never have been so comfortable with a stranger. This smuggler was very...confident.

"Let me show you." Makoa led Xinyi to stand on the skiff. It was barely wide enough to hold them both, and she'd lost count of how many times she tripped today alone. She didn't want to be here. She held her breath, clenching all of her muscles tight. Makoa paused a few steps ahead of her. Setting down his basket, he lifted a large fan, nearly human sized, that had been hanging off the side of the ship.

"Watch carefully," he said in an enticing voice. With great flourish, he flicked the fan open. It was painted with a lovely scene of undulating mountains in various hues of green, surrounded by beautiful blue ocean. Xinyi stepped forward, something about the image soothing her so she entirely forgot the precarious boat. But just as fast as he had opened it, Makoa snapped the fan shut, and Xinyi fell over again. But she didn't land in the water; she landed on the boat. The true *River Serpent.*

"Marvelous," Xinyi gasped. Flat on her back, she stared up into the green canopy that hung over the middle of the boat. It was much larger than it had seemed. It was wide, with a green canopy over the center, and a cooking pot and some seating near the front bow. And room enough for ten people at least to walk around or sit comfortably. As Xinyi took it all in, she caught sight of the captain on shore, her gaze so intent on Xinyi that even with her glare, Xinyi felt...admired. She jerked her gaze away.

"How amazing!" Xinyi accepted Makoa's hand. He pulled her up easily, which was good as she was far too busy avoiding the captain's gaze to worry about little things like her balance. "It looks so much smaller when one is outside. Flimsy even." She spun around and around as Makoa led her further onto the ship.

"That's the idea," Makoa said. "It wouldn't make for much of a smuggling vessel if it were obvious."

"Does it always look so...unassuming?" Xinyi used the nicest word she could think of for the floating piece of trash she'd seen. "From the outside? If you were to pass another boat on the river, would they see us all floating on a few pieces of wood?" She giggled.

"Sometimes yes, sometimes no." Makoa shrugged. "Once that particular illusion is revealed to you, it doesn't work on you ever again. So anyone who knows about it sees the ship's true size. But the illusion adapts to what is reasonable. If the ship were full, one wouldn't see fifteen people standing on a few planks of—"

"Oh!" Xinyi didn't mean to interrupt, but she rushed forward laughing. There at the front of the ship was the pole that had fallen off the gem trader's ship. "It was you! I did see a red panda stealing the necklaces!"

Makoa laughed hard. "Yes, you nearly got me caught, princess trouble. That hasn't happened to me in years."

"Sorry." Xinyi didn't think her apology was very convincing, beaming as she was, but really, she wasn't sure she was sorry at all. This was all so wonderful. And she hadn't even left the river market. She was sure Makoa had only told her a few of the boat's secrets. Hopefully she'd get the chance to see them all in action.

The Brooding Captain Resents Her Cargo

As the boat sailed along the river, the perky positive princess peppered Makoa with questions. Shiraz was at the stern with her steering pole propelling the ship, *upriver,* by the power of her muscles and her know how...and fine a slight enchantment on the ship that made it easier to move under the power of one person.

The princess was bouncy and energetic as if the whole world had opened before her and she wanted to understand it all. Shiraz found it annoying, for multiple reasons.

One: All of the woman's enthusiasm was directed at Makoa, when it was Shiraz who was doing the work! Makoa would do his part when it was his turn, but that didn't stop it being annoying right now to be the only one working. The only one who'd stolen funds and food, the only one working the pole, the only one referred to as scum for having done it.

Two: The princess had such a *perky* way of looking at everything. Oh, wasn't Makoa's *curse* wonderful? Oh, how delicious was each individual piece of fruit? Wasn't *Makoa's* thieving cute? Shiraz was scum, but he was amazing. The princess loved the cool of the river, the song of the river, the rush of the water pushing against Shiraz's work. She was fascinated by the various spells Shiraz had collected.

Makoa had given her a rather benign account of the illusion spell on the ship and an overview of a few others. Saying things like it was achieved by magic or a spell. When building this boat was achieved by Shiraz stealing enough Dinga berries from an underwater cave in a period of seven minutes. Sucking in air and swimming back and forth from the surface to a cave thirteen feet deep, with electric eels stinging her, and tiny fighting dragons nipping at her heels as she brought as many berries as she could carry to the witch waiting on shore. Shiraz had been bleeding, stung and breathless, with her eyes pounding and her body aching, but it was worth it. Because in exchange, the witch made the boat as adjustable as a snake, larger on the inside, and able to almost fully compress its form without compressing anything within its walls. A smuggler's dream! Shiraz's dream.

Shiraz had spent years imagining her perfect vessel, and more planning out its every crevice. Then she had bartered, worked and stolen to get all the spells she needed to make it work.

The River Serpent was her creation! Even if she had to nearly drown to get one spell. Burned a patchwork of scars into her back to get another. She'd earned this fabulous steering pole (made of elfwood, thus four times as strong as the world's strongest man, more supple than the swaying trees of the Feffa islands so it would never break, and magically enchanted to return to the boat should it ever be dropped) by transporting the youngest of the elf king's world scattered children through secret byways in the war torn country, so she couldn't be kidnapped and used to draw elves into the human war. By the time she'd realized Princess Helima hadn't wanted to enter her father's kingdom, it was too late to refuse and escape with her life. Every spell cost a compromise of some kind. And every piece of this ship she had earned. Only with this last spell would it finally be the ship she had imagined.

One more spell and she could take it anywhere. She could slip between the volcanic spouts that bordered the last group of islands in the Ooloo'a chain and find the Singing Hills.

Despite all the magic she had seen, and how little it inspired in her, still Shiraz had to know if those hills were real. She needed them to be real. So she worked and she compromised and she achieved.

But Makoa and the perky princess talked about it all like magic was something extraordinary, something free of suffering. Something from another realm where things just happened because they should.

It was soooo annoying.

C: Makoa had not stopped wearing Ayinde's form. Shiraz regretted everyday that she had gone to Maltuba after returning to Glen Harrow and realizing both her brothers had left. She didn't want to know that her brother was dead. That Noam had left the island she had celebrated. He deserved to be out in the world where he could be seen for all of his beauty. But to know that she would never see him again made all of the magic she'd gone seeking seem pointless. She never should have left without him.

For all she knew, both of her beloved brothers were dead. Ethan had left home to hunt witches apparently. A foolish endeavor. Magic did not make one indestructible, but magic having limits did not mean a sheltered boy from *the steadfast island* could find and stop them. Nor should all witches be viewed as equally culpable as the only one he knew of—who harmed their entire family in an attempt to punish father. And none of them should be *hunted* for their mistakes.

Seeing Makoa in Ayinde's body made her sad. Took her back to the angry girl she'd been before she left Glen Harrow. She wished he would change into something else. Anything. Even a goose, and those things were the stuff of her nightmares.

Which brought her to four: Regrets.

"So you were the people who helped the thieves come to Hi'mau?" the princess had asked.

"My boat is the only safe way between borders," Shiraz bragged.

"Then you would also be the ones who helped a group of kidnappers try to take Princess Qiu. Five-year-old Princess Qiu," she said, her voice laden with judgement.

"Seems so." Shiraz lifted her chin to challenge the woman to say more. Though she regretted that.

"I see." Xinyi looked Shiraz over as if she were something despicable, incomprehensible. As if Shiraz had taken on that job with pride and would have carried away a child with pleasure.

It was part of what was making her...disinterested of late. She hadn't known they were after kidnapping when they asked for passage. Shiraz would not have helped them if she had known that. She didn't think. Part of a deal she'd made to get one of the ship's enchantments was that she would not turn away any paying passengers until the war was over. So it had become something of a habit, even now that things were settling. But she wasn't sure of herself. She might have turned them away if she knew. She surely would have turned them away if she knew they were after a child.

It was Makoa, in the shape of a jungle cat, who had led a jumble of animals to save the child and chase the kidnappers to a group of ogres. Human was a particularly special delicacy to ogres, but having formed friendships among humans over the years, most ogres restricted themselves to eating only bad humans. Murderers, abusers, scheme payout advance lenders—fathers in law.

The last kidnapper had not even been that lucky. Ogres killed humans quickly before cooking them to perfection. But the last kidnapper fled back to Shiraz's boat and was carried down the Nanghi River, into the Tranquil Sea, then down around the mer reef of Loqwan until she came to the Cave of Suffering, thus named because of the group of female water spirits who lived there. They were not mer, but often confused for them, they would call out in songs of avarice, beckoning wicked men. Once there, the men were fed delicious and hallucinogenic fruit that would cause their nightmares to become real as the spirits consumed them alive. The men would cry out in agonized suffering and the spirits grew strong, not off the human flesh, but off the suffering.

Shiraz hated people who hurt children. She hated herself for having unwittingly had a hand in it. Even though the child was safe now, something like that was bound to haunt her for the rest of her life. And Shiraz had a hand in it.

She was scum.

The princess's words rolled around in her mind, angering her, annoying her, torturing her.

And also five: the woman reminded Shiraz of how exciting it was leaving home. Entering a world of magic and wonder. She reminded Shiraz of fruitless hope.

Shiraz pushed the boat on faster. She wanted this woman gone.

That was until the woman in question approached Shiraz looking uncomfortable. She'd been fidgeting for the last half hour, but Shiraz didn't have any fancy cushions for royal behinds.

"Excuse me." The princess leaned near, her voice at a whisper. "How does one…" She looked around and her red face got redder. Shiraz had never seen a face look so like a tomato in her life. It was interesting.

Not attractive on its own, though it didn't detract from her appeal. Only made one want to throw some cold water over her to extinguish her visibly burning skin.

"How does one what?" Shiraz said at her usual volume. The woman gasped and leaned nearer.

Oh. Shiraz laughed internally but managed to keep her expression bland. This was going to be fun!

The woman drew in a deep breath, steeling herself for an ordeal. And Shiraz basked in anticipation. There were plenty of reasons to resent her cargo, but at least one not to.

1. Fun!

She wondered if she could get the woman to say the word piss. That would be everything. The prim woman in the confection of a dress brought down to human things like *pissing* and *shitting!* Ah, sometimes life was very good.

Kaagok- A Delicate Delay Worth an Additional Four Percent

Utterly humiliated, desperate, shaking, and very warm in the face and chest was not how Xinyi imagined she would die, but she began to suspect it would be. Certainly if the captain of the ship had anything to say about it. Xinyi was having trouble with her character, making it make sense. How could a woman be part of bringing kidnappers to take Qiu? How could she be so cold and unkind, but have such a warm and lovely friend?

The woman's blank expression made Xinyi want to return to Makoa for the answer, but...women were not supposed to discuss bodily functions with men. And here was a woman she could address her concerns to and the woman was being obtuse.

The worst of it was, Xinyi had a feeling it was intentional. The woman was awful. But Xinyi had never bowed to awful people before and she would not do so now.

"Might there be a place where I can relieve myself?" Xinyi managed to ask in a whisper and maintain her dignity.

"Ohhhhh." The smuggler stretched the word out as her smile was stretching and made no attempt whatsoever to lower her voice. In fact, she might have raised it.

Xinyi couldn't bring herself to look at Makoa.

The captain jerked her left hand over her shoulder, indicating the hull of the ship.

"See the handles, and the bowl-shaped dip in the hull? Back into it, lift your skirts and do your business. There is a lip to sit on, and the handle will make sure you don't fall in after it."

Xinyi gasped, horrified. She was not doing that! She opened her mouth to protest, tears coming into her eyes. But nothing came out of her lips or her eyes. She stared at the other woman helplessly.

The smuggler snorted, dropping the pole with which she steered the ship to cover her own amusement. "Azaqif." She chuckled as the pole slid away into the water. Xinyi jerked forwards after it, but the woman was too busy being rude to notice. "I've never seen anyone that offended by the ship's seat of honor. Settle your feathers, there is also a piss pot behind the screen. Toss it after. I don't want a smelly ship."

"I—" It wasn't so much the pronoun that escaped her lips, as the sound the letter made, or a tiny noise of shock. The woman couldn't be serious.

Xinyi had used a piss pot. She had even cleaned them when she was younger. But not in gowns like this. Not on open ships. Not *in public*. And she certainly hadn't then disposed of her waste in such a public fashion.

Xinyi jumped, yelping in shock and barely managing to keep the urine in her body, as the steering pole appeared on deck between them. Still Xinyi couldn't force words out. The other woman was clearly loving every minute of making Xinyi uncomfortable. She bent to retrieve the pole with a wide grin.

"What did you think you would do in the jungle? Maybe we should turn around and leave you in the market. Bring you the treasure when we find it," the captain offered sweetly. Too sweetly.

Xinyi hardened her spine. If this untrustworthy, unkind woman thought she was going to trick Xinyi out of her treasure, she had another thing coming. Fine. They thought she was a princess; Xinyi would behave exactly how they expected.

"I would like you to take me aground to handle this. Now, please," Xinyi said firmly, lifting her head higher with every word.

"No," the captain replied, her grin more than her tone indicating her pleasure in refusing. "We cannot stop the boat every time you need to piss. Delays cost me money."

"I will not subtract from our agreement for doing what I requested," Xinyi argued.

"I meant it costs me money from taking *other* jobs. Or did you plan to cover those?"

Xinyi narrowed her eyes. This woman was so greedy, and seedy, and low!

"I'll stop for an extra two percent of your treasure."

The longer they spent in each other's company, the less Xinyi regretted not telling the woman her treasure was nothing but paper and ink. It served her right.

Externally gracious, but internally vindictive, Xinyi dipped her head, accepting the new terms.

The princess's enraged expression lit fires in Shiraz! Her whole body tingled with it. Who knew the sweet princess had a glare inside of her? And wasn't it delightful that Shiraz was the one to wake it? She felt like skipping! The woman definitely looked angry now. At least five tenths of the way to fully pissed. Halfway! Shiraz had been all set to give in, with the poor thing floundering so hard. She'd thought this was not a woman built for adventure. You couldn't worry about modesty if you wanted to roam the world. She'd been feeling bad for taunting the sheltered princess and was ready to tell her about the little room below deck for just her purpose. Then the princess squared her shoulders and started making demands like a champ! And Shiraz was in love.

Momentarily. She had no illusions about lingering loving feelings. But she enjoyed it when it passed through her life. More than anything she loved a woman who fought back, and so sweetly. What could Shiraz do but give in?

She scanned the magical map tattoo on her left forearm. There didn't appear to be any immediate danger nearby, nor were they on the territory of any criminals. There was a part of her tattoo that was...sort of filmy, and unclear, but it was much farther into the jungle than they needed to go.

Shiraz hopped out of the boat first, into about a half a foot of water. It splashed up, sprinkling her legs, but when she stood in it, the water didn't reach above her boots. The princess wouldn't want to soak the bottom of her gown, so Shiraz reached up to lift the baggage free. That was the only reason, naturally.

"Oh, no. I am sure to be too heavy for you," she protested shyly.

It took a great deal to restrain the words— *"Oh, I build up my strength daily, so I can carry pretty princesses through puddles."*

It sounded cute and flirtatious in her head. Makoa who, in deference to the woman's discomfort was pretending rather well (without transforming) to be a plank of wood, would have laughed or winked. But Shiraz had a feeling the princess would take it as an insult.

Which it wouldn't have been. And anyway, she was already upset. Shiraz ought to save some ways of annoying her for later.

So she only coaxed her forward with curling fingers. "I carry all sorts of cargo much further. You're wasting minutes."

The princess clenched her jaw as if she expected to be dropped, but she allowed Makoa to hand her out without further protest. A weird choice. Shiraz never would have trusted Shiraz in the same situation. But this woman gave over, and Shiraz gathered the bundle of perfume, fabric, and warm woman into her arms happily. She carried her for all of fifteen seconds and enjoyed every one. It was fun how the other woman held her breath and scrunched up her face, preparing to fall. Lovely how soft and alive she felt against Shiraz's chest. And fun to contemplate playing with her, she could pretend to drop her! But the princess didn't seem ready to play. And Shiraz had no desire to be pissed on, so she set her down away from the water.

"Thank you," Xinyi said in a small voice.

Shiraz popped her brows and led the way into the brush until they found an area with bushes on most sides.

"Here is a nice spot for a kaagok." Shiraz waved grandly.

"A what?" the woman inquired seeming both curious and annoyed, a fun combo.

"Kah· gok," Shiraz pronounced slowly. "It is a Maltuban word. Means shit-hole. It sounds better in Maltuban." She grinned at the other woman's narrowed eyes. Shiraz was tempted to tell her about the collection of Maltuban curses back on the boat. Shiraz had met a young woman compiling them with little stories between and had been gifted an unfinished edition, because her brother had inspired the idea. The princess seemed the sort to be offended by things like collecting books of curses and insults. But Shiraz read it constantly. She treasured it, partially because it was funny and she loved knowing new ways to insult people. But mostly because it was a connection to Noam; she was proud to know that he had touched other lives. It made her happy that other people loved him, and missed him, and understood his humor.

"Shall Your Majesty dig her own kaagok?" Shiraz asked with a wide grin. "Or will I be getting another two percent of your treasure?"

"Two?" Xinyi demanded. "For a hole?"

"I run by the rule of scum. Wherein the person with the supply, *me*, gets to set the price. I suggest making up your mind quickly. I add on a delay surcharge of one percent per minute."

"Just dig the hole and give me some privacy," the princess snapped. Looking fully six tenths of the way to pissed.

Ah yes, life was good to Shiraz some days.

Never Wake A Sleeping Pixie— Definitely Not Fifteen!

Xinyi tried to be as quiet as possible as she…utilized her *shit hole*. She could hear the other woman humming as she walked away. It set her more at ease. She didn't know why she was so embarrassed. Everyone did this. And from the sound now coming from a ways off, the captain was taking this opportunity to do it as well. But she didn't like these strangers knowing something so personal about her.

As soon as she was finished, Xinyi rushed to cover up the hole and right her clothing. She wanted to wash her hands before the captain lifted her once more. She heard a stream up ahead so she moved that way, instead of heading back towards the boat.

She'd been entirely shocked when the woman carried her, seemingly without difficulty. She was strong. Xinyi had been clenched up in preparation for a fall when the woman set her gently down. She'd nearly fallen from her own clenched muscles, it had been such a shock.

Xinyi moved through the jungle. The air was cool and damp, and she could hear little animals scurrying around and birds singing. The further in she went, the more melodic the noises sounded. Even the stream. There was a cadence. It was so beautiful. Everything about the area called for peace. The canopy of trees decorated the sky with an interwoven pattern of green shades and soft blue lights. There were hummingbirds and butterflies hovering around patch of flowers, seeming most connected to the closed buds. They did not try to drink from their nectar but hovered about them attentively as if caring for them. Their wings created a gentle buzz, and a soft breeze that carried the scent of the flowers.

Xinyi swayed with the sounds. The fingers of her right hand twitched with a desire to pick up a pen and write the words drifting through her mind.

The tune ran up from the ground, tickling between Jian's bare toes and through her being until she was swaying. Her arms extended away from her body but curved back around towards herself. There was a bundle there, something warm and pulsing with life. Something small and soft. A baby! Whose she couldn't say, for she knew it was not her own. But she swayed with it, danced, holding the little bundle to her chest and humming in time to the music. She blinked down, into the cradle created by her arms, but she could not see what she felt. There was—

"What are you doing?" the captain demanded. She came up alongside Xinyi and her voice grabbed her with a shocking harshness in the midst of that vision, though the woman had not touched her.

"I..." Xinyi blinked several times, trying to pull herself fully into the present. It was hard sometimes when the story caught her, to recognize that the "real" world was as important as the one in her head. Some people would say more so, but never her.

"I wanted to wash my hands."

"And this couldn't have been done in the giant rushing river we are traveling along because?" the woman prompted. Her eyes looked sharp and annoyed. But Xinyi wasn't having that. Her temper was much faster to flare when yanked out of a forming story.

"There is a stream right here!" Xinyi moved roughly around the woman, wanting to shove her, but they didn't touch. "You do not have to be so grouchy about absolutely everything."

Xinyi crouched by the stream and shoved her hands into the flow of the water, scrubbing them together.

"Wandering off in a jungle full of things willing and able to kill you is not nothing."

Xinyi scoffed at the melodrama, but the captain wasn't finished.

"You're paying me for your safety, and I take that seriously."

"Why?" Xinyi demanded. "Because I haven't paid you yet?"

"Mostly, yeah!" the woman shouted. Her voice broke through every bit of peace surrounding them.

The air shuddered then went still. Even Xinyi stiffened. As one, the butterflies and hummingbirds turned towards them. The closed buds they attended fell slowly open.

"Kuffik szou," Shiraz cursed in a tiny breathless whisper.

Xinyi didn't know the words, but she knew a curse when she heard one. She also knew from the violent contracting of her heart that something very bad had happened. A hand fell on her shoulder, jerking her, trying to make her stand, but Xinyi couldn't move.

"We need to go," the captain whispered. "Those are baby pixies."

Each of the blossoms had a glowing ball inside of it. *Rising* from it. They started out mostly in a soft of yellowish light, but the wider the petals went the brighter they became. And no longer only yellow. The balls grew brighter and brighter, red, and yellow, and pulsing purple light spreading wide and collapsing in, again and again, with such violence it hurt to see. Xinyi's ears pounded with sharp pressure. Her eyes watered and her head pulsed.

She felt the captain pulling on her but didn't realize until she tumbled onto her back that she was also yelling.

She couldn't hear her. It was hard even to make out her face with the lights pulsing and the world screaming at Xinyi.

The captain bent down suddenly, and with a hand under Xinyi's armpit yanked her up. Xinyi saw her mouth very clearly *"RUN."*

So she ran. Or she thought she did. They were both moving, running away from the pulsing light. The trees moved around them, but...it made no sense. They moved *around*—in a circle.

Xinyi and the captain ran forward, but the jungle moved too. Xinyi tried to find an escape. But there was none. They were going to run forward, in circles, forever. She giggled. It made no sound, but the trees shuddered with it, as if amused by her amusement. This was nonsense.

The world shifted again and suddenly there was a cliff ahead. Xinyi could see out over it to the river, where the River Serpent and Makoa waited. A daring look entered the captain's eyes that was as frightening to Xinyi as the cliff before them. The woman didn't slow down. If anything she ran faster, towards the edge. She reached out for a hanging vine with one hand and Xinyi's waist with the other, but Xinyi pulled backwards just as the woman raced off the edge, alone. Not how she meant to be from the look of shock on her face.

The whole jungle shook with laughter as the smuggler swung out above the jungle, her face contorting with confusion.

"Sorry," Xinyi tried to shout. She was terrified of heights. The woman was swinging back towards her, and light enveloped the criminal. When it cleared, there was a tiny grouchy looking fox, with hummingbird-type wings and beak where the captain had been. She hung in the air over the baby pixies on a vine, spinning around and around on a loop like a baby's mobile. How did she look so grouchy and so adorable at the same time? Xinyi had the silliest urge to reach out and snuggle the frustrated creature.

Xinyi giggled. Then screamed as her body was lifted into the air. She flew the same loop as the captain, waving about wildly to stop herself being pulled from the ground. When her arm flapped in front of her face, she realized she too had been transformed. She was some sort of combination flower and bird. She had bright pink wings with flower-petals for feathers and a round fluffy body like a sparrow.

What in the world of whimsy was going on?

Xinyi's mouth opened to laugh, to scream, she couldn't tell. She was floating above the ground, it was terrifying, but what came out was bubbles. Bubbles of many different colors. They floated towards the flowers and the fifteen balls of light, currently being inundated by the manic attentions of a full swarm of butterflies and hummingbirds.

One of the bubbles—POPPED—on the back of a hummingbird. It was shocking how loudly it popped. Shattering all the pressure of the silence. The light in the glen shifted; the angry reds and flashes of purple cooling to become vibrant pink and neon violet.

Xinyi and the captain bobbed around, bumping into one another. Their impact jarred their floating forms. They fell to the ground, back in their original bodies. Xinyi landed with a pained laugh-sob as the impact struck her right in the small of her back. Why was it always that spot? Her bottom alone was in the stream, her feet tossed up on one side, and her back slammed hard into the other. The captain fell atop her diagonally, her face cushioned by Xinyi's upper arm and her torso stretched across Xinyi's.

The captain shoved up with a pinched expression, indicating something had been jarred. But she paused, hovering over Xinyi's chest with their faces nearly touching and grinned warmly.

"Well, I can't say I didn't want to get on top of you, but maybe at a less dangerous moment, alright?" Xinyi heard her words as if from very far away. They floated around her, not really registering until long after the woman's wink, even after she had regained her feet and yanked Xinyi up.

They raced away, the captain far faster, as Xinyi's partially soaked gown fell at odd angles. Xinyi laughed as the woman's words finally hit her. She was outrageous. Xinyi didn't understand what was going on around her. Everything was bizarre. All she could do was run, tumbling over her gown as usual.

She fell once and became what felt like a tumbling ball. She cried out in shock as she bowled over the captain running ahead of her. The other woman let out a giant guffaw at the sight of Xinyi and gathered her into her arms.

"Come on, fruity princess, let's get you out of here."

She lifted Xinyi and ran. Xinyi tried to look at herself, but she was all curled up and couldn't move. It was the oddest feeling, she ought to be scared, but as the captain ran Xinyi saw trees with faces waving at them, and the air was full of color, and somewhere along the way the captain's face had fully transformed from its earlier grouchiness to one of amusement. She wasn't so bad, was she?

Xinyi felt oddly safe with this grouchy, loud voiced criminal. And as if that safety were what transformed her, she was suddenly tickled by the flying tail of her sash. It flew up and hit Xinyi in the face. She shoved it away, only to have the wet fabric get caught in the captain's legs, sending them both tumbling forward into the river with a giant splash.

The *Not So Great* Escape

S hiraz was in rare form. Makoa hadn't seen her smile like this in months. The princess didn't seem to like it much, but Makoa was happy with the return of Shiraz's playful side. Even if it was leading to unnecessary delays.

What was her plan? How did she expect to find the thieves? That they had dropped them a few miles from the Mushroom Grotto they knew, but that was all. Shiraz had been **unwilling** to take **her ship** to the grotto in the month since Makoa and Aiattaua had announced their bonding. As if she thought the absence would change things.

Makoa knew Aiattaua took it personally. He thought it had to do with his multiple other partners. But Makoa knew better. Shiraz was afraid that one day Makoa would leave her for good, choosing Aiattaua over her. She was frightened of seeing if she would choose to stay, when she hadn't been able to do that for her real brothers, or leave him behind. She didn't understand that one of Makoa's favorite things about Aiattaua was that Makoa didn't have to change at all to be loved by him. He could come and go in any skin and be loved for who he was inside. Just as he could with Shiraz, though there was nothing romantic to his love for or from Shiraz.

Shiraz and Aiattaua were actually alike in several ways. They tended to accept people for who they were. Aiattaua was a bit better at it, but he'd been doing it longer. And they were drawn to the same sort of people. It was mainly the ways that they differed that built the wedge between them.

But her dislike of Aiattaua wouldn't help their current situation. They didn't know the names of Xinyi's thieves. Or where they'd gone. They would need to go to the Grotto for their answers, and she hadn't mentioned it once. Surely, she was practical enough not to have taken this job out of spite. Surely, she had a plan to get them paid.

Not that you could tell with the way she'd walked off, carrying the back end of Xinyi's dress as if it was a train, and making jokes about dirt and unsullied princesses, which anyone could tell her was not the way to make friends. In the past months, she had been bored, depressed, and grouchy. But today she was teasing a pretty woman and intentionally taking her time getting her where she wanted to go. She was having fun again.

Bright colorful lights shifted through the trees in the distance. Birds took off, flying away from the clearing, and rodents and small animals followed along on the ground and in the trees. This didn't bode well. Makoa tied off the boat to go in after the women, only to see Shiraz come running out of the jungle carrying a giant nectar fruit and giggling.

"What in all the fairy nonsense?" Makoa shouted.

The bright colorful lights shifted into softer hues of pinks and purples and golds and the nectar fruit transformed into the princess.

Shiraz was yelling breathlessly "pixies," when she tripped on the other woman's dress and they both fell face first into the river.

It wasn't very deep, no more than two feet. But Shiraz went down hard, and both women yelped.

Shiraz groaned and shouted from her back, "We woke a nursery!"

"Damn." Makoa didn't stop to help the women onto the ship. He untied the moorings and ran to the stern. Shiraz would get the princess on board. The only other time Makoa and Shiraz had encountered a baby pixie, *a single* baby pixie, their ship had been transformed into a duck and the pair of them were lice on its back for two days until an adult fairy was able to convince the little creature that they would be more entertaining as themselves.

Pixies were to be avoided at all costs.

Makoa heard a loud wet thump-slurp, as someone, most likely the princess, hit the deck. Soaked through from the sound of it.

"Are you both on?" He shoved the steering pole into the water. All around, the trees were shaking. One particularly close to the ship stood up, shaking the dirt off it its roots and threw its branches up to the sky.

"Go!" Shiraz shouted. Her voice sounded low but if she could grab onto the ship, it would pull her along, so Makoa shoved the ship out into the flow of the river.

The standing tree began clapping, the force of its amusement shaking the river so hard that the boat rushed forward with the waves. A dizzying array of giggles rushed after them in a whirl of leaves and flower petals.

Makoa had a feeling they were being pursued. Just once, it would be nice if they needed to make a fast escape while following the direction of the river. It was much harder against the current.

The boat listed violently to the left, nearly flipping over. Makoa managed to keep his footing, braced against the wall of the ship, and using the pole as leverage. But the baskets of food went tumbling. He heard the princess stumble and cry out. There was a second plop, far louder than Shiraz should make, and the boat rocked violently.

"Shiraz?" he called out.

"Here!" Her shout sounded odd, deep and angry. But Makoa had no time to worry about it as an explosion of color and laughter and bright flashing lights was trailing them upriver. From every tree, birds fled. The jungle was chaotic with rushing creatures and deafening noises as they screamed out to one another.

"Ack! Oh, I'm..." There was a crash accompanying the princess's voice, and she stumbled around the canopy, tripping over the spilled fruit and rushing, drenched, to Makoa's side.

The ship wobbled wildly as *something* came forward.

"Shiraz," Makoa called out in concern.

"She's...she has..." Xinyi's eyes were bright with amusement and fear. She made a downward slashing motion in front of her face with both hands. Apparently unable to find words to describe Shiraz.

Then *Shiraz* lumbered around the corner of the canopy. In a whole new form. She was gigantic, frustrated, and in the mighty tusked form of a walrus.

Makoa couldn't help it; he cracked up. *Hard.*

"Never seen a look more suited to you," he teased, his eyes tearing.

Shiraz made a grumbly noise he supposed was meant to be a growl and lumbered forward awkwardly. Ohhh. It served her right, *the poor thing*, always so confident and agile, teasing the tumbling princess. It was too perfectly her just desserts to be real. But it was. Makoa cracked up all the more.

The ship veered left, banging into some rocks. A loud crunching noise accompanied the splintering of wood on the aft hull.

"Don't break my ship!" Shiraz shouted, her voice bark-like.

At her shout, the pixies, following in clouds of foliage, birds and butterflies, cried out as well. They were mimicking her cadence, but not her words, and the sounds painted the river. The waters rose and fell with the same rhythm as her words: a giant wave of red shot them up and forward, sliding down with a whirl and splash of orange that crashed over the side of the ship, soaking them all anew.

Xinyi giggled. The pixies painted the air with her amusement. Bubbles filled with tiny flowers or individual petals pursued the boats progress. And despite the danger, Makoa was tickled. This was a whole new sort of adventure.

Shiraz was the one transformed into an animal for once. And learning her limitations. And she didn't like it. But Makoa was neither foolish enough, nor mean enough, to point out that they were moving far slower because of Shiraz's extra weight. Or that walruses could swim. At her size, she could probably push them along.

"I'm sorry." Xinyi held out a hand, gently towards Shiraz. "I shouldn't have run. You...startled me." The pixies transformed the sound of her nervous laugh into an explosion of color.

The boat moved through the painted breeze, becoming spotted in different colors for every laugh they encountered.

"I don't care." Shiraz's growl-like tone belied her comments. "Get us out of here! We'll find a fairy to turn me back later."

The pixies seemed to like the rumble of Shiraz's voice and made the waves bubble and roll with it. The oddly helpful transformation changed the flow of the river. The boat raced upstream. And though Makoa had wished for that sort of luck only moments ago, he was so unprepared for it that the boat veered towards the shore.

The princess cried out as the boat lunged towards a giant rock along the shore. Shiraz shouted "NO" between her tusks. And Makoa only had time to throw up his hands before they struck.

Or rather before they—*landed*.

I Knew You Were Trouble

Having deposited Shiraz and her companions in a new impossible scenario was enough to satisfy even the most vindictive of the fairy babies. Their nursery attendants were now able to distract and round up the babies, leading the swarm back to the nursery. Leaving the River Serpent perched at a precarious angle atop a pointy rock, and Shiraz in the body of a walrus with no idea how she'd get out of this mess. Typical.

Pixies! She'd seen a whole pixie nursery. Shiraz wished she could enjoy that fact, but at the moment it felt like her body weight was all that was balancing the ship. If she moved, it would tilt. If she didn't move...what then? Stay exactly here, forever? She couldn't get the boat back in the water without seriously damaging it. At least not in this form. If she were in her own body, maybe she could shrink it. But her walrus flipper didn't appear to be wearing any of her jewelry! Already being in this form had harmed her boat when she'd used her tusks to climb on board. She couldn't let that happen again.

Shiraz needed to think. Then Xinyi started to cackle. She looked around at where they were poised, a large boat, balanced on the pointy tip of a bolder. Shiraz supposed there were more dangerous scenarios. If they fell, they were most likely to land in the river, from a height of no more than fifteen feet, so they likely wouldn't die from the impact.

But they would probably be injured, unless they landed in the deepest parts of the river. Unlikely. They were at the bank! But even if they managed to land in the center of the river, the boat would be following after them, and that impact alone was enough to kill.

"Why are you laughing?" Shiraz demanded.

Even once the princess stopped laughing, her smile spread and spread. She waved her arms, shifting the boat.

"Look at what we survived! Isn't it amazing? I've never seen anything magical! But we were transformed into weird bird creatures, a ball and a giant tusked creature."

"I'm a walrus, and you were a nectar fruit," Shiraz said without inflection, though she was possibly in awe. You wouldn't think a sheltered princess from the Jade Valley would handle this sort of thing well, much less enjoy it. She was soaked, had been magically transformed twice, and a huge delay had been added to her journey. She should be upset. But she was overjoyed.

"Really?" the princess giggled. "A nectar fruit?"

Shiraz dipped her head carefully, so as not to move the ship.

"Look." The princess stretched out her hand towards a blue and purple tinted bubble floating past in the air. "This is my laughter. I can touch my—"

"Don't!" Shiraz and Makoa shouted in unison, but it was too late. The princess touched the side of the bubble. It popped and out fell thousands of shadow spiders.

They fell through the air and landed everywhere, on everyone. They raced over the ship, over the fruit, over Makoa and Shiraz and the princess. Makoa spun around, batting at himself and stomping at the ground.

"They aren't poisonous." Makoa shuddered. Shaking, he knocked as many off of his skin as he could. "They aren't poisonous. They aren't poisonous."

Shiraz wanted to reach out and help. Makoa hated spiders like nothing else. But any slight move of her giant wiggling form set the boat tilting.

The princess rushed to help. Apparently she was no more afraid of spiders than she was of pixies with massive magical powers.

"You're safe. You're safe. Look, watch." The princess lifted a spider on her open palm and blew it away. It floated off with string trailing behind it, but as soon as it was a few inches away, the spider vanished. A wisp of mist floated where the spider had been. "You can make them become anything you want."

Makoa froze. He stared at the woman the same way Shiraz was, *suspiciously*. What was she? A witch? A fairy? An informal god? She didn't look particularly magical, but...looks could be very deceiving.

"You have to realize that you are safe," the princess said.

Xinyi approached Shiraz. Her wide sleeves hung heavily from her arms, dripping across the boards of the ship, leaving her more balanced than she had been thus far. "You can turn back too, without anyone's help. When you were carrying me, when I was a nectar fruit," she giggled. "I realized that I was safe, that the babies were playing, and everything would be okay. And once I realized that—I was myself again. You are safe."

Makoa didn't seem convinced, but he shut his eyes, holding in a breath, and when he opened his eyes, the spiders all blew away as leaves.

The ship was silent for a moment. Shiraz stared at the other woman. She was entirely unique.

Shiraz laughed. It was quiet and breathy, and disbelieving. But it was definitely a laugh. It occurred to her that she rarely felt safe. She was so used to looking out for danger and preparing for it so that she was always ready.

Neither she nor Makoa trusted easily. Although, it seemed from the vanishing spiders that it was an easier task for Makoa. The princess trusted the world enough that while transformed into a fruit and carried by a woman who'd been teasing her, she knew herself to be safe.

Azaqif. Was there something wrong with Xinyi? Or with Shiraz? Because Shiraz didn't even want to be that trusting.

"So what you're saying is, you think you're belief in your safety transformed you?" Shiraz asked.

"You said you would keep me safe, and...I hadn't paid yet. So I knew you meant it." The woman's lips lifted at the corner with that sly bit of humor, and Shiraz's chest was suddenly home to a thousand burning fireflies. "And since you haven't retrieved my treasure yet, you are safe with me too."

Shiraz chuckled. Hard. The boat tilted from side to side, tilting one moment towards the rocky shore of the river and the next towards the river's edge.

"Get her off the ship," Shiraz snapped as they rocked.

"No, we're fine. You're safe," the princess was calling out, but Makoa tugged at her. "Even if you were a walrus forever, I am sure Makoa would still love you."

Makoa choked briefly on a laugh. "Speak for yourself." He grabbed the princess around the waist and, breathing out, transformed himself into a large chimp. He leapt off the deck of the ship and made it into the branches of a near by tree still gripping the princess tight.

They were safe.

This felt somehow exactly like the lessons in belief that the elders had preached and also nothing like it. She watched Makoa and Xinyi land safely on shore. The princess's words rang in her ears and the woman managed to do what no one ever had before. She made Shiraz listen.

She was safe. *Shiraz was safe.* And just like that, she transformed. And the truth became a lie as the boat tilted towards the rocks, ready to topple with her on board.

Shiraz jumped toward the river, hitting the right eye of her snake bracelet five times to change its size.

She hit the water with a splash, in deep enough to only jam her legs, but not so deep as to be pulled along in its current. She managed to see the last of her boat's shrinking transformations. It was now five times as small as it had been. It tumbled into the rocks, getting bumped and losing some cargo. But it wasn't shattered, as shrinking it also changed its mass. It stopped in a little pool of water between rocks.

Shiraz waded through the water towards the shore with creaking aches shooting up from her ankles to her knees. She heard clapping and cheering from the edge of the jungle. Makoa was watching her with concern on his big chimp face. But the princess was all excitement.

"Oh, princess, you are going to be *a lot of trouble.*" Shiraz sighed with that burning feeling in her chest. There was something about this princess. She just didn't make sense. Shiraz could barely believe that her speech had worked, and yet—

It was magic. Like *real* magic. The unexplainable, unfathomable type. The type she'd been seeking her whole life. That, or there was something about this woman that she didn't know yet. Like that she was a sprite in disguise, a skin slipper! Or...some sort of trap. That had to be it. Because she didn't make sense otherwise. She didn't make sense at all.

Shiraz snagged a piece of nectar fruit floating by her in the water and took a big juicy bite. She needed to be careful of that woman.

Shiraz shoved up her sleeve to check her tattoo, unwilling to take any more chances at the moment. The vaguely unseeable area caused by the pixies was retreating, and for the moment at least, they seemed to be alone. Hopefully they stayed that way long enough for Shiraz to make some repairs to the ship. She made it to the rocks and lifted her battered and currently toy sized River Serpent into her arms.

The tattoo on her arm was magic. The bracelet she'd shrunk the ship with was magic. There were no less than fifteen spells on her ship. And Shiraz had encountered, sought out, and been injured by magic for years. So why was it that the first time the magic felt...special and unfathomable and monumental was when a prissy princess was telling her she was safe?

You said you would keep me safe... I believed you.

No one but Makoa trusted Shiraz like that. But...No. This was the same woman who called her scum a few hours ago. Shiraz shouldn't let her imagination run away with her. The princess didn't mean it. Not the way Shiraz took it. She just meant...exactly what she said, that she trusted Shiraz to keep her alive until she'd been paid. Anyone would trust Shiraz that way.

Itchy Writing Finger

"**I** am sorry I woke the pixies," Xinyi informed Makoa trying for apologetic, but from the smirk on his face she had not succeeded. "I don't mean to cause trouble."

Xinyi could barely catch her breath. Pixies! She'd seen pixies. She felt bad about the ship, and everything that had happened to its crew. She just...also felt *very* excited.

"That is a shame. If one is bound to cause trouble, they might as well mean it." Makoa winked. He had transformed again, into a fairy fellow of some years younger than Xinyi, likely in his early twenties.

He had lighter brown skin than the last man, and short cropped black hair, showing off his pointy ears, and a neatly trimmed beard. He looked nothing like the last fellow, but Xinyi knew Makoa from his voice, and his bright green eyes, and his beautiful energy. She felt very at ease with Makoa. His partner was another matter.

I can't say I didn't want to get on top of you... Xinyi shook off a shiver down her spine, glancing back at the captain. She was glaring over. Clearly the woman said wildly flirtatious things to everyone, even people she openly disliked.

The captain had waded out of the water a while ago, carrying the ship under one arm. Now she sat further down the bank with the boat.

She'd increased its size, so it was now the length of an average human adult, and she was making repairs.

Makoa and Xinyi had been tasked with gathering any of the cargo they could find. And *keeping away from the captain*. She was in an, if it was possible, even grouchier mood than when they had set out.

Xinyi supposed that was because her boat had been injured. But it was slightly diminishing Xinyi's enjoyment of her adventure! Who knew adventures were so fun? She wished she had her journal to take notes. She had been able to see her bag shrunken on the deck of the ship before Makoa dragged her away to do as the captain asked. At least she knew it was safe, but she needed to write. Pixies, transformations, escapes on the river. The captain a walrus, and then the boat magically shrinking right before her eyes! This day was amazing! She didn't even mind the dull throbbing in her lower back.

And for a few moments, as they ran from the pixies, as the captain carried her, with a smile on her face and laughter in her voice, Xinyi had been enjoying the woman's company. Not so now.

"I will try not to cause more trouble." Xinyi wasn't entirely sure she meant the words. That sounded awfully boring.

Her heart was still racing, and her mind was whirring like their bodies had through the air. She'd flown! Maybe she wasn't afraid of heights any longer. Maybe she wasn't afraid of anything. And this might be her only adventure. She didn't want it to be boring. She wanted it to be...outlandish, wild, silly and magical.

"I've never seen a pixie before. Before they made me a nectar fruit," Xinyi chuckled. "They transformed us into strange birds and made us float over them. The captain looked like a fox with wings."

"A hummingfox? They are generally considered to be the cuddliest of the fey animals. An interesting choice for her." Makoa smirked.

Xinyi smirked as well; she wouldn't call the other woman cuddly either. "What were you?"

"I don't know. A sort of flower bird with lots of petals for wings."

"A winged dhalia most likely. They are incredibly rare to find in the wild; they've been hunted so much to only exist in captivity. Their many petaled wings are said to make medicinal music."

"Goodness!" Xinyi said in soft delight, and horror. "The world is so full of amazing things. And you two are out here all the time. Is it always like this?"

Makoa let out a loud, single laugh. "Almost never. We encounter magic here and there, and the ship has many spells upon it, but in general we avoid any magic that can do us real damage."

"Why?" Until today Xinyi had avoided many things: inclement weather, awkward conversation, missing her tea. She was a creature of comfort in her ordinary life. But it seemed to her that criminals with a magic boat ought to be getting into all sorts of trouble and having a grand time of it. Otherwise what was the point? "Aren't you *adventurers?* Shouldn't you want to see all that is magical and wild? Why would you avoid danger when it is bound to lead to fun?"

"Because it can also lead to more danger than we are equipped to handle. Not all magic is sweet and playful. Pixies are born orphans with massive power. When they are little, they play with everything, trying to understand it. But a grown pixie might be sweet, or might not, and still has that massive power. If you get on its bad side, you are unlikely to come away unscathed."

Makoa stood before her transformed for the fourth time that she had seen. "And you were cursed." Makoa nodded but said nothing. "Was she?" Xinyi nodded behind her.

Xinyi could feel the smuggler's eyes on her again. They burned her through the layers of damp silk. She had been shivering for a while now, in her damp clothes and the cool of the breeze, but that woman's gaze could melt a glacier. Xinyi bent into herself to avoid the feeling and smiled at Makoa.

He glanced warmly at his friend. "Not as such. But that does not mean magic has always been kind to her. But...even though it has not always been kind, she still loves magic. It simply isn't in as...effusive a way as you love it."

Xinyi blushed. She had been called overeager and overly emotional as a child. But it had been many years since she let any of that out. She needed to calm herself. To conceal herself. But the way she had learned to do that was to write. She put her wilder side on paper and lived as others preferred.

"I am sorry, I—"

"Why ever for?" Makoa interrupted. "Your joy is beautiful! Do not apologize for loving life and embracing wonder. Be true to yourself. Always. But she must be true to herself as well."

Xinyi didn't know what to say. She wanted to ask so many more questions. About his travels. About his curse. *About his friend.* And he seemed to sense it.

"Shiraz is not very good at making new friends. It took us three random meetings and an additional two years of travel before she started trusting me. But," he leaned close and winked, "don't mention the number. She only knows about two of the times. I had not yet been cursed when first we met. And I was not...my best self. It might annoy her to realize how we first met."

Xinyi leaned in, delighted by his energy and the freely offered story, feeling in on a secret joke already.

"The second time we met, I was a fish. She was wet, hungry and fishing in a river amidst a rain storm. She caught me in a net and was planning to make me her dinner before I began speaking and gave her the fright of her young life."

Xinyi laughed in delight! How exciting that would have been. But before Makoa could say more, a thought leapt from her lips.

"How young was she?" Xinyi had been all alone in the garden of her future family when she was only three. She didn't precisely remember it, but she felt it inside. Xinyi hoped the captain had not been on her own that long. But even though she traveled with Makoa and called him friend, there was something about her that felt very alone. One could not imagine such a woman having ever been a child.

"I believe she was nineteen. She had left the island where she was born the year before and been traveling alone."

"Traveling all alone!" Xinyi shook her head. "At that age, I had not even left the home of my adoptive family," Xinyi confessed quietly, and rather unexpectedly. She rarely told anyone about any part of her life prior to marrying Wei. "My husband, Wei, was the first person to...coax me into the world."

All was quiet for a moment. Too quiet. Xinyi looked up, a blush spreading up her neck. She had no idea why she kept sharing today; it was not like her. But Makoa put her at ease. He would listen to all she had to say, if she wanted that. But she didn't. She wanted to listen.

"Please, continue your story," Xinyi begged.

Makoa did not speak immediately. After a moment, he nodded. "As soon as she had dragged us up on land, I let out a shriek—

Delusions of Dignity

"*D*on't eat me, for it will curse us both!" Makoa cried out in as dramatic and high pitched a voice as he could muster. A fish talking ought to be enough to get this girl to drop him. But he didn't want to take the risk that she was hungry enough not to care that he had feelings. Meat eaters in general appeared not to care for the feelings of their dinners, so it was prudent to lie. And fun!

Nothing in Makoa's curse implied that it would curse others to kill or eat him. But this carnivore didn't need to know that.

"Sea spirits!" the girl exclaimed and tossed Makoa away.

He flipped about on the ground very much like the fish out of water he currently was. He could change shape. He should have when she caught him. That would have been funnier. He liked scaring boring, non-cursed humans. But he also liked for it to be a hilarious story for the next fun person he met. He should have turned into a bear as she was lifting him out of the water. That would have scared her and unbalanced her, sending her face first into him and the water at the same time.

As he flipped around, thinking of all the better jokes to be had, the girl recovered. She had fallen backwards with her eyes wide and her not very impressive curse falling from her lips. But she was up, with tears in her eyes and her voice racing after him.

"I'm sorry. Please, I am so sorry. Let me help you. I will get you home."

Makoa lay still, allowing her to scoop him up. She was crying in earnest now, tears streaming down her stronger than the rain fall. But she raced with him down to the river, sunk to her knees and slipped him into the water, still offering apologies for having yanked him from his home to begin with.

Weird.

Makoa floated there, staring up at her on the shore with her hands braced on the ground and tears still falling. That was awfully dramatic. He was a single fish, and she looked hungry and wet, likely to die soon if she didn't toughen up.

Makoa hadn't recognized her at first, but he did now. She was that hungry pickpocket he'd hired for his wedding. She'd seemed confident and enthusiastic then, overconfident really, and that had suited his purposes fine—three months ago. A lifetime. She must be fast on her feet if she'd gotten out of that mess. Though clearly she wasn't the savviest runaway in the world.

As she was now, braced on her knees, with hairs coming out of her clearly a few days old crown braid and sticking to her face, she looked much younger. A child really. He ought to feel worse about his role in her current situation. The witch would have him feel worse. It made him wonder if she wasn't some trick. Her clothes were overlarge and unsuited for the rain; the wool vest and linen tunic and trousers hung pathetically off her as though she'd been starving. And here she was appearing out of nowhere to remind him that he had to *earn* a true love. Earn his freedom.

Annoyed, Makoa blew out a breath of—delicious to eat, but not so much to smell second hand—broccoli (his hexer's mode of spell delivery) and transformed into a rabbit. He hopped up on land, nudging her knee with his head.

"What's wrong with you? I'm fine."

The girl gulped. Hiccupped. Sat up straighter and stared at Makoa, panting. She didn't seem nearly as startled to hear his voice coming out of yet another animal as he would have expected from a boring (non-cursed) human runaway. Hadn't she been from one of those exclusively human islands? She should never have seen magic. Unless he was right, and she was some trick from that twisted witch.

Or... Makoa supposed the witch might have cursed her too, for proximity to Makoa's mess. Oops. If so, he *should* feel at least—a little bad. But he was just mildly curious.

"Have you been cursed or something?" he demanded. She had remained silent up to this point, but at least her sobs had stopped and her crying was slowing.

"No." She shook her head. "No. I wasn't cursed. I...am glad you are alright."

"So why were you crying? I'm not dead, no harm done."

"I..." She shook her head. "It wasn't about you. I'm just...tired, and hungry. And every time I find magic, it either hurts someone else, or it hurts me. And nothing is working out, and...I heard your voice and all I could think of was Elder Trent saying we were the *steadfast people* and we fed our dead to the sea so that they could be given new life. I always thought he was an idiot!"

The girl all but screamed before Makoa could say, *he sounds like an idiot*. This made Makoa laugh, his little bunny nose scrunching up and down and his fluffy tail wiggling. It also made him fairly certain she hadn't been sent by the witch.

"But what if I was wrong?" she shouted, coming to her feet. "What if I'm the idiot? What if you were some village boy come back as a fish? What if my mother is swimming around somewhere about to become someone else's dinner? And I left the island because of the way they treated us, but I really was the problem, like they always said."

"Okay," Makoa bobbed his bunny head and long bunny ears from side to side. "Fair enough, that was a lot. Go ahead and cry. But one cursed man's opinion to a non-cursed...?"

"Woman."

"Sure." Makoa rolled his bunny eyes. This was a girl if ever he'd seen one. But if she had delusions of dignity, who was he to contradict? "If you want my opinion, your elder was an idiot. You were right to leave. And in general, bad stuff happens to everyone. It's just a matter of deciding which sort of bad stuff you want. Being frightened when not-fish shout at you and questioning your whole existence. Or living in a place where you are treated like shit for knowing the people in power are fools."

"Well damn." The *woman* dropped on her ass in front of bunny Makoa. She crossed her arms, flipping her head to get some of her sopping hair out of her eyes. "That isn't the sort of speech you expect from a fluffy little bunny. Guess I won't cook you either, though you look more appetizing now than before."

They both laughed. And Makoa got a feeling he might wind up liking this kid.

How You Steal a Princess

The boat was as good as Shiraz could make it in the moment. When they got to another town or the grotto, she could buy some supplies, or find someone to make more permanent repairs. But she had patched the holes from her (temporary) tusks. Now she sat back, sighing in-between annoyance and amusement.

She hated having to make repairs to her ship. Hated watching anything happen to it and threaten her dream, her livelihood, her home. But...in the past few hours, she'd had more fun than she'd had in years. It was the same river, the same sights she passed every time she transported someone up the river. But today was interesting. Today was threatening. Today was special.

She watched the princess leaning on her knees, listening to Makoa with rapt attention. Shiraz had partially convinced herself that the woman was some sort of magical monster. But the rest of her— The rest of her wanted to be nearer to that trouble magnet.

Shiraz stood, stretching. Her knee was bruised, it made a jerking catch motion when she stood, and there was an unpleasant squelch in her wet boots. She wanted to get going so she could get changed. In a moment, she'd take the boat back into the river and change it to its ordinary size. But she'd want Makoa near for that. She came up behind them quietly enough that she caught the end of Makoa's story.

"We passed the storm together," Makoa said. "Sharing stories of our journeys. When the storm cleared, she went her way, towards a local harbor in search of passage to the Ooloo'a islands. And I mine, in search of someone to kiss me and free me from my curse." Makoa winked, as if inviting a kiss now. But he didn't wait for Xinyi to respond. Shiraz could tell that even if the princess hadn't noticed her, Makoa had. "I lived off that story for months, people paying for my meals to hear how I frightened her."

Shiraz rolled her eyes. She remembered feeling so confident after they parted all those years ago. She'd made it through the storm, she'd confronted magic and not been defeated, she'd survived being robbed and tricked and run out of town. She was so sure that as soon as she got to Ooloo'a, she would find the magic she was seeking. She hadn't even minded going on alone, thinking that every encounter would be like that. She would find magical, wonderful people and learn so much about so many lands, and all of it would be exciting and inspiring.

But Makoa was one of a kind. And their encounter as well had been special. She was lucky that they had found each other again.

Shiraz used to hate being alone. But since traveling, unless it was with Makoa, she preferred it. She was safer alone. Somewhere over the years she had stopped looking for encounters like the one she had with Makoa, and she hadn't really had another. *Until now*—Maybe.

"I did ask her for a kiss before parting. But she assured me that her true love would be found in a more magical way. Which I took very poorly. I may have been a bit curt with her." He wasn't looking her way, but Shiraz raised a brow at her friend.

A *bit curt*? He'd lost his temper and told her she would never find better than him. And if she thought she would, she should go back home. He was a very sore loser in those first years after being cursed.

Shiraz wondered now, when had he gone from being angry with the magic to being easy with it? Was that shift anymore permanent than his transformations? Which man would he be if he managed to break his curse?

Shiraz had a feeling she would lose him if he ever broke his curse. He didn't travel with her constantly; they would part ways when he grew antsy, or when she did, but would make plans to meet up and go forward as if they had never been apart. But if he broke his curse...that would be it, wouldn't it? He would find his *true love* and want to be with them forever.

She didn't like the idea. But she loved her friend. So she knew... when that happened, she would have to accept it, and sail away from one more brother. But she couldn't understand why he'd agreed to be bonded to Aiattaua when his kiss clearly didn't break the curse. Was it just that he feared being alone? She wouldn't let that happen. Or maybe he didn't even want to break the curse anymore?

"What could have been more magical than my transforming three times in the middle of a storm and reminding her of all the reasons she left home?" Makoa said as if annoyed by the lack of a kiss still. It was all pretense, the showman. She'd kissed him eventually anyway, and it had done him no good.

Xinyi giggled. "It might have felt more magical if she were dry and hadn't cried the moment she met you."

"You see." Shiraz startled Xinyi. The princess didn't jump this time, but it was a close thing. She leaned back so far, she had to grip the tree trunk she was seated on to keep from falling. "The princess understands. That is exactly what I have been telling you for years."

Makoa chuckled. "What have I told *you* for years? It is your need for magic to look pretty that hinders your search for it."

Shiraz bobbed her head from side to side.

You said you would keep me safe… I believed you.

"I don't know," Shiraz said softly. "Maybe it's like the pixies, and if I *believe* enough, I'll find that special magic I've been looking for."

Makoa chuckled hard, and Shiraz could tell from the stiffening of the woman in front of her that Xinyi also thought Shiraz had been poking fun. But the truth was so much scarier, so Shiraz kept it to herself, letting them mistake her words for a slight.

Makoa had been enjoying the princess's company. She was eager and bright, but she had depths to her. Her questions were insightful and sympathetic. Makoa was on his way to getting her to like Shiraz. When they were interrupted.

A group of monkeys were grabbing at the food he and Xinyi had collected. Shiraz looked around for something to scare them off with and Makoa was up and racing towards the little thieves. But monkeys in general were pretty fast, and this particular group were exceptionally well practiced. They jumped around, screeching and laughing, never letting go of the food. The Golden Paw Gang were the most feared thieves along the Nanghi river, ruthless, clever, fast, and… just rude.

A stick went hurtling through the air, past Makoa's ear and smacked one of the smaller monkeys in the gut. It cried out, dropping the fruit and fell backwards.

"Oh, leave them be," Xinyi called. "They just want food."

Shiraz and Makoa ignored her. They had experience with these creatures. If you gave a monkey a mango—it came back for *every bit of cargo* you had and drove you crazy. Shiraz let a second weapon fly, right at Screecher's head. Screecher, the largest of the monkeys, managed to catch the second stick and threw it straight back at Shiraz. He screamed out his success in an ear shaking tone. But it wasn't the success he'd thought, as Makoa managed to grab ahold of his tail and lightly toss him towards the river.

Shiraz raised her hand to throw a stick again, but the princess grabbed onto her arm. "Don't."

Makoa chased after the two remaining monkeys, each with a pair of fruits in their palms. The pair escaped into the trees, rushing off. Makoa turned around to find Shiraz and the princess staring each other down. Damn. All his fine work ruined by the monkey gang, leaving the women at odds again, over the silliest of things.

"You don't want them following us the whole way, *princess trouble,*" Shiraz snapped.

"They weren't hurting anyone," Xinyi insisted.

"They will, thanks to you. Now they see us as easy marks."

The princess put her hands on her hips, glaring at Shiraz. Then gasped, jumping backwards as Sweetums ducked out of a tree right between them. Xinyi nearly fell over, but Shiraz steadied her with a casual hand at the other woman's elbow.

The littlest of the monkeys squeaked softly. She tilted her head with her lower lip trembling and her big round eyes glistening. Makoa couldn't see the monkey's face from this angle, but he'd seen Sweetums at work before. And Xinyi's misty smile said she was falling for it.

The monkey was doing the work for which she was famed up and down the river. With one hand she held out a flower, gently settling it behind the princess's ear, and with the other, she stole a pink ribbon that had been tied around the princess's throat. It wasn't much, but that was only because Xinyi had come to them without gems.

"Aren't you the sweetest little thing ever?"

"Not even close," Shiraz muttered. She pulled a face, scrunching up her eyes, and hissing at the animal with all her teeth.

Sweetums shrieked and raced into the trees, making a whining noise that could be best compared to a crying child.

"Did you have to?" the princess demanded, incensed. Apparently Sweetums was better equipped to win her favor than Shiraz.

"Yep," Shiraz replied in a similar tone. "You don't know them like we do, it is never just— No!" Shiraz gasped. She shoved the princess towards Makoa. Spinning around, she ran back the way she'd come.

"Zaagok!" Makoa steadied the princess then raced after Shiraz. Twelve other members of the Golden Paw Gang had the River Serpent over their heads and were carrying it away. He should have known better. The monkeys always employed distraction. Things were about to get messy.

A stick struck one of the back monkeys in the legs. It fell, letting go of the ship, but the others kept on. A monkey dropped out of the trees, screeching wildly, bragging!

"Scabber, you back off. Or you won't like what comes next," Shiraz shouted. She knew a way to efficiently stop the monkeys, but up to now, she had not been brought to killing any.

The monkey atop the boat screamed his refusal. They were halfway into the tree line. There was nothing for it. There was no point in negotiating with monkeys.

Shiraz pressed in the left, aquamarine eye of her snake bracelet. The boat doubled in size and toppled sideways, too heavy for the monkeys to carry. Most of them jumped out of the way without injury, but a few got their tails caught beneath the toppling boat.

Shiraz heard the princess gasp in horror, but didn't stop to examine her annoyance. Once she was close enough, Shiraz pressed the bracelet's right, amethyst eye. The boat shrunk enough that the monkeys could yank up their tails and run into the trees.

Shiraz hit the amethyst again twice and grabbed the now easily carried boat into her arms. The trees were filling with monkeys.

"Will they be alright?" the princess asked. Likely of Makoa, Shiraz had her back to them, but it was Shiraz who snapped.

"They'll live, which is more than they could have hoped for if they stole my boat. Grab what you can and let's get going." Shiraz waded into the river with the shrunken boat under her arm.

"I'd just started to dry."

Shiraz rolled her eyes but otherwise ignored Xinyi's quiet lament, trusting Makoa to bring the whiny princess. Her fear of dampness notwithstanding.

Not My First Time Doing Monkey Business

The trees shook with jumping screeching monkeys, so many. And Makoa looked more concerned than he had with pixies transforming things. So Xinyi grabbed as much of the food as she could and waded into the water after the captain.

Xinyi barely had time to appreciate the ship jumping in size. Or to be impressed watching the captain grab some of the rigging hanging off the side of the boat and pull herself onboard as it drifted backwards with the current. But she was impressed! This wasn't just the woman's source of income; it was where she belonged. She threw herself over the rim of the ship, dripping wet, and without hesitation raced to the rear and dug the steering pole into the river, forcing the ship forward against the current.

By the time Xinyi and Makoa were far enough into the river, the boat was back alongside them. Makoa took the food from Xinyi's arms and threw it onto the ship. Then he lifted Xinyi until she could grip the side of the ship and pull herself up.

"Let's move," he called out before he was even onboard.

Xinyi landed with a plop and leapt up, leaning over the rail to help Makoa. But he didn't need it. He leapt straight out of the water and onto the deck, landing beside her with a grin.

"Find a place and brace," Makoa suggested. "I doubt we're through with them yet." He moved under the ship's canopy, away from her.

Xinyi was soaking wet for the second time today and she didn't even think it was noon yet. She raced towards where she had seen her bag earlier. She would grab it, find a corner and hide. Because there were clearly things going on she didn't understand, but that the smugglers were concerned was clear.

Xinyi spotted her bag on a ledge built into the wall of the ship. She rushed to grab it, only to have her hand struck away. Xinyi cried out in pain and dropped her hand to her side. The blue faced monkey gripping her bag released a high screech and an angry growl, shaking his bright orange fur.

"Oh! Hello there," Xinyi greeted it, breathlessly polite.

This monkey wasn't as friendly as the one who'd given her the flower. It held the bag hostage in one paw and swiped angrily at Xinyi with the second, its sharp claws threatening to tear her open. There was rage on the monkey's face. A tingle of fear raced up Xinyi's spine.

Stepping away to seem less threatening, she tripped on the slippery ends of her gown and fell sideways. She landed against the rail of the ship, nearly falling into the river, but managed to catch herself. "Please, may I have—NO!" she shouted, unable to finish her request.

The monkey leapt away, onto the canopy of the ship as Shiraz rushed over. The monkey ran back and forth on the canopy with Xinyi's wedding bag, hissing and chittering angrily.

"I did warn you, Scabber." The captain came forward, addressing the monkey as he continued to screech. "I had my eye on that bag. Bring it back, or I'll make a scarf out of you."

"You will not!" Xinyi glared at the woman. Couldn't she try being polite and respectful even for a few seconds? The other woman met her gaze, and a smile tugged her lips.

"Scabber," Xinyi called out. "Will you please give me back the bag? I will give you some food."

"Soft touch." The woman shook her head. "Don't bargain with what isn't yours."

Xinyi turned to Makoa. The other smuggler was at the back of the ship steering them forward, but he grinned, shaking his head.

The monkey stopped chittering. It held onto the bag, stretching it out behind him like a child at a game of keep away. Then it grinned and held out its second paw with fingers splayed. "I...It...I would swear it is asking for payment."

Makoa laughed. "You made the offer. Exchanging goods for goods is the way of the world. It is good business to receive payment first."

The monkey grinned and nodded, showing off both its sharp teeth and its humor.

"For instance," the smug smuggler said, not missing a beat, as Xinyi gaped at the mercenary monkey. "We can get that bag back for you, princess. But it will cost you another four percent of your treasure."

"That's ridiculous!"

"How much is it worth to you?" Shiraz countered with a wicked grin. Crossing her arms, she leaned against the canopy, nearly putting her back to the monkey. But Xinyi noticed one eye still tracked its pacing.

"I'll get it back myself. I offered him food," Xinyi protested this woman's penchant for demanding payment. Xinyi looked around for a piece of fruit to throw to the monkey.

"He isn't fool enough to take that." Shiraz shrugged. "He knows an item of value and will more likely throw the bag to them to extort more." She nodded above.

Xinyi tilted her head up, and up, and up. To a tree, no, two trees filled with utterly still, grinning monkeys! Great Gods! Xinyi didn't know if she wanted to giggle or scream, but either would be full of fear. In a story, this might be a threatening scene, or a dramatic one, even amusing. She would spread their number and at the peak of the tree would sit—*Oh!* The biggest monkey yet. Xinyi stepped back. But there was no back left. She tumbled.

"Aaaah!" Xinyi cried out as she fell towards the ship's edge for a second time in as many minutes. But Shiraz was there with a sure hand, catching Xinyi against her chest. As if she'd expected the fall.

"Another two percent or I let you go in," she suggested playfully. Confirming Xinyi's suspicions. She had expected her to trip.

The captain's face was right next to her own. But it showed no mercenary threats or superiority, just an exceptionally warm smile. This was amusing her. Her eyes were fixed on Xinyi's and so close she could see her pupils expanding and her gaze shifting down to Xinyi's lips.

Oh! She was *flirting?*

She wasn't very good at it. Or...Xinyi revised the thought as she felt a lovely tingle lightening her chest and fought the urge to lick her lips. She *was* good at flirting. Xinyi rarely felt caught like this for anything but fiction; she was breathless and warm and...something she wasn't ready for but was very much enjoying. The captain was a good flirt, but she chose terrible moments. Yet, Xinyi *wanted* to participate.

"One percent," she countered, her mouth a little dry.

Shiraz made as if to release her. But Xinyi caught onto the woman's forearm and clenched her fingers around her as tight as she could. She wasn't going anywhere.

"Deal." Shiraz winked.

Then she did away with Xinyi's flirting theory. She shoved Xinyi so far forward so suddenly that Xinyi landed on one knee with an umph and a jerk in her lower back.

Shiraz reached into a bag that hung inside the canopy and held something towards the monkey. The monkey leaned forward to look, then tilted its head up.

Groaning, Xinyi followed its gaze and saw the largest of the monkeys squinting down. It cried out with a loud screech that shook the tree. Answering screeches followed shuddering branches, wider and wider the echo grew until it reached the bottom layer of the tree, leaves showered around the boat and rocked them so much they bobbed with the resounded cacophony of monkey voices.

It was overpowering and inspiring. Xinyi pushed to her feet. She wished she could ask them if they were mere opportunists, or if this was a regular practice, robbing boats along the river and ransoming the best bits? She wished she could speak to their leader and learn its style of rule. Then speak to the thief army and see if they liked their leader. She wished she knew the language of monkeys. She wondered if Makoa did.

What fun that would be! She should write a character who could do such things. Xinyi imagined herself as such a character walking into the monkey court in an ornate gown, bowing low before speaking as monkeys did. It would be such fun!

Shiraz stepped towards the canopy still addressing the monkey. "You know that was no way to treat a lady, Scabber. It's only because she isn't bleeding that we're having this conversation. I never negotiate with monkeys."

"Rule number nine, isn't that?" Makoa asked casually.

"Indeed. But...my cargo has a soft heart, so...hand over the bag and you get the shiny."

The monkey rolled its eyes as if it understood human speech even if they could not understand his. He stretched out the bag to make the exchange. But as he grabbed whatever the shiny was, he screeched loudly, showing off his teeth, and the monkeys in the trees did as well, jumping up and down and shaking loose a new shower of leaves. Scabber threw the bag towards the ship's edge.

"No!" Xinyi lurched after it, throwing herself off the ship.

Water sprayed up Xinyi's nose and in front of her eyes, so befuddling her senses that she couldn't see or hear for a moment. She cried out in shock and fear. She was getting pulled away by the river. Then she felt an arm close around her. Or...something. Xinyi touched the squishy, slimy thing around her waist, shuddering but unable to blink enough water from her gaze to make it out.

Too much was happening too fast. She felt the hard surface of the ship's hull against her face, but it wasn't until Makoa, in the body of a giant octopus, dragged her on deck that she could understand a single thing.

She had been rescued. But what happened to her bag? The captain stood over her with the bag hanging from the end of a pole wearing an incredulous smile.

"Really," she laughed. "What were you hoping to achieve?"

Makoa blew out a breath, transforming into an older man, and headed towards the back of the drifting vessel.

"What? How?" Xinyi wasn't making sense. But the captain understood. She grinned, leaning over Xinyi.

"Not my first time doing monkey business. Never trust a monkey," she said smugly.

She held out Xinyi's bag. Xinyi grabbed it but the woman didn't let go. "Two percent," she said.

It took a moment, but Xinyi's senses were returning. "We agreed to one," Xinyi sputtered as firmly as she could muster under that very confusing stare and with water still dripping out of her nose from the pointless dive into the river.

The captain smirked and let go of the bag. "You're learning. Let me change into some dry shoes and I'll trade posts with you," she called towards Makoa. "I swear, the day is only half gone, and I'm exhausted already."

Xinyi felt exhausted too, but so alert, her mind filling with a thousand details and contradictory feelings. Xinyi watched the captain walk off calm and confident and— *intriguing*.

Never Deal, When You Can Steal

"So we've had half of our goods stolen, and all these monkeys are lining the trees with their hands full of gold, demanding the only thing we could not give them, our secret cargo." Makoa invested the story with all his energy. He was in the form of the person they'd been smuggling, General...General...azaqif! Shiraz forgot his name.

He was a man of about sixty with a slender face and nervous posture. He'd been smuggling some of the king's treasure to him across the border, unaware of Makoa and Shiraz's secret cargo, food for the families along the border whose farms had been destroyed.

Makoa entertained their guest with stories of the past as they worked. Shiraz pushing the ship upriver, and Makoa and the princess cleaning the mess from the monkey visit and getting started on a midday meal. Makoa loved to talk and share and befriend. So he made a point of telling the princess about the food they'd been taking to the villagers. Shiraz would not have. If the princess disapproved of them, that was her business. And, brief flirtation aside, she really seemed to disapprove. Of Shiraz anyway.

"How the monkeys saw through the enchantments, I'd still like to know," Shiraz put in. "I burnt my back in seven places collecting that soil from beneath the lava flows. I couldn't lay on my back for months.

And our deal was for an enchantment that would fool *anyone* looking at my deck."

"Anyone, or any being?" Xinyi asked insightfully. The woman had barely helped clean, lifting her damp journal to make more notes or flavoring the story with her questions. Shiraz wanted to be annoyed, but she actually found it cute.

"Anyone," Shiraz answered.

"Perhaps whoever sold it did not consider animals to be *anyone*."

The wizard who'd made that enchantment was sort of a ngok. He lived in a colony of humans shipwrecked on Great Island who had been allowed both by the fairy and the dragons to make a home there. The wizard insisted on being called Merl the Magnificent and kept taking credit for the spells of nearby lake spirits or using magic to manipulate the developing political system.

He'd needed the lava dirt for a spell to make a rock solid for some and permeable for others. And Shiraz had needed the spell by which he hid his fortress, so she hadn't cared. If people were willing to trust their government to a child because he could pull a weapon out of a rock, it wasn't her business to point out it was a trick.

"I suppose I might have worded that request more vaguely than others," Shiraz accepted responsibility for the mistake. "Maybe I should see if someone else can improve on it."

"Anyway," Makoa interrupted, and Shiraz knew why. She winked. She had been about to go find her journal of witches, enchantresses, wizards and fey and see who she thought might help her fix the spell. She did this from time to time. No one but Makoa and the enchantress who made the spell knew that this boat was seaworthy. It looked like a river boat. It should only be a river boat. But Shiraz had spells to transform it when the time came.

The River Serpent needed to be perfect because she had made herself a promise not to be disappointed by magic any longer. If she could not find the Singing Hills within the next year, she was done searching.

For good.

She would just be—a smuggler. And a thief. And a reader of books.

"There was nothing for it, it was run or fight. And we didn't want to start a war with the monkeys," Makoa continued the story. Shiraz's eyes were running over the scratches on her ship, looking for any flaw that would prevent her from getting to her ultimate treasure.

Makoa wasn't sure any longer that she even wanted to go back to the islands. She kept making excuses, more spells the ship needed, slight alterations to the tattoo spell on her arm. And he was a little scared of returning to the home of his childhood while he was still cursed. So he didn't push when Shiraz came up with any excuse to prevent herself being disappointed. He wondered if she needed more for the possibility to live on than she needed to find the magic she'd longed for most of her life.

People often questioned why they traveled together. Makoa had no need of a vessel to live on, or to travel. And he might be more likely to find a true love and break the spell if he stayed in one place long enough for love to develop, like his friend Henri was trying. But Makoa loved Shiraz; he couldn't leave her alone. And perhaps what they had most in common was that neither one was ready to live without their curses. Hers of seeking magic, his of seeking *true love*. They needed the search. And they needed each other. More every day, as each of them lost faith in that thing they were seeking.

Makoa hadn't really thought about true love prior to his curse. And once he was cursed, he thought of it as something he would find to break his spell, then leave behind like so many other things. But...in the process of seeking it, he'd met Shiraz, who he loved, truly, if not at all romantically. And he'd met Aiattaua who he loved completely, flaws and foibles and fourteen other partners included. But apparently even that love was not enough to satisfy the curse. How much more could he possibly be expected to love someone?

But now wasn't the time to focus on that. Makoa entertained their guest, watching Shiraz out of the corner of his eye.

"So we ran. The monkeys saw this as shameful. As did our cargo who started shouting at us to get his gold back." Makoa shook his head. "So he was shouting, the monkeys were screaming and all of the sudden we were being rained on with clods of monkey feces."

Xinyi giggled, then looked down apologetically. But Makoa only grinned wider. He liked the woman. She embraced her feelings better than either himself or Shiraz. It was a pleasure to have a perspective around that was brighter than his own. Shiraz's certainly never was.

"But we escaped. They stopped following us once we moved outside their territory."

"But not before Scabber jumped on board with a few of his friends and scratched up my arm," Shiraz put in. "And our passenger's face. That's how he got his name. You're lucky he only swiped at you," she said to Xinyi.

"So is he." Makoa smiled slyly. If that monkey had hurt this woman, Shiraz would have grown a touch more violent than was her nature. It was clear to Makoa that someone was smitten with their passenger. "From that adventure came two things." He intoned the next words to get Shiraz's response. "Rule number nine—"

"Never negotiate with monkeys," Shiraz provided. "They won't hear reason, and they scream right over you."

Xinyi grinned, and for a moment the two women were caught up in each other's enjoyment.

"And our name for the monkeys, the Golden Paw Gang," Makoa interrupted the sweet moment, making a kissy face at Shiraz over Xinyi's head.

"Oh, I thought it was because of their fur." Xinyi looked back at Makoa, missing his look and Shiraz's extended tongue in return.

"That too." Makoa nodded. "We like that it works on multiple levels."

"But I do not understand," Xinyi pondered. "You negotiated with the monkeys the first time and they double crossed you."

"Yep. Cheats. Came back in the night," Shiraz began to reiterate.

"That I understand, but...why didn't you go back for your passenger's gold? Did he not offer you more in exchange?"

"He offered us a quarter of anything we recovered," Makoa replied. "We refused."

"But...you got my purse, even though my treasure is something you have not seen." Xinyi sounded lost.

"It was easily done." Shiraz lay the pole aside, looking over the back of the ship. At nothing.

The conversation had turned serious, so Shiraz must move.

"Why not let the monkeys keep it?" Xinyi pressed.

"We like you much better than we liked him," Makoa answered.

"And anyway, we went back for his gold. Just…not with him on board. Why take one quarter when you can have it all?" Shiraz said brazenly.

Makoa chuckled. "Gave the queen four baskets of dates to get that gold back for ourselves."

"Was that not negotiation?" Xinyi asked cautiously.

Shiraz grinned wide and smug. "The dates were laced with a sleeping spell. Once they slept, we stole back the gold."

"Cheat!" Xinyi accused.

"Smart business," Shiraz countered. Makoa could tell what Xinyi could not, that Shiraz was still hurt by this woman's disapproval. So she would do what she always did when faced with disapproval. Jerk up her head and boast her way through, never giving an inch. "Rule number seven," Shiraz said pointedly, "Never deal when you can steal."

Walking Would be Faster

Captain smug stood at the back of her ship with her head high. The sun was behind her, and the pole was in her hand, and she pushed her boat. The tail of her hair rippled in the wind and her arm muscles corded as she steered. Her expression wasn't visible against the sun, but one could not mistake her. She was the silhouette of a proud river pirate.

And Xinyi found her itchy-twitchy writing finger recording just such a character despite her continued uncertainty about this woman. Up one moment and down the next, she was never sure how she felt about her, or how the woman felt about Xinyi. But her presence was inspiring something.

> Pride and practice held the pirate's back straight. Her hair ~~rippled behind her like rushing water over a cliff~~.

Bleh! Xinyi crossed out the line.

> Her hair rose and fell with the wind, blowing off her neck and allowing sunlight to glisten across the mist of sweat clinging to her skin. A delicate hand settled on her shoulder, one finger

tracing patterns on the pirate's damp skin. She leaned into
the caress—

Xinyi put down her pen before she could get too caught up in the exercise. *The fantasy.* She cleared her throat and forced out a question in the most biting tone she could muster. "So when I get my treasure, I should hold onto it tight until you've delivered me back home?"

Makoa nodded. "Yes, certainly."

"It's what I would do," the captain remarked.

Xinyi stared after her at a loss. That whole story seemed designed to tell Xinyi not to trust them. But…she thought perhaps Makoa's remark that they liked her better was closer to the truth than the captain's insistence that it was easily done. There were so many things about the woman that did not make sense.

She liked to tease Xinyi, liked to flirt with her, but turned grouchy the moment Xinyi said anything remotely kind or returned the teasing. She had worked *very* hard, by Makoa's accounts, to get the spells to make her ship. But if she was willing to work hard, why not at something good? Why smuggling?

Not ten minutes earlier, Xinyi had watched the woman joking and teasing as she exchanged alcohol and children's puzzle games for safe passage with a group of soldiers. She'd had it all ready and waiting, and warned the soldiers to watch out for the monkeys that were sure to follow. They teased her saying they weren't "afraid of a few fur balls." And all she'd done was laugh and shake her head. "You'll see."

And Xinyi was inspired. It had never occurred to her that such characters might have friendly, playful relationships with the people they paid off, the people they swindled. The people who were meant to stop them.

Xinyi was running out of pages. She had more notes on this boat alone than she had taken on any new idea in years! What had begun as a wish to write something new was quickly becoming a reality. And Makoa kept her fed with a steady stream of stories and answers. But it was the surly captain who provided the most intrigue.

Xinyi wondered more and more about the guarded woman with the sure feet, the surly attitude, and the incongruous moments of humor, understanding, and playfulness.

"She likes you," Makoa said out of nowhere. "Or more specifically, she likes your joy. She has been having trouble feeling joyful since she learned of her brother's death."

"She had a brother?" Xinyi asked softly, leaning nearer to Makoa.

"Two. She knows nothing of her eldest brother's fate, but her second eldest died some years ago. She feels now that she should have forced him to leave their home with her. They were not well treated, but her brother worse than herself. She hoped he would find joys like she had. Now she feels responsible for his pain. So she sees your joy and it makes her miss a time when she felt it."

"What did her people do to her?" It should feel wrong to talk about the woman behind her back, but Xinyi wanted to know everything.

"Only she can tell you that. But," he smiled, "she would always have risked the return of the Golden Paw Gang to get you that bag. Because she could tell it was precious to you. And...she has had many precious things taken from her."

"Thank you, Makoa." It was strange. Here he was in a new body, and they were all so different. This one was older and more unsure in his own skin than most Makoa had used in front of her. Yet Xinyi could clearly see Makoa in it. His beautiful, fun, loving spirit.

She understood Makoa far better than the captain. Makoa preferred to share about Shiraz rather than himself. The further along they went, despite any story Makoa told, the worse Xinyi felt about lying to them about her treasure.

It was easier with the captain, but even to her it was getting difficult. She'd saved Xinyi's bag and carried her through the jungle as a piece of fruit. And the captain had done it as though it was nothing. Surely most smugglers would have left her and saved themselves.

If she knew nothing else about the woman, she knew that the captain loved Makoa. There was an intimacy to their conversations and the way they moved together. After their encounter with the monkeys, as the captain was disappearing below decks to get new shoes, Makoa had pulled her near. She had laid a hand on his heart, and he'd leaned his head against hers. They loved each other.

If Xinyi could do something to help break Makoa's curse, she must, and they would surely both appreciate that. Despite the lies Xinyi was telling them.

She flipped to one of the few remaining empty pages in her journal. "May I ask you about your curse?"

"Of course." Makoa lifted his hands from the bread he was flattening and waved them wide and welcoming.

"Do you share the memories of the different bodies you take? And if so, is it only when you are inhabiting their form?"

He considered the inquiry deeply. "I do not precisely share their memories. But I feel more connected to their experiences when I am in their forms. I can, for instance, recall how to make the pnupa bread I am preparing for you without being in Ayinde's form, but when I take on his form, I do not need to think to make it. My hands follow the rhythm I watched from him when we met in Maltuba."

"So now that you are in this other form, what sort of thing would come more easily to you?"

"Giving orders." He chuckled. Then grew more serious. "There is a certain feeling he carried beneath his skin, a discomfort with the world. When I am in his form, I feel more cautiously aware that—everything is a threat." His voice slipped away, and his eyes grew distant, as though he was only now realizing the truth of his words.

"But that was not true with the one who taught you to make the bread? Ayinde." Xinyi consulted her notes.

"No. Not at all. He had a great deal of faith, and it translated to a form of confidence. He was taking a religious order. This was a dish he prepared for his gods! I do so enjoy eating like a deity." Makoa winked. "You are lucky we had enough pnupa left to make it! It is a grain found only in Maltuba, it has a lovely tangy quality, and makes the smoothest batter for the bread. Maltubans make two special styles of this bread: one shaped with a dip in the middle, the other flat for serving food on. I am preparing the flat, as it is easier to make on the boat, but if you ever get the opportunity, the shaped bread, filled with spices and vegetables, is a delicious treat." His attention shifted back to the rolls he was flattening on a wide dish. He was doing it again, speaking about someone else to avoid speaking of himself.

She wondered if it was a direct effect of the curse, or a byproduct of its pain. Leaving him unable to speak of his old life or inhabit his old form, the spell had in a way taken the *self* from him. But in another sense given him a greater sense of self. For surely he could feel which of the emotions belonged in other forms.

"Being in Ayinde's form would be helpful for preparing this, but he taught me to make the bread. Somewhat by accident, he thought he was talking to one of the animal servants of his gods." Makoa filled the silence as Xinyi's mind ran away. "Poor thing thought it was proof that his faith was being honored by his gods. Even after I revealed myself, he believed it," Makoa said wonderingly.

Xinyi smiled at the playful story, though she thought it unkind to fool someone into thinking you spoke for their gods. She did not personally believe in gods. Few people she knew truly believed in them the way their ancestors had. But they honored them on feast days, out of respect. And many were the people who loved the idea of gods and the function of them in a story.

That was why she'd included the river gods from the region in her story; it lent the whole thing more authenticity. So when Jian escaped Nanghi, the god of death and namesake of the river, it was with the help of his rivals. The shape shifting trickster siblings provided Jian with disguises. They were even the reason she met Kinmei, using the romance between Nanghi's servant and a human as a means of stealing the god's most efficient hunter. In a story, gods always made sense, but in reality, Xinyi could make no sense of them, so she didn't believe. But it still felt unkind to trick someone for whom the existence of gods not only made sense but served to give them strength.

"I believe *everyone* should try the foods of other lands," Makoa interrupted her thoughts brightly. "So after I was exposed I made Ayinde a sweet-rice ball recipe I learned in Ayowi."

"Are they called sweet balls?" Was that man back at the market calling her a food from the island nations to the east?

"That is the fairy word for them, yes. What do you call them?"

"I have never had them." Xinyi flipped back a page to make a small note on an already crowded area. She had barely stopped making notes the entire time Makoa talked. She was getting so many ideas, not just for new stories either, some she could add to Jian's adventures. It didn't always have to be pirates or soldiers. Some of her adventures could be travel and wonder! She could even add some ideas, like new foods, to her own life.

"A man grabbed me in the market and called me sweet ball."

"We saw him. I am sorry he touched you. Shiraz stole his funds because of it and put a small curse on him. I believe it was his funds she gave to the monkeys. But...you do look a bit...confection-like in that dress." He laughed. "Sweet balls are sticky rice balls formed into two stacked half-circles, one much larger then the other, then they are dipped in a thick pink syrup and decorated to look like a woman."

Xinyi chuckled at such a description of herself. She supposed she did look like two pink circles in this gown. She filed away the information that Shiraz had tried to avenge her but did not respond to it. Makoa was clearly trying to make her like his friend, but the woman was a thief. Thieves did not need reason to steal, did they?

"So it was a compliment," she said. "I wasn't sure how to take it in the moment. I hope we get to try some sweet balls while we travel. How long will it take to reach the border?"

"It should not take more than three days."

"*Three days!* Walking would be faster! We are a mere fifteen miles from the border. I expected we were about halfway there."

"Walking is perhaps faster. But not safer. And miles are measured as birds fly, not as humans walk, in jungles without marked roads, to newly established borders. Even the river is not a fast nor safe journey. But we promised to get you there safely, and that is what we will do."

Xinyi nodded an apology. "That was unfair of me." She would be with them two days more at the least. Xinyi wasn't sure if she was worried or pleased by this. Perhaps a bit of both.

Xinyi was getting so many ideas her wrist hurt. She didn't used to have pain from writing all day. Nor did her back used to hurt from nothing but sitting. But here she was wishing to be at the back of the ship, with the surly smuggler, if only so she could be up stretching her back.

Yes. That was the only reason. Not any of Makoa's stories about the woman that made her out to be as fascinating an inspiration for writing as anything else on this boat. Not the tingly memory of her intent gaze on Xinyi's lips.

"You are hardly the first passenger to claim we are taking too long. But don't let Shiraz hear it. She takes any insult to her ship as an insult to herself. She went through a great deal to get it."

Xinyi recorded his exact wording: *she went through a great deal to get it*. The captain had mentioned burns. Had they healed? Was she permanently scarred? Did she still feel the pain? Why go through all of that for a ship to smuggle other people on? Surely there was a deeper reason. Xinyi longed to ask what it was. Longed to write it. Longed to understand these two. With the thought, she realized that Makoa had distracted her again. Rather than press and too shy yet to approach the captain, Xinyi walked to the edge of the ship, smiling. She had plenty of time.

Kindred Chaos

Makoa shuddered as Xinyi walked away. She was unnervingly perceptive. Her questions began to make him uneasy, and only part of that was because he was in the general's form. Makoa felt very much like changing skins and he didn't like it. He changed bodies because he wanted another, or because it fit the moment, or because it was entertaining. Or, on some rare occasions, because he wanted to impress someone. Not because the form made him uncomfortable. But there was something about Xinyi. He couldn't tell if it was magical, but she was certainly special, maybe even dangerous. She was an element of chaos.

Makoa began to think it would be best if they got her home very soon.

One at a time, he heated the flat breads over the warming plate, watching as they puffed up and steam was released. He felt a kind of comfort sooth through him, knowing exactly the moment to flip the bread, feeling the prayers in the back of his mind.

Makoa startled.

His hand had changed. He stared at the darker skin, rotating his hand, noting the longer fingers and soft, unwrinkled skin. Had he changed form without intention? Without blowing out a breath of the curse? In the fifteen years since he had been cursed, outside of the very first time it happened, Makoa had only ever changed form intentionally. And always the same way. By calling up a form and forcing out as much of that broccoli flavored spell as he could find. He'd done it in desperation at times, changing from a drowning human into a comfortable dolphin, or in jest, transforming from a tiny bird into a giant bear to terrify Shiraz. He'd even slipped through thirteen bodies in as many minutes—and kisses—as part of a drinking game with Shiraz's last girlfriend, which led to Shiraz abandoning him at the grotto, ending her relationship with Michaela, and Makoa meeting Aiattaua for the first time.

He'd changed forms and regretted it, or been saved by it, but always, always intentionally. But...he was back in Ayinde's body. And feeling comforted by the young man's faith and his certainty that all things were as they were meant to be. And Makoa did not know what he'd done to make it happen. Or even if he had. Makoa felt tears gather in his eyes. What was happening?

Instinctually, he flipped the bread, knowing inside what to do, as if he wasn't only mimicking the other man's shape, but allowing his spirit to share this space with him. A few tears fell, and Makoa shuddered, but Ayinde kept his hands moving, preparing the food. Preparing the prayers and the offerings.

Makoa sought Shiraz's gaze. She would understand. But her gaze was once again on the princess wandering their deck.

Shiraz was changing too. Did she realize it? He'd thought it was good, her infatuation, the return of her playful side. But now he didn't know. Even in Ayinde's skin, he felt a shiver of fear. What would become of him and Shiraz with this new element in their orbit?

The boat dipped, Shiraz focusing too much on the princess to steer straight. A piece of fruit rolled across the deck, striking Makoa's foot. He lifted it from the ground and raised it to his lips without thinking.

Kup oxtia nav uli akil bozou urilla, szo havio. Un mur gibo. Makoa heard the other man's voice in his ear as if he were here, as if he could feel Makoa needing comfort.

Makoa only knew a little of the Maltuban language but right now he understood every word. It was as comforting as it was terrifying.

The gods embrace you in their light, my friend. All is well.

When one lived inside a jungle, it wasn't as obvious that it dipped and rose. It wasn't as obvious how sheltered the interior was from the light. Xinyi took off her wrap and stood in the sunlight drifting onto the river. She was nearly dry, but still any breeze stirring across the river found the damp spots in her clothes and made her shiver.

The bushes lining the water stirred. Xinyi leaned on the ship's edge, wondering what new and exciting thing she would see. Maybe she would see a not-panther come out and sip from the river. Between their encounter with the pixies, and Makoa's habit of changing into animals, Xinyi wondered how many animals were animals at all.

Xinyi had the oddest feeling. She was always content, *always*. Anywhere she was, there were beautiful things to see, wonderful people to speak to, life was beautiful, even when it was full of struggles. So she was always content. Sometimes the people around her complained about the level of joy she carried inside, but just now she felt *sad* for Makoa, and for the part of herself that understood fully why he must change the subject to other people whenever the conversation grew too close to things that hurt. She felt an answering fear, of never belonging. She imagined his was more of never knowing himself. But her fear recognized his.

There were tears in her eyes, but there was also a smile on her face. Because there was so much beauty to see. She wanted to reach out and hug him, to tell him he could be any self he needed to be with her. But she didn't want him to be more uncomfortable. So she kept it to herself. He might belong with her, but she didn't know that the same could be said of her.

The vines shuddered and a bird ran to the water's edge. It had a brownish body with an elaborate fan of purple feathers decorating its head, and its long tail ran along the ground with a similar fan at its end. She didn't know what sort of bird it was. Surely, they were not so far from home that she could see birds that were unfamiliar. It looked up, right at Xinyi. It let out a long strand of jibber with an upturned tweet at the end. Then went back to drinking.

A gathering of colorful feathers descended through the air like silk scarves twisting in the wind. The long plumes and wide outstretched wings of several different types of parrots! It was mesmerizing.

She should add such a scene to her stories. Only it would not be the wonders of nature that inspired the birds to descend so magnificently. It would be V, calling forth fanfare.

Furtively she reached down to the basket of nectar fruit they'd been gifted. Xinyi leaned further out of the boat. She doubted the captain or Makoa would approve, what with the way they responded to the monkeys trying to get food, but Xinyi loved to share.

It was like the old woman had said, *it was a genuine pleasure to share.* Some mornings, Xinyi took sliced fruit into the garden with her while she had her tea, and little song birds or parrots sampled her meal. Why should it be different in the jungle?

Xinyi used her teeth like a knife, biting out little sections of the juicy fruit. She couldn't help slurping up the juice, and munching on a bite or two herself as she held out the offering in her palm.

"Hello," she cooed. "What is your name?"

She did not expect an answer, merely that a bird would hop nearer and come investigate her. So it was quite the shock when the bird with the purple fan atop its head met her eyes and opened its beak.

"Come, jungle deep. Come, your heart we keep. Come, home is here. Come now, sister, near."

Xinyi caught her breath as the words sang inside her mind. Sang like a twisting scarf, falling again and again, before her eyes, before her ears, before her mind, shrouding any thought but those words.

Come now, sister, near. Sister?

Did they know her? Was this her true...*home*?

The birds stepped forward as one, and all their beaks opened together—inviting.

"Come, jungle deep. Come, your heart we keep. Come, home is here. Come now, sister, near."

Xinyi could feel the homecoming, the love. She'd always known she belonged somewhere. She must. And at last...she'd found it.

Pause—*Before* Drowning

Shiraz dropped the pole and began running seconds before the splash. Had she not been outright staring at Xinyi, she might have noticed literally anything else and realized it was the Soul Parrots she was trying to feed.

"Azaqif!" Shiraz shouted running towards the ship's edge. "Makoa!" She didn't bother giving an actual explanation. Makoa would understand. They always brought an offering to appease the Soul Parrots. She'd known they were near by but hadn't worried; their long-standing bargain generally protected Shiraz's passengers.

Shiraz didn't think before vaulting over the side of the boat. Just threw herself into the water after the princess. Were she to have paused to consider, she might have realized that the woman's bag was still on the deck and worth some coin. And the princess had gone out on an adventure of her own free will, causing nothing but calamity since setting foot on the River Serpent. Also if Shiraz wanted, she could still go after the thieves and try to steal whatever they had taken from the woman on her own.

It shouldn't matter to her that a group of jungle spirits had appeared as beautiful birds and whispered words only her passenger could hear, beckoning her off the ship, so that she could be devoured by the river *god*, Nanghi. It wouldn't have mattered with most of their passengers. And surely a princess born and raised beside the river had heard of the river god. This shouldn't be on Shiraz. The woman should know how to fight her own gods. Not that Shiraz believed he was a god, but he definitely was a super old, apparently lazy creature who arranged to have the jungle spirits hunt for him. He consumed the bodies, and the Soul Parrots took the spirits.

A neat arrangement for him, but a pain in the ngok for Shiraz. She swam towards the pink swirling fabric. The dirt on the river floor was stirring. Shiraz pushed her muscles harder. She was not about to let this overeager princess throw herself into the mouth of a gigantic alligator to avoid a three-day journey with Shiraz.

Shiraz managed to grip onto the silk, but in the same moment, it gave a jerk, pulled towards the bottom of the river. Shiraz wrapped the sash around her hand, using it to pull herself closer, until she could feel the woman's warmth radiating towards her and saw her face.

Her eyes were wide, and she was struggling to get her dress untied as Shiraz dragged her one way, and the dark bumpy mouth and pointed teeth of the god dragged her another. Far more fabric than was practical for an afternoon swim billowed around her and a long sash was wrapped about her waist and tied behind her back.

Shiraz held onto her end of the sash but pushed Xinyi's hands away to work at the knot herself. Xinyi made a slashing motion with her hands like a knife.

Knife!

Yep, that would have been a smart thing to bring. But Shiraz hadn't stopped to plan before she dived to the rescue. Perhaps she should swim back to the surface and get one, she thought snidely. Sea Spirits, this woman was annoying. Shiraz struggled in vain as the river creature dragged them deeper. She could barely make out the other woman's face. But she could feel her trying to push Shiraz away.

Save yourself, the motion seemed to suggest.

Like she would do that. Like she was the sort of scum to bring a sheltered woman into the ugly world and watch her die.

Fine.

Shiraz let go of the sash. Her store of breath was beginning to fail. She could hold her breath fairly long. She had been born on an island, and to this day, she spent much more of her time near water than away from it. But this was exertion and breath holding. She could die drowning.

Shiraz swam deeper. Past the princess. She grabbed onto the other end of the sash and followed it towards the river monster. Nanghi was said to be large enough to swallow two men whole and not even burp. Said to have teeth sharper than blades, and no heart to speak of.

Shiraz had never encountered him directly. She paid attention to local legends in each new place she visited. Paid attention to where people died and how. She made it a point to be two steps ahead of any malevolent force. Which was why she had offerings for his hunters, to barter safe passage. She had spent the last fifteen years learning to question everything. It was what kept her alive.

Until now. Because she hadn't paused to think before drowning. Nanghi (the alligator) was so dark Shiraz could barely distinguish his full features, as her breath grew thinner and thinner, here in the depths of Nanghi (the river). But she could see his teeth, and one eye. She kicked at the area around his teeth. It had no effect. So she kicked off of his face, and aimed herself straight for his eye. If she could hurt him badly enough, he might release Xinyi.

She dove fingers first at his eye. But the creature blinked. She slammed her fingers into its shockingly leathery eyelid with a sickening crunch and a yowl of pain that released the last of her breath. She shook and felt her chest crack; before all went black, the only thing she could see was the creature's mouth opening around her and a soft flutter of pink floating away.

Makoa leapt up at the first splash, rushing to help. Then came the second splash, and the voices. And Makoa...paused.

Wait, traveler there. Wait, we have a gift to share. Wait, try out no tricks. Wait, your worries we will fix.

Makoa knew how to fight the voices. He and Shiraz had learned the tricks before they'd sailed this river. But he paused. He'd wanted the princess gone. Not eaten but gone.

Wait, traveler there.

Makoa heard bubbles over the side of the ship and Shiraz's face flashed through his mind. What was he doing?

"Shut up," he said aloud. That wasn't the way, but he needed to get himself moving.

Wait, we have a gift to share.

"Is it better than four in exchange for two?" Makoa asked. His voice was rough, but he felt the question working. The birds were the ones pausing now. "And human flesh, prepared by Ogres, for your god?"

He'd hesitated. Shiraz was down there, and he'd hesitated.

A soul parrot settled on the rim of the ship. *"Souls first,"* it demanded in his mind.

"No. Save them now! Or I'll see you starve for months." He wasn't exactly sure how he could do that. But he knew he would do worse if they let Shiraz be eaten. If *he* let Shiraz be eaten.

Shiraz rolled away from a putrid scent and the pain in her chest. She vomited water onto the ground.

What was happening? Everything smelled sour. Her head was killing her, and her sight was fluctuating between bright light and utter darkness. She thought she heard voices but couldn't make out words.

Someone turned her onto her side, patting her back hard. "Shiraz!" Makoa shouted in her ear.

"Shhh," she hissed in response as the attack of it reverberated through her aching skull. "Am I dead?"

"Not for want of trying, no." Makoa's arms tighten around her, pulling her against his bent legs in an angular hug. "You're gonna kill me with this new hero shit, you know that?"

Shiraz didn't care that she felt his bones in her back, she leaned into the embrace, twisting one of her arms behind her to grip him back. She was shaking, everything hurt and smelled; everything was awful, as usual. But Makoa was here. Makoa was here and she was alive, so it was their sort of awful.

"Did it eat her?" Shiraz asked in what sounded very close to a sob.

"Of course not," a huge rumbling voice growled, filling the air with more of that putrid smell. "The princess is a delightful creature. You should be more like her."

Shiraz managed to peel open an eye. There was a giant alligator behind her, with a stinky mouth a quarter the size of her boat. "Don't tell me. The legends are all lies and you're just a nice boy cursed into the body of a giant mud dragon?" she muttered achy and annoyed.

Makoa helped Shiraz sit up. "I paid for our safe passage. So Nanghi *generously* spit you back up," Makoa informed her in that special tone that told her to temper her response to this new danger.

"I am so blessed," Shiraz observed, without even a hint of sincerity.

"You are indeed!" the princess's bright, but teary voice sounded from over the alligator's shoulder. Her words were so charged with genuine feeling, it was a wonder there was sincerity left for anyone in the world, much less Shiraz who had rarely been sincere regarding anything but insults.

Shiraz's chest eased seeing the bright-eyed, tripping princess. She hadn't fully believed she was alive. "Thank you for saving her." The princess threw her arms around the alligator god.

"Him save me," Shiraz squeaked. She felt like crying. She had just saved this woman and almost died in the process, but Xinyi was thanking the river monster for—*not eating*—Shiraz! As if he'd set out to rescue her from drowning.

"It was my pleasure. As it was my pleasure to meet such a beautiful light. Even had your way not been paid, I could not have consumed such bright energy. The world needs it."

"I'm going to vomit." Shiraz shoved out of Makoa's arms and stumbled towards the bushes. She caught her breath and swallowed bile as the Soul Parrots descended right before her with feathers fluttering dramatically.

"Ugh." Shiraz stepped over them where they landed and stumbled away. She couldn't stand one more moment of this smell. One more moment of all those positive perspectives on her brush with death.

Magic was an extra ordinary, multiple times a day, extremely annoying pain in the ngok.

Clinging to Death's Good Side

Xinyi couldn't calm the rushing river in her veins. She'd nearly died. And...Shiraz, who she had insulted, been annoyed with, and flirted with had nearly died to save her. Xinyi would lay awake tonight and shake, probably also cry. And definitely think. But at the moment no one would know how chaotic her feelings were.

She smiled at the river deity and made light conversation, expressing her gratitude that Shiraz and herself were still alive. She knew enough of this legend to know he was volatile, likely to spare a soul one moment only to devour it the next. She intended to keep them all on the good side of the god of death. When Shiraz fled looking like she might cry, Xinyi almost chased after her. The poor woman, she looked so distraught. But the birds came between them.

She should have known these birds were Soul Parrots. She'd heard stories of them since she was little. She had even written them into her story. **She should have known.** The thought kept eating at her mind. Look at all the trouble she was causing because she couldn't control herself. Or because...she could. This was her bad luck spreading, wasn't it?

Must you always race into danger, Xinyi? If you are so sure bad luck trails you, why go seeking it?

She heard her adoptive mother's long distant voice in her mind and shuddered, her being compressed by the shame.

Xinyi was in a state of half-chaotic worry and joy at surviving another dangerous encounter with the river, and half-wonder at all the magic around her. River spirits and deities. Watching Nanghi swallow Shiraz whole and then scoop Xinyi up in his claw like she would be his next snack. It was all racing through her still.

For the first time in her life, she realized that perhaps her imagination was not wilder than reality. Perhaps Yinuo was right and she had hidden in the castle because she was afraid to want more. But even with that fear, her imagination had built her more, because she… never was as content as she'd thought. Never was as small or as quiet or as safe as she meant to be.

Maybe she was just afraid to be useless. Afraid to be alone. Again.

Makoa stood. His breath escaped him with a loud shudder, and he transformed, this time into a woman of very small stature and loose wrinkled skin a shade between Shiraz's warm brown and the darker skin of the man he'd been before. The body also had a great deal more age than Makoa's playful attitude suggested was his own. He glared at the Soul Parrots.

"We have always done good business with you. What you did today put that in jeopardy," Makoa snapped. This was the first time she'd heard his voice in a rage. It was disconcerting, but not frightening, though there was violence in his voice. This was the expression of his threatened heart and despite the virulence, it was beautiful.

Why had she always feared such passions? Xinyi did not have the sort of company here she had at home. The sort that offered love. The sort that she knew in and out. Out here everything was new to her except her.

But maybe...if she had any good luck at all, maybe she could be new as well. Oh, she loved herself, but Yinuo was right; she wanted to grow. If she could not do so at home without her fear of rejection stopping her, perhaps she could do it here.

"You knew it was us, don't play that game," Makoa was shouting, though Xinyi had not heard the birds argue. "No! You apologize to her for nearly getting her eaten, and you make promises to approach us for payment next time."

Xinyi wanted to ask how this magic worked, but she stumbled on her wet clothes. She was beginning to grow cold standing here in the shade. And she would only get colder as she had brought no other clothes, thinking this a journey of a single day. Three times she'd been soaked in these clothes today. She had expected to be home before bedtime. Had expected river travel to be faster than on foot. Expected to be (mostly) comfortable until she faced the thieves. Nothing was as she expected.

"You think because we're leaving Loqwan you can do away with our deal? Now that he's spit her out, it won't be so easy."

"You're leaving?" Xinyi asked. Not the words she expected to be saying nor could she credit her own tone of unhappiness. Makoa seemed only then to realize she was here.

His eyes touched on hers and Xinyi could see what she had not before. His fear. His pain. His coming undone.

"We rarely stay anywhere this long."

"Oh." Xinyi managed only the one word. Why did she find their leaving unsettling? Xinyi put on a smile. "How wonderful. But," she dipped her head to the side reproving, and looked on the magical spirits, "it is not very kind to take advantage of a situation like that."

Nanghi responded, "She would cheat us as soon as pay us were she given the chance. She has no heart."

Makoa was shuffling angrily towards them. But Xinyi took on the river god. "Along the river, they call you Nanghi the hungry and Nanghi the heartless. Only one of those is true. And just like you saved her, at cost to yourself, she saved me at great risk to herself. She has a heart."

"Perhaps," the alligator conceded, smiling at Xinyi's defense and even the names he was called. "But I would not be so quick to trust her. She dove after you on impulse. Because there was no money or magic being offered her not to. But with thought, and with something worth her while to trade, she would let you die every time."

Xinyi wasn't sure the alligator was entirely wrong. But...she could have given up. In the water, Xinyi had tried to shove the captain away, but she kept trying. And she'd saved Xinyi's bag and rescued her (sort of) from the pixies. She'd apparently cursed someone only for grabbing Xinyi. The woman was certainly a mercenary, but that wasn't all she was. There was more to them all than good or bad.

"I have imagined you, Nanghi, and the Soul Parrots. But you are so different. You are marvelous, and dramatic, and powerful," she spoke to the Soul Parrots. "And you, Nanghi, you are larger than life, and full of nuance that I might not have written for you. The same must be true of her. She loves her friend, and she risked her life for me. She is more. You are more. I saw you as a tyrant, giving the Soul Parrots power, but only allowing them to use it to feed you. Before I ever let my readers hear you through your own voice, you loomed over my Jian, frightening her away from the water."

Makoa let out a snort of air that was only noticeable because he did not change shape with it, but his humor was massively overpowered by

Nanghi's laughter. It knocked Makoa down and Xinyi off her verbal stride before she'd made her point.

"Ah, you are the delightful mystery writer who has fed me so many a curious fisherman or woman. I quite like your Jian, and I do not mind making her heart tremble in fear."

"We do not speak aloud. But otherwise we don't hate the depiction," the medium bird said.

"Speak for yourself," the largest bird disagreed. *"We are not servants. We do not work alone. No one is forced into this role. We hunt the humans, Nanghi devours their bodies, and their last share of cosmic energy comes to us. This is a labor. We have wider lives than fluttering at the river, beckoning the heedless into Nanghi's mouth."*

Xinyi nodded. Why did she speak? She rarely shared that she was the author of Jian's adventures, but—Shiraz needed defending.

"Of course. Thank you. I will consider how better to represent you in future stories," Xinyi said respectfully.

"Ooooh!" The littlest bird fluttered up. *"Maybe one of us could visit Jian and tell her no one is angry with her. Or join her on an adventure so she is with someone with power and cannot be attacked by V."*

Xinyi shrugged. It wasn't a bad idea. But she hated saying yes to suggestions. She wrote in moods and might never get around to any number of ideas she had. Also—she was proud of her work as it was. There would always be things to improve, but everyone seemed so sure they knew better than her how to write the story. It felt like they found her work wanting. Why didn't they write their own?

"The latest adventure does end with Jian having re—

"A-a-a-a!" Nanghi shouted. "I haven't read it yet!"

"He hasn't read the last four," the youngest soul parrot laughed derisively. Could he hear them when they spoke in other's heads?

And why had they used those specific words to tempt her? It had felt so real. Her soul burning with certainty that at last she had found where she truly belonged, though she'd thought she'd given that up years ago. And though they were birds and she was human. She had not thought herself so desperate for kin that she would believe such obvious lies.

"Send for food and wine," Nanghi shouted excitably. "At last, we have met the author! We must celebrate before you press on with your journey!"

Xinyi shuddered uncomfortably. Cold and fear and disappointed hopes trying to poke through the sheen of smiles and positivity she was presenting. She glanced at Makoa for help. He lay on his back on the ground, having been knocked over by the alligator's laugh. He was still in the old woman's body, but his gaze was all his own. He stared at her full of suspicion.

Solitude or Something Close

Shiraz returned from *not* vomiting, not that anyone cared. She overheard the river *god* demanding a celebration. Since she was in no mood to indulge seemingly immortal pains in the ngok, Shiraz took the opportunity to run ahead and collect a few necessities off the boat. She stuffed a change of clothes, soap and a sponge, a towel, food, the recent installment of Jian's adventures, and a machete because her mama—well, no her mother had never advised her to take weapons with her, but life had taught Shiraz it was best to never be caught empty-handed—into a basket and ran down the bank of the river to a smaller creek they'd passed earlier.

She bathed in solitude but for the animals, bugs, plant life, and any invisible or well hidden magical being who might be in the vicinity. So...the illusion of solitude. It was something she had accepted over the years—not enjoyed or forgotten about but accepted—that she could never be entirely certain someone wasn't watching. Her brief stent in prison made her a touch less shy, but she'd always been a private girl at heart. A time or twenty, she had considered buying a spell for total privacy, but spells like that tended to have unforeseen consequences, like somehow killing every living person or thing in the vicinity, or finding oneself thrown onto a deserted island with no way off, or smelling so foul no one would come near you. It wasn't worth the risk.

Nor would she ever completely trust someone selling her a spell. Thus she accepted bathing far quicker than she had when she lived in a home with walls and doors. Even at roadside inns, one never knew when someone might try to break in, or a fire might break out. Or Makoa might *play a prank*, faking smoke and screams outside so she jumped out the window of her inn wearing nothing but a towel. She still needed to get him back for that one.

She felt a moment of unease as she rose from beneath the water. She spun in circles, searching for the eyes she felt, but all she noticed was a tail slipping into the trees. After another moment, submerged to the neck, nothing happened, so she emerged, dried and dressed speedily. Would it have been nice to have someone check her for leeches, rather than using a handy stick? sure. But she didn't think the princess would be as open to the chore as Shiraz was eager to have those deep eyes running over her or those soft fingers on her skin.

All bathed and changed, and having washed out her dirty clothes, Shiraz walked back towards The River Serpent. She didn't like leaving it unguarded. Makoa would look after it, but he was inclined to trust other creatures. Shiraz would never understand it. How could he, after his curse, trust random strangers? Someone else might curse him as dramatically. But she couldn't and wouldn't change him for the world, so she had to accept him as he was.

Shiraz settled against a tree a short ways away from the ship. Laying out her wet clothes on branches touched by sunlight, she pulled the story out of her basket. It was the second copy she'd bought earlier today. The first, as well as her extra copy of chapter seven were ruined, as she'd still worn them in her book holster when she jumped into the river after their encounter with the pixies. This was why she didn't like spending money. What was the point if everything you bought got ruined anyway?

Shiraz shivered as the heavy pile of her wet hair soaked the back of her shirt. She should have taken a brush, but she wasn't going back for one. So she settled in to read. She could brush her hair later; tangles were an acceptable exchange for not having to deal with the cheerful group socializing on the deck of The River Serpent, and Nanghi swimming along side it.

A laugh went up among them, Makoa's loud boom. Shiraz glanced over to see the princess lift Makoa, in the body of a red panda, and begin to dance with him as the Soul Parrots made music with found items around the boat, and the alligator sang in a gravelly voice. It looked like a scene from a story. Not the sort Shiraz read, something silly, something almost pointless, and yet...absolutely pivotal.

Eh. Shiraz preferred dramatic fiction. She lifted the leaflet and soon enough forgot entirely about the party going on without her.

Jian tilted her head back and bellowed unceasingly. It shook the air and the waters of the river, making waves crash up over the shores. Rain joined the river waters rising all around until Nanghi's home stretched up over the grounds of the jungle. The waters raced ahead, making way for the river god Jian was beckoning with her cry.

The pirates would not be allowed to get away with this. They had taken her love. Now they would taste her vengeance.

As the waters rose, Jian screamed on. She screamed with pain. She screamed with rage. She screamed with all the force of seven long years absence from this power. It was always angry and vengeful, but with its years pent into the cage she built it, the power had grown—voracious. Not to be satisfied with merely waking the river god and capturing the souls of those who had killed her love. It might never be satisfied again.

The ground rumbled as the river god awakened. His heavy feet climbed the bank, shuddering trees and creating waves in the tide crossing the land. From her perch high in the trees, V watched. Her eyes took in Jian alone. Jian with her arms collapsing under the weight of Kinmei's lifeless body. Jian shivering and bloody, clinging to the last vestige of her human life as water rose. How lovely it was, her lingering love.

But how necessary it had been to rip him from her. Look what she had done. What no river spirit ever had before. Jian in her grief was commanding the river god and flooding the Jade Valley. One day very soon, she would stand at V's side and they would be unstoppable. All would kneel to their power, or flee from it, and their combined power would remake the valley as a land where magic sang.

Festival of the Not-god

One of Nanghi's temple attendants arrived at the River Serpent with a dour expression. He'd pulled Nanghi away from the celebration for a serious chat, but Nanghi ignored the man, teasing him until he agreed to ride into the depths of the river on the alligator's back. The Soul Parrots flew after them squawking encouragingly, leaving Makoa and Xinyi alone a moment. In the body of a red panda, he built a tray of food for Shiraz. Xinyi had spotted her a while ago and asked if someone should go get her. Makoa just smiled and said it wasn't her way to join. He was making her food now because he worried she would go hungry before coming over.

"Did she truly curse that man at the market for grabbing me?" Xinyi asked, her voice shivering with her body.

She sat near to Makoa with a blanket around her shoulders, watching him work, and feeling tired inside and out. Tired from dancing and laughing and putting on a bright face for the overpowering magical creatures around her, despite having nearly been drowned and eaten by them. She had been holding together exceptionally well; no one must suspect how shaky she felt. How much of her wished she was back in the palace with a warm cup of tea, dry clothes and a blanket around her.

She shivered again. She should stand, she should walk, because with the unexpected question voiced, she began to feel small, and frightened, and weak. The dam around her unspoken fears might burst at any moment.

"She does not like presumptive men," he said.

It sounded like he meant Shiraz might have cursed the man for grabbing any woman in her presence. Not just Xinyi. Which actually made her like the woman more. It was a kind of morality, wasn't it? Not strict. Shiraz was still...Xinyi didn't know what she was. But a woman of high morals she was not.

The sound of squawking and wings flapping alerted them that their guests were back. Nanghi burst out of the water, splattering the deck and throwing his attendant free. The man had clearly done this before, as he did an impressive flip, landing on the deck, holding up two bottles of wine.

Xinyi forced a laugh and clapped. The attendant took one of the bottles and poured it down the waiting throat of the alligator. Where had they gotten wine?

Nanghi burped so powerfully, it shifted the ship. "Your turn, author?"

Xinyi shivered and shook her head, smiling as broadly as she could muster. "Oh no. Thank you, I am only now beginning to dry."

Also, river god or no, friendly or no, Xinyi didn't want to ride on his back back to the depths where she had nearly died.

"Oh, but you must try," the alligator insisted. "It will make such a great adventure for your next story."

Xinyi's heart was beginning to stamp against her ribs frantically; if he continued insisting, she was bound to give in, but she didn't want to. Perhaps if she told Nanghi she had written thirteen stories ahead of the one released today, and his character only lived through two of them, he might be heartbroken enough to leave her alone. But she didn't have the heart. Even thinking of his sadness made her think she should alter a story, perhaps include such a scene to...

"She is about to take her attempted rescuer some sustenance." Makoa placed the tray of food into Xinyi's hands. She had never been so grateful for a chore.

"Some other time." Xinyi dipped her head and cast the creature her most charming smile.

"Any time you wish, lovely one. Ah, but this is the most fun I've had this age. What about you, curse friend? Shall I carry you into the deep?"

Makoa blew out a pungent breath and transformed into an alligator of considerable size, though no where near as large as the river god.

"I do not need your assistance, but what say you to a race?"

"Ahhhh!" The alligator god shook the boat rancorously, laughing and attempting to clap while still clinging onto its side. Xinyi barely maintained her hold on the food. "I knew there must be an adventurer among you! Come, I will show you why age races always before beauty."

"Ah, are you calling me a beauty?" Alligator Makoa asked with sly tilting smile. "Could this be love?"

That question shook squawks of laughter from the Soul Parrots and a rather grim look from Nanghi's attendant. Xinyi slowly backed off the boat.

"Come give us a kiss and find out," the river god invited.

Makoa puckered up. The Soul Parrots watched with rapt curiosity, and Xinyi felt discomforted. She wondered if Makoa agreed merely to avoid more awkwardness. Because she didn't think love was like that. Didn't think you could find it in a mere acquaintance. It had to grow. One had to know the other, inside and out and accept them all. And she didn't think Makoa thought any differently.

The kiss was remarkable only in that it passed between a giant alligator and a much smaller one. When it was over, nothing had changed. Two of the birds clapped their wings, and the other rolled her eyes. But Xinyi relaxed enough to find the humor when Makoa threw her a look, rolling his eyes.

The world was full of wonders. She never would have imagined someone like Makoa, nor getting to be confronted by her characters. She'd never thought them real. Not until she was shaken out of her routine.

The birds cheered Makoa on, their motions clearly indicating they wished him to defeat the ancient alligator. She giggled as one bird patted his shoulder with its wing and another encouraged the attendant to offer him a drink from Nanghi's bottle of wine. Apparently, this was a race of great amusement to the Soul Parrots.

She could see now that she had not done them proper service in her story. Not that she did not love her story, but it was good to see the ridiculous and the joyful as well as the serious in her characters.

Xinyi made her way carefully along a strip of dirt and plant life on the riverbank. Her focus was so centered on her steps, on not tripping one more time in front of this confident and very surefooted woman, that it was not until she was just before her that she realized what Shiraz was reading.

Immortal Hunger, number sixteen, the one that was released today. She could tell from the numbers marking the bottom of the page. Had the captain read all of the others? Her face was screwed up into an unpleasant expression. Did she dislike the stories? Why keep reading them? Perhaps she had found that one lying around and picked it up for something to do other than join the party. Had Xinyi brought a copy in her bag? She didn't think so. Volume sixteen was a terrible place to start the adventure.

Xinyi opened her mouth to announce her presence, not to ask Shiraz what she thought of the story. Certainly not. But it hardly mattered. Shiraz made a noise of frustration and tossed the leaflet aside before Xinyi could speak.

"Oh!" Xinyi exclaimed accidentally. It was a shock to see the story tossed as if it were foul. Shiraz looked up, her raised brow asking any number of snide questions.

Why was Xinyi here?

Had she brought Shiraz food? Did Xinyi think that was thanks enough for having saved her life?

Why wasn't Makoa here instead?

Why had Xinyi left a party she was so happy at?

Xinyi didn't answer even one of the questions she saw in the other woman's expression. But she asked one of her own. Could not resist the inquiry as the beautiful story that had been pulled out of her being was tossed aside like trash.

"Do you not care for Jian's adventures?"

Tears, Leeches...all that Romantic Stuff

After months of wishing Kinmei dead, Shiraz was thoroughly dissatisfied with how it played out in the story. V should not have killed him! It was bound to bite her in the ngok. And she knew that!

V had considered killing Kinmei plenty of times, but always stopped herself, knowing that if word ever got back to Jian, it would ruin anything that they could have had otherwise, any partnership, any adventure, any love—though in no specific wording had the author offered that. Shiraz always felt it. But there was no chance of it now. She could see where the story was going.

Jian would briefly join forces with V. Wreak some havoc in her grief. Then discover it was V who had killed Kinmei and everything would change. She might briefly try to kill the sorceress, but more likely she would repent. The good girls always did. They sank under the weight of their misdeeds and let the world crush them. Jian would give up her power again, like Kinmei wanted. She would think it was ugly.

When it was never the power that made her kill. It was the pain and the rage. She wouldn't be *better* without the power, only less influential.

In the midst of all that annoyance, Shiraz looked up to see a very damp and disheveled good girl. The princess stood above her with a tray of food.

"Do you not care for Jian's adventures?" She looked almost hurt. Read them, did she?

Shiraz shrugged, pulling the pamphlet near with the heel of her damp boot, not one to disturb the natural beauty of the jungle with her refuse. Her heel squelched against the water still logged in her shoe. Along with a brush, Shiraz had forgotten a change of boots, so she must suffer the icky feeling.

"Melodramatic, don't you think?" Shiraz said, intentionally insulting. She didn't need to bond with her cargo. Just to get paid.

The woman didn't say a word. She held out the food.

"Thanks." Shiraz took the tray, immediately dipping her pinky into her favorite spicy sauce and licking it up.

"Was that the first of the adventures you've read?" Xinyi inquired.

"No, but it might be the last. I can see where it is going."

"Oh?"

Shiraz took a bite of flat bread dipped in all the sauces at once. "Good girl forced to see the error in her ways, giving up her power for the good of the world and living as a small, broken, obedient bit of baggage for the rest of her life," she spoke with her mouth half full.

"Goodness," Xinyi chuckled. Not the response Shiraz expected. The woman shivered and pulled the blanket closer about her shoulders. "All of that from Kinmei's death. Perhaps you should write a story."

Having been very neatly put in her place, Shiraz scooped up a bite of the tangy mix of vegetable and beans to hide her grin. "Is Jian a favorite of yours?"

Xinyi hesitated a moment before giving her head a half-hearted dip. "I...thank you," she said. Without warning she let out a gasp and began crying. "Thank you for saving me! I...I have never been so scared. And you were there though I was unkind to you." She huddled into her blanket intent on hiding.

Shiraz was too startled to react. She'd cried earlier, nearly dying could do that to you. But this woman had been smiling and bubbly and so bright, it seemed almost as if she didn't know what had just happened. Now she was spouting like a geyser and Shiraz froze.

It wasn't that she had never comforted tears. She had, Makoa's, her brothers', her mother's. Her own. More than anyone else's, she had comforted her own. It was what one did when they traveled alone, and she had done that for a great deal of her life. But it wasn't the tears themselves that got her, it was seeing them come from someone so happy. So bright and colorful and alive. Shiraz had begun to think of tears as things reserved for people who were less than impressed with life.

She stood, patting the woman on the arm carefully, unsure if half a day was long enough an acquaintance to offer a hug. "It's alright. It was frightening. It's natural to be afraid."

"Butitsovernow," Xinyi sobbed, blending all of the words together.

Shiraz was fairly certain she understood. "Many things are scarier after they are over, when you have time to consider how dangerous it was. Come on. I know what you need."

Xinyi hiccupped and stared at Shiraz, befuddled. Shiraz glanced past her to the boat. The three jungle spirits were perched on the side of the ship, waving their wings as if clapping, and there was an unfamiliar human there in robes.

"Do you know where Makoa is?" she asked.

"He…" *sob,* "challenged Nanghi to a…" *sniffle,* "Race as an aaaaalligator," she finished through one more sob.

"Bet you another ten percent of your treasure Makoa wins."

The princess gasped and cried all the harder. Shiraz rolled her eyes. "You can't hang onto your money with tears. My heart isn't made of gold, it's bought with it."

Xinyi gurgled on her tears like she was laughing. Shiraz draped a hand around the woman's shoulder and led the crying princess to the creek, rubbing a hand along the woman's soft arm to comfort her. Once at the creek, she suggested she bathe; Xinyi resisted. *She **had nothing else to wear**,* and *it was only starting to dry.*

"You can wear the damp clothes after. They might even dry faster off of you. Luckily for you, you weren't vomited up by an alligator so there is no need to wash them." Shiraz used sarcasm to avoid more of the sexual innuendoes the woman seemed to dislike. She was fragile right now. She'd tease her once her spine was back.

Xinyi bit the edge of her smile and tingling flames raced through Shiraz's chest. Those must have been some strong chillies.

The sensation had nothing whatsoever to do with having made the woman smile when a moment ago she'd been sad. Nothing.

Shiraz turned her back as Xinyi undressed. When she heard the other woman enter the water, she retrieved her damp dress and carried it to a near by sunny spot.

"I am sorry." The princess's soft voice drifted from behind Shiraz. "I nearly got you killed. I should have known better. I should have resisted. I am the reason you were vomited—"

"Alright," Shiraz interrupted brightly. She didn't turn, grinning into the trees. This princess was too sweet. "That's enough blame eating. You'll get a big head. None of that was your fault. Soul Parrots speak in your mind, offering your heart's desires as if they are real. Of course you were tricked into the water. The rest was Nanghi's fault. We had an arrangement that he broke. Never take responsibility for someone else's actions. It lets them off too easy."

All was quiet behind her. Shiraz desperately wanted to turn and see if the woman was still crying, or smiling, or deep in consideration. She had seen that look on her face a few times, like she had in the market. It was a lovely expression when she disappeared into the jungle of her thoughts. It filled Shiraz with that same thirst for adventure she felt when reading. She was sure if she could only steal into that woman's thoughts, she would know what magic looked like. But as much as she wanted to, she couldn't bring herself to look. Magic had let her down so many times.

And she knew how much she valued her own privacy. She couldn't take it from Xinyi. She scanned the area...waiting.

"Have you ever been tricked by them?" the woman asked, her voice moving nearer.

"No," Shiraz answered, flat and honest, and was oddly saddened by the facts spilling from her lips. "I pay attention to local legends, so I knew they might be here. The first time I traveled the river, I had an offering and knew how to resist them." When had she gone from seeking out all the magic the world had to offer—willing to lose her life just to find it—to avoiding any force that might cut her life short?

Like herself, Xinyi was a quick bather; after only a few dunkings beneath the water, she was finished in the creek. Shiraz extended her arm behind her, holding out a towel for the princess.

"The towel will do a decent job of it, but there is also a stick down there to brush over your skin and check for leeches."

"Leeches?" the woman exclaimed in horror. "Will a stick work?

"It's what I use. Of course I'm willing to check you, if you like," Shiraz offered. "For a small fee."

"You expect me to pay you to check me for leeches?" The incredulity in her voice was strong enough to knock over an elephant.

"Of course. Mine is a full service smuggling vessel, but all services have a fee. Why? Are you implying that checking your body for blood sucking pests would be a favor to *me*? How?" Shiraz's very innocent inquiry was met with a little snort from the princess.

"How much for the stick?" Xinyi asked dryly.

Shiraz's teeth dipped into the bottom lip of her smile as the princess teased her back. "Seeing as there are a few in the vicinity, you can use that one for free. I'm endlessly generous."

Xinyi laughed, and without more teasing, dressed once more in her damp clothes. "I've heard," she said softly. "Makoa told me what you did."

"That's too long a list. I was only gone half an hour." Shiraz made light, wondering uncomfortably what her friend had said.

Xinyi did not laugh; she walked around in front of Shiraz. "Cursing the man on the docks. The one who grabbed me," she explained and watched Shiraz in a deep thoughtful way.

"Oh, that." Shiraz started walking towards the ship. "When you have traveled alone as long as I have, you learn to appreciate some things and to strongly discourage others. If you mean to keep up this adventuring, there are a few lessons you should know."

"Please, share." Xinyi seemed more entertained than alert. Maybe even— flirtatious.

Shiraz looked away, forcing out even breaths and focusing on education alone. "One: Be wary of all strangers. Two: Never trust any offer of free assistance, food, or gifts."

"You never accept kindnesses?"

"No. And don't interrupt," Shiraz said in a playful tone, but she did tend to lose her train of thought when interrupted. "C: Never trust an injured stranger."

"You began with numbers." Xinyi bit on her grin.

"D—I mean—" Shiraz pulled in a deep breath, counting the letters into numbers in her head.

Xinyi chuckled softly.

"Four: Never drink from someone else's wine, even if you have seen them do so first. And *five,*" she said with great emphasis pulling a snide face at the other woman, "don't let anything you love or value out of your sight. The world is full of thieves and liars. People much worse than me."

"I am genuinely sorry about calling you scum. It was unkind," Xinyi tried to apologize, but Shiraz was blazing on with her instructions.

"You want to start being more suspicious. People will call you friend then rob you while you sleep. I learned all of those lessons the— Kuffik szou!" Shiraz shouted, startling birds from the trees. They had reached the spot where she sat to read, but something was missing.

"You see?" She waved angrily at the empty spot where her boat ought to be. "Lesson E, or five, or whatever the kuffik I said. Everyone is a liar!"

Lesson D or 4— Not Just Good Advice for Women

Makoa swallowed the wine Nanghi's attendant offered unthinking. If Shiraz were here, she would have stopped him. So paranoid was she. He nearly spit it back out with the thought, but that would be very rude. They had settled their differences. This was all fun and games now. And...he needed to relax. Makoa was still shaken from nearly watching his best friend be eaten. By nearly causing it.

He couldn't believe she'd thrown herself into the water like that without thinking. Well, yes, he could. She put a brave face on it, but she was still upset about having helped the kidnappers. It was as much his fault as hers, but she couldn't let it go. There were very few things that she could not find a way to forgive or excuse. But hurting children was where she drew the line. And their bright-eyed passenger calling her scum then asking if they had helped the kidnappers had brought it all back. Shiraz was desperate to feel redeemed.

She didn't need to be. But despite appearances and sarcasm, Shiraz hated making mistakes. She was too hard on herself. And today she had nearly died.

When Nanghi spit her up, she wasn't breathing. Makoa felt his heart rupture, wide and aching in his chest. What would he do if he lost her? She was his constant. His sister.

So he swallowed the wine to shake off the fears that still clung to his skin no matter how many changes of form he made.

He climbed up the side of the ship agilely. Nanghi flopped back into the river. Makoa had not thought the alligator's kiss would break his spell. But nor had he cared to offend him. Anyway, he was curious about Nanghi's kissing skills, having never kissed an alligator. The accolades of wet, smelly, and very pushy lips were all the alligator could boast. If love existed, the sort of which his curse suggested, Makoa was certain his *true love* would not be found in someone he'd seen nearly eat his friend. But it was possible he spoke about his curse too often, as it seemed to be of great entertaining interest to those he was least interested in loving, and of least interest to those he loved.

Neither Aiattaua nor Shiraz ever behaved as though his curse would be broken. Makoa didn't really think it would be broken either, but...what if it could get worse?

He'd grown accustomed to this version of himself. What happened when the curse started changing him against his will, as it had earlier? Who would he be then? Would he even retain his glowing teal eyes to be known by? Or would every change make him a stranger to those he loved?

With two arms and a third of his body up on the railing, Makoa shoved himself forward, leaping into the water. He was looking forward to the race. He loved competition without purpose. Loved a good swim. Loved the pointless and the ridiculous. He wished Shiraz was here to watch; she would be taking bets. Or hopping into the water to race them herself, knowing she could not win, but enjoying the game.

His body hit the water with a shock. It felt almost as if a painful charge rushed up and out of his body. He shuddered and tried to focus.

Nanghi was speaking. "Are we going to race? Or are you too dizzy from my lips?"

Makoa had some choice words to respond to that. From the breath of the creature, Makoa doubted alligators ever cleaned their teeth, but he couldn't get the words out.

Nanghi swished his tail through the water and took off swimming. Makoa shook his head to clear it and swam after.

Something was wrong with him. Everything seemed slow. He noticed the Soul Parrots moving away from the boat, no longer watching him. That wasn't right. They were looking for something, or —No. He watched as a horde of brightly colored parrots descended on the ship; there must be twenty of them. Thirty, they covered the entire ship. And Nanghi's attendant was struggling with the steering pole.

Makoa turned back. They were trying to steal the boat. Makoa had to stop them. A giant claw fell on his back.

"Not so fast, cursed one." Nanghi dug into Makoa's back and dragged him deeper into the water.

Makoa's scream bubbled up through the water as he thrashed. Damnit. Maybe Shiraz was not paranoid.

Makoa fought, wriggling his body and gnashing his teeth. But he could not catch the much larger Nanghi. With a shout of pain, Makoa dove towards the river floor, yanking himself free of the alligator's claw. He turned onto his back in time to see the giant diving after him, mouth agape, ready to swallow him whole.

Damnit! He was about to be eaten by that rotten breath rough lipped kisser, and he couldn't even clear his mind enough to focus up a new form. He wished he'd spit in Nanghi's eye when he asked for a kiss. Nanghi didn't deserve the satisfaction of having tricked him.

A Great Way to Get Kidnapped

For the past few minutes of travel by foot, the woman before Xinyi had been so angered as to be reduced to mere grunts and growls in response to Xinyi's myriad of questions. Xinyi wished she could stop asking questions, but it was something she did when she was nervous, or happy, or interested, or scared. She talked. She questioned. She rambled. And though the captain did not seem to be enjoying this, she hadn't told her to shut up. Or yelled, or blamed Xinyi for having lost her boat.

Xinyi knew it was not her fault, but it felt like her fault. But she had learned to stay positive. She needed to stay positive. So, at first, even though they could not find Makoa, or Nanghi nor the soul-parrots, or the boat, Xinyi was convinced that Shiraz was overreacting.

"Surely they just sailed it upriver to follow the race." Xinyi received only a glare.

"They'll be back. We should wait here. That is what mother told me. Wait, and someone will find you. And they always have."

That was the first thing to encourage a word that was not profanity out of the captain's lips. Her eyes widened in what appeared to be horror.

"That is terrible *advice! Wait and someone will find you! Who? No one is looking for us. We were tricked off the ship, robbed, and Makoa was*

kidnapped or...injured." The words were spoken with Shiraz's teeth clenched so tight, it looked painful and sounded precisely like the pent in rage Xinyi was used to seeing before people grew tired of her. Before she became a nuisance.

She'd been a nuisance to this woman since she agreed to take her upriver. It just...hadn't seemed like it by the creek. She'd stood there with her back to Xinyi, without her even having to ask, and spoke to her like a real person. But now the captain was back to resenting Xinyi's existence.

The captain searched up and down the banks, in the water, under bushes. Xinyi thought perhaps she was looking for signs of what direction the others had gone, because surely the boat could not become so small as to be hidden under a single bush. But when Shiraz pounced on a tiny lizard, pulling the terrified creature up to her face and examining it, Xinyi understood why they were still on the banks of the river. She was looking for her friend's body.

Xinyi fought the dark thoughts tumbling through her mind, but they would not be silenced. "Would he be a serpent? Or a man? Or an alligator? He was an old woman briefly. Would you even recognize him?" She instantly regretted her question as the other woman's eyes glassed over with tears. Then anger shuttered her expression and she growled.

"Come on. We're going after them."

Xinyi was shocked to feel relief sing through her body. She had been worried she would be left behind. Worried she would have to stay in this spot where she'd seen this fearsome woman be spit out of the alligator's mouth. Worried she would do what she had done all her life: wait to be found. She scrambled to her feet, managing to stand firmly even as the gauzy material of her dress got caught up under her. She gathered it in her hands, holding it high, out of her way.

"Are you sure you'll be able to find them?"

A growl again, this one clearly in the affirmative. She dropped the basket of things she'd carried, taking only a long, curved knife. Shiraz held out her left arm, indicating an intricate tattoo with the butt of her knife.

Xinyi had never seen a tattoo this involved on a woman. The only tattoo she'd ever seen on a woman was the small bird behind Yinuo's ear. This was nothing so delicate. It was a map, with color and depth and—

"It moves!" Without thought, Xinyi closed a hand around the woman's wrist, leaning in close.

There was a shimmering golden snake swimming along the river on the map. It was astonishing; she couldn't take her eyes off of it.

Shiraz stiffened, alerting Xinyi to what she'd done. She started to apologize for grabbing her, but Shiraz interrupted, pointing at a spot on the tattoo where a golden snake slithered.

"I can find it. They're headed towards the temple," she said tightly. She yanked her arm back and started forward. Xinyi followed, filling the air between them with nervous words.

"I've never seen such a tattoo. Never even imagined one. How did you get it? Was it put on you with needles or magic?" She did not slow down much between questions, but all Shiraz did was grunt anyway. "Could it slither off your arm, if it went beyond the map?" Xinyi snorted. She appreciated the distraction, because the look in Shiraz's eyes when she had asked if Shiraz would even know Makoa's body...it was a haunted look. A look that said today was not the first time Shiraz had felt that fear and had no answer.

So Xinyi embraced the other topic. She didn't like seeing people she imagined as invulnerable as mere mortals with fears.

"Now I am imagining your tattoo leaping off of your arm and slithering away into the ocean. Sailed by monkeys." She giggled high pitched. "Perhaps monkeys stole it, and not the soul-parrots. You said

they'd come back. And they were trying to take it before. What would monkeys even do with a river boat?"

Shiraz kept walking, though it seemed more of her attention went to the trees. And Xinyi kept talking. Her voice carried out random musings, thoughts on tattoos, magical wonderings, questions about the name of Shiraz's boat. There was no silence between them. But no matter what she asked, nor how complicated the answer ought to be, Shiraz had only growled.

"At least we are heading upriver," Xinyi observed now, no longer expecting a response. They had been walking for about twenty minutes without a word exiting the other woman's lips. "I thought it all so simple. Sail upriver, demand my treasure, return home for evening tea. I expected to be heading back now. Without these bruises, without being soaked to the bone multiple times. Or getting fifty bug bites." She slapped her arm as she felt something crawling beneath her sleeve. "I should never have left home. Yinuo said I would not be a burden, even without my treasure. But I am always a burden eventually. Everyone says I will not be, but I am.

"When my family found me, they were so happy." Xinyi spoke as if to herself alone. Speaking things she had never been able to, even with Wei. "Their other daughter was ill, but now she would have a companion. Kai-ming could not leave her bed, but I sat with her and told her stories, and we built a wild world together. And her parents, *my* parents," she corrected herself, "doted on me. But she died. Only four years after I came to them. Then I was a reminder." Her voice fell away. But the silence began to close in, reminding her to be grateful for what she'd had. It could have been so much worse. She should be grateful.

"Oh, they loved me still," she rushed to assure the silent air. "They kept me fed and clothed. But I could feel how I was a burden to them. Everything I tried to do to help went wrong. And I could see their frustration and sadness. I am always a burden eventually." She didn't let the words hang for long this time. Not risking their weight upon the air. "So I need the treasure back. I need to earn my place in this family."

"No one should need to *earn* their place in a *family*," Shiraz bit out, violently angry. She slashed unnecessarily hard at the overgrowth around them.

Xinyi was so shocked to receive a response that she stumbled, stubbing her toe on a root.

"Eeech!" Xinyi attempted to strangle her exclamation, covering her mouth as Shiraz stopped. "I'm sorry," Xinyi whispered, trying to hold up her dress and hop around one footed and follow, and be quiet and calm and…prepared like the woman in front of her.

"I'm so sorry. I can't stop talking and I'm a burden to you."

Shiraz set down the machete, and her hands came up gently to frame Xinyi's shoulders. Their eyes met. Xinyi felt like crying again. The other woman opened her mouth, but Xinyi beat her to speaking, needing to get the words out.

"You should have left me behind. You would be better alone."

Shiraz crouched, shaking her head, and reached out for Xinyi's injured foot.

"One." Shiraz brushed rocks and twigs off the bottom of Xinyi's silk shoes. She tsked her tongue at the holes already forming in the soft soles. She reached behind her for the machete and cut off a pair of tall thick leaves from a near by plant that stretched up to Xinyi's thigh. She began wrapping a leaf around Xinyi's left foot. "Never apologize for expressing your pain. You have every right to feel it and make it known." Her voice was so...soft. Comforting. "You have a right to make a need for love known. Not because you've earned it. But because you exist and you deserve to be loved. Especially by your family. Love hurts, and it is frightening. But it is never a burden."

Xinyi felt the air evaporate from her lungs, felt her pulse and her blood slow. Felt tears slipping down her cheek and brushed them away with the back of her hand. Who knew this woman had such kindness in her? *Love hurts and it is frightening. But never a burden.* That was beautiful. Comforting even as it broke her heart.

"Seems no matter where I go, someone always feels that way though." The smuggler's voice dropped, sounding remote and morose for a moment. "I've been on my way to Ooloo'a for years because there is a legend about their Singing Hills. *If you find your way to their secret shore, you are promised love forevermore.*" She looked up through the curtain of her hair briefly, smiling, but it was a sad smile. "Supposedly the island chooses you. If you are outcast, or lonely, it picks you and gives you a home where you are loved for all of the things the rest of the world hates most about you. The things that make you different become the things that make you loved." She tied off the leaf, cradling Xinyi's foot gently. "It's just a legend, I suppose. But I search for it, because I still think everyone should be loved like that. Loved for who they are, not for what they've done to deserve it."

Shiraz set the injured foot back on the ground with a leaf wrapped and tied around the center of the shoe. Xinyi tested it out. It made for a stronger sole, not as smooth but much sturdier.

"Two: talk as much as you want. You aren't hurting anyone," she said in a much brighter voice, but Xinyi wasn't fooled anymore. This was a lonely woman, criminal but kind. "C: and I cannot believe I am going to be this nice to you, but." Xinyi grinned as the captain switched to delineating her list with letters instead of the numbers—again. And at the same number. "*You* are paying me, princess! Never let someone you are paying for a service act like it is a burden. If it is, they should have negotiated a better price."

She had a point. Though, she doubted she would still mean it once she learned what Xinyi's treasure was.

"And four: *this isn't your fault.*" Shiraz was now making improvements to Xinyi's second shoe, her head pointed towards the ground. There was a calm to her cadence and her casual work that Xinyi found comforting. "They attacked the ship though we've had safe passage for years. Then they did something to Makoa and took the ship. And you were right, the Golden Paw Gang were after the ship earlier. Something is going on. But it isn't about you, it's about the River Serpent. It's a negotiating technique. That's how I know Makoa is alive. Because I wouldn't negotiate with them otherwise. This is how business is done, in the world of scum."

Shiraz winked up at Xinyi from the ground, making Xinyi swallow uncomfortably. She wanted to ask why she was so easy about needing to negotiate with people who had kidnap her friend when a moment ago she'd been reduced to growls. Or to ask if she was this nice to all her clients. But she couldn't open her mouth. She felt connected to this woman. Too connected to speak and risk breaking the link.

Shiraz broke it. Lifting her machete again, she started forward. "Go on and talk if it helps. Tell me all about that treasure. What form is it? Gold, gems, clothes, spices, *magic?*"

Xinyi felt sick. Look how kind the smuggler was being, when she didn't have to be. Xinyi ought to tell her that she was walking into the jungle, with her equivalent of a smile on, for a treasure Xinyi had seen her throw into the dirt an hour ago.

It was possible Nanghi and the Soul Parrots had stolen her boat as a negotiation tactic, but it was still Xinyi's fault. Bad things happened to everyone who helped her. Wei's family, Yinuo and the other women. Now this woman and her friend.

Xinyi was ashamed. She'd left the palace intent on going after the thieves and using her bad luck against them. Felt it was only right after their crimes. She'd wanted trouble to befall the River Serpent as well. And now it had. She needed to get to the thieves as quickly as possible, before this surly but secretly considerate woman's life was ruined.

"Fine," Shiraz remarked. "Keep it a *secret* treasure. I'll see it eventually. Tell me more about your mother's ill-conceived advice. *Wait for someone to find you*, ha! Great way to get kidnapped that."

Xinyi opened her mouth to reply, but her thoughts were oddly tumultuous. One could look at how she was found as a sort of kidnapping. If one wanted to take everything poorly. She'd waited in the basket where her mother left her and she'd been found...she'd been taken to a new home, a new life. She'd been rescued. Just as her mother said she'd be. Right?

How Business is Done in the World of Scum

Clouds of bubbles rose through the water. Nanghi dragged Makoa to the surface of the river. Makoa could not have transformed into a worse form, damnit. It was lucky that the river god was after kidnapping and not eating, because he'd taken on the form of a young gorilla and was flopping around, losing air every second, unable to make his long arms and short legs work properly.

Why couldn't he have instinctively changed into a stingray? Or a boa constrictor? Ugh. Because his head was still too fuzzy. Even though he could now think the names of animals he should have become, when he imagined a stingray, he saw a small hard-bodied bug thing with a long hooked stinger coming out of its back. What were those called? And when he'd thought of a boa, he saw merely a long, feathered scarf fluttering in the air. An unlikely means to strangle an alligator.

Nanghi threw Makoa onto smooth stone. Makoa blinked. The world was bright before him for a moment, then dimmed, then brightened, then dimmed. It evened out into a grayish green bumpy surface as the alligator stepped out of the water, towering over Makoa.

Ugh. He didn't want to die looking at the underside of Nanghi's chin. It was no more attractive than the rest of the creature.

"Someone bring our guest some water, he's had an ordeal." Nanghi walked over Makoa. Makoa hastily shut his eyes and turned his head aside. The rest of him was ugly enough; Makoa didn't want to become closely acquainted with the alligator's personal appendage.

Nanghi shook the ground as he walked. Makoa only relaxed when Nanghi's tail dragged across him. *Open your eyes*, he told himself. *Clear your head. Think.*

Makoa managed only one of the three instructions. Blinking, he held his eyes open by the force of his will. He was inside some sort of stone structure. There were stairs leading away from him, stairs Nanghi was climbing and Soul Parrots were lining.

That was an awful lot of Soul Parrots. That or he was seeing double. Maybe triple. But he thought he was seeing as many as were there, but that they weren't all what they looked like. Well, they weren't all *more* than what they looked like.

They were parrot parrots. Not Soul Parrots! That was what he was trying to think.

They were in Nanghi's temple, weren't they? Groaning Makoa, managed to turn to the other side and saw the open pool of water and the little canal leading to the river. There in all her dinged-up glory was the River Serpent, covered with yet more parrots, parrot parrots, or Soul Parrots; he couldn't say. Nanghi's attendant was at the helm, looking grim. Other than the uninvited guests, the ship looked magnificent. It looked like home.

He'd always called it Shiraz's ship. She had been the one to dream it up, and the one to do the work of getting its spells. And she worked to keep it in good condition. He helped here and there, but he hadn't wanted to get attached, and he had. Not just to her, but to her home as well. Their home.

"Get off my boat," Makoa attempted to shout. The birds ignored him. And to be honest, Makoa wasn't entirely sure that the slurred words came out as he meant them. He needed to get rid of the poison.

"Alert our buyer," Nanghi said, and a pair of parrots took off.

"We need the woman for the full bounty," an attendant remarked.

Bounty. Damnit. Makoa needed to get clear, and figure out what they had done to Shiraz, and save their home. Her face flashed through his mind, not as it was now, but as it had been that second time they met sitting across the fire from him, laughing as she described a prank she had pulled on one of her elders after he insulted her brother.

"Have you ever smelled sheep vomit? They don't digest things right away, and it smells like it. Smells like it's been rotting inside of them. So I dropped his prized sermon sash into the vomit before washing it." She chuckled hard. "That smell never came out! And he couldn't have another made because even the idea was tainted." Shiraz chuckled so hard.

She was so full of life, so wicked in the best ways. And so full of useful information about sheep. Makoa took a deep breath, digging to where his curse lived, and blew out. He hoped for the best. And weirdly, it worked! He transformed into a sheep and at once felt himself gagging, his body regurgitating the sleeping drought he'd ingested.

Nanghi raced towards him as Makoa was gagging and spitting. Makoa spit out the last of the drug slowing his reflexes. Nanghi was closing in on him, was going to eat him. Makoa needed to be big and threatening. Powerful. He needed to be a dragon. Makoa breathed out the spell again and transformed.

Only it didn't exactly work.

He transformed not into a gigantic, fire-breathing beast, which to be fair, he'd never actually met, or even seen in person. And not even into the dragon form he'd been imagining, capable of thoroughly burning the death god with her lava, like she had Shiraz's last ship. But into Felicia's—humanish—form. Apparently his mind wasn't free of the muddling effect. But it wasn't all bad. Her humanoid form's spiked joints had some value.

Makoa kicked Nanghi in the face with a spiked ankle, drawing blood and a scream, then raced away, breathing out curse breath, hoping for a very large bird of prey. He transformed into a secretary bird, near triple the size of the parrots. He leapt into the air. He flew straight up at first, barely escaping Nanghi's teeth as the alligator leapt to bite him.

Avoiding the alligator's teeth, he flew with his wicked beak straight at the ship, startling up a swarm of parrots. Many of them squawked and fled. Nanghi's attendant rolled under the canopy in an attempt to hide, but the Soul Parrots stayed with the ship, some taking flight to attack Makoa, others sitting on the boat like they could claim it.

He was pecked at and bit. But he was a much more impressive bird; the power from the flap of his wings had other birds falling back.

"Get off my ship before I go in for the kill," Makoa shouted. They didn't need to know that in general Makoa preferred not to kill. He could be pushed to the point of letting that go. But he wasn't there yet.

To reinforce his threats, he yanked a parrot out of the air in his beak, and another in a claw. He didn't bite or squeeze hard enough to kill. But he didn't let go either. He flapped to the ship, settling atop the canopy like a god, and glared at Nanghi.

"Explain yourself." Makoa managed to slip the words out around the purple and green parrot in his mouth.

Nanghi had been pacing back and forth at the base of his stairs, watching Makoa. Now he shrugged, laying down with an arm in the pool stirring the water, as blood dripped off his nose.

Another attendant slipped out of the shadows at the top of the stairs, carrying a platter of raw meat and a cloth.

"After I generously spit out your friend, my attendant informed me there was a bounty in the offering for your ship," the river god said nonchalantly. "It seemed foolish to spit in fortune's face. The bounty for the ship is worth far more to me than our bargain, especially with the pair of you leaving our nation. Shouldn't have announced that."

Makoa nodded aside. He didn't really have room to argue with that. Had the Golden Paw Gang been after a bounty as well? That implied some sort of relationship to humans or the fey.

Makoa squeezed the bird in his claw tighter. It let out a squawk in the minds of everyone around, an exclamation of pain.

"Kill her," Nanghi laughed. "As you can see, I have many others."

"You *have* others?" one of the parrots on the ship squawked. Aloud.

It was unsettling. Makoa had never heard any of the Soul Parrots speak outside of his head. Also the creature's voice was so odd coming out of its body. It sounded like a squeaky field mouse.

He wondered if they all had mouse voices. It would explain why they spoke in minds. Not that there was anything wrong with squeaky voices. But they didn't inspire feelings of awe or fear.

The Soul Parrots flew in sharp waves, attacking Nanghi. He leapt up, his teeth snapping in annoyance, though Makoa doubted in much fear. The attendant with the food on the other hand kept ducking. Makoa wondered about the attendant on the ship. Looking around, he spotted him attempting to pull a weapon off the wall of the ship.

Makoa leapt up, flying around behind the man and frightening him into jumping off the ship. Makoa took up his prior roost and watched Nanghi fight with his forces.

"You're falling for his ploy. He wants to turn you against me. He isn't going to kill them." Nanghi was not gifted at double dealing. Too used to having his meals provided to handle real world scoundrels while maintaining alliances.

Makoa was more practiced. He didn't release the birds, fully aware that the parrots would be attacking him if he did.

"What about to you?" Makoa asked the Soul Parrots. "What is the bounty worth to you?"

A trio of Soul Parrots flapped up in front of him, beating their wings to stay level with him. "Quite a bit," one said aloud.

"More than your friends?"

"One," the bird replied.

Damn, they were cold blooded. "Which one?" Makoa asked.

"Not one of our friends," tiny voice countered. "Which bounty do you want to trade with? There are bounties available for the ship, and the princess. We will trade their lives for one."

Oh. Reasonable. Makoa's claw curved around the canopy. His home. Shiraz's home. As opposed to the *princess* who had been lying to them about who she was at the very least and might be lying about a great deal more. Makoa was surprised not to need more time to consider. Not to feel conflicted.

He used to feel conflicted. After he was cursed, he felt conflicted whenever he did self serving things. It didn't stop him doing them, but he'd felt it and he hadn't liked it. But now he felt fine. Perhaps he was more his old self than he realized. Or...perhaps it was just the right choice.

"We'll take the ship." Makoa spit out the bird in his mouth.

The Turtles at the Temple Path

All Shiraz had to defend them with was the one nectar fruit she had yet to eat, and two nectar fruit pits that she kept playing with to settle her nerves. And the machete. Shiraz had never killed anyone with the knife. Certainly not a giant alligator that had lived for hundreds of years. Shiraz was a run over fighting, steal over asking, argue with words over fists sort of woman when it came down to it.

But Makoa was missing, possibly hurt. Her boat, which she had worked years to get, and dreamed of for even longer, was taken. And at her back she had a nervous princess intent on blaming herself for every incident that befell them. When in reality they were mostly the result of Shiraz trying to tease her.

How many times had Xinyi repeated that she should have stayed behind and waited for someone to find her? How many times had she said she was sorry? And that story of her "family." That was heartbreaking. Shiraz had thought Noam had it bad, and he had, but not like that. At least Noam had her and Ethan and Mama. Xinyi had been forced to find her joy alone. And find it she had. Shiraz couldn't let anything happen to this bright bundle of resilience.

Today—she had to be prepared to fight.

Shiraz was as nervous as Xinyi.

But Xinyi's constant chatter soothed the fiery rage she'd felt when she noticed her boat missing, making it calculated. The Soul Parrots and their river god would pay. They would pay twice as much if Makoa was hurt. Even *Makoa* would pay for scaring her like this.

Shiraz stopped, and Xinyi, much more sure footed with her more appropriate footwear, managed to stop without falling. Shiraz watched her tattoo a moment, waiting for her golden serpent to slither away further. But it didn't.

It was ahead of them, past the clearing, around the back of Nanghi's temple. In the pool of reflection most likely. With any luck, Makoa would be there. If not—

Shiraz shoved her arm behind her back. She couldn't think about that, not yet. Her fingers brushed against her old, wool lined vest. It was worn, overlarge, and had a few holes, but still she hung onto it. It was the only piece of clothing she still had from Glen Harrow.

She remembered Ethan dropping it around her shoulders when he'd found her smuggling herself to market under a pile of wool. She'd popped out, felt how near they were to the sea and been chilled in her slip of a dress. He'd taken off his vest and dropped it around her shoulders, eyebrow raised. *Don't you ever think ahead, whirlwind?* He'd laughed and whispered for her to hide if the elders came near, then ordered Noam to guard her. Noam had grinned. This had been their plan all along, to get her to market so it would be too much work for Ethan to do what he was supposed to and drag her home. She'd wanted an adventure, and she got one. She met her first fairy that day, because she *had* thought ahead, just not of dangers. She never thought of the dangers then.

But she did now. And she wasn't letting anyone take one more brother from her.

"Right." Shiraz spun around, smiling with false confidence, her body slouching into a casual posture that had succeeded many a time before in convincing others she cared not at all. "Up ahead will most certainly be a few Soul Parrots. It will be easier for you to resist, now that you have heard them, but when they speak in your head, ask them questions. If your heart's desire is to...climb the world's highest mountain, ask if there will be sweet balls waiting for you. The more ridiculous the question the better. It throws them off. When we were first negotiating, they tried their tricks on me. Offered to show me the secret source of magic in the universe."

"Is that your heart's desire?"

Shiraz shrugged; she didn't know anymore. "I asked them if there would be geese. When they said yes, I said oh, then I guess I won't go, I hate geese."

Xinyi giggled, relaxing, which was good, though not Shiraz's aim. "Just ask them any question you can think of. And don't trust the alligator god; he might eat you for fun. Stay behind me, don't say anything, and smile pretty. What? It can't hurt," Shiraz added in response to Xinyi's dirty look.

Xinyi moved closer, trying to close Shiraz's hand in her own, and her eyes glowed with such gentle comforting energy that the woman was lucky Shiraz didn't kick her.

"Makoa will be fine."

"Naturally." Shiraz turned away to shake her off. Surprised and annoyed that the woman saw through her confident veneer.

They made their way forward boldly. Well, Shiraz walked boldly. Xinyi walked very carefully, holding her skirt high. They stepped out of the lush overgrowth of what, a few years ago, had been a footpath and into the temple clearing.

The grasses around the temple were overgrown, and weeds had climbed over the statues that marked the path. The temple of Nanghi was devoted to the alligator and was bound to have large renderings of him within the walls, as there were on the upper porch of the building supporting the ceiling. But the smaller statues that guarded its entrances looked like turtles.

She and Makoa had never stopped to view the temple, both nonbelievers in nature. Under other circumstances, she might have been excited to see it though. She enjoyed a decorative temple. But she likely would not have been *as* excited as the woman behind her.

"It is lovely. I would have thought to wish it not overgrown, so I could see the effect of the divine mazes shaped into the grass. But this is like stumbling across a ruin in an adventure story."

Shiraz resisted telling the woman the temple was not a ruin, just… neglected. Five years of disuse did not a ruin make. The pillars, arched roof, and stairs all looked fine, if dirty.

The trees overhead began shaking, and she heard chattering, not like birds, like monkeys. *Great.*

The Golden Paw Gang were all she needed. She was growing exceptionally annoyed with this day. This year. This trip. There were likely monkeys in the trees, and though the woman beside her seemed not to notice, parrots of every variety were on outcroppings or weed-covered statues. Shiraz had never seen this many Soul Parrots. She hadn't even thought there were that many. This day was never going to end, was it?

"It's Nuan and Feng!" Xinyi pulled weeds away from the faces of the turtle statues. "They mark the temple entrances, warning the unwary that they are about to be eaten." Xinyi giggled then the sound faded away. Apparently, she had caught sight of their audience. Her voice when it returned was quiet and thoughtful.

"They are rival gods. Changelings, like Makoa. Only not cursed to be so. They take on many forms. But in stories with Nanghi, they often wear armored shells that he cannot bite through for defense. You see they are pacifists who want Nanghi's carnage stopped. Nuan is the goddess of friendship and mischief. And her brother Feng is the god of romance and irony."

Shiraz chuckled. "Romance and irony go together well." She knew some of this already but had not sought out such detail.

"I never thought Nanghi existed. But he does. And so do the Soul Parrots. So Nuan and Feng must also," Xinyi continued.

"Let's look for them after we get your treasure, eh?" Shiraz offered, starting up the steps to the temple, past a sea of sinisterly silent parrots. "Got my hands full at the moment."

"No, I was just... wishing I had something to feed them."

"What the birds *again*?" Shiraz demanded. "Like it went so well last time?"

"No!" Xinyi said, just short of snide. Shiraz turned back. "Nuan and Feng. Worshipers of Nanghi feed the trickster gods for protection when they enter the temple. And the gods provide them with...*tricks* to escape Nanghi's carnage. In the past I wouldn't even have considered it; before I started on this journey, I thought they weren't real," Xinyi spoke in a wondering fashion, bobbing her head from side to side as she spoke as if she was speaking more to herself than Shiraz.

Shiraz was mystified. A surface observer might think this woman so oblivious she didn't see the danger. But that wasn't the case. Xinyi was aware of the danger. She was just so optimistic that she had room to hope the existence of gods meant they were bound by the rules of their legends. And her hope was infectious. She was infectious. There were a small collection of jungle creatures fanned out behind her, watching her in awe. Of course Shiraz had been inoculated against optimism by years of reality, but...it was still lovely to witness.

Xinyi shrugged. "I don't have anything to feed them, but if I did what could it hurt?" She focused on Shiraz, truly seeking an answer.

Shiraz should be annoyed with Xinyi for delaying their rescue of Makoa to feed statues. Which weren't gods at all! Even if the gods they represented were real. But Shiraz was touched. Xinyi was trying to help. Was willing to look foolish in her attempt to help.

Shiraz slipped her hand into one of the loose pockets of her pants and pulled out the nectar fruit. She didn't say a word, just sliced it in half with the machete and held the fruit out to Xinyi.

The princess grinned like this was the greatest gift she had ever been given and, heedless of the dangers, yanked the fruit from Shiraz's hand. She spun around, racing back towards the statues. Shiraz watched that fluttering pink skirt waft behind the princess, brushing across the high grasses. A lovely lady rushing out to the rescue.

The birds squawked and cried out. Shiraz brandished the knife.

"Come, temple in," voices sounded in Shiraz's head. *"Come, your brother is within. Come—"*

"Which one?" Shiraz cut the birds off aloud. She was very skeptical that this was the case, but—they had only started calling out to her as Xinyi ran back towards the statues.

Were they afraid of the turtle gods? Was Xinyi hearing their voices? Hearing and resisting. She was deceptively strong, wasn't she? Powerful.

Xinyi yanked away the weeds covering one statue and knelt, bowing her head. She presented half of the fruit in two hands, placing it at the feet of one turtle. Then she repeated the process with the second statue. Lights didn't flash, the air didn't fill with fog, or magic noises. But as Xinyi returned, Shiraz felt, ever so slightly, hopeful.

And that was such a powerful shift in the universe that it left her feeling more than a little nauseous.

Grabbing Adventure by the Hand

"*R*un*, princess sweet. Flee. You must retreat. Run, princess far. These aren't the friends you hope they are.*" The words sang through Xinyi's head as she fed first one god and then the other. She removed the stone from the center of the fruit, wanting both offerings to be the same, and licked juice from her fingers.

This was madness. But...it was also exciting and hopeful, and...fun. She was terrible. Makoa was injured or worse. And she was having fun!

When Shiraz had produced the fruit and sliced it in half—like she was a character in one of Xinyi's books, possessing exactly what the heroine needed in exactly the right moment—that had been *everything!* Her heart pounded and it was all she could do not to jump into the other woman's arms. It surely would have shocked Shiraz. Why did that excite her? Xinyi wanted to shock that woman. She'd never felt this way in her own skin, like she was one of her characters.

She felt like someone totally new, but very old. Someone she kept silent, except when she was writing. She felt herself believing in the strangest things, gods, rituals—*destiny.* Things she had been entirely certain were pretend until today. Until she lay on her back in the market and her eyes had met the deep brown eyes of the smuggler. She'd set out to find the lowest of scum, expecting to be disgusted. But there Shiraz was all fierce and confident, the embodiment of all those things Xinyi had been raised to despise. Avarice, selfishness, immorality. But she didn't feel the disgust she was meant to, well, some of it. But more she felt *intrigued*. Felt like she was meeting her villain, the character that was secretly Xinyi's favorite to write.

That was why she lasted so long in the series. Xinyi hadn't set out to create a villain so strong Jian could never defeat her. But when V was on the page, Xinyi felt charged. Like she did now. She had never had so much fun in her life!

She didn't argue with the birds aloud, not wanting Shiraz to know what they were implying about her. Because she began to suspect the villain had a softer heart than the princess. So she queried the voices in her mind with thought alone. *Am I the friend they think I am?*

"You are just as you appear. They are far worse we fear."

As Xinyi reached the stairs, the captain stretched out a hand, likely to wave Xinyi on, but Xinyi gripped that hand in her own. A charge rushed up from their joined hands to shudder through her. Xinyi walked forward, holding on tight to this adventure. She had the strangest, most exciting feeling that now it was her turn. That she held in her hand, or her mind, or her heart, exactly what this villain needed to get through the scene.

Promise? she asked the voices in her mind. And heard peals of laughter.

Shiraz and Xinyi mounted the stairs and the temple rose before them. It was an open shrine, its columns held up by stone renderings of Nanghi, each with a different expression. The roof's tiered slats were made of wood, rotting in places, but overall the green, moss-covered roof bore up under the weight of...perhaps *all* the parrots in the jungle.

According to legends, Nanghi worked with many jungle spirits, but the Soul Parrots were small in number. She had written about it.

> The colorful consumers of souls knew Jian would recognize them. Knew that having been a priestess at the god's temple, she knew their small number and their secret ways. So the elder devised a plan. They would bring the god his servant, and he would devour her, releasing that bright soul unto those who had fed him. But to do this, they must confuse the naiad. So she dispatched her squadron of fifteen parrots, but split them amongst all the birds of the jungle. Thus no place, no bird, no tree was safe for the girl as she fled her duty.

He's copying me, Xinyi thought. Then puzzled aloud. "In volume four, Nanghi and the Soul Parrots capture Jian. But she escapes using her knowledge of the temple rituals!" Xinyi began to form a plan, expecting Shiraz, who didn't like her writing, would need it explained.

"Sure," the captain agreed. "She offered up everything she had in exchange for her freedom. She had only flowers, and Nanghi wanted none of them, but because she had made the offering in accordance with his rules, Nanghi had to let her leave. Then he followed and attacked her later, away from the temple."

"You remember that awfully well for something you found melodramatic." Xinyi grinned. Shiraz had been fibbing, hadn't she?

Shiraz shrugged. "Are you suggesting we copy Jian?"

Her cautious eyes were focused on the birds as she started through the nearest archway, but Xinyi pulled her back.

"Yes...and no." Bowing low before a statue, Xinyi kissed the alligator's clawed hand.

"If you think I'm going to…"

"Come on." Xinyi dragged her towards the statue chuckling softly. "It will be over in a moment. It never hurts to respect tradition."

"Oh, trust me, sometimes it hurts very much," Shiraz said with a laugh, but no measure of humor at all.

Xinyi startled. "Oh. Yes. Alright, I concede it can." Xinyi didn't know why she'd said that. It was something she'd heard but never particularly considered. It just slipped out of her mouth. But from the captain's response, the words meant a great deal to her. All bad. "I am sorry. Please trust me. Kissing the statue is part of the ritual, and maybe it won't work, but it's one more chance." Xinyi stared at the other woman with entreating eyes.

Shiraz didn't move.

"For an extra two percent?" Xinyi sweetened the deal.

Shiraz rolled her eyes, but she conceded to Xinyi's request. Bowing with extravagant sarcasm, she kissed the statue's hand.

"Is that it? Magic achieved? Do I get my boat back now?" Shiraz asked with a snide disbelief that might have offended Xinyi earlier, though she herself hadn't believed. But now she recognized it as this snapping turtle's armor. She was scared.

Xinyi slapped her playfully on the arm. "This is my world, smuggler. Just stand beside me, do as I say, and smile pretty."

Xinyi expected argument, but the other woman allowed herself to be dragged. And she came along wearing an expression of amused wonder, her lips lifted, her eyes sparkled, and a dimple appeared in her left cheek, highlighting her spray of freckles. The smuggler took direction very well. That was a lovely smile.

They passed an empty plinth with statue remnants scattered around it. "Do you suppose he rested but woke when the war broke out and there were so many more bodies to feed him?" Xinyi wondered aloud.

"I suppose the statue broke."

Xinyi slapped Shiraz again. Her hand barely touched the other woman, but her meaning was clear, and it seemed not to bother the smuggler at all. Not once had she tried to reclaim her hand. The air in Xinyi's lungs tickled so wildly she nearly shuddered.

They stepped around the broken statue and made for the back exit where they could see The River Serpent floating. Atop the ship were yet more birds, most of them parrots, but one was a huge eagle with a parrot gripped in its claw. At the base of the stairs, Nanghi lay half in half out of the pool, with a few bloody scratches on his back and face.

"Makoa!" Shiraz jerked forward. "Did he hurt you?"

The eagle shook its head. "Mostly just my ego."

Nanghi pushed to his feet and began pacing the bottom of the stairs. The parrots shook their feathers.

"I said don't talk," Xinyi whispered in playful reproach.

"You failed to give that instruction." How she managed to sound flirtatious when speaking out the side of her mouth, Xinyi did not know. "But—*I'm yours to command*, princess."

A tingle raced up Xinyi's spine at the captain's tone. It danced under her skin, making her want to curl up into the feeling. But she had no chance to properly enjoy it.

"How helpful of you to deliver our prize right to us," Nanghi intoned from the base of the steps.

Xinyi had to literally bite her own cheek to shake her gaze off Shiraz and focus on the task at hand. What was wrong with her?

"Greetings, Nanghi, great god of death, namesake of the river, and devourer of evil." Xinyi gave the traditional greeting. Nanghi smiled. But a few of the birds tensed, and the two attendants exchanged looks. It seemed the god was not nearly as observant as his servants. She wondered who had thought to copy her story. "Who won the race?" Xinyi inquired.

The alligator god chuckled. "I did, naturally."

"I don't have to drug my competitors," Makoa muttered.

"I was sure you would win." Xinyi took back her second hand to clap for the god, ignoring Makoa entirely, as gods tended to demand. "I only wish I could have followed along to witness on the boat."

"But did you not have an adventure worth the writing, author?"

"Author?" Shiraz asked in a whisper.

Xinyi focused solely on the alligator. There was little chance of her hiding the truth now. "Indeed. And Shiraz was a helpful guide. We thank you for the opportunity. But now it seems we must part. I have another journey to complete."

The alligator chuckled loud enough to shake the waters and even the stone steps Shiraz and Xinyi stood on. Several of the parrots took off, flying around in weaving circles so fast one could see a colorful pattern drawn in the air from their wake.

"You are a delight, princess author. But I cannot allow you to leave."

"Oh?" Xinyi pretended shock. "Have we offended you?"

"You've delighted me in all instances. But as I warned when I rescued you, you were saved merely because there was no money in the offering to prevent it. Your traveling companions have traded you for a boat."

Now Xinyi was confused. "I...why would you want me? Or a boat?"

"We told you princess sweet to flee. Now your fate is far from free."

"It is not I, but your father. There is a king's ransom to be had by any who delivers you to him."

Oh. They thought she was *Yinuo.* Had the kidnappers worked for the king? Why not invite his daughter to join him? True, Yinuo likely would have refused but...jumping straight to kidnapping seemed extreme. Should she continue pretending to be Yinuo, so no one went after her?

The answer wouldn't alter her plans to escape the alligator god, so she pressed on. Though it was disheartening to realize Shiraz and Makoa had exchanged her. How? The Soul Parrots perhaps. Otherwise, how would Shiraz have known about the exchange?

"You made a bargain with Makoa *and Shiraz* that they might leave peaceably, if they give you myself in return?" Xinyi asked.

"Just so. I had wanted the boat as well, but I have been pressed to exchange the life of one of my parrots."

"It is not the business of a mortal to counterman the bargains of a god. Particularly not in his temple. But, great god," Xinyi bowed. "I have a request. I have kissed the hand and bring an offering in good faith." Xinyi lay the seed from the center of the nectar fruit on the stairs. "I offer you all I carry that you might agree not to collect your bounty until my stolen property is retrieved." She could find a different way home. Surely. This wasn't particularly honest of her, but having told a few lies now, it was getting easier.

Nanghi laughed loud and long. "Ah, author, you are fun. Do you think life will be as easy for you as it is for your Jian?"

Shiraz jerked, looking at Xinyi in disbelief. Xinyi wondered how long it would be before the smuggler realized that she had lied about more than her identity.

"I read that story," Nanghi said smugly, unaware that Xinyi had been counting on this. "And I paid attention to you humans and your double dealing ways. Fine, I agree to your terms." The alligator showed all his teeth. "But my dear, you must wait with me, *here*, until I am ready to collect my bounty."

The Princess Saves the Day

"Uzaok," Shiraz muttered as Xinyi's face fell. Xinyi had been so sure she could outsmart the river god. Shiraz far preferred cursing in Maltuban; there was something about the language that just...worked. Even if the being you were insulting didn't know the language, they knew they weren't being complimented.

Shiraz had not expected Nanghi to be anything other than his usual camel feces stench of a self. But she had been oddly optimistic that the cheerful princess beside her would triumph. The little liar beside her was a better description.

Xinyi was a much better liar than Shiraz had credited! No wonder she'd looked hurt when Shiraz threw the story. *Her story*. Azaqif. She doubted Xinyi would believe her now if she confessed how much she loved the stories. Shiraz felt bad about that. Only that. Not the look on her face when Nanghi said Shiraz and Makoa had agreed to trade her for safe passage. Definitely not that.

Shiraz had agreed to no such thing. But...if she had been in Makoa's place she would have. It was the practical move.

Being the quiet member of the party was a role Shiraz was used to. Though being ordered to smile pretty by the princess was a tingly new turn on she hoped to repeat. But the benefit of playing silent crew member was oh so much more attention for details.

The River Serpent was unmoored and drifting toward the river. There were no humans onboard, nor near enough to stop it. And Makoa had a Soul Parrot captive. All Shiraz really needed to do was get to the ship with the princess. It hadn't worked too well the first time she tried it, but there were handy vines hanging all over the place. If the princess would cooperate this time, they could swing out to the ship, lean into the peddles and speed away.

"Oh," Xinyi said, deflated. "I hadn't thought," she said with such sincerity it was hard not to believe her. But Shiraz—*didn't.*

"You *liar*," she whispered. And Xinyi, in very uncharacteristic move, jerked away.

She moved several steps from Shiraz, sniffling, focused solely on the alligator. "Yes. Yes, of course, I will stay, but...how will I know that you will not exchange me before the property is retrieved?" she asked in a desperate attempt to change the god's mind, nothing like the infectious confidence she'd entered with.

The confidence with which she'd convinced Shiraz to kiss a statue. Shiraz didn't honor gods or kings or anyone in between. But she had because Xinyi was certain it would make a difference, and Shiraz had loved seeing that faith. That...force of energy. Not forceful, or harsh, but so *powerful.*

"If I make a bargain, I honor it." The river god mounted the steps, examining Xinyi's offering. "If I agree, they will bring it back to show you it has been retrieved. Then I will collect the bounty on you."

Shiraz snorted. "My hidden pot of bronze we would," Shiraz remarked snidely. "And let you try and capture us again? No."

The princess gasped anew, releasing yet more tears. How did she have such faith and confidence one moment, and not the next? It was a game. Wasn't it? But Shiraz needed her to stop moving away. Every time Shiraz inched near, she moved. Did she even want to escape?

"You are lucky your friend negotiated your safe release. I wanted to bite you. But for the princess, I will offer one additional term. When you bring back her treasure, I will allow you to leave again safely."

Shiraz raised a brow, looking to Makoa—*Safe*. Now they had to see about getting away. All of them. "There were terms?" she inquired, playing casual.

"There is a bounty out for our ship and for the princess," Makoa remarked, equally bland. Shiraz felt her heart catch. A bounty for The River Serpent. Her dream. Their home. Someone was after it? Azaqif, she'd known they needed to move on.

"In exchange for promising the parrot will live, I negotiated the safe release of our boat. They promise not to follow until I release the bird, which is to be done before we reach sludge pass. And they are not allowed to sell any knowledge of our location, in exchange for being allowed to do their best to take the ship again," Makoa added. That was an excellent clause.

"Reasonable," Shiraz undersold. "And the princess?"

Makoa dipped his head gently in Xinyi's direction. She let out a sob. "I am sorry, princess. But...it is our home. I could negotiate for only one thing."

Shiraz refrained from adding that they would have much better chance of rescuing her with the boat than retrieving the boat with only her. She imagined the princess could work that out herself.

"Nanghi will collect the bounty on her, though it was negotiated that if we felt so inclined, we could attempt to bargain for her release with her treasure when we retrieve it. I hadn't enough knowledge of it to prove it was worthy of such a trade now."

"If you feel safe enough, cowards, you ought to leave, while my benevolence lasts," the alligator said, having taken Xinyi's nectar pit into his teeth and spit it across the room.

Shiraz took a few steps down the stairs. "Tell me, Nanghi," Shiraz asked snidely. "Is this the treatment all of your followers should expect? To pay homage to you, only to be sold to the highest bidder?"

"Do not be so dramatic. It is her father. She should be pleased he wants her near."

Shiraz shook her head. *"Zagok!* If she wants nothing to do with him, he did something to cause it. Forcing that relationship makes no more sense than the concept of worshiping a god who has no care for you. We'll make our own way."

With that, Shiraz lunged towards the princess, grabbing hold of the nearest vine. She caught Xinyi around the middle, the startled princess didn't struggle this time, and for one glorious moment as she leapt, it seemed like it just might work. Book type hero stuff.

Until the beam holding the vine whined and cracked and the two women stumbled back onto the stairs. The only positive was that they'd barely left the ground and so landed rather well. Nanghi's attendant reached out to grab Xinyi, but Shiraz brandished the machete. Nanghi laughed and raced forward, teeth bared.

"It is called obedience and fear." Nanghi's eyes flashed, and his tone deepened. He looked at Xinyi alone. "One fears a god's wrath, so one honors him. And the god in turn accepts his accolades and offers what protection has been paid for."

Xinyi nodded, moving around Shiraz. Shiraz's protests were stopped by Xinyi's head shake and entreating eyes.

"It's alright," she said softly. "We made the exchange. He accepted my offering. I'll be safe."

Zagok! Shiraz had no intention of leaving her.

"Come on, Shiraz," Makoa called out. "We have a bargain."

"With a god," Shiraz mocked. "Is worshiping you strictly mercenary then?" Shiraz asked brightly. "I can understand that."

Shiraz walked backwards slowly. Halfway to the water's edge, she stopped. Nanghi wasn't looking her way, but Xinyi was.

Xinyi bit her lip, but her eyes had that far away look in them, like she was trying to write a solution in her mind. That's what the look was, her writing look. She seemed truly to believe that Shiraz would leave her. She probably thought if she waited here, Shiraz would come back and rescue her. Or someone else would. That lone kernel of advice she held onto from her mother.

Xinyi focused suddenly, catching Shiraz's gaze. She winked. "Nanghi," she said in a softly wondering voice. "When you made your deal with Makoa, did you agree not to collect my bounty until he had returned to negotiate with my treasure?"

"I..." The alligator god startled, backing down the stairs a step. "Perhaps."

"Then...you did not accept my offering in good faith?" she asked. The water in the pool began to shift and splash. And Nanghi's attendants stood straighter, staring at Xinyi, not their god. Seriously? Shiraz looked around fully disbelieving. It couldn't be working? The splashing water was a coincidence, right?

The alligator appeared concerned. "My bargain with you was with you alone!"

"But if it had already been made, then—"

"Bargain anew then, author," he growled deep and low, interrupting Xinyi. "But know this, I said only that they could have the ship, not that it would be in one piece. Which will you bargain for, yourself or your means of escape?"

Herself. Obviously. Shiraz and Makoa would handle the ship.

But Xinyi's kind heart was not defeated. She nodded. "Very well, I request that you allow their vessel to leave unharmed."

Shiraz groaned. With the alligator god, Xinyi gave in, but with Shiraz, she really was pressing to get her money's worth. Fine. "One more thing, before I leave." Shiraz swept a hand behind her back and bowed. "Nanghi, great god of death, namesake of the river, and devourer of evil, *I* have kissed the hand, and I come with an offering, in good faith."

The alligator looked like he might fall over, so great was his shock.

"YOU *HAVE*?" Makoa's shock was as dramatic as Nanghi's.

But it was Xinyi, with her eyes alight with adventure and fun that caught Shiraz's attention. Shiraz made her offer to the river god, but her eyes remained on the lying manipulative schemer with the full lips and the sparkling eyes.

"In exchange for all I carry, I ask to take the princess into my protection and carry her away from this temple in *good health*."

Shiraz tore her eyes away from Xinyi, dragging it down to the glaring alligator. In Shiraz's head, she heard gales of laughter. Around the room, parrots took off, swooping down before the god in a mocking fashion that she might have felt bad about were he any less of an uzaok.

"No," he growled.

"I followed the ritual," Shiraz pointed out. She set her nectar pits on the ground.

Xinyi was rushing down to her, her dress wafting around her, and the long sash—No! Xinyi stepped on the sash and went stumbling. Shiraz jerked forward in time to catch the woman against one arm, jamming her shoulder painfully.

"Umph."

Xinyi looked up, and both women giggled.

"That isn't enough," the alligator shouted, annoyed not to be the center of attention. He banged his feet, shaking the temple.

"The knife," Xinyi whispered. Shiraz gave her a dirty look. "You're carrying it."

"Better stand on your own feet then before he demands you in exchange for you." Shiraz shoved Xinyi away, trying not to wince. Xinyi took it well; chuckling, she stood on her own power.

Shiraz set the machete on the ground. "Satisfied?" she asked the god belligerently.

He stomped again. "NO! You are no worshipper. I owe you nothing." Nanghi jumped up and down, angrily.

But the water it the pool splashed high, shaking the River Serpent and even the temple. Shiraz pulled Xinyi to her side to keep her steady. And near. Water splashed over the temple attendants, and they began to glow. The shells of armored turtles appearing on their backs.

"You have no sway here!" Nanghi shouted.

In Shiraz's arm, Xinyi managed another small bow. "But, Nanghi, I invited their protection at the temple gates. Promising to follow your rules, and theirs, that I might pass safely through the realm of gods."

"GET OUT of my temple!" His shout shook the air. "Never write about me again!"

Shiraz grabbed Xinyi's hand and pulled her quickly towards the ship. This was too ridiculous. The whole world was upside down and insane, if the god of death was letting them go for a bunch of trash in her pockets and a machete he couldn't use, not possessing the necessary digits or range of motion. All because his attendants were glowing with the shells of turtles. Turtle gods. When the nearest one looked her way and his eyes flashed, Shiraz was half convinced he wore a familiar face. But he turned and the impression passed.

"Do you think I should mention he dies in three chapters?"

"Don't spoil it," Shiraz hissed. Makoa had knocked down a plank and the two women raced on board, Shiraz holding tight to the accident-prone princess. "I was going to enjoy that surprise."

Xinyi smirked. "What happened to sixteen being your last?"

Shiraz laughed.

"This isn't over." Nanghi was hopping mad and generally ignored. He muttered to himself, "I'm tearing down your statues, I swear."

"Take a seat, princess. It's time to beat a hasty retreat," Shiraz said once they were both on board. She wasted no time running for the stern of the ship and grabbing her steering pole to get them moving.

Birds took off, and Makoa blew out a puff of heavily scented air, taking on the shape of a long-limbed young woman. Still gripping onto the bird, Makoa made certain the princess was seated before shoving aside the stool near the cooking pit and opening the little hatch that concealed foot pedals. As he peddled, propellers under the ship spun, moving them much faster as they fled the temple of the alligator god.

The Slightly Greater Escape

"You kissed a deity statue? *You?* The temple burner?" Makoa called back to Shiraz.

"I never burned down the temple! Just—Elder Trent's robes." She added, sounding in no way repentant, "And they—happened to catch the temple on fire."

Makoa laughed.

"I put it out before more than the back wall was gone!"

The princess laughed, which seemed out of character. But Shiraz's general belligerence towards faith of any kind grew infectious after a time. Makoa's legs pumped hard. Michaela, whose body he was currently inhabiting, was one of the fastest humans he'd ever encountered, and he was using her strong legs for all they were worth while managing to hold onto the bird in his hand gently. He hadn't exactly expected to get out of that temple with the princess. Not that he'd thought Shiraz would leave her behind permanently. But...it was odd how sideways things went with her along. They got into so much more trouble than usual. But then through the oddest turns of events— were fine. Was she a witch?

"She did kiss it. Bowed and everything," Xinyi called out from the bench, but her voice was muffled. She was looking around under things. "Did someone take my bag?" she asked. Shiraz and Makoa shook their heads.

The boat turned out of the temple canal and reconnected with the river, headed north, against the current. Usually Shiraz pushing them was power enough, but they needed to move. There was no way the river god was going to keep the entirety of his bargain. And none of them wanted to see what powers beyond a long life and sharp teeth that giant had.

"I was being paid," Shiraz answered, groaning hard.

"Ahhh, now I understand." Shiraz was sweating already and looked to be in pain. "You okay?" Makoa asked.

"Are you?" she countered. "Your shoulder is bleeding."

"I was sure it was here," Xinyi muttered. She was now on hands and knees, crawling around the deck, shoving aside feathers.

"Eh, little scratch," Makoa responded. "My own fault. I forgot rule number four."

"Still his fault," Shiraz growled and shoved the steering pole deep. She looked down at her left arm and made a loud whining noise. "We're being followed. I knew I spotted monkeys back at the temple. Today may be the day we test your invention if you're up for it."

"We aren't letting our home go without a fight," Makoa agreed. Shiraz's eyes briefly filled with tears, but she shook them off.

"Is it me, or does this trip seem a lot more eventful than our usual ones?" she asked rhetorically. It was sooo much more eventful.

Makoa gave up peddling and moved over to the cook pot. Most of the food from earlier was gone, but there was some left cold in the pot. He dipped in a finger, pleased to put something back in his stomach yet still annoyed by the mess. Makoa hated dirty guests.

He spotted the princess, still crawling around searching. "I hope you understand about the negotiations," Makoa remarked. It was both true, in the sense that he'd no desire to hurt her. And untrue in that he still felt he'd made the right call. Moving aside the half empty pot, he pulled a deep mixing bowl near.

"Of course." Xinyi said nothing more. There was something wrong with her.

Shiraz remembered her mother saying a good cry was good for you, but a bad one left you with a headache. Shiraz didn't think she'd had a cry that hadn't left her with a headache after. But today she felt like having a good cry. And there wasn't time!

It was maybe an hour to sunset. And in the space of one afternoon she'd been transformed by pixies, attacked by monkeys, nearly eaten by an alligator, feared for her best friend's life, nearly lost her boat, and if the shaking, squealing trees were any indication was about to be attacked again. So yeah. She felt like crying. She felt like running to Makoa and wrapping him in her arms and never letting him go. She felt like turning the boat around and leaving Loqwan before someone else could threaten her home and her family. She felt like taking the princess with them, even if she was a trouble magnet. She felt entirely lost over the...possible interference of the trickster gods. She **didn't** believe in gods. She'd told Elder Trent and meant it that she was going to find his god and drag it back to the island and prove it was nothing but a magical creature he didn't understand. She felt that way about all gods but tried not to interfere with other people's beliefs—unless she saw them being clearly harmful. But now...now she was...she didn't know what. All she knew was she felt like having a good cry, or like running below decks and hiding for a month.

But none of it showed. Even her jammed shoulder wasn't enough to make her show how drained she felt. She smirked over the head of their passenger and teased the woman's, ridiculous, easy acceptance.

"Our passenger is very accepting. Her mother told her once to wait where she was and someone would rescue her—*once*—and she still follows the advice."

"Did you ever follow your mother's advice?" Xinyi muttered from the ground.

"Yep." Shiraz said and was unable to strangle the teary sound of her voice. "Go west, my daughter, my mother said to me. Go, north or south or east. Find the Singing Hills you dream of. Find anything. Just get off this island and live," Shiraz relayed one of the last things her mother said before she died. To get off the island. To have a life she loved, and to never let it go. Shiraz wanted her words to sound casual. But Xinyi stopped searching.

They had half of Shiraz's, annoyingly messy, boat between them and they barely knew each other, but Xinyi's eyes pierced her with their desire to understand, to befriend. Shiraz wasn't sure she wanted that, but the world was frozen, and she felt a similar nausea to what she'd felt outside of the temple. A feeling like something was turning so far upside down that she would never get it the right way round again.

The ship slammed into some rocks and swerved, the princess fell, and their moment of connectivity was broken. Shiraz could breathe. She focused on steering the ship.

Xinyi swallowed hard, freed. She was liking this woman more and more the longer they spent together. Wanting to know her more and more. She spotted her wedding bag and released a huge sigh. She reached in and found her journal. Relief sang through her, but not for the reasons she would have expected. She was glad to have the bag, but more she was relived not to have lost all her notes from this adventure. She'd never done anything like this, and she didn't want to lose a moment of it.

"What is so amazing about that bag?" the captain demanded. "Was it actually made by elves?"

She sounded mocking, but Xinyi, with the bag in her grip, answered sincerely. "It might have been. It was a wedding gift from my husband, a way of honoring how his aunt and uncle found me. Showing me I truly was a part of the family."

"Found you?" Makoa asked.

As Shiraz asked, "You married your cousin?"

"Adopted cousin. When I was three, my mother left me in a basket of nectar blossoms outside the gates of a grand home and told me to wait for someone to find me." She touched the embroidered basket on the bag. "Wei's aunt and uncle found me. They took me in and... provided for me."

"Loved you?" Makoa asked.

There was a distinct catch of doubt in his voice. And Xinyi did not know how to respond. Very pointedly, she did not look towards the captain. Xinyi had always known the answer before today. Had they loved her? Even before she became a burden? Was it ever love?

Screeches filled the air before Xinyi found her words. Monkeys leapt out of the trees to land on the boat. Yet more monkeys threw sticks and small stones from the shores. Xinyi hung the bag across her body and began waving at the monkeys.

"This isn't very polite. You were bested. Now you give up," she shouted, waving her arms, trying to scare the animals away.

Xinyi was not the most effective of monkey deterrents. They merely screeched and swiped at her. Still Xinyi didn't feel right about trying to hurt them. They were small and fragile.

"Aaaah!" A rock hit Xinyi in the back and jarred her forward. It wasn't very large either, but it *hurt*!

She heard a clank from the stern of the ship and saw the captain rushing forward with the pole, using it like Mei would a broom to frighten the animals away. She swung and the monkeys jumped. Most managed to hop over the pole as it swung forward and back, but a few lost their footing. A pair fell into the river. One jumped into Xinyi's arms.

It was the sweet one who had given her the flower. It made a whining noise, clinging to Xinyi's neck gently.

"Oh, hello there," Xinyi said softly.

Makoa was busy by the stove, shoving away monkeys with one hand. He released the Soul Parrot he'd been carrying. Shiraz was still waving the pole. It was chaos. But in Xinyi's corner, all was sweet.

The baby monkey reached up and pet Xinyi's hair, her wide eyes staring lovingly at Xinyi.

"Ohh," Xinyi cooed at the baby. She returned the petting, running a hand down the monkey's head. "Aren't you sweet?"

"No!" Shiraz shouted, groaning as she lifted the pole over her head, trying to throw off the monkey who'd grabbed onto the pole and was swinging around on it. "She's stealing from your bag."

"No she—" Xinyi broke off. The monkey indeed had her hand in Xinyi's bag.

The baby grinned unrepentantly. This morning Xinyi would have been horrified by a baby monkey thief. But she chuckled and kissed it on the head. "No, you don't." She gently removed the monkey's hand from her bag.

The boat lurched as a group of monkeys landed on one side all at once. A nectar fruit rolled into Xinyi's foot and as she bent to retrieve it, Makoa walked by, with a hand over something fizzing. Shiraz noticed him and redoubled her efforts to get rid of the monkeys. Xinyi didn't know what was going on, so she focused on the monkey in her arms, handing her the fruit.

"Do you want this instead?" she offered.

The monkey smiled, her bottom lip bending out. She yanked the fruit to her and took a giant bite. She seemed afraid that Xinyi would take it away. But when she did not, the monkey climbed to Xinyi's shoulder and kissed her cheek. She held the fruit in front of Xinyi's face.

"Oh, you want to share, how swee—" but the word was ripped out of Xinyi's throat as the world around her *exploded.*

The River Serpent Slithers Free

Water exploded around the ship as Makoa dropped the speed bomb into the river over the stern. There were screams all around as the force of the bomb shot the boat upriver and the unprepared monkeys flew off. Xinyi fell forward, which was lucky. Her tendency to fall off the boat would be a real problem now. Sweetums, the monkey she'd been befriending mid-fight, leapt off her shoulder and into the trees after her brothers and sisters. The boat was pushed along by the momentum of the bomb and the answering waves. It was quite the lurch, bigger than expected, but luckily Shiraz was braced.

Everything on the boat was tumbling about but Shiraz managed to hold onto the steering pole. Yanking Screecher off the end, she threw him towards the trees. Makoa raced forward and threw himself over their bright pink trouble magnet cargo who was rolling around the deck.

There were monkeys howling and racing through the trees behind them. But the boat was covering almost half as much distance as Shiraz had earlier in only a matter of moments. Wahoo! She wished she could enjoy the moment more, but very soon now the momentum of the bomb would slow, then the monkeys might catch up. The younger, faster monkeys were still visible in the trees.

This was the first time they'd tried out the speed bomb. It was a backup plan Makoa came up with a while ago, but as yet, their trips upriver were too uneventful to have need of it. This was anything but a typical trip.

Shiraz rushed around Makoa and the prone princess. The ship was slowing. They would slow much more when they made the turn, but at least they would be out of the domain of the Golden Paw Gang and the troublesome river god.

Shiraz raised the steering pole. She glanced down at the tattoo on her wrist to be sure how close she was. Another few seconds—

"Brace yourself," she called forward. Makoa nodded, still holding the princess flat to the ground, but his feet stretched out, catching in one the grooves along the hull as the princess strained her neck to see. Shiraz shook her bracelet into a more convenient spot.

Four seconds, two—Shiraz slammed the pole deep into the river and held it steady with all her weight and dug her teeth into the head of her snake bracelet, both eyes at once. The boat stopped. It shuddered, yanked backwards and to the side at such a sharp angle, it would surely crack in a moment, turning on the pivot of Shiraz's pole shoved deep into the riverbed.

A person's body weight should not be able to turn a ship this size, not by standing on a deck and holding a pole in the river for certain. But Shiraz had built this piece of floating artwork. It defied reality, defied nature, defied even a few rules of magic. The only thing it did not defy was Shiraz. For her, The River Serpent did exactly as she willed.

The River Serpent shimmied; its timbers rolled softly, glistening as green scales unfolded themselves across the deck, and the boat uncoiled like its namesake. It divided into little sections, precisely mirroring the self-consuming snake bracelet Shiraz wore. Then it stretched until it was twice its original length and able to slither and coil around itself. When Shiraz yanked the pole out of the river, the boat darted forward at an impossible angle to slither into a tunneling offshoot of the river.

The boat sucked itself in, condensed its outer walls, while allowing those inside the ship to hold their shape. It slithered through a gully no more than a foot wide and down, down, down into the crevice along which the tiny trail of water stretched.

The boat was low to the ground and shrunken in size, though on deck it appeared nothing had changed. It slithered along the gully with high muddy walls and blades of grass bending over them to offer shade. The boat's momentum slowed immensely; the water in the gully was nowhere near deep enough to hold a vessel afloat. But Shiraz dug her pole into the little stream. Her shoulder and lower back ached, and she was sweating profusely, but she shoved the boat forward.

A sparrow was pecking at the ground up ahead in search of worms; it poked its head up at their approach and stared at the unusual sight of the green shimmering boat shaped creature, with Shiraz at the back grunting and sweating. She watched the bird from the corner of her eye while searching for something to throw if it got too near. Anything she threw would leave the ship at a tiny size but transform back to its real one as soon as it was free of the spell. Shiraz kicked at a spoon stuffed into a basket of nectar fruit, causing a fruit to fly into the air. She caught it in one hand and shoved it in her mouth, taking a bite.

Umm. This one was delicious too. How were they all delicious? But that wasn't the reason she'd sought one. The stone in the center of the fruit would be a decent size to throw at the bird without killing it. She couldn't risk the bird getting too near. The sparrow was about their size at the moment, if not as long, but if it pecked at them, it might shrink part of itself, or it might stay its size and capsize them, or it might shatter the spell entirely and leave them wrecked. Most of those things had happened with some animal in the past. Of all the spells on the ship, this one was the most unpredictable. But this bird found them so disturbing, it fluffed up its feathers and took to the air with an offended tweet. Shiraz relaxed slightly.

Xinyi gasped in wonder, wiggling to get her head out from under Makoa's arm. Her head tilted back to follow the progress of the bird, who shook the boat with its beating wings.

Shiraz shoved the pole straight into the mud to steady the boat as it rocked from side to side. When the air was steady enough, she shoved against mud instead of water. Her muscles were burning, particularly the one she'd jammed catching the princess, but she didn't stop. She had to keep them moving. And she did, slowly, slowly, so slowly.

Makoa poked up. "Safe?"

"We're at sludge pass, so," Shiraz spoke around the fruit in her mouth, bobbing her head from side to side, "maybe." She slurped, sucking up some escaping juice.

"How are we moving at all? Are we shrunken?" the downed princess filled the air with questions. "Or in a cavern? Was that a sparrow?" The princess lay on the ground but was reaching out towards a flower bending near their boat.

"Don't!" Shiraz snapped.

The remains of the fruit fell from her mouth, but she managed to catch it. Makoa fell to his knees next to the princess, putting out a hand to stop her.

"It's best not to reach out of the boat. The magic works only inside. You could lose a hand, or shatter the spell and wreck the boat, perhaps even kill us all," Makoa said gently. The princess jerked her hand down, horrified.

"Sorry," she whispered.

"It was our mistake for not telling you first. It is quite the shock the first time." Makoa smiled, a gentle guide, while Shiraz could only be a sweaty worker.

"How many times have you—" Xinyi looked around apparently without words. "Done this?"

"We are shrunken, and about to slip underground where this gully will grow larger and run off to join another river. And we've done it several times. I stopped counting at about eleven. Though this was the first time we took it at such speed."

"Amazing." The princess looked at the giant world, giggling as she saw a line of ants rushing up a vine.

"Listen to the music of it." She shut her eyes. "Every blade of grass that brushes the ship slips across with a *shush, shush, shush.* And the birds are so much louder. You can even hear the ants progressing like drum beats in the distance. It is magical!"

Shiraz kept her eyes on her work—mostly. But she'd told Xinyi she was hers to command and it seemed at least partially true.

Shiraz began looking around as she had not done in years. She was too used to looking out for the dangers. The sparrow flew away today, but others had not. The boat had sustained a lot of damage from curious rodents and birds.

Once, they'd been overrun by ants that were basically their size. Makoa had transformed to an antelope to fight them off, while Shiraz had only a frying pan. She chuckled thinking of it now, but in the moment, it had been scary.

Another time they were stranded in the mud, forcing Shiraz to transform it back to its true size, causing the ship immense damage and injuries to both herself and Makoa, not to mention the jungle. So she was used to watching for threats.

But now, she noticed the shiny ore in the walls of mud as they approached the underground tunnel. Noticed the flower petals drifting in ahead of them. Noticed the earthy scent of the air, and the coolness brushing over her sweaty skin. The water was beginning to rise. Shortly it wouldn't be as much work and they would be underground, and the walls of the cavern would shimmer with the gold and green and purple lights of the raw gems the earth held. They would even reflect back in the water, creating light where there should be none. And the water ways would be dotted with flower petals and leaves that were so large they would appear like the floral pass of the grand palace waterways in Lu.

Shiraz wondered what her eager cargo would make of that. Her eyes drifted that way, watching Xinyi watch the world. And in her distraction from the dangerous world, Shiraz missed entirely the shaking of the trees behind them, and the tail of golden fur that swept right over the ship, trailing them to the byway.

The Dragon's Whisper

Tears filled Xinyi's eyes. This was so beautiful. So new. Incredible. All her life she'd thought her imagination was so much bigger than the world. But she was wrong. Look at all this wonder.

The boat was shrunken. And *she* was shrunken with it. Here she was in the mud, in the deepest parts of the shade, looking up at an interlacing tapestry of grass, trees, sky, leaves, even a few bugs and animals. It was such a new view. Different even from when she would lay on her back in the grass as a child and stare up into the trees. Stare up through the leaves and imagine that pattern as a dress drooping down the shoulders of some grand lady, some sorceress, or queen, or goddess, even then the view had not been so startling a perspective.

Today something surpassed her imagination. And to think, that something had been here all along. It had only taken looking through smaller eyes. Tears of joy and wonder fell from her eyes as they drifted through a curtain of twisted roots, out of the already dim world and into the darkened cavern.

Who could have imagined it? And she was living it!

The air in the tunnel was cooler, and the sounds closed in around them. The water was at first a quiet trickle with an uneven pattern of dripping from the wet walls. But the sound was growing. Every now and again, she heard an odd shuddering she did not understand. She longed to stick her head up and investigate, but it was dark, and she did not know how high her head was allowed.

The captain was standing, and Xinyi was shorter, so surely she could stand, right? But she didn't move. Just listened and let her tears fall. She did not want to miss a moment.

She could smell the earth! She used to smell it on her fingers when she was a girl, when she was working in the gardens for a brief while. But this was different, it was all around, and she could smell the water. There was a freshness to it. And a pulse. She heard a scratching noise, and the smell of earth grew stronger, and something more solid than water splashed in the rising *river* they were floating down.

Xinyi looked towards the sound and gasped.

"Glow worms," Makoa whispered, understanding that this place called for quiet. This place was sacred. "In the daylight out there, if you saw one you would think nothing of it, but here they are magical."

The worm's tail wiggled over a hole in the cavern above them. It was visible one moment and gone the next. She had almost missed it. She had spent so much of her life missing things.

The boat began moving faster, and the cavern began to take on light. Not much, surely not enough to make out words were she to try reading, or even to find her wrap on the ground. But enough to see the cavern and the bounds of the ship.

"Poke your head up and have a look. Makoa will stop you if it isn't safe," the captain said in a quiet, neutral voice.

How could she know for exactly what purpose Xinyi's heart pattered against her ribs, but not feel an answering softness inside? Xinyi could not make out the other woman's face to understand her, so she merely rose cautiously.

First to her knees, expecting to be shoved back. Then when her eyes took in the water, and the walls and the wonder, then caution laid down in defeat beneath the tidal wave of awe rising inside her and shoving Xinyi to her feet.

Stones in the walls of the cavern poked out with iridescence in shades of green and purple and gold. They provided that bit of light that fell down to reflect off the surface of the water and...

"Ah! There are more beneath the water aren't there?"

No one answered, but they didn't need to. She could see it. There were precious gems beneath the water and in the walls. They lit the cavern and tinted the water like a flowing brush stroke across a canvas. There were even tiny blossom boats floating in the water. In this moment, they lived inside a painting. Outside of time, outside of reality. Living an immortal moment. Xinyi half wished she could write this all down, half longed to stand right here and soak in all the moment had to offer.

She was still crying, her tears blurring her vision before she blinked them away. But even blurred, this moment felt so much more precious than anything she had ever imagined for herself. Only creatures of fantasy could have such moments. And she was so ordinary.

She cried harder, sadness and fear mixing in with awe. What if this was a dream? What if she woke up? What if not one moment of this adventure had ever happened? She—

Xinyi stumbled back, covering her mouth with both hands and tripping once more on the hem of her dress as something rose out of the water. She remained upright only because of Makoa behind her. He caught her shoulders in his hands and steadied her as that shuddering sound she had not understood revealed itself.

A giant snake lifted its head out of the water. She could see its weaving body beneath the surface, but its head stared right at Xinyi. It was so big, the size of the boat. It could unhinge its jaw and gobble her up!

Her heart raced, and her tears dried as she and the snake stared eye to eye. It was skinny and green. An ordinary garden snake most likely. But here it might well have been a dragon. And as it stared into her eyes, Xinyi felt the creature's message.

The time before was the dream. This is the waking world.

Xinyi was shaking with so much life, perhaps too much for her being to hold. She took a step forward, intent on reaching out, on touching the dragon. On touching life, but Makoa caught her back. Something loud splashed behind them, and the ship rocked hard from side to side, upsetting the water. The snake looked towards the other end of the boat, then slipped beneath the surface of the water and rushed away.

But it didn't matter that the snake was gone. Or that she had not had a chance to touch it. To ride upon its magic scales deep into the secret heart of the water where magic first was born. None of that mattered. Because she had seen the dragon, and she had heard his words. Her tears were dry. And her eyes were open. This was not Jian's adventure, or any other character of her invention. This was Xinyi's adventure, and she would not miss a moment of it.

The Pessimist on the Pleasure Cruise

Shiraz licked the last of the nectar juice off her fingers as the snake swam away. Lucky she'd had that pit to throw, or Xinyi might have reached out of the ship and shattered the spell. Shiraz's heart didn't seem to know what to do. This was the calm place, the safe place, but it wouldn't stop pounding and tears drilled at her head.

Would he be a serpent? Or a man? Or an alligator? He was an old woman briefly. Would you even recognize him?

He was in Michaela's body, but Shiraz saw none of the woman with whom she'd had a brief relationship. She saw her brother. His soul. But what if he were dead, would she recognize him still? Would his soul remain in the body? She hadn't believed in an actual soul when she left Glen Harrow, but she believed now. Because of him. And it terrified her because she'd almost lost him. She *wouldn't* know him, would she? Her heart couldn't take more thoughts like that.

Find a life you love, that loves you in return, and never let it go, her mother's firm voice insisted.

Anyone who can call someone friend and not believe them when they say they were cursed is unfeeling. And scummy.

Shiraz felt it all building up, shoving against her throat, and her eyes, fighting to be freed. She was so tired. She'd nearly lost so much today but she kept shoving those feelings away with wild escapes and amusement and wonder. And watching Xinyi encounter the world. But it wasn't working at the moment.

They were only in the tunnel for a few minutes before the water began to rise. They could all hear the rush and spit. She had expected the princess to be vocal with her wonder, an unending stream of excitement and questions as they drifted. Shiraz had been looking forward to it. But Xinyi was quiet. She cried, the tears glistening in the refracted light of the gems. And Shiraz had felt it.

Felt that wonder that used to keep her up at night for fear of missing out on some new beauty. Felt the excitement she'd been missing. Felt the conviction with which she'd left Glen Harrow. The certainty that she could find the Singing Hills of Anolani and all the magical wonders of the world. See them and prove, to herself if no one else, that the world was so much more wondrous and loving than the island she grew up on. And she had...somewhat, but—

"Come with me, both of you. I need the three shield." Her voice broke at the words. With Ethan's name for their sibling group. "All we need is each other and we can have a beautiful life."

"So let's have one here." Ethan was always so reluctant to break the rules.

"That is the only thing I cannot do for you. Please," Shiraz begged her brothers. "We don't have to go to Ooloo'a. Come with me anywhere. *Let me show you how beautiful the rest of the world is."*

"We can't leave him like this," Noam said softly. "He's broken without Mother, and she—"

"Mother never wanted you to spend your life taking care of him. He would never do the same for you! You can *leave him. She would rejoice to*

see you out in the world. You deserve to be loved and happy! And you never will be here! None of us will."

Her brothers were the only people left who she loved completely, no piece of her heart guarded against the pain they might cause. She looked at them with her heart laid bare knowing, even as she fought, that they were going to break that heart. But having to try.

"Mom knew love could be more beautiful than it is here, and I'm going to prove her right. I'm leaving, with or without you. But I want you with me, and I always will. I love you. Isn't that a good enough reason to come?"

Noam had nodded. Stepping forward, he wrapped his arms around her. "Of course. Of course it is," he said. But there was no conviction in his voice. And Ethan merely stretched out a hand to lay on her shoulder.

She knew right then, even though she had pretended it would be different. Even though she had prepared as though they were coming. She'd known. So when in the morning they each had their excuses, her heart was broken, but her mind was firm, even excited. She made her way out of her village and down to the shore where she'd arranged to meet a fisherman from off the island. She walked away alone. She broke the shield of three. She left her brothers behind. So certain that out in the world she would find love, and acceptance, and magic enough to bring back and show them what they could have elsewhere. And by the time she'd come back, they were already gone.

She hadn't felt as connected to the dreams that led her off the island in the past few years. Feeling like she broke their shield for no reason. Why wasn't she searching for those hills? Why didn't she embrace things anymore? Had she given up on even finding magic? She did the same things everyday, desperately clinging to what she had. And she had nearly lost even that.

"Coming up on the turn," Shiraz called out hoarsely, trusting Makoa to know what that meant.

The tunnel split off ahead of them. The right would lead into a ditch that was a true pain to get out of. The left led to a tributary of the Nanghi river, Chi'hu. But to get to the deeper tunnel meant a steep drop. Shiraz steered towards the left, cutting through a spout of water coming through the thinning ground above them. More light came through as water sprayed in. The downpour showered across the deck, making Xinyi laugh and twirl around. She just enjoyed *every bit* of the world around them.

"We're about to go over a drop. May I protect you?" Makoa asked, laying a hand on Xinyi's shoulder.

Xinyi nodded, allowing him to lead her to the aft wall and help her sit. She tilted her head down shyly. "May I watch, if I stay down?"

"We're here on your coin," Shiraz grumbled. "By all means, let's make this a pleasure cruise."

Shiraz shouldn't be such a grouch and she knew it. But she was her uneasy self, and she could not shake it.

"Of course you may," Makoa answered gently and sincerely. He helped her see how to brace, with her head tucked into her shoulder, and her shoulder braced under the lip of the hull. "Watch the bow of the ship. This, princess, is the safest way, to go over a waterfall."

"Over a waterfall!" she cried out, elated.

Shiraz's eyes burned as she dug the pole into the rivulet and shoved. She felt an uncomfortable mixture of annoyance and kinship with Xinyi's pleasure. It dragged Shiraz back to the first time she'd done this. When it was adventure, when she hadn't been sure she would survive, but had to try. When she'd still believed in her dreams.

"We did it! We did it!" Shiraz jumped up and down. She held tight to the pole. If she lost it, they might never get through. But she had never felt so exuberant. This was it. She was making it work. If she could shrink this boat down to the size of an actual snake, with her on board, and steer it still, she could do anything.

Makoa was quiet, braced at the side of the boat in the form of an octopus with each tentacle holding onto another part of the ship. He hadn't believed that this would work. Not for a moment. But he looked at her now, without much semblance of a face, but those giant eyes. And yet, such expression. His eyes stretched and his tentacles loosened. And Shiraz felt his joy rise to match her own.

"We're going to find it. I know we will!" Shiraz shouted into the depths of the little underground tunnel they were moving through, uncaring as she heard the walls shudder with her shout.

She grinned as she dug the pole into the sludge and shoved them forward, grinned as she pushed and pushed and pushed them through the underground runoff of the river. Grinned.

"Oh! Makoa, listen," she laughed. "Can you hear the water building? We're coming to a spout!" She nearly bounced, so excited as she pushed her pole into the sludge, leading them towards adventure headfirst.

Shiraz gripped the hull with one hand and gave the boat one last giant push. The force of the water against their vessel did the rest, dragging them over a steep cliff. The drop sent their stomachs flying and the boat plunging. It lifted Makoa and Xinyi off the deck and raised Xinyi's voice to a scream of excitement that rang out as a sharp note of music in the air.

Shiraz dug her pole into the wall of dirt behind them, slowing and steadying their descent as she had learned to do over the past years of using this escape. They got wetter than necessary, but when the boat hit the river, it was at a nearly level angle. It bobbed up and down but didn't go under. Makoa scooted away from Xinyi. She was drenched. A flower petal had fallen into the ship at its real world size and lay over Xinyi's shrunken head like a fitted hat. It suited her. Making her look like a bright pink fairy poking her head out of a giant blossom. Makoa brushed the flower petal off her head, grinning.

Shiraz pulled the pole into the boat. Here they followed the flow of the river, and while she could push them along faster, she didn't feel a need. There was more light in this part of the tunnel, birds having pecked little holes into the ground in search of worms. It wasn't a deep tunnel. That was for the best. If they had to stretch the ship, it might not kill them. There weren't many threats down here but the occasional spider, snake or pecking bird. Shiraz breathed out, trying to pull herself together, taking the moment to relax.

Xinyi was still surrounded by an aura of joy despite being drenched. Despite having been catapulted down river without a word, and attacked by monkeys, and almost trapped by Nanghi. She smiled way too much. Makoa helped her to her feet. She looked up into the tunnel, and the holes in fascination. All of a sudden, she gasped. Shiraz tensed.

Xinyi rushed towards her, then past. "A double rainbow!"

In the tunnel? Shiraz glanced back and saw nothing. Xinyi grabbed Shiraz's free arm, pulling her to the ship's edge.

"Look." She took Shiraz's chin in hand and led her gaze to the spout they'd come over, where sunlight fell against it. And there were indeed a pair of the most vibrant rainbows Shiraz had ever seen. They...created a light all their own, colorful and luminous it shimmered in swirling clouds of mist. She'd never seen a thing like it.

Makoa came up on Shiraz's right. "And to think we might have missed it if we hadn't needed to escape."

"Yes," Shiraz had to reply sarcastically. Had to. Because her heart was pounding and nothing made sense and she was fighting off tears. "I mean we might not have almost died, but how sad would we have been to miss the rainbows we didn't know existed."

Makoa and Xinyi turned disappointed looks her way. What? It was rainbows, not pots of gold. She moved away from her overly cheerful companions, annoyed to be outnumbered by positive attitudes.

She could admit they were pretty rainbows. She might even have snuck another look over their shoulders as she walked away. She had never seen a thing like it, despite years of searching.

Years of nearly starving one week and being robbed the next. Years of sleeping with no shelter or lying awake at night in fear. Years learning to be more prudent than the girl who left her sheltered island. She'd spent years searching for magic and beauty and wonder. Years learning not to be tricked or cheated. Years developing the sarcasm her companions disapproved of and keeping herself safe. But…maybe things like that, beautiful magical rainbows and hidden wonders, were only spotted by the optimists of the world.

Sort of put a damper on her life goals.

I Also Believe in Thieves and Desperation

Xinyi felt her heart stumble as the captain walked away from the rainbows with her snide remark. She didn't even know why. No, that was a lie. It was just...so new and unusual that it was easier to lie. She knew why. She liked Shiraz, but she didn't understand her. She was friendly, flirtatious, and funny one moment, then transformed into a snapping turtle. She was easier in moments of crisis than calm. And she looked like she wanted to cry, but she wasn't doing it.

Xinyi didn't understand that. Many people called Xinyi too cheerful, too positive, too accepting. They thought her smiles meant she felt nothing else, but that wasn't true. Xinyi cried. She cried often. She felt sad, and lonely and fearful. She wouldn't be on this boat at all if she didn't know darker emotions.

She'd come in fear of being cast aside again. But...the dark feelings didn't chase her like they chased the captain. Perhaps because Xinyi was not afraid to cry or laugh. Fear might have driven her from home, but she was here now having adventures instead of writing them, and she was seeing such marvels, understanding the world as never before. If she was injured, she would cry; if she was happy, she would laugh.

And if she found herself liking and longing to befriend the surly captain, she...would go about it carefully. She laughed softly, thinking of the monkey who'd climbed into her arms to make friends, even as she was trying to rob Xinyi. This world was full of complicated women. Smiling, Xinyi turned her attention to the rainbow until they drifted too far for her to see it.

The boat bobbed along with the flow of the river. It was slow; the water was far from clear, covered with leaves and bits of algae.

Xinyi nudged Makoa. "Did our escape add much time to the journey?"

"It might have shaved off half a day." He shook his head. "With any luck, we've put our troubles behind us and can pass along the river without further incident."

"Hey!" the captain called out from across the ship with an offended tone and incredulous look. "You want to tempt fate?"

Makoa smirked. "You don't believe in fate."

Shiraz laughed, and her face was transformed. She grinned at her friend like an entirely different woman, one with a sense of humor and fun, one who trusted little but loved greatly. Not for the first time, Xinyi wondered about the nature of their relationship. Because with nothing else did Shiraz look as warm and happy as with Makoa.

"You don't?" Xinyi asked quietly. She'd never met anyone else who did not believe in fate.

But the boat bumped something in the water and veered towards the wall of the tunnel and Shiraz seemed not to have heard. Xinyi rocked sideways, but the captain steadied her with a casual hand. Her eyes never separated from her friend's gaze though. "I believe in being careful with what I love."

The friends regarded one another, but the gaze was broken when the boat again shifted course. At once, Makoa moved to the rudder and redirected the ship. Shiraz lifted the pole from where it had fallen on the deck. Gripping it in two places, she twisted her hands in opposite directions and the pole shrunk up to the length of a walking stick. She hung it from a clamp at the rear of the canopy.

Xinyi took it all in silently. All her life people told her one thing or another was her fate. She used to argue that there had to be more. It couldn't just be fated. But by the time she was twelve, she'd learned that people who believed in fate could not be swayed. And whether she believed or not did not change things. It might not have been fate that led her to Wei's family, but that was where she was raised. It might not have been fate, as Wei believed, that led their relationship to grow from friendship to love, but it had. It might not have been fate that started the war and left so many widowed, but the widows found one another. Fate did not rule you, but you were where you were and you made the best of it. That was her theory.

The captain looked back at Xinyi now her work was done. "No. I don't believe in fate," she answered as if no time had passed. "I believe in chance, hard work, good food, good money, betrayal and endless frustration. Why, do you think it was fate that led you here?"

Xinyi shook her head. "That was thieves and desperation."

The captain laughed, really laughed. It shook her whole body, sending a tiny shower of water shaking off her to encircle her on the deck of the ship and sparking the tiniest of rainbows as her head tilted right into a beam of sunlight.

"Fair enough." She winked. "I also believe in thieves and desperation."

A tiny catch interrupted Xinyi's breath as her gut seized up in amusement at this smuggler's funny side.

The captain turned to Makoa. "I think we should take the tunnel slow. Rest in here, it's much safer and our trouble magnet," she nodded her head at Xinyi, "shouldn't be able to attract monkeys or pixies or gods in here."

Makoa laughed. Xinyi found that assessment of herself unfair. Although she did have a slight bad luck curse, she surely couldn't be blamed for everyone in the jungle trying to collect the bounty on this ship. That seemed likely to be a result of all the spells on it.

"Not a bad idea. You taking first shift, or should I?" Makoa asked.

The captain shrugged. "You pick. But first I want a look at your shoulder."

Xinyi wandered away; she wasn't involved in this conversation. She could vaguely hear the captain and Makoa in the background, but tried to put them out of her mind, so they could have privacy. She got the sense from the evenness of their voices that they talked all business. Did they not need to hold one another? To assure themselves that they were both safe? To worry over the bounty on their home? That's what she would have been doing in their place.

<center>~~~</center>

"So, we don't find nature impressive anymore?" Makoa prodded sarcastically as Shiraz wrapped a bandage around his arm. "Not even double rainbows?"

Shiraz changed the subject. "What do you think we'll do about her thieves?"

"Rob them, naturally."

"Naturally. But I only know where we dropped them. I did not ask for directions to their homes. Or their names," she added as an afterthought.

Makoa nodded. "I was surprised you agreed when we don't know that. What were you planning?"

"I thought it would be funny to get her upriver, then ask for directions, watch her flounder at how ridiculous her entire plan was and then take her home empty handed but for the lesson on how the real world works." Shiraz's shoulders lifted dismissively.

"You'd be empty handed too," Makoa pointed out, used to Shiraz's particular brand of justice.

"We," Shiraz corrected. "And no. I planned to steal the bag."

Makoa smiled knowingly. He could practically hear her thinking that she still could steal the bag. Trying to convince herself. But he'd seen her in the temple, holding onto the other woman's hand. Trying that ridiculous hero swinging on a vine stuff. He'd seen her nearly in tears at the sight of the rainbow. She liked their baggage, and it was scaring her. She always was walking away from people, sailing away, but always wishing they would come along. And every time they didn't, growing more afraid to ask.

She wouldn't steal from that woman. And she might get upset with Makoa if he did. He hadn't seen her this vulnerable in...maybe ever.

"We should put in at the Mushroom Grotto," Makoa suggested.

"Ugh, no." Shiraz shook her head, but her protest was mild. She knew Makoa was right.

The grotto had no end of useful criminals. Elves, fairies, humans, wizards, and nymphs. Of all the fey creatures, nymphs were the best trackers, the most willing to work with any species, and the most...

devious. Shiraz loved to meet up with a nymph. But the grotto was one of her least favorite places in Loqwan recently. As she'd said to the princess, Shiraz most definitely believed in thieves and desperation.

When she was younger, when she had nothing to lose, she had *loved* thieves and desperation. She'd ran with a group of thieves and grifters. But it ended poorly. So she found another group of thieves to work with. When that landed her in jail, she stopped working with anyone. Until Makoa joined her again.

Makoa knew why he trusted Shiraz. But he didn't always understand what made her trust him. But she did. When they separated, she trusted him to come back—he thought.

"I'm sorry about ear—"

"What will we do about the bounty?" She changed the subject quickly, her voice breaking. She tied off the bandage, stepping back.

Makoa knew she'd be ready to talk at some point, but not yet. "Carry the Serpent with us. You can get back your book. You haven't stopped talking about it since we left."

"Aiattaua probably burned it. You know he's never read a book in his life."

Makoa rolled his eyes. He wasn't rising to such obvious bate. Instead he smiled and needled her, mentioning one of Aiattaua's other bonded mates, one to whom Shiraz was in fact closer than Makoa was. "As I recall, Valerian enjoys a fair amount of reading during his hibernation years. Perhaps Aiattaua gifted it to him."

Shiraz narrowed her eyes but did not respond. She'd met Valerian in one of the quiet corners of the grotto last year while hiding out from Michaela. She'd disappeared with five books in hand and emerged hours later laughing and chatting and having traded books with Valerian. A type of ice fey, Valerian's people hibernated for three years and went about in the world for two. And he was already somewhat shy, so he rarely made friends. Even among Aiattaua's spouses, he was withdrawn but polite. But...seeing Aiattaua with him had in fact made Makoa like the prince better; few people cared to love people as they were, always trying to force out someone who better suited their world, but not Aiattaua. He was quiet and intent with Valerian, helping the other man to feel comfortable. And it worked. Only with Aiattaua or with Shiraz had Makoa ever seen Valerian light up and share himself.

Shiraz's friendship with Valerian made Aiattaua like her a bit better; before, he'd liked Shiraz about as much as she liked him. But with Valerian between them, the two could converse almost politely. Though Makoa knew Shiraz hated the connection to Aiattaua, almost as much as she liked Valerian. But she wanted him for a friend. It was cute. She was far more likely to make passing friendships than lasting ones. But now she kept adding to a bundle of books she planned to give him when next he came out of hibernation. Makoa wouldn't be surprised if *Immortal Hunger* was one of them.

"Have you told our passenger how much you love her stories?" he needled a bit more.

She pointedly changed the subject. "The monkeys came after us twice. I don't know if I'm underestimating them, but it makes me nervous. I think they are working for someone. Why would monkeys care about a bounty?"

Makoa bobbed his head from side to side. "A fairy or an elf would know how to make the bounty appealing to the Golden Paw Gang. As they apparently knew how to make it appealing to Nanghi. But the thought of the Golden Paw Gang having a more humanoid leader had occurred to me. There are certainly plenty of fey who can talk to them. That teenage witch who made your bracelet had a thing for monkeys and knows about the boat. Even Felicia could communicate with animals, or I wouldn't have known where to pick you up. The list is far too long for us to narrow down alone. Where do you suppose we can find help with that?"

Shiraz rolled her eyes. "It'll mean spending some of our share of a treasure we have yet to see. If she's Jian's author, she probably has a fair amount of coin. But we know that isn't Princess Yinuo, and she felt no need to correct Nanghi. What if she's tricking us?"

Makoa nodded several times, letting the silence stretch. He had felt discomforted by the princess. Happy to trade her for his ship. But he began to think that the same things that made them uncomfortable with her were the exact reasons they should give her a chance.

"What if she isn't?" Makoa countered. His friend could stand to trust someone new. Especially someone as open and loving as their passenger.

Shiraz rolled her eyes. "Right. Since you're doing so well, I'll leave you to it and go show our guest where she can sleep."

"Take your time." Makoa winked.

The Cause of all this Dampness

"*What if she isn't?*" Makoa's intentionally provoking question lingered in Shiraz's mind as she crossed the deck.

If Xinyi wasn't tricking them, then she was exactly what she appeared. A sweet woman, full of wonder and a positive enough attitude to embrace an adventure when she hadn't expected one and certainly hadn't spent her life having them. If she wasn't tricking them, then she was the creator of Shiraz's favorite thing in this nation.

Shiraz wished she could make Xinyi sign a copy of volume seven. That was her absolute best! Poetic, sinister, deeply emotional and yet so fun! It was the first time Jian met V. V had been lurking in the background causing trouble, but when she and Jian met, sparks flew and the world was new, and Shiraz was hooked.

If Xinyi wasn't tricking them, then she was the sort of person who deserved to have her treasure back. And...she was the sort of person who was embracing every moment of this adventure, because she knew it was coming to an end in a few days.

Apparently, Xinyi heard her approaching. She was making notes in her journal, but she looked back, smiling at Shiraz. "Your ship is astounding! I cannot imagine there is anything else like it."

"There isn't," Shiraz agreed proudly. This boat was her work of art.

"How does it work? I mean, magic, I know. Makoa said you worked to get all kinds of spells. But...does it only work for you? Does it answer your thoughts? Or are there specific spells you must use? You seem to strain to steer it. Where did you get the bracelet? How does it work?" Xinyi asked question after question, pausing mere seconds between them as she had when they were walking through the jungle.

Shiraz rolled her shoulders. It wasn't as calming now. It nudged Shiraz's worries. What if she was tricking them? Shiraz couldn't afford to be taken in by a beautiful smile and a compelling personality.

"I'm not telling you my boat's secrets so you can sell them to the highest bidder," Shiraz said flatly.

"I..." Xinyi gasped. "I wouldn't do that."

"No?" Shiraz asked, quietly serious.

"Of course not!" Xinyi said with great sincerity. But that alone was frightening so Shiraz played light.

"You write down everything Makoa says. And there is a bounty out for my boat. I'm not sharing more information about its abilities. I can't risk you dropping that journal the next time you trip and sending it into the hands of my enemies."

The princess opened her mouth but seemed to have trouble finding words. Shiraz shouldn't be baiting her. She already believed her. She just didn't trust her own trust. And her more practical side was trying to assert itself. She could still feel the moment Xinyi had tangled her fingers with Shiraz's and smiled at her with such beautiful faith in herself and their ability to triumph. She'd looked like magic manifested into a single being and Shiraz's attraction had gone from a spark of enjoyment to a raging fire.

She liked this woman too much. And she knew how things went with women like her. Sweet, moral, cozy women who followed all the laws of their society. They played at making friends, made you believe it, made you think you were loved for yourself. When they wanted to *restore you to morality.*

Xinyi's eyes narrowed. "I don't trip that often. And that isn't the reason I am taking notes. And you shouldn't have enemies if you can't protect yourself from them. I wouldn't sell your secrets. I just…" She snorted at herself, making Shiraz snort as well. "Okay. Maybe I would sell your secrets, but changed slightly and written like they are someone else's secrets."

Shiraz laughed hard, thrown out of her maudlin thoughts. Were there even any other women like her? That was excellent!

"Goodness, that makes you quite the *scummy thief,*" she teased, her voice warming in pleasure. "You may be worse than me."

"Not possible." Xinyi scrunched up her nose in a playful glare.

Shiraz nodded, still smiling, but slightly more serious. "I've been told."

Xinyi had nothing to say for a long while. She shook her head. "You were told wrong," she whispered. "Sort of like you don't mean your insults whenever I'm being nice to you, I didn't mean to hurt you."

Shiraz felt her smile stretch. She could see her own cheekbones at the bottom of her gaze. But they weren't in any sort of focus, because all her eyes wanted to take in was Xinyi. And Shiraz let herself enjoy it. Enjoy how their breathing matched up. Enjoy gazing into her deep brown eyes with little flares of light that made them sparkle. Enjoy the tension clenching up her gut with nerves and anticipation. Enjoy every — single— second.

The princess broke their gaze, spinning away. She held her gown out as she twirled.

Shiraz felt the delicious tingle of her pulse racing. The sort of rush she'd felt the first time she opened a fairytale and was transported to another world. Maybe...maybe she hadn't given up on finding magic. Maybe she hadn't spoiled her chances of finding it by becoming stronger alone. Maybe Makoa was right, and she'd been finding magic all along. It was just different than she expected. Maybe she was exactly where she needed to be. Exhausted, a little sad, with her heart still pounding from all their brushes with death today but smiling as she met the world anew.

"Dancing with anyone in particular, princess?" Shiraz asked playfully, though her heart burned in her chest.

"Why? Would you like to be asked to join me?"

Shiraz shook her head. "I don't dance."

"Not at all?"

"Not really. Do you," Shiraz waved a hand at the twirling steps, "do this often?"

Xinyi rolled her eyes but continued to spin. "I'm trying to get dry. Never before I met you had I spent a day so wet."

Shiraz snorted so hard it felt like her chest cracked from the humor. *Same*, she thought and began to cough. Tears came into her eyes as she fought to hold in the humor. It was a futile struggle. Shiraz spit out an appallingly loud laugh. Xinyi fell still.

"And me barely even trying," Shiraz gasped.

"Are you alright?" Xinyi asked genuinely concerned. "What did—" But she cut off her own question, her eyes narrowing on Shiraz and a faint blush dusting her cheeks. Shiraz returned the regard with unbroken eye contact and a world of desire clearly displayed therein.

Xinyi rolled her eyes, but a smile kept tugging at the corner of her pursed lips. "Don't you think about anything else?" she said like an offended elder.

"Around you?" Shiraz was impressed she could get the words out past her own humor. She bit her bottom lip and shook her head *very* slowly. "Can't come up with a thing."

Xinyi was turning red, from her neck up to her face, but her cheeks were lifting in what appeared more amusement than discomfort. And when she replied, her words were clear and strong, and—encouraging. "You aren't exactly dry yourself."

Shiraz gasped for breath. Who knew sweet Xinyi had that in her?

Makoa crossed to them, concerned.

"Is everything alright?" He reached towards Shiraz.

"Fine," Xinyi answered, her voice reaching an impressively high pitch. "We were discussing possible culprits for all this dampness."

Shiraz braced on her knees laughing. Her gasps for breath grew desperate. This was too much. Xinyi was too much. Someone so positive all the time couldn't also be this fun! This—

Shiraz's breathing became more pained, her vision blurred, and though she knew Makoa's hand was on her shoulder, she couldn't feel it. She bent forward, fighting against the army of tears pummeling her eyes. But she couldn't hold them back.

This day was too much.

Makoa didn't say a word. He settled on the deck and pulled Shiraz against his chest. Michaela's chest. Shiraz giggled wetly. Michaela turned out to be a bit of an uzaok, but her chest was nicer cushioning than most Makoa wore. He pressed his lips to her head, and Shiraz turned into his arms, clinging on tight.

"It's alright," he said softly.

"You don't even know why I'm laughing," Shiraz argued through tears. They came more gently now, but she still preferred not to acknowledge them. And anyway, the tears weren't for their troubles. They were over the frightening realization that today, with all its dangers, had been one of the best days in her life. She didn't know what to do with it. Did she really want to keep being scared out of her wits one moment and laughing the next?

"Sure, I do," Makoa replied. "You've remembered that you kissed a deity statue and realized you now owe Elder Trent a case of Shadowien elk wool."

Shiraz yanked herself out of his arms. "Uzaok!" He was right. She'd sworn no power could ever compel her to bow down before another god and Elder Trent bet she would. That zagok won. All because of the princess who was retreating to the other side of the ship, unaware that though it was uncomfortable and new, she was definitely wanted here.

Shiraz glared at her friend, annoyed by the reminder, at least as much as she was grateful to him for breaking her bubble of restrained fears. "I hate you sometimes."

Makoa pulled her forehead back to his lips. "Never."

In The Dark of the Tunnel Confessions Will Find You

Makoa had been steering the ship for sometime. The captain slept on the ground near him. There was such ease to their relationship. Xinyi missed that. She used to be so with Wei. Their ease had developed long before desire. At least for her. Their ease had led to her desire. Quiet as each of them went about their day, not needing a word to know what the other was thinking. Or lying in bed speaking of all their wishes and strange dreams. It had been lovely, before the end.

She had been avoiding such thoughts in the last years. It felt different thinking of Wei today, thinking of their relationship. She knew, but was not entirely ready for what it meant, that she was thinking about him *because* of the woman she'd been traveling with. Because of the feeling she was stirring in Xinyi. It made her feel quiet, her mind shying away from the thoughts by focusing on their dim environs.

The tunnel pressed its walls closer, and little roots poked out threateningly. Even the bugs were in cahoots, skittering along the walls when she least expected it, making the world feel...sinister.

Yet Xinyi's thoughts were drawn back to the moments right before the captain broke down and let go of all the tension she'd been carrying. Xinyi was a part of that. She'd said things that hurt her. And the captain had certainly called Xinyi trouble more than once. But Xinyi honestly thought Shiraz wanted her around despite the trouble. She seemed to like Xinyi. Liked her best when she let out the parts of herself that stayed quiet at home. Her silliness, her demands, her fight. The captain seemed to like it all, and not just be attracted to her.

Xinyi wasn't sure what to do with that. She liked her far more than she would have expected. Liked laughing with her and even flirting. But desire had never come as quickly to her as it clearly did to other people. Desire for Xinyi was rare and perhaps all the more special for it. She'd only ever truly felt it for Wei, who she had loved with all her heart. But she was definitely feeling something now, though this relationship was so—new.

"Xinyi," Makoa's soft thrown voice interrupted her thoughts. She could barely make out his face. "Would you help me light the lanterns? There is a flint beneath the pot there, and some kindling. If you bring it over, I will show you with the lamp nearest me." Xinyi knew how to light a lamp. But she didn't mind that he gave instructions. He thought she was a princess and they might not know. As soon as she stood, something sticky, thin and difficult to see caught her. She tried to brush through it, but it clung to her hands.

"I would like to let Shiraz sleep as long as she is able," Makoa continued. "She has been pushing herself hard today."

"Eager to be rid of me," Xinyi said in a teasing voice as she fought the sticky stuff trying to cling to her dress. She broke free but still couldn't see the substance to make it out. She shuddered.

When she was next to Makoa, he shook his head. "Eager to get the forty percent of your treasure." He winked. "The longer you are with us, the higher percentage she will wiggle out of you, one percent at a time."

Xinyi's lips stretched, *it was already forty-seven percent,* but the boat jumped, making Xinyi yelp loudly.

"Oh, I am so sorry."

Makoa chuckled. "Please, scream whenever you are startled, laugh when you are amused, and cry should you feel the need. Neither Shiraz nor myself will hesitate to do so." He showed her how to light a lamp and was sending her to light others when the boat was struck by another wave and she tumbled against him again, crying out.

"Are you alright?" Makoa asked, pulling her back.

Xinyi nodded, eyes wide. She couldn't speak. Not because she was too scared—though she was pretty scared. But—a spider hung by a thread directly behind Makoa's head. It was illuminated now the lamp was lit, throwing all its terrifying features into sharp relief.

She'd been mildly amused by his fear earlier. But seeing a spider face to face, having been shrunken to just a bit bigger than it, and a million eyes to two. Yeah, now she understood his fear. And she couldn't let him see it. He started to turn.

"I'm fine, just clumsy. Don't tell the captain," she rushed out the words to distract him. Makoa laughed, and the boat drifted slowly, further from the fear-inducing arachnid.

"Here." Makoa took Xinyi's hands and wrapped them around the rudder with which he steered the ship. He placed a finger at his lips. "We will keep this our secret. Stand here and hold the rudder at this angle. See how it is aligned with that beam? Keep it there."

"But...how do you know the boat won't hit anything?" Xinyi panicked anew. This was the family garden all over again, and the laundry she'd ruined. Her bad luck curse was going to cause a catastrophe. "I'll wreck her ship and make an enemy for life. I don't want to be hunted by V."

Makoa chuckled as though he knew the character but would not allow her to remove her hands. "The boat will bump a few rocks very likely, but it will not run aground if you steer it at that angle. This will only take a moment."

He was away, without giving Xinyi more room to argue. And without seeing the spider. Hopefully there were no more out there. Her heart pounded, and her breaths were tight and yet...she might not have argued. As soon as he removed his hands, and the responsibility was hers alone, she felt a tingle. It started in her hands and raced up her arms and all through her body. She felt...adventurous. It felt like those few moments outside of the temple again. When she had imagined herself as the protagonist of her own adventure.

She wanted to jerk the rudder aside and see if she alone could move the whole boat the way Shiraz had.

That had been...astounding! At first when the boat shot upriver and there was water exploding and monkeys shouting, Xinyi had been so overwhelmed she was sure she was about to die. Then Shiraz slammed that pole into the water, bracing herself with her feet angled against the back wall of the boat and her arms holding the pole, making an angle of her body, and the whole boat turned with her power. She was *spectacular.* Even more compelling than V.

Then she bit her bracelet and scales rolled across the ship and it broke apart into tiny sections with visible joints between them, and the ship stole Xinyi's attention. The ship slithered and raced like a snake, and Xinyi lost the ability even to think. All she could do was lay there watching the captain work wonders until she saw the sparrow and realized that they had shrunk!

This trip was a fabulous dream! And she didn't want to wake up. She didn't want to be quiet Xinyi with her ordered life and her polite smile. She wanted to be loud. She wanted to be a force. She wanted to wreck the ship! Just for the fun of it. She could almost hear Wei's laugh in her mind. He'd always wanted adventure for her, but she'd been too scared. Not so now. Now she wanted to confront the thieves herself. And get her story back, but not for the same reasons anymore. She didn't want it only so she wouldn't have to edit and revise the same chapters over, throwing her off schedule and threatening the steady pay. She didn't want it to keep her place among the other women. She wanted it so she could...end it. So she could focus all her attention on new kinds of stories.

Stories of adventure, but not danger. A story of a happy character, who simply could not live quietly. Every chapter would see her facing a new adventure. A court of monkey thieves. A gaggle of giant birds. An army of ants so loud the shook the ground as they marched. Terrifying spiders. A whole world of adventures waiting for her!

Makoa didn't try to take the rudder back from Xinyi. He settled against the boat, dipping a hand into a basket of nectar fruit. He selected a piece and bit in.

"Enjoying the work?"

Xinyi nodded. The river was illuminated now; she noticed rocks coming up on their right and jerked the rudder in the opposite direction. The boat jerked with her, making Makoa stumble, and the sleeping captain roll into the canopy and groan. She did not wake. But Xinyi stayed steady! She giggled. Was this what made the captain so sure footed?

Makoa was smiling but not as easy as usual. He arched a brow on the woman's face he was wearing that made his expression look cautious. His hand settled on the rudder behind Xinyi's.

"You don't need to move so forcefully. There is a spell on this ship to respond more readily than others. Shiraz is building the Serpent for a special purpose. She needs it to move faster than other ships, be small one moment, and giant the next. She has dreams…" His voice drifted off and Xinyi could hear the love in it.

Xinyi shifted the boat right, still too hard. The captain rolled again, and water splashed over the back. But she was getting better.

Xinyi wanted to do this in the day. On a wide river. Wanted to see the jungle from this perspective. The captain groaned. Xinyi glanced her way, afraid she would wake, afraid she would become angry with Makoa for letting Xinyi steer.

"I have an apology to make to you," Makoa said out of nowhere. His voice had softened and grown heavier. Xinyi pulled her gaze back.

"When we spoke of my curse, I began to feel unsettled. You raised questions I had not considered and the feelings it caused frightened me. I worried that you were not who you seemed and had come to… destroy my comfort. So, when I made the deal with Nanghi," he said slowly, "I meant it."

Xinyi let his words sink in and shock her. She'd never frightened anyone before. But he was right to doubt who she seemed to be. Maybe he should fear her. He should certainly fear her curse.

"It was the more prudent trade. But…you were upsetting our routine and I felt it changing me beneath all of these skins. You frightened me. So I leapt at the chance to be rid of you."

Xinyi nodded, looking out to the light cast ahead of them. "I understand," Xinyi whispered. "Change is frightening."

"But fear is not an excuse. I am sorry, and I hope you can forgive me. I will do everything in my power to make it up to you."

"Why?" she asked, the words escaping on a bumpy breath, not quite laughter but far from steady. "What makes you trust me more now? I *was* lying to you about myself."

Makoa looked away. "I lied to Shiraz about myself and my intents all three of the first times we met. Yet each time she trusted me more. I rarely share all of myself with anyone, and yet I am offered love. It is what I should have offered to you. Yes, you hid pieces of yourself. When approaching criminals, that is the wise course of action. But...I've realized your questions didn't change me. They illuminated things of which I had yet to become cognizant. You are not someone to fear. You are someone who inspires change, that is a beautiful thing. Do not forgive so easily that you fail to recognize your own value."

Xinyi shook her head, far from offended by Makoa's actions. They only made her thoughtful about her own.

"Wei told me I inspired change *in him*. My husband," Xinyi explained. "He had been loyal to the king when the war broke out. But I told him people's stories that I overheard. Their reasons for fighting. He said *I* was the reason he joined the rebellion. I fought with him over it. His family disowned me when he left. Blamed me for his going. They exiled me from our home. My wedding bag is all I have left of our life together. But..." She laughed. "None of them knew we fought before he left. I told him *not to go*. Said there were other ways to resist. I said—" Tears raced down her cheeks as the memories washed through her. "I said he would be no use as a soldier. *Then he died.*

"I started writing Jian as a way to...go with him, instead of holding him back. But only recently did I realize I was never writing myself as Jian. I was Kenmei. Still holding the one I loved back, in fear of losing them. So I killed my story self, to set him free." Xinyi couldn't help thinking of Shiraz's assessment of the story. Was she right? Had Xinyi saddled her character with grief instead of fear?

Makoa's hand rested beside her own on the rudder. Not touching. Just there, offering comfort, drawing her back into the moment. "My point is I don't forgive because I am endlessly forbearing. I forgive because I am immensely flawed. So I **understand**."

Makoa bowed, kissing the back of her hand. "If you are immensely flawed, then those flaws are precious treasure. Thank you," he said softly. They were quiet for a bit, just drifting along the river. "You look tired, new sister. If you follow the stairs down, there is a bed."

"When will you rest?"

"Soon. She will wake, and we will trade. Get your rest. Sleep good and have bad dreams."

Xinyi smirked, touched though the words were strange. He'd said the same to Shiraz earlier, so it felt like being invited into their world.

"Why bad dreams?" There must be a deeper meaning.

"We get the bad out while we sleep," Makoa said instructively. "So we can wake and **create** our good dreams."

Xinyi liked that. She took a lantern and climbed down the six steps to a part of the ship she had not realized existed. It was a tight space, but there was a bed stuffed into the wall, and shelves all around it held a horde of books that would have done the librarian dragons of Wehu proud. Xinyi was wandering around, intent on studying the books kept on shelves with netting. Then she noticed a door at the back of the room. Opening it to peer inside, she did as Makoa had suggested earlier and held back none of her emotions.

"You lying scum!" she shouted loud enough to run a shiver through the ship. "There was a toilet on board this whole time!"

On a Scale of Deadly to Harmless

The sun was out, the air was cool, and Shiraz was in a lovely mood. She had woken to the princess's scream last night, and despite the unfortunate dream she'd been having, and the searing pain in her forearm, Shiraz had woken so amused that it carried her through the remaining hours of night.

"Oh, do you prefer enclosed room toilets to holes dug in the jungle? When you demanded to go ashore, I assumed..." Shiraz had let her words drift off.

Xinyi was glaring with such fire in her eyes it was a wonder the ship hadn't been struck ablaze. "I won't forget this," she said ominously. "I will get you back."

Shiraz was still chuckling about it.

While Makoa slept, Shiraz guided the ship through the underground tunnels and out to join the river Chihu. They were still shrunken and elongated like a snake. She planned to change back the size shortly. She hadn't decided if she should wake the princess so she could see the process; the scales rolling over the deck made the ship sparkle in a way no other could. Or if she should let her keep resting. Shiraz had heard her moving down there for hours.

At first, she thought Xinyi was up writing. And the idea of what new adventures she would write for Jian was electric and exciting. Then she spotted her bag laying on the deck. Shiraz was tempted, so tempted to see what she wrote. If she had described Shiraz and Makoa. If she had written about their adventures. If it was poetic, or dramatic, or silly. She wanted to peek into that woman's mind.

But Shiraz didn't peek. She didn't want to see herself written of as an uzaok. She really had been one off and on yesterday. Mostly on. Until she'd broken down and *cried* in front of her. And yet...she did feel better for having cried.

But she didn't peek, and she didn't wake Xinyi, or even Makoa. He was going to need his sleep. She was certain of it.

Shiraz twisted her aching left arm to see her tattoo. She'd felt it changing in her dream.

She found the Singing Hills. And there was a home waiting for her, with her mother and brothers, including Makoa and a bunch of people she hadn't recognized, then a searing pain caused everyone to cry out, but the pain was hers.

Her glowing tattoo was no longer a map of Loqwan's river and mountains. It was a map of her failures, every island in the Ooloo'a chain she had already searched. Her childhood home on Glen Harrow, and the port in Jaccada where she learned of Noam's death. It was a tattoo of pain.

She hadn't asked for that. Hadn't made promises and risked her life for such a tattoo. That wasn't magic! It was torture.

On the positive side, her waking tattoo had not transformed to a map of her failures. But...on the negative side, it was changing. The edges of the tattoo had been eaten away. The river Nanghi was almost gone. It showed largely where she was and perhaps twelve miles of jungle in every direction but even that was scraggly and unclear, showing none of impediments it usually would. It was being eaten more and more the longer she was awake.

She ought to tell Makoa. But…he'd warned her not to get the tattoo. Prior to their bonding, Makoa was a bit more cautious of Aiattaua. And Shiraz agreed Aiattaua wasn't to be trusted. But he'd offered her the tattoo so she could smuggle in *his* contraband. Why turn on her?

It probably wasn't him pulling the magic from under her skin and closing the net around her. He wouldn't do that to Makoa.

Shiraz could barely credit her positive attitude. Shouldn't she be more worried? Someone had taken out a bounty on her ship. She'd seen at least two monkeys that looked familiar in the trees, and someone was using the tattoo with which she tracked dangers to track the River Serpent. She was overrun with threats.

Why did that put her in such a good mood?

She kept thinking about yesterday. She'd nearly died. Makoa had nearly died. The ship had nearly been taken from her. But she also laughed more often than she had in months, and she looked at the world more positively. Maybe being hunted agreed with her.

Not bothering to wake anyone, she gently bit down on both eyes on her bracelet. The ship jerked, shuddered, scales folded over one another in an iridescent display that refracted the light, creating a beautiful rolling array of color. When the scales rolled beneath him, Makoa leapt up, blowing out a breath of spell and transforming. He jumped in Michaela's body and hit the deck in the body of the fisherman who'd rescued Makoa, Shiraz and her cellmate off the coast of Minn. When Felicia sunk Shiraz's last ship.

"Why didn't you wa—" Makoa began.

But as soon as the boat regained its usual size, grappling hooks were fired into the hull from either side of the river. Six elves stepped up to the banks gripping the ropes and pulled the River Serpent to a stop.

"Kuffik! Doesn't anyone ever just ask?" Shiraz muttered. Wasn't that exactly like the universe. She was in a good mood so what did it do? Throw her into the path of the Immortal King.

Shiraz didn't even think about it. Years of being boarded had prepared her to act on instinct. She kicked over a basket of food and ducked away from the rudder arm, knocking the door below deck shut.

"Keep quiet." She managed to throw a handful of starlight dust from the bag beneath the canopy and drop the bag over her shoulder.

Just in the nick of time too. Dao, the commander of the elf king's guard, dropped silently out of the trees, landing on the deck.

With the door to the lower decks closed, the smuggling spell Shiraz had gotten from Merl the Magnificent automatically concealed the existence of their lower deck. But it didn't silence anything. Hence the starlight dust. It surrounded any area in a bubble of awe that rendered all who viewed it speechless.

Technically Shiraz was *friends* with the Elf King. And if one were to judge on a scale of deadly to harmless, the Elf King fell somewhere in the middle. Being as he was dangerous when riled, but so slow to temper that this rarely happened. Of all the things she could encounter along the river, human soldiers, soul collectors, monkey gangs, rapids, even the fey guard at the border to the northeast, the elf king was in no way the worst thing Shiraz had to face.

However on Shiraz's scale of preferred impediments, which was something she was not foolish enough to have written down, the Elf King was near the bottom of the list, with only encounters with the elf prince, Aiattaua and his gaggle of bonded mates (Makoa excluded) and wood-eating termites after him.

Shiraz could escape a pack of monkeys with a black eye and scratches that were bound to get infected but still feel like her life was worth living. She could escape human soldiers with holes in her vessel and a new sketch put up marking her and Makoa as criminals but still have a chance to repair the damage. She could even escape the fey guard by paying half her cargo, knowing she could earn back the funds. But she never left an encounter with the Immortal Elf King without feeling he'd sucked years off of her life. *Years!*

So it was typical of the universe to shove him in her path when she was in a good mood. Although...today didn't seem like their usual encounter. In her experience grappling hooks in the hull spelled out trouble. The Immortal Elf King had never used them before. So, yay! Maybe it was more trouble!

Dao walked forward as silently as she landed. The ankle length skirt of her uniform and its deep sleeves caught in the breeze, dancing around her, quietly dramatic. She observed Shiraz suspiciously. Marrying her impressive flair with her tranquil expression, Dao stomped a foot on the deck. It struck so heavily that the deck jumped. The spilled fruit and the basket that had held them flew into the air. She yanked up the basket and spun around in a whirl, gathering up the fruit.

She stopped directly in front of Shiraz, her skirt still twirling. "You dropped these." Her voice betrayed no feelings.

"Had to." Shiraz bit her lip, gazing provocatively at the other woman. "I love to watch you work."

The elf raised a brow infinitesimally. "Would you also enjoy being tied up as my prisoner?"

Shiraz gave a low, intrigued hum. "Am I about to find out?"

Crude Awakenings

The door to the lower deck fell shut, startling Xinyi awake. She barely heard it, but the captain's voice hissed "keep quiet" as she woke.

Xinyi's heart raced before she'd even gotten out of bed. She blinked, managing to catch the book she'd fallen asleep reading so it didn't fall. She had to keep quiet. She just didn't know why. She looked in the direction of the door, and her heart stopped. The seam of the wood matched up with the door so well you couldn't see where the door was. She was trapped. Why? What was going on? Why had she started trusting smugglers? Her heart was pounding, and she couldn't decide if she should obey the woman's dictate or shout for help.

It didn't help that Xinyi had been reading all of these twisted tales of animal spirits emerging to speak to humans and consuming them when they answered questions wrong. Or of vines that came to life and yanked humans into the jungle and fed on them. The enclosed deck felt like a trap. Like she was being punished by some malevolent spirit.

A shockwave of light slid around the room. A softly sparkling veil made up of millions of tiny pricks of individual light. It was like seeing the night sky, only it wasn't dark. It was brilliant!

Awed, Xinyi sunk her fingers into the mist twisting around. The starlight twirled between her fingers, shifting so she could never grasp onto the stars. They drifted away, clustering and weaving apart in the cool damp mist. Dancing! The stars were dancing.

Her fingers were tingling again. Desperate to write. Everything she had seen on this trip was so beautiful, so inspiring. She needed to get it all down. She would hate herself if she forgot even a moment.

She wanted to write about the grouchy captain transformed into a furry winged fox. Or about racing through the sound of color! Every second a new, ridiculous adventure. Even this—trapped in a net of stars! And surrounded by books.

The ship's library had kept her up for hours last night, though none of it was the sort of thing she would usually read. The entire deck was full of books from around the world. Most were written in fairy, but there were a few whose languages she did not recognize. She wouldn't have expected the captain to read this much, but there were a few books that could belong to no one but her, like:

Kaagok Obaaz

"Filthy Mouth"

A guide to Maltuban curses and insults.

And Xinyi couldn't resist it. She'd skimmed the whole thing, stifling her laughter so no one would know. She loved it. She loved every book she found. Each tale had some element of magic. They were very...*dark* or very sexual, or both. She paged through several. One— she'd opened to a random page and nearly dropped—multiple body parts were being simultaneously explored by multiple tentacles.

Alright almost dropped was a slight exaggeration. She might have in fact gripped the book a bit tighter. And definitely finished the scene. *As a professional courtesy.* Who wouldn't, with so many tentacles working so creatively and so...diligently? Xinyi had never imagined. But the door was open now, the door to so many new worlds. So many books ended with the ghoulish deaths of mortals who interfered in the realm of gods and fey folk.

Xinyi was captivated. She would not have expected to like such stories. With otherwise good people coveting powers not meant for mortals, only to be eaten alive or tortured by their greatest fears.

She wouldn't have expected to curse her growing exhaustion as her eyes kept drifting shut. She'd given in to sleep while reading a story of forbidden romance between a sea god and a mist woman. They had run from their homes to be together but were being pursued. Xinyi's body failed her completely, just as the couple had found a cave to hide in.

But now, moved to peace with the starlight surrounding her, and given the marvelous excuse of being stuck, Xinyi curled up in the blanket and lifted the book. A storm raged outside the cave where the couple hid, slowing their pursuers. Things were about to get steamy. Maybe one of them had tentacles! A girl could dream.

Makoa had woken uneasy. Shiraz was in a good mood, which was unsettling enough. Then the elves arrived before he could get out a sentence. There were a new set of holes in the ship, and he was hungry. Add to that Dao was acting suspicious. This was a terrible way to start a morning.

Dao escorted them off the ship, unbound despite her poor attempt at humor, and was marching Shiraz and Makoa through the jungle. The rest of her soldiers followed with the River Serpent borne above them.

Clearly Shiraz's instinct to hide the princess was a good one. They weren't prisoners, but they weren't being treated like friends either.

"We aren't usually invited into the Mushroom Palace in this fashion," Shiraz probed casually, though any moment the princess might make a noise, alerting their escorts to her presence.

"The king didn't want to miss you." Dao had a way about her, using the minimum of expressive words but expressing quite a bit.

"How flattering." Shiraz's eyes drifted into the trees.

Makoa followed her gaze, spotting monkeys—again. That did it! The Golden Paw Gang had never been this persistent. Something was definitely up.

Sweetums leapt onto the deck of the ship. "If you are holding our ship hostage, you ought to be protecting it from thieves," Makoa admonished the elves impatiently.

Dao paused. Noticing the monkeys, she subtly shook her head. "Your *possessions* are safe. It isn't hostage. We are carrying it for your benefit."

"I could carry it easier," Shiraz countered slyly. Shiraz and Dao never met without some manner of flirtation striking up between them. The two weeks she'd spent aboard as they snuck Princes Helima across the northern boarder had been excruciating. Particularly since nothing beyond flirtation ever came of it. Dao liked the game, but in terms of interests hers were exclusively focused on Prince Aiattaua. And nothing would come of that either.

Aiattaua was very good at accepting one as one was, but he did not believe in exclusivity. A body needed to be bathed in love, he believed, not bound to one mate, expecting all things from them. Dao was his opposite. So her infatuation would come to naught. For Makoa's part, he was happy with Aiattaua's perspective. His love for others did not lessen his love for Makoa, and nor was it so fragile that it needed to pin him in to feel that love was returned. He understood that Makoa must continue trying to break the curse. Though it was done halfheartedly. Angrily, Makoa supposed. He had such ready love and acceptance from the prince as he was. Why did that not satisfy the spell? What even was true love?

"You look so sore. We do not want you entering the palace at a disadvantage," Dao teased Shiraz.

To most observers, Shiraz would appear entirely enraptured by the elf. But Makoa had seen her enraptured. She was playing and laying it on very thick. She sidled up to the elf and not very subtly brushed her arm against Dao's.

"Why is today special?" She laughed softly to make it seem like she just spoke to speak.

Makoa knew what Shiraz was up to. He just couldn't think how she expected to make it work. There were *seven* elves.

Elves were certainly bores. Elitist. Confident to the point of being excessive, and then looping back around to justifiable, as they were better at most things than most creatures. They were fast, cunning, agile, and excellent hunters. And there was the ship to consider in an escape. Would she shrink it with the princess on board alone? Was that even safe? They'd only ever shrunk people when Shiraz and the bracelet with her were onboard.

"The king will say all that needs saying." Dao put some space between herself and Shiraz.

"Ugh, will he ever," Shiraz complained. She turned to Makoa. "This is your fault, you know?"

"Mine?" Makoa asked in a tone of incredulity.

*"**With any luck we've put our troubles behind us**,"* Shiraz mocked Makoa's voice. "You jinxed us. It's the only explanation for all that's gone wrong on this trip. Pixies, alligators, fights, our boat thrown into the air, cargo lost to who knows where, separation!" she shouted.

Makoa shook his head. *No.* "You aren't jinxed," Makoa tried to get her to see reason. Even if he managed to transform and grab the boat when she shrunk it, it was unlikely he would get away. And certain that she would not. "The king is a reasonable man. There is no reason to think we are being threatened."

Now that was a bald-faced lie. Even placid Dao raised an eyebrow. But Makoa felt he had to say it. The elf army were unlikely to tell their king anything the pair said, but there was always a chance. He'd met the elf king before but was not bonded to his son at the time. One wanted to make a positive impression.

Shiraz snorted. "Are we talking about the same elf? His majesty of the life sucking conversation, otherwise known as the Immortal Elf King!" Shiraz said, trying and succeeding at annoying their escorts. A few elves were beginning to glare. Their tempers were their undoing.

"Just being welcomed into the palace by him is sanity threatening! Headache inducing! Ear suicide encouraging." One by one, every elf began to show signs of anger, their arms shaking as frustration weakened their holds. Their eyes narrowed, and with it, their focus. As Shiraz did what she had always done best and broke the wills of the calmest, most patient creatures in existence with her incessant sarcasm.

It wasn't any lack of loyalty that would keep the elves from telling the king what had been said of him. It was a combination of loving devotion and self preservation. Because the man didn't know how to form a succinct sentence.

Thus when the elf king would eventually ask, it was bound to go like it had a year ago when the elf king sent for them to "request" they retrieve his youngest daughter from her mother, with the djinn of Reethurn. *"Ah, and did our guests, that is our forced visitors, but always welcome guests and dear friends, Makoa the cursed and Shiraz the disbeliever, have anything to say for themselves when you fetched them to us, honoring them with our request for a visit? It is a request naturally, though you were escorted by guards; it is the way things are done when one is royal, a great inconvenience it is, although I do not like to complain; some I understand offer invites—my dear friend Hamol for instance—I say friend, of course he was a general from a foreign state who came to me seeking my advice in how to overrun the local government. I sent him away without much word on that; it wasn't my affair you understand—Elves, you know, like to keep to their own affair—but then, they do not always. My own children have been known to cause a ruckus here and there, but mostly there, that is in worlds not their own, the rascals. My children, not my friend Hamol who was telling me, oh, this must have been three or four years ago now, during that dreadful human skirmish, just around when we met you, Shiraz the nonbeliever. He came and spoke of a grand affair he'd thrown for the neighboring rulers—Hamol that is—wanting to get to know them, and,"* the king chuckled softly, *"poison them, as it were. I do believe his original goal was to become powerful enough that I might gift his daughter with a royal offspring of my loins. He'd heard of my copious interspecies offspring and mistaken me for wanting children of great power, when of course my aim was to offer my own greatness into the world through my progeny. But wouldn't you know it, his plan failed in all instances for, though they all promised to come, not one guest attended his party, and there was all that food, wasted. He couldn't eat it himself of course, as it had been poisoned, so he had to dispose of it. The waste was appalling. An elf, I must have told you before, hates nothing so much as waste, so clearly his daughter was not an option for procreation. And as I told him eventually, I attempted human offspring years ago to no success; humans appear not to be a strong enough species to mate with elves. But Hamol's fate, my unfortunate friend, would never have befallen a king, all my guests—you, in this instance—must attend. So I should not complain that I must send guards, for at least I am never forced to throw out a meal."*

The commander having impressively recalled the question from within the ramble replied, *"They said nothing."*

Makoa didn't know why he was trying to present himself well to the king. He clearly didn't respect humans and had only asked their help because *"no one would suspect the Immortal Elf King to risk his progeny in human care."* Makoa wondered if they would have taken the job if they'd known what the learned later. That Helima hadn't particularly wanted to meet her estranged father, and that all his children were in effect trapped in the Mushroom Court once delivered to him. Probably not. Though it was hard to imagine having refused and lived to tell the tale. It was also difficult to imagine someone placing a bounty high enough on The River Serpent that even the Immortal Elf King was after it. Makoa didn't like it, so he played along as Shiraz began her distraction technique and prepared himself to enact her suggestions for escape.

Those sucked into the Mushroom Court rarely left without permission.

The Even Greater Escape— from Some Perspectives

"You were never cursed at all, were you?" Shiraz demanded. Makoa knew what to do. Clearly, he didn't want to do it, but he would.

Dao had nodded to the monkeys and *they backed off.* There was no reason for the Immortal Elf King, who was not immortal at all in Shiraz's opinion, to work with the Golden Paw Gang. Something was wrong, and Shiraz preferred finding out what through her connections.

"You *are a curse.* You were sent into my life by some vengeful god to make me pay for stealing sacred flowers or not marrying that furry guy with the temper and the castle you sent me to meet."

"How do you know he had a temper?" Makoa asked.

"He wouldn't stop yelling at me! All because I came in through his rose garden. I couldn't get a word in, and his servants were super creepy, peeling themselves off of wallpaper, or the banister decorations and peeking out all excited as if they thought having some big guy scream in my face was a kink for me." Shiraz invested all the energy she could into the story, drawing the attention of their escorts. "I was seriously angry at you for months. You're lucky we ever spoke again. I can't believe you thought *that* was my true love."

"You're telling me that you went into Henri's castle, looked around, and didn't stay?" Makoa demanded.

"Stay there? With him and the army of creepy servants?"

"But..." Makoa sounded confused. He was getting much better! In all the times they'd used this story as a distraction, he'd never sounded so convincing. "You did go inside, right? Did you at least rob him?"

"I never made it past the garden. I just gave him a lecture about manners and ducked out."

"Shiraz!" Makoa yelled, the fisherman's face he wore growing red and sweaty. Damn. His acting was really improving. Makoa's real temper ran cooler than the south sea. But now—he stopped in the middle of the jungle, shaking with false rage; it was inspired. "Don't you think I know you at all?"

"That incident left me with som—" but he cut her off.

"The whole east wing of his palace is a library. Books from *every* nation in the world!"

"*WHAT!*" Shiraz's shout could have woken the dead, set off volcanos, shook the core of the earth. Azaqif, she was loud! But as they were near a waterfall and deep in the jungle, it merely frightened away the birds, rodents and small animals in the vicinity. It also brought the elf guard to such a sudden stop they nearly dropped the River Serpent.

"I thought you'd like it there," Makoa said more softly.

"You mean—" Shiraz's eyes filled with tears and rage heated her skin. Horrendous, *deep* regret. Shiraz recalled the actual moment when she discovered that she had stood outside of the world's largest personal library and never even set foot inside it. It was seriously depressing. It was easy to tap into the emotions.

"Are you telling me all I had to do was marry some hairy guy with anger issues, and my whole house could have been a library? And I would have had servants? They weren't *that creepy*," she said morosely, slipping the knife she'd lifted off Dao's belt into her hand.

"Yep." Makoa patted her on the arm. "Look on the bright side. If he was that rude, maybe he isn't married yet."

"Do you think?" Shiraz asked with a hopeful catch in her voice.

"Definitely. Once the boat is back on the water, we can sail over and find out."

"Yeah." She looked only at her friend. "He was a real uzaok, shouting at a stranger in the rain. Who'd marry that? Unless they know about the library."

"I'm sure no one knows."

She nodded. "I suppose. Anyway, a temper is better than droning on so long your guests wish they were dead." Shiraz smirked. One of the younger elves holding the ship started forward.

The ship tilted, Makoa rushed at it, Dao turned to do the same, and Shiraz threw the elf's knife into the trees. The blade sliced cleanly through a branch and sent a quartet of monkeys hurtling down atop Dao. Shiraz saw the monkeys land, attacking the woman as if she had knocked them from the tree.

Makoa rushed bodily into the tilting elf, knocking him over. The others might have managed to hold the ship, had Shiraz not pressed on the aquamarine eye twice, quadrupling its size. They lunged out of the way. Before the ship could hit the ground, Shiraz hit the amethyst eye seven times, shrinking it to the size of a small fish. It got kicked into the air by one of the tumbled elves.

Makoa leapt high, breathing out his curse, and scooped up the ship in the beak of a pelican. Shiraz saw him fly away and threw two large handfuls of stardust spell into the air above the elves before she took off running. She did not look back, rushing into the jungle with the sounds of elves and monkeys pursuing her.

They were bound to catch up, but at least the ship would be on the other side of the jungle with Makoa.

Ewsax: A Fast Paced, Nausea Inducing Ride in the Jungle *not an exact translation

The first bump was startling but not harmful. Xinyi felt the ship tilt down and she rolled with it towards the wall, managing to catch herself with an outstretched hand. She thought she heard a screech near the door. The starlight that had coated the room began to fade. When the second bump hit, it was so startling that she cried out. Books flew over their nets, pummeling her. Then the whole ship flew into the air and rolled, tossing Xinyi upside down. She tumbled through the air surrounded by books, pillows, and her shoes. She ought to be screaming.

Oddly, she had time enough to consider if she wanted to scream before she hit the bed. At which point she began laughing.

It was a sort of shocked to be alive, desperate for air laughter. She lay, tumbled on the bed, beneath a sea of books. Libraries were dangerous places. She chuckle-groaned at all the bruises and paper cuts she must have. What would today's fairy nonsense be?

The ship was bumping up and down. And Xinyi remembered suddenly the captain's voice telling her to keep quiet. How long ago was that? How had it slipped her mind? Her laughter faded and her breathing evened. She felt a hand soothing her head.

Opening her eyes, she looked into the tiny face of a monkey. The same one she'd fed on the ship yesterday.

Xinyi smiled up at the little creature. "Hello."

The monkey squeaked once, an equally calm greeting. She tilted her head to the side showing all of her teeth.

"Do you know what is happening?" The monkey nodded.

Xinyi sat up, the ship was still bumping, but in a fairly even rhythm now like it was caught on a loop. It would rush forward only to be yanked back over and over again. It made her woozy. Xinyi scooted against the wall. The monkey sat beside her and held out her free hand, offering Xinyi a half-eaten piece of nectar fruit.

She could hear Shiraz in the back of her head admonishing her to **never trust any offer of free assistance, food, or gifts.** She probably shouldn't. Outside of even being drugged, animals sometimes carried diseases. But the monkey tilted her head to the side, eyes wide, lips pouting, looking so heartbroken that Xinyi felt monstrous.

She accepted the fruit and took a bite. It wasn't as juicy as some had been, but still delicious. The monkey jumped around happily, making little whines and chirps that sounded like singing. She played among the books, throwing them or flipping through the pages until she found one to her liking.

Xinyi peeked over her shoulder. This was not a book at all, but a journal. There was a poor sketch of a person, some notes, a wobbly map. The monkey was turning page after page. She stopped on one with the clearest drawing yet. A boat. *This* boat. There were notes about what it needed, and where to get each feature.

And she'd said she would not tell Xinyi, lest it fall into enemy hands! What would the captain say to know that it was in the hands of a monkey right now? A monkey she didn't trust.

Xinyi wondered if she should take the journal, but that was ridiculous. Monkeys could not read. Still, Xinyi's hands slipped out and lifted the book.

The monkey climbed up Xinyi's arm and settled at her shoulder as if they would read together.

Xinyi flipped away from the page about the ship. And the next and the next. She came to a page where there was a sketch of Shiraz, clearly drawn by someone else. She was laying on one arm staring at the artist with a soft smile. It was lovely. Peaceful and *inviting*. Not what one would expect. Her gaze lingered on that expression a moment, but it began to feel intrusive, so she flipped the page and found a journal entry.

> She was but one drop of water in the sea of existence. Amid a crowd of her siblings, one might not even see her. When their voices were raised in song, hers was so small it vanished into the cloud of sound. And she was neither bold, nor striking to look upon. She was small—insignificant next to the vast expanse of the world. But to Anolani's heart, she was blood. To her lungs, she was air. To her mind, she was the fire of inspiration.

The story broke off there and little doodles of swirling lines were drawn around it. The page was softer than others as if it was often returned to, and Xinyi could see why.

Maybe the captain really should write stories, because Xinyi wanted to know more of this one with only a paragraph to go on.

Xinyi closed the book around her finger. The surface of the page brushed softly against her skin. But...her head was starting to pound, and the constant bumping of the ship was turning her stomach. Xinyi pressed her hand, the book gripped in it, against the bed. She breathed slowly, very opposed to vomiting.

"Right," she said, softly. "Shall we see if we can get out of here?" she asked the monkey.

Sweetums pet her head gently, clearly a mark in the affirmative. Xinyi stood, weaving, and made her way towards the stairs.

Makoa took the ship in his mouth and flew up, up, up, and out over the treetops. He could hear monkeys pursuing him through the branches, but he didn't think he heard anything as large as an elf. Elves were especially quiet in pursuit, but in a situation like this, even they would make noises. He was tempted to look back, but he resisted, beating his wings as hard and as fast as he could. He needed to get the ship away from Shiraz.

How she expected to get away herself, he couldn't say. And if she was caught by anyone who knew about her tattoo, they would easily find him. It was fair to say she didn't advertise her tattoo, but nor did she hide it.

Makoa broke through the trees without being caught and set out to the other side of the river. There were splashes loud enough to be elves, and some that were likely monkeys, but he kept flapping. Once across the river, he dipped into the tree line. He was not the most maneuverable of birds, and he had a plan to transform. He always transformed a number of times when on the run. But he couldn't do it until the right mome—

Makoa shuddered. Something was moving inside of the deep pocket where he carried the ship. Something light fluttered at the pouch, tickling him from within.

He held his breath, fighting the urge to cough.

Makoa dove face first into a tree full of squabbling parrots. They took to the air concealing him. Makoa spit out the curse and the boat along with it. He heard a tiny scream but could only focus on transformation. He picked out a common bird among the mix and took on its shape. He snapped up the boat in the long Tucan beak and flew.

Makoa felt a nauseous sort of hunger as he zipped between trees. And the stress of the escape wasn't helping. But all he could do was carry the ship and try to get away. He heard another scream, tiny in volume and intense in fear, but couldn't angle his head to see the boat.

Damn, he hoped what he thought had happened hadn't happened. All the same, he willed the princess to hold on. He'd find a way to help her shortly.

Xinyi screamed at the top of her lungs, "*MAKOA!*"

She should never have left home. She should never have started writing adventures. She should never have longed for adventures. She was nauseous, she was bruised, she had a persistent ache in her lower back, and she was about to die, shrunken and falling off a boat in the middle of the jungle.

She had stumbled dizzily to the edge and fallen in an attempt to see where she was. It had been so dark. Just based on the smell, she had to assume she had been in Makoa's mouth! Ugh. She couldn't think about that smell. It made her smell it again. It made her so sick, death sounded comforting.

Her eyes were burning, and her skin was clammy. She was definitely sweating. Holding her breath was all that stopped the vomit from spilling out of her and flying back into her face. She'd never wished more acutely to be someone else.

Sweetums was on the ledge of the ship, jumping up and down and screaming! She tugged on Xinyi's arm, trying to pull her back on the ship, but there was just no way.

Xinyi wished she could be the her from yesterday and watch the world zoom by with delight. But she could barely make out the different shades of color, much less what they were. The only steady thing she could see was a beak, closed around the middle of the ship.

"Makoa?" she called out again. Much more weakly.

She hoped that beak was him. What happened if she lost her grip on the boat? Would she stay shrunken? Would she plummet to the ground and be lost forever? Would she even survive? Would she return to her normal size? Would that be better? Or worse?

Xinyi sobbed as the bird breathed out that same pungent breath. Her stomach turned and tears ran down her face. The boat flew into the open air once more.

"Ewsax," she whined a Maltuban curse, leaning her face against the cool surface of the ship, and held on for dear life though her fingers screamed in protest.

No Such Thing as Fate, Right?

Very quickly after making her escape, Shiraz realized that she hadn't made an escape at all. Nearly all of the elves had followed her, which was the plan, but she'd hoped to get ahead of them. It didn't seem to be the case. They just weren't catching her yet because they were playing with her. She was lucky that Dao was their leader and not Princess Abeo. That particular, giant, elf princess had a fondness for musical theatre and had been known to instruct her father's army to sing and dance as they performed their duties. It would be very insulting to have to hear them perform a song about luring her into an obvious trap—while actually succeeding in doing so.

On the other hand, Shiraz thought as her sore ankle started to smart and her breathing grew heavy, they were apparently very entertaining. Shiraz was tempted to stop and sit down. So tempted since this was only a game to the elves. But her purpose was to give Makoa more time to escape, not to feel triumphant against the elf army. If he could get to the Grotto before she was caught, maybe he could find a spell to hide the boat from her tattoo. Or if Aiattaua was there, perhaps Makoa could convince him to remove the tattoo altogether. Shiraz would prefer that Makoa not take the ship anywhere near Aiattaua without her. But she would have to have told him about the tattoo being burned slowly off her skin for him to know that. She wished she'd been able to give him the bracelet before running. It made her nervous thinking of the shrunken ship with Xinyi locked onboard. What if Aiattaua *was* the one after it, and Makoa flew right to him? What if he was after the princess and would mistake Xinyi for her?

Azaqif! Why had she hid her? Xinyi free was a whirlwind of contradictions. A sweet, sheltered woman who somehow both got into and got out of more scrapes than Shiraz had in the last four years—with a war going on! But trapped…Shiraz didn't know. It made her uneasy.

Hopefully Makoa was making it much further than her. Hopefully Xinyi was safe. Hopefully in some, weird, unlikely, perhaps so ridiculous it felt fated sort of way, Shiraz would get away from the elf guard. Because even locked up, the princess's good luck curse had rubbed off on Shiraz.

She stumbled over a root—nope, no luck there—managed to keep her feet, jarring her hip on the opposite side to the shoulder she'd jammed yesterday so…ughhhh, that was nice. Probably wasn't going to escape then, but she ran as fast as she could. There was a body hurtling in the opposite direction that felt vaguely familiar, though she couldn't make out specific features.

Shiraz moved left in an attempt to avoid the other runner. And, as if it were her mirror self, the other body matched the move exactly. Shiraz moved right and again was matched. The body hurtled by her, clipping her hard in her good shoulder. Uzaok! But it was only as Shiraz felt the spiked shoulder slam into her own that she knew who it was.

The woman, annoyed to have **bumped into someone else,** kicked an equally spiked ankle into the back of Shiraz's knee and knocked her to the ground.

"Felicia?" Shiraz shouted from her back at the blue skinned, spiky jointed woman towering over her. Shiraz had not thought to ever see her former cellmate again, nor wanted to. And certainly not while fleeing a gaggle of elves.

"Speedy Hands!" Felicia screamed excitedly. She stretched down and pulled Shiraz to her feet, dusting her off far more thoroughly than was required.

"What are you doing here?" Shiraz demanded. She saw green moving in ways plants did not. *Elves*. She took off running, without a response.

Weirdly, Felicia followed alongside her. "I was going to ask you the same thing!" Felicia laughed, so easily keeping apace with Shiraz that she began to run backwards. *Showoff!*

"Fleeing, clearly."

"Do you owe elves money or something?"

"Something," Shiraz replied. "Why are you here? Are you a part of this?"

"Of running?" she teased. "Obviously. What's your plan? You do realize the elves are luring you into a trap where they will surround you, right?"

"I just need to run!"

The months Shiraz shared a cell with this woman were more than enough. She appreciated that it was mostly Felicia's magical power that broke them out. But it wasn't worth it, as her magical power had also burnt a giant hole in Shiraz's last ship, *The Island Rebel*, and nearly drowned them both and Makoa.

Well, Makoa became a dolphin; he would not have drowned. But the annoyance remained.

"We should catch up, Speedy Hands. This can't be anything but fate."

"Ha."

"I'll tell you what I'm doing here." Felicia stopped running. She grabbed Shiraz's arm in a viselike grip stopping her as well. "Saving the day."

Felicia pulled a long thin blade from behind her back and sucked in a breath. Before she could use the magical power that had gotten her banned from fifteen countries, Shiraz shook her.

"No! No need. It's...I'm...They're training me to run faster. *Don't kill* anyone!"

Felicia threw her head back and laughed wickedly. "Still the sweet steadfast girl, I see. I promise, Speedy Hands, I won't kill any of your *enemies*. Get running. I'll find you again. I have so much to tell you! But no one messes with my cellmate. I always keep my word."

"I..." Shiraz really ought to try harder to stop her. But she also needed to run. And it wasn't a good idea to get on Felicia's bad side. And...she did promise not to kill anyone.

Felicia had looked after Shiraz in prison. The guards were fond of picking on the weaker inmates, and at twenty-two, Shiraz wasn't nearly as savvy as she was today. Felicia, on the other hand, with spiked joints, transformative powers, and stomach acids that expelled lava? Felicia was always self assured.

Shiraz took off running. Dao and a few of her soldiers emerged from the tree line and onto the sun-drenched ground. Shiraz only had time to see Felicia's sword come alight with fire, and a few elves surround her in dance-like choreographed unison, before she ducked back into the shadowed jungle. It was odd that she should bump into Felicia in the jungle while on the run.

There was a Maltuban adjective that seemed to suit; there was no perfect match in fairy. *Vivipo;* it meant something that was divinely weird. A connection so *improbably perfect,* it could be nothing but fate.

That seemed to fit this turn of events. Which made Shiraz—*suspicious.* She did not believe in fate. Not. At. All.

But she had been wishing to escape miraculously, and now she was. That too was odd. The only question was if it was a good odd or a very, very bad odd. She suspected the latter.

Makoa transformed into a squirrel monkey, catching the ship in his hand and leaping onto a tree branch. He raced down the tree, running around and around the trunk, with his eyes peeled for pursuers. It looked like he'd lost them. But he couldn't be too careful. Slipping into the cover of some bushes, he stopped to examine the boat.

He settled down, surrounded by bugs and leaves, but no other animals or fey that he could see. A shudder shook his body as he examined the ship, relief and fear in one. Xinyi was hanging off the side of the ship! What happened if she fell out? He thought, hoped, she would return to her normal size, but he didn't know.

How had she even gotten out of the lower decks? Once closed you—oh!

"Sweetums, you troublemaker," he whispered, his breath uneven. "Princess, I am going to tilt the ship sideways, do you think you can climb up on deck?"

Xinyi nodded with her head pressed to the side of the ship and her eyes closed. She had a distinctly seasick look about her.

As slowly and carefully as he was able, Makoa tilted the ship. A number of loose objects on the deck rolled to the opposite side. Sweetums let out an angry screech, but managed to hold onto the netting the princess was clinging to.

Makoa had hoped something on the deck would roll wildly enough to fall off, so they might see for certain what would happen to the princess. But most things were bolted or tied down. And the rolling fruits and vegetables were caught by the bow of the ship.

Xinyi crawled back onboard. When she had a leg over the side, Makoa helped her along by slowly tilting it the other way. When she was standing on the deck, and the ship was upright, Xinyi looked at Makoa, opened her mouth, and immediately jerked forward to vomit over the side of the ship.

Makoa jumped back, holding his arm out away from his body.

"Sorry," he whispered. He hadn't meant to shake the ship more. But the sheer volume of vomit coming off the deck at least answered one of Makoa's questions. If Xinyi got off the ship, she would return to her normal size. But he didn't think she wanted to do it right here.

Nor did he. That smell was worse than his transformation breath. At least they were safe for the moment. Now they needed to find a place to hide, to wash off, and to formulate a plan to meet up with Shiraz.

"I'm so sorry," Xinyi called when she was finally done vomiting. There were tears streaming down her face, and her visible skin had a mottled red and white pattern. Sweetums held back her hair, petting the princess soothingly. Maybe that one monkey wasn't all bad. "Where is...is the captain alright?" Xinyi asked haltingly.

Makoa nodded, though he had no way to be sure. "She distracted the elves so we could get away. They were trying to take us captive. I'm sorry. That must have been a rude way to wake up. I'm going to carry you somewhere safer. I'll keep the ship as steady as I can. But...vomit if you need to." Makoa winked.

He stuck his head out of the bush. The area seemed clear, which was strange. He'd been moving fast, and he had intentionally taken nonsensical turns, but he'd expected to still have a tail of some kind. Or to hear his pursuers run past. Makoa walked as slowly and steadily as he dared. Putting the still rising sun at his back, he walked west, the general direction of the Mushroom Grotto. If nothing else, Shiraz would find them there.

He got three steps before an unfamiliar bird of white and brown with little blue patches on its wings and a short beak fluttered down in front of him. Its feathers flew apart in a dramatic whirl and spun upwards, expanding and changing shape to form a woman with rich brown skin, dressed from head to toe in black fabric. Makoa estimated her age was near his own, in her middling forties. Her face was full and good natured, putting one at ease, despite her sudden appearance and the fact that Makoa was on the run with the ship in hand.

"Greetings, fellow skin slipper—" she began.

"I am not a skin slipper," Makoa interrupted. His response one of habit. "I was cursed by an old woman to never again take my own form unless I learned the meaning of true love and earned a true love's kiss."

"Indeed?" The woman considered this, a sly smile growing. "Did you betray her love? Or did your original form give some offense?"

"Neither!" Makoa nearly slammed the boat onto his hip, incensed, but he heard Xinyi tumble and remembered the vomit. "She was an angry bitter woman. What is it to you?"

"You brought it up," the woman shrugged. "My apologies. I saw the elves and monkeys pursuing you, and..." She put a finger to her lips as if she were confessing a crime. "I sent them running towards the river. I hoped their pursuit of you meant you know someone I am seeking."

"Who?" Makoa asked suspiciously.

"A world traveler by the name of Shiraz, born on Glen Harrow Island."

Makoa debated the merits of lies and truth for, at minimum, half a second. "Nope. Never heard of him."

"Makoa!" Xinyi exclaimed, catching the attention of the skin slipper.

The woman smiled down. "How marvelous! I so rarely see humans exploring the world in any new way. But at such a size, it must all seem awesome and inspiring. Did you request this transformation of size, or were you also cursed?" She chuckled.

"I think it was an accident," Xinyi groaned, blinking several times.

"I'd step back," Makoa advised. "She's a little travel—"

He didn't get to finish the statement. The woman crooked a finger at Xinyi and the area filled with a shimmering mist of golden light. When the light cleared, Xinyi towered over Makoa at her usual height, with the monkey still seated on her shoulder. But the boat remained shrunken and in Makoa's monkey paw.

"Perhaps you will feel better on solid ground," the fairy remarked. "Tell me, friend, have you heard of this Shiraz?"

At her natural height, Xinyi was slightly taller than the other woman. And having been transformed, some caution was finally sneaking into her nature. She bit her lip, looking between Makoa and the stranger. But Makoa hadn't much faith that she'd do the prudent thing.

Be Careful What's Wished *For* You

Queasiness aside, Xinyi felt like kaagok. No. Wait. What was the word for shit? Kaagok was a shit *hole*. Eh—close enough. Her head pounded, she was thirsty, Makoa hadn't especially been reassuring about the captain and Xinyi was worried for her. And then there was the fairy standing in front of them, asking about Shiraz.

Makoa was doing her rules proud and flatly ignoring someone who claimed to have helped them. But Xinyi suspected that the captain's rules came about because she was used to taking care of herself alone. She must not have learned that there was more to taking care of oneself than maintaining one's bodily safety. One must also strengthen one's heart. Shiraz had a heart worth strengthening.

"May I ask why you are looking for this person?" Xinyi inquired. Makoa, in the body of a small monkey leapt up, catching onto Xinyi's left arm, and climbed her so she had a monkey on each shoulder and began to feel like a perch.

"That is practical." The fairy looked amused. Then Sweetums took a swipe at Makoa, and Makoa answered the attack in kind with Xinyi right between them and the *skin slipper* looking on with a few fingers concealing her widening smile and sparkling eyes.

"Please." Xinyi threw a hand between the squabbling primates, managing only to get slapped from two sides at once. "Makoa!"

Makoa leapt up, blowing out a heavy breath, and transformed, landing in one of the bodies she had seen already, the fairy.

"Sorry." He didn't sound all that serious.

The woman took the opportunity to answer. "I am a part of a collective of fairy; we bless the wishes of the dying. In particular the wronged dead. Shiraz was sent such a wish, but we've had trouble locating her. She goes by many names, lives in many lands, and rarely stays in one place for longer than a year. I was seeking another," she said with great emphasis, examining Xinyi closely. "When I heard heartening news! There is a bounty out for her on this very river."

There was humor in the woman's tone, *heartening news*, but Xinyi felt the words fall heavily upon her. Shouldn't it be lovely that Shiraz was owed a wish from some loved one? But it made Xinyi miss Wei. Made her sorry for all the people who must be visited by this otherwise friendly woman, to be reminded of what they lost.

And the idea that Shiraz never stayed anywhere for long saddened her.

"We do not know where she is. We were all fleeing, but in different directions," Makoa offered up.

"Oh! You have heard of her?" the fairy teased, getting a good chuckle at her own joke, which was fortunate as no one else was. The woman lifted her skirt in one hand like she would leave.

"She—" Xinyi started forward. Both Makoa and Sweetums tried to hold her back, the monkey pulling her head sideways, Makoa putting out a hand. "She has promised to deliver me safely home in a few days. We will be in Hi'mau. You can find her there."

"Tell me," the fairy asked with an intrigued upward tilt of the lips. "Is that what you would wish?"

"What?" Xinyi startled. Was the woman offering her a wish? Why? She felt like Shiraz would tug her away from this kindly woman and tell her to wish for nothing? And strangely she wanted to agree with the Shiraz in her mind, though she'd been doing the opposite of everything she said only moments ago.

"Safety," the woman explained. "Would you wish to be brought safely home? Would you wish to stay safely there?" The woman grinned. Her round features stretched so wide and welcoming, she appeared to be the most good humored woman alive. When Xinyi would have thought that was herself.

"You needn't answer me. But I suggest thinking on it. Because I can tell you that it was *someone's* wish for you. That you be *always safe*. But having met you, I am not at all sure that it suits you, adventurer."

She glanced over both her shoulders before leaning near to whisper, "The elves are closing in. In thanks for your assistance, what say you I speed your journey along?"

Makoa and Xinyi both opened their mouths to protest, but the fairy never heard. She lifted her skirt and waved it like a fan through the air, the material seeming to stretch wide enough to form a full circle of black swirling fabric before her. When it dropped, Xinyi and Makoa were some place entirely new. Shoulder deep in a rushing river.

Ahhhhh! Relief. Xinyi ducked her head under the water with a grateful groan, despite Sweetums claw digging into her shoulder. Lovely cool water. Just what she needed.

Shiraz hit the river and waded in. Another pair of boots soaked. She only had one dry pair left and they were…expensive. Beautiful and largely decorative. A frivolous purchase if ever she made one. But if anyone came across a cobbler that was also a leather artist, who offered to put a sea dragon on one boot and a fire dragon on the other like they were fighting! And they said *no*—for any reason other than a lack of funds, then they were someone Shiraz did not trust.

She dove and started swimming down river. She was an excellent swimmer and going with the current made her even faster. It was one of the few things she had been good at most of her life. Several times in childhood, it had taken fisherman being launched from the island to bring her home when she had made it out past the break waves and into the open channel between Glen Harrow and Great Island.

This was not pertinent to her current escape attempt, but she always felt bad for Great Island. It had been thusly named by the world's most pathetic explorer. An eager young thing from a tiny little island in the frozen southern sea. Who set out exploring the world and was so awed by the—*first* place— they encountered, they became convinced it must be the biggest, most important place ever. And thus recorded the rather middling size continent as "Great Island" in their records and never bothered to amend it when they learned differently. The island's fairy and dragon inhabitants, caring not at all what nonsense humans said about their land, gave it no other public name. So it stuck. People from other, bigger, and possibly better places would say *Great Island* and chuckle. Such a shame no-one spent any real time in naming it. Even Glen Harrow was better, and it was only named that because it was the *glen* where someone (not a god, if you asked Shiraz) taught the citizens to use a *harrow* to till the fields for easier planting seasons and was worshiped forever after by the steadfast people.

Still the sweet steadfast girl.

Whenever anyone called her steadfast, Shiraz felt an itch under her skin. An itch to act out, an itch to leave, an itch to be as dramatic and loud and wild as she could be. She was not a steadfast girl! Ask anyone on the steadfast island, they would tell you. She never fit.

But apparently she didn't even fit among criminals, all because she was mildly opposed to murder. *Mildly.*

Something weird was going on, but it wasn't fate. And yet Shiraz felt that old crick in her neck from standing in the stocks, her back and shoulders ached, and she could hear Elder Trent's voice admonishing her for her lack of faith.

You are too concerned with yourself, Shiraz. Our faith is not about what you believe. It doesn't matter if you believe in fate. A better question is, does fate believe in you? Does it have a purpose for you? Or are you merely a clod of dirt to be broken down and fed back into the soil?

Shiraz swam angrily, arm over aching arm. Legs pumping. Speeding down the river, until she slammed into something.

"Ouch!" Shiraz grumbled as her fingers crunched against something solid. She rolled over in the water and put her feet down. She wasn't in the deepest part of the river. Clearly, as there were two people just standing there in front of her.

"Makoa! Xinyi!" Shiraz exclaimed.

"Shiraz?" Xinyi lifted her drenched head out of the river. It looked like she'd been trying to swallow the whole thing.

Shiraz started to joke about her being thirsty, but a loud screech stopped her. "Sweetums? How did you all get here?"

"Talk later." Makoa set the shrunken River Serpent in the water and held on with both hands. "Let's get out of here."

Shiraz was not about to argue with that.

Not Suited to Safety

Once they were all on board, Shiraz shrunk the ship. Only much smaller this time. They were about the size of a water bug, *and just as fast,* Shiraz had insisted brightly, as if her surly attitude of the day before was a thing of the past. But Xinyi wasn't fooled. There was something under her surface, something angry. She was just trying hard not to let it out. Playing positive.

"Have you ever tried to catch a water bug? Being this small moves the boat at triple speed."

"Why not do it all along?" Xinyi asked in a small voice. She wasn't facing the others. Makoa and Shiraz were putting the boat to rights, but they had insisted she sit on a bench staring straight ahead because this was a bumpier ride than usual. And it was. They were tossed from side to side by spraying water and arching rocks. But Xinyi was feeling much better in terms of her stomach and head.

Her thoughts were worse, all caught up with what the fairy asked her. And what she had said about Shiraz. Makoa had yet to tell her, and Xinyi didn't feel right bringing it up first.

"We were moving against the current on Nanghi; it would have tossed us out to sea." Shiraz came up at Xinyi's shoulder. Xinyi tilted her head back. "Feeling better?" Shiraz asked with a smile.

"Much."

"Good." She held out a plate of food and a vessel of water. "Eat up, then we'll find you something dry to wear."

Xinyi had finished eating a while ago. She hadn't been able to clear the plate, but Sweetums helped. It was surprising the monkey had been allowed to stay, but aside from watching it suspiciously, Shiraz had barely acknowledged its presence.

"Ready to change?" Shiraz called out from behind Xinyi.

"I won't fit anything of yours. I should just let this dry—"

"*Again*," Xinyi and Shiraz said in unison. But where the other woman ended with a grin, Xinyi's voice died and her expression fled with it. She blinked, unsure if her mouth was open or closed.

Shiraz had disappeared below decks while Xinyi ate and changed clothing. She was back now and looking—*spectacular!*

She wore a black vest over nothing at all apparently. Low cut and tight, it boldly displayed her cleavage. The vest had many pockets of different material, some decorated with chains or odd pieces of jewelry. Her legs were covered in tight hose of teal, and a truly unique short skirt. It was made with diamonds of fabric, but no two pieces of fabric were exactly the same or even exactly the same colors. They were fitted together around a circle, in several layers, so they looked like the multi-colored petals of an inside out flower. Xinyi wanted to flick the pieces and watch it move, but with the way it clung to the captain, she didn't dare. The smuggler had also added a brand new and amazing pair of high boots. The left sported a blue serpent dragon, and the right a red fire breathing dragon. There were extra rings on her fingers, a high wrapped bracelet that curved around her arm with sharpened points at either end. And to her head she added...a crown. A golden snake curved around her hair, with its mouth open and a forked tongue sticking out. Her hair was left nearly loose but for the front twisted out of her face, letting one see the incredible volume of wild curls like the churning waters shaking up the boat.

There was not one subtle aspect to her attire. She no longer looked like a common criminal. She was a queen, or an infamous assassin, or a wicked fairy of temptation. It was everything. Xinyi couldn't breathe. And when Shiraz moved, she jangled! The woman had tied a strand of bells around her right boot. No. Nothing subtle at all. How had Xinyi never realized before how wildly her pulse could race for a look so… obvious.

"Wow!" Xinyi breathed out. It was the first word she could manage, and the blush and flattered smile on the smuggler's face was well worth the embarrassment. Maybe it wasn't just the look speeding her pulse.

"Come on." Shiraz held out a hand. "I think I have something for you. If I can make myself look this good, imagine what I can do for someone so beautiful already."

Xinyi startled, and the captain rolled her eyes.

"Quit pretending, you know you're gorgeous." She stepped forward. Taking Xinyi's hand in her own, she dragged her to her feet. Sweetums hopped off Xinyi's shoulder, chasing a butterfly that was circling the ship. Xinyi saw it from the corner of her eye, and surely she should be distracted by a butterfly that was bigger than her, but she was all caught up in the captain. "If you don't get moving, I'm going to start charging by the compliment."

Xinyi grinned at her back, unable to resist touching a few of the petals on her skirt. As the captain walked, the petals swayed and shifted. She couldn't take her eyes off them. She'd never stared at someone's behind before, but she might have to take up the practice. This skirt was obscenely entertaining. "Where did you find this skirt?"

"I made it," she replied.

Of course she did! No one else would have.

"Over several years. Every new place I went I bought or *stole* fabric I loved. Like the Serpent, I had a vision of who I wanted to present to the world, and I needed to make it a reality. It's a bit much for everyday wear though. But you always want to dress for the grotto."

Below deck, Shiraz had laid out a selection of skirts, pants, dresses, and extra fabric of different hues. "I wouldn't have thought you the sort of woman to know anything about fabric or sewing," Xinyi admitted.

The captain laughed. She lifted a long tunic with an asymmetrical v neck that made it appear to be a vest. It was long, but had very high slits on either side, and tie closures. Nodding, she set it aside and lifted a bright pink jacket that was clearly made in Loqwan. It had the signature deep embroidered sleeves and ribbon tie closures.

"This was not my size, but I couldn't resist the shade of pink, or these wicked birds on the sleeves. I stole it right before we met yesterday."

Xinyi shoved a hand over her mouth so as not to encourage Shiraz with a laugh. Bragging about her thefts. *Yesterday.* Was it truly only yesterday? It felt like they'd been together so much longer.

"I had plans to turn it into a cape, but I think it may fit you just right. Why don't you take that dress off and get dry?" She turned her back, looking over the other bits on the bed. Her voice sounded pensive as she built Xinyi an outfit. "I grew up among a community who refer to themselves as the 'steadfast people.' Steadfast in their commitment to staying on their island, no matter how the sea eats it away. Steadfast in doing the same things generation after generation, reading the same stories, wearing the same clothes, saying the same words. *Steadfast!*"

Her shoulders stiffened, and her hands fisted. This was an enlightening new side she was displaying, with her face turned away.

"We weren't allowed vibrant colors, or really any colors. All we wore were shades of brown and black, or white at funerals. Always in the same combinations. I hated it. I used to collect flowers in this exact shade of pink and make crowns that could only be worn in secret." She breathed out a small laugh. "Anyway, the first thing every female is taught is to keep her eyes on the ground and say *yes elder*. The second is how to sew. How to measure, and cut, and seam. I was convinced that both of those lessons were pointless. I took every opportunity to escape saying *yes elder* or sewing my father's and my brothers' clothes. When I was forced to sew, I made things no one was allowed to wear. Wasting fabric and getting punished but rebelling because I must." As she spoke, a picture formed in Xinyi's mind of a young woman who knew she was meant for a different life. One who questioned and was full of passions in a quiet world.

She was an interesting character. The type Xinyi might enjoy writing. The type who did the things Xinyi could not. Did not. She couldn't picture Shiraz ever looking at the ground and saying yes. But she could imagine her with a hand on the back of her head, forcing it down as she fought to shout her true feelings. Growing more and more defiant, until she turned criminal just so the world could hear her voice. Qiu could have been such a girl if she had grown up as a princess. Yinuo might have been such a girl before Xinyi knew her. Would either of them have fought back and forged a path alone, as this woman had? Or would they have borne it?

Xinyi never felt like she fit either. Yet no one had to teach her to bow her head and say yes. She taught herself. She found comfort in making other people comfortable. But she was glad this woman had not done so. It would not have suited her at all.

The boat lurched to the side. Xinyi swayed with it, nearly reaching out to steady herself on the captain, but she managed to keep her footing. Shiraz had not even turned around. Was she sure Xinyi could handle it, or afraid to invade her privacy?

"What do you think that was?" Xinyi asked in a small voice.

"A fish most likely. We're pretty small. All they have to do is swim beneath us to create a wake that tosses us. Makoa can handle it."

"What goes on first?" Xinyi held her hand forward. She wanted more of the story. And she wanted to see the captain's face as she told it. But she had a feeling Shiraz would not turn around until Xinyi was dressed.

Shiraz lifted a pair of pants that were loose at the top but got progressively smaller. They had a string to tie at the waist, but when it was loose, they appeared to have enough fabric to fit two women at once. They were in an even deeper pink than the jacket on the bed; they would look well together. Shiraz set the pants on Xinyi's hand. Their fingers brushed as she pulled away, leaving Xinyi breathless.

"When I finally left," Shiraz continued, sounding tingly and short of air herself, "I was sure I would never use *any* of their lessons. I set out to prove that they were nonsense." She laughed at herself. "I was right about that first one. Never let someone tell you it is your duty to say yes, when you know the answer is no."

Xinyi didn't say anything this time, just stretched out her hand and Shiraz passed her the tunic vest.

"But I am grateful to know how to sew. It has been endlessly useful!" Having given Xinyi enough time to pull on the tunic, she turned to observe the effect. The tunic was very tight, slightly smashing Xinyi's chest, though it was almost entirely covered, the tunic having only a tiny v shaped dip above her collar bone.

"May I?" Shiraz had a wrap skirt in her hands that was far too small around to cover Xinyi, but she reached around Xinyi's back and draped it like a train, tying the long ends at the side. She lifted the tunic to cover the ties. Then loosened the ties along the tunic's sides until they hung open. It gave Xinyi more breathing space around the chest but revealed two triangles of skin at her sides.

"Are you comfortable?" the captain asked.

"Yes. Sorry," Xinyi whispered. "I'm stretching your clothes."

The captain grinned. "Excellent. Then I'll get to remember how close it was to your skin the next time I put it on." She bit down on her bottom lip as Xinyi stared at her, unable to speak.

Shaking her head, the captain stepped back, indicating the extra fabric on the bed. "I can use the swaths of fabric to make a sash beneath the tunic, or tie them around your torso instead of it," she offered. "Cover any skin you like. I want you to be comfortable."

Xinyi was surprised by the offer. But she shouldn't be. The captain talked all manner of sarcasm, but she behaved considerately. "This is fine. Fun. Like pretending to be someone else."

Shiraz went back to adjusting things, making it comfortable.

"I am surprised you are grateful. Even if it was useful. You still seem angry."

The captain lifted the jacket and held out the first sleeve. Xinyi slid an arm in easily. "I am angry. Just not about the sewing, nor about learning to cook, or clean, and to respect the tides. Someone told me, after I first left, when I talked about these things more, that I should be thankful for *all* the lessons, because they shaped me. But that is nonsense." She helped Xinyi into the second sleeve, adjusting the front so it fell open at an angle and tying an exceptionally neat bow at the base of Xinyi's throat. "I thank them for the things that served me, and condemn them for the lessons that were false or harmful. A thing, a people, or a place can be bad and good at the same time. I learned that long ago."

They were quiet for a long while before Shiraz stepped back to observe her work.

"You look...stunning." Shiraz's voice was soft and warm. "Like an adventuring princess. But it's missing something." Xinyi wondered if she would somehow miraculously produce a pair of shoes of the right size.

She bent down, lifting Xinyi's wedding bag, causing the oddest catch in Xinyi's throat. Her heart raced and she thought she might cry. Shiraz slipped it over her head, hanging it down to the right, following the line of the vest. And Xinyi heard her words from the day before again. *Don't let anything you love or value out of your sight. The world is full of thieves and liars. People much worse than me.*

"Perfect." The captain smiled softly.

Xinyi gripped onto the bag with one hand. There was so much kindness in this woman, but she was so used to fighting to be seen and respected. Apparently Xinyi had stirred up all that inner strife in their first moments of acquaintance. But look at this thief, this liar, gently honoring the things Xinyi loved.

Neither one of them was wholly bad or good, were they? And she might never have seen it if she were *always safe.*

No. Xinyi didn't dare voice her stirring thoughts, but she had to acknowledge them inside. *No. She didn't want to be* always *safe. That wouldn't suit her at all.*

Much Scarier than Adventure

"We failed to negotiate this before, but princess makeovers are not a gratis service on the—"

Xinyi reached out and covered Shiraz's lips with her hand. She was grinning, and her pupils were dilated enough to look like tiny black whirlpools devouring everything in sight. It made Shiraz tingly all over just having those eyes on her. Xinyi's hand on her. But she needed to stop thinking this way.

"Two percent. No more." Xinyi's tone was firm but playful and Shiraz couldn't help but grin beneath Xinyi's fingers.

She knew the other woman could feel it. Xinyi's gaze shifted down to her own hand. But she didn't jerk away. Shiraz didn't move either. Tempted as she was to kiss those fingers.

This was the strangest job. Perhaps of her whole life, but she hadn't had time for comparisons. She wasn't used to talking about Glen Harrow, and certainly not in a way that acknowledged its bits of good. Yet that had been easier than saying what she really wanted. Easier than telling the princess again and again how lovely she was to be near. How her joy felt like sunshine and cool breezes. How her energy and enthusiasm were an inspiration. It was easier than telling her she need never pretend to be someone else. Who she was already was staggering. It was easier than telling her that seeing her standing drenched in the river next to Makoa had been such a painful relief. They'd only known each other *one day*, but Shiraz was already caring not just for her safety but her happiness as well. She wanted to tell her so much, so she kept her mouth shut.

"Unless you have shoes in my size." Xinyi removed her hand.

It took Shiraz a second to remember what Xinyi was talking about. Payment. Shiraz shook her head.

"Sorry. I'll try to remember to take up a collection of women's footwear." Shiraz headed for the stairs to the upper deck. "For now, your slippers are drying by the fire. Provided your new buddy doesn't throw them in for sport, you should have some crunchy, but dry and thoroughly impractical footwear."

"I didn't expect this level of adventure," Xinyi grumbled.

"Always expect adventure on The River Serpent, princess. Always." It was said flirtatiously, but today Xinyi was returning all Shiraz's wit with thoughtful expressions. It was uncomfortable. Why wouldn't she laugh, or tease, or tell her to stop? Shiraz tensed as an uncomfortable urge tickled her tongue. It had to be done, her mother would never approve of her if she didn't do this, and...she wouldn't either. Azaqif paax.

"I am sorry, about...some things. Yesterday, you...got on my bad side and I was a bit of—"

"Ewsuul," Xinyi supplied with a giant, tickled grin.

Shiraz's eyes widened in horror, and she had to fight a grin. Even she had never used that curse. "Do you always snoop through other people's things, princess?"

"Only when they tumble onto me while I'm locked in tiny rooms without warning."

"So you read the book and decided to start with perhaps the worst, certainly the most disgusting curse inside?" Shiraz asked, a small snort escaping. Though she fought it, she could feel herself turning red.

"It jumped out at me," Xinyi said, looking a bit embarrassed herself. "Like I said, the room was somewhat unsettled."

Shiraz shook her head. "I'm not apologizing for saving your life."

"Was my life under threat? I thought it was your ship."

Shiraz bit down on her lip, moving in on the princess slowly. "It's no wonder you were seasick. You should never read while carried in a pelican's throat pouch."

Xinyi threw a hand over her lips like she would vomit again, but her shoulders shook with laughter.

She dropped her hand. "Imagine adding that to a story."

They both giggled. "Jian wouldn't know what to do with herself."

"Oh, and here I was imagining V."

They both exploded with laughter.

"I wish I had a collection of books like these. Books from all over. So different from my own, and so lovely. Everyone should see stories different from what they might imagine. These books, they pull me out of my own imaginings and into another world! Are..." she hesitated. "Are many of them Makoa's?"

"Not one. He reads, but he doesn't collect." Shiraz felt her lips opening, felt herself wanting to tell Xinyi everything. Tell her about Snapdragon, the first fairy she'd befriended who brought her stories from around the world. Wanted to tell her about Elder Trent finding her favorite, the Book of Anolani, and ripping it to shreds and setting it on fire while she was held before the village to be shamed. She wanted to tell her about searching the world to find that book again and about waking up in the middle of the night with words from the story filling her consciousness and having to write them down, having to get up and go searching again.

Wanted to tell her about the Singing Hills and her quest. Wanted to have her copy of Jian's adventures so she could pick the author's brain about her favorite bits. Wanted to invite her to stay.

But they'd only known each other for one day. And it was frightening. And there Xinyi was smiling at her with bright, interested eyes, ready to hear it all, and take it all in, because—it was part of her adventure. Shiraz was just *part of the adventure*.

Like Makoa had been when he'd first transformed in front of Shiraz. Like becoming a thief had been. Like spending a year with Danesh running around Reethurn taking vengeance for money. Like the tattoo on Shiraz's arm and the deals she'd made to make her ship. Everything had felt like an adventure at one time and Shiraz had embraced it all. But she wasn't looking for adventure any longer.

Xinyi didn't feel like an adventure. She felt much scarier than that. Much more real. So Shiraz smiled.

"Pick one, before you leave. Start your own collection. For a small fee of course."

This Is Why We Can't Have Nice Things

Shiraz ran up the stairs from the lower decks. Ran. The princess followed behind at a more considered pace.

"Presenting Princess Xinyi, the adventurer," Shiraz intoned dramatically as Xinyi stepped onto the deck.

Makoa cheered as Xinyi blushed and twirled, playing with the wrap skirt she was wearing like a train. Sweetums hopped off the canopy where she had been running around shouting at water bugs that got too near the ship and rushed at the princess. Xinyi laughed as the monkey climbed all over her before finding a comfortable spot on her shoulder, curling her tail around the woman's neck.

"You know, the monkey sort of completes the look. You could be one of your characters," Shiraz teased.

"What would you know about my characters?" the princess probed coyly. "You think they're melodramatic, right?"

Makoa snorted, ready to reveal the truth. And Shiraz could tell, changing the subject to rules for the princess to follow at the grotto.

Makoa had listened to the pair of them below deck, their laughter and their quiet. Shiraz really liked the princess, but clearly, to Makoa anyway, Shiraz wasn't ready for her feelings. Something was putting her on edge, and as soon as he told her about the skin slipper and the wish, Shiraz would go back to feeling her brother's loss as acutely as she had for the last year.

He wondered if Shiraz realized that she was no longer driven by the Singing Hills. Over the years, her quest to find them had morphed. When she first set out, she was determined and enthusiastic; she was going to find this place that everyone told her wasn't real, Makoa included. Could he have perhaps tried a little harder? Explained that even in the story of Anolani, a legend from his birth nation, the Singing Hills were never meant to be taken as an actual place? Should he have explained that the love story that pulled her around the world was a tragedy? That Anolani and Omea never found a home where they were accepted and free, but in fact died in the volcanic eruption in the last chapter and went to a mythical paradise?

Maybe. But...well it was more fun this way. At first.

Then she got older, was disappointed a few too many times and the Singing Hills became a quiet promise to her heart, some beautiful reward waiting at the end of her suffering. Which was a fairly accurate description of the Singing Hills, so...Makoa...just let that be. But in recent years he probably should have explained, because her quest changed again. After her brother's death, after she returned to Glen Harrow and saw her father happily remarried with a new daughter. After she'd seen him honored among the elders who had ostracized their family as a result of **his** choices. Since then, her quest for the hills had altered again. It was now an angry weighted chain around her neck. She must find the islands, because it was her purpose in life. Now it seemed meaner to rob her of the quest. It might break her spirit. She no longer loved them. No longer loved magic, or quests. She had given away so much of her love with hoping that she was no longer willing to love anything she did not already have. Which was likely what held her back with the princess.

Would it change anything, knowing her brother had thought of her in his dying moments?

What if the thought wasn't a blessing? The Battle Born exacted revenge for the dead as well as granting wishes of comfort. He wanted to be hopeful. But he had been worried for Shiraz for a while now, protecting her when he could, and he didn't know how to stop.

As the conversation fell off, Xinyi wandered towards the aft bow, examining the rocks in the river that towered over them like mountains making it seem like evening though it was only shortly after noon.

Makoa watched the direction of her eyes, noticing the moss growing up the side with little spots of white and purple flowers. One of the rock-mountains had a water carved peak that bent outward, nearly a hook and was a darker vein of rock than the rest.

It was entirely ordinary; he would have looked past it another day, but today it was inspiring. He liked the addition of the princess. The novelty of her. But it would wear off, he was sure. He was sure.

"So I bumped into an old acquaintance in the jungle, and the more I think about it, the more certain I become that I know who is after the boat," Shiraz remarked casually in the silence. She was perched on the bow beside Makoa, snacking on a nectar fruit.

She appeared annoyed, stiff, and pensive. One of her hands was clenched around the hull of her ship like she would prevent anyone from taking it with her hand alone.

It hadn't occurred to Makoa to ask how she escaped. He'd sort of thought that Dao had let her go. The elf occasionally did things against the king's wishes because she knew Aiattaua would be pleased.

"Felicia," Shiraz said the name as if it was an answer to all questions.

"What, she needs to sink another of your ships?" Makoa snapped, quickly set to anger by that particular woman.

He felt Xinyi's attention turn their way, but Makoa and Shiraz were focused on each other.

"She just…ran out of the jungle as I was running through it. And offered to distract the elves, **but not to kill them**, so that I could escape." Shiraz shook her head disbelieving.

None of that sounded like the woman who claimed to have been birthed of a goddess and a human. And though he knew Shiraz had never believed the woman's mother was indeed a deity, Makoa was more easily convinced. Felicia, the fiery demigoddess of Xichotyl, did possess superhuman strength, speed, and temper! In addition to her powers of transformation. They hadn't seen her since she and Shiraz escaped prison together, hopped on Shiraz's old boat and fled Ninn. They only made it to a few miles off the coast of Minn before the demigoddess threw a fit and burnt through the hull of their ship, sinking it! One acquaintance was enough for Makoa.

"The thing is—it feels narcissistic to assume she is only here for me. But I think that's what she's counting on. She wants the Serpent for something, and she's willing to do anything, pay a bounty, trick me into thinking she's on my side." Shiraz snorted. "For a moment, I was running away, and it felt like fate had stepped in to save me for some greater purpose."

Shiraz chuckled hard; Makoa worried she was about to cry again. But her eyes rose to his with piercing rage.

"But *fate* doesn't have any plans for me. I just can't say the same about women who transform into dragons and spit lava."

"Spit lava!" Xinyi breathed out, excited.

There was nothing exciting about it. Lava heated the air, burnt holes in ships, and singed flesh without actually touching. It was not exciting.

"Right," Makoa said, unsettled. He and Shiraz weren't fighters. They were happy to help fighters. But they were runners by nature. And they couldn't do that with the princess on board. "So…how do we want to handle this?" Makoa asked carefully.

"Ideally," Shiraz said, but just let the word sit there as her gaze fell on Xinyi. When she started up again, Makoa wasn't at all sure her words were what she would have said before. "Meet with her. See if she is open to chartering the ship. For nothing short of all the money in existence as collateral for my ship's inevitable smoldering demise."

"Wouldn't it be better to…run?" Xinyi asked what Makoa was thinking. "If this woman is so dangerous and is after your ship. I mean…I want my treasure back, and I know that must be part of why you—"

Shiraz shook her head. She stepped into the space between Makoa and Xinyi and held out her left arm. She removed the leather bracelet she'd put over her tattoo.

"Azaqif!" Makoa exclaimed. He dropped the steering pole, uncaring, and took Shiraz's arm in his hand. The pole slid into the river, entirely ignored.

There were red, bubbling burns around her tattoo, eating in on it. "How long has this been going on?"

The steering pole shot out of the river, landing on the deck with a clatter, thanks to one of Shiraz's many spells. Only Xinyi jumped.

"Just since last night," Shiraz said dismissively.

"Doesn't that hurt? Where is that cream I saw you with?" the princess asked and immediately ducked under the canopy rummaging through baskets.

Shiraz went on thoughtfully. "I get the distinct impression she'll find me wherever I go."

"Aiattaua has to be a part of this," Makoa growled. "Is that why you didn't tell me? Did you think I would take his side?"

"No. I just thought you'd tell me you told me so and I never should have gotten the tattoo from him in the first place." Shiraz shrugged.

"And you were right!" Makoa shouted only to be cut off.

Xinyi returned, undercutting his justified rage. She took Shiraz's wrist gently in her hand and rubbed cream over the burns.

"I told you so! I knew this would come back to bite you in the ass."

"Ngok," the princess said under her breath. Apparently someone had found Shiraz's curse book. She didn't pronounce it right, ignoring the n as if it were silent. Makoa ignored her, but it was clear Shiraz could not.

"Nnn-ghok," she said quietly, making it two syllable word, the second sounding like a click in the back of her throat. Xinyi tried it a few times.

Shiraz's eyes rested warmly on the princess's fingers, and there was a smile on her lips though Makoa was chastising her.

"Now we can't do what we always do and run! Now we might lose the Serpent. When it was finally what you needed! Now we may have to start from scratch," Makoa continued his lecture.

"Thank you," Shiraz said softly and pulled her arm away. Then she met Makoa's eyes sadly.

"No." She shook her head, eyes shiny with unspent tears. "No more starting from scratch. No more searching. I made a promise to myself to quit putting us through this. I swore if I couldn't find the hills by the end of the year, I was done searching. Same goes if we lose the boat," she said with a shrug, as if it wasn't the most painful thing she'd ever said. "If we lose the boat, we...get another, or find another means of travel, and we...go find a way to break your curse, and I travel around with you collecting stories. No more searching for the Singing Hills. You were probably right about that too. They were never anything but the invention of a beautiful story that I needed to be true."

"Shiraz." Makoa's heart sank. "I never wanted you to give up."

"I haven't yet. Not exactly. I mean...maybe we can still manage to get to the grotto, find the princess's thieves, get her treasure, and get out of here before Felicia catches up to us. Maybe we can get Aiattaua to just remove the tattoo. I'm not giving up. I'm just...thinking ahead. I'm not about to fight her and risk someone I love over a boat."

She pulled Makoa's cheek to her and kissed gently. His sister. A tingle ran down his spine, and his head felt light. He felt all his skins at once. Every form he'd ever taken on, shivering, like a fever had spiked within his soul.

Had it not been for the sudden and unexpected disaster, he might have stumbled in fear of what he felt inside.

Instead, he fell over from a massive impact with something invisible, shaking the entire vessel and making it leap to its regular size without warning.

Azaqif! What now?

An Introvert's Nightmare

E uphemia Precocious Arrow was a witch of some years, some dimension and some (but very little) repute. And she liked it that way. After some centuries of existence, she had found a glen near a quiet river with a particular stone in its soil that worked wonders with her magic. In this glen, she made her home, placing a pair of its short legs into the river and planting another two into the soil. There she waited with joyous anticipation for the end times to come and destroy that most disgusting of nuisances: *other* beings.

Euphemia had always been fascinated with the concept of "end times." Fascinated with how different legends dreamed the world would end, and why all of them seemed to believe this would come to pass. But in this secluded glen, left to her own curious devices, she learned a particular legend that spoke of the end times being ushered in by four dragons of doom, well, five, if you counted the chaos dragon who was to awaken the others. But the main four each served to rid the world of a particular evil: one hunger, one illness, one war, and one that would free the world of death. Which all seemed too chipper to her, until she read the text again and realized their method of freeing the world from suffering was to end all life. Death of all meant no death ever after, or so she read it. And all of it would start right here!

Ah, bliss. So she stayed reading portends and waiting for the dragon of chaos to arise and start the end cycle. She had not stepped beyond the small outer porch of her home in a good seventy-five-years.

She called them good, despite how long the doom dragons were taking to get here, because she had not much been bothered by the outside world. Had drunk, once each morning and twice in the afternoon, her own brew of caffeine and chocolate. Had eaten once a day a slice or three of pie, though, some slices were more circular and larger in nature than one might strictly call a slice. But when one did not associate with other people, one did not need to stick to any strict understanding of language, mathematics—or any other rule.

She sat, nude, in her comfortable chair, next to her chilly fire—she enjoyed the dance of flames but abhorred the heat and had thus spelled them to work properly years ago. On Wednesdays if one of them was not busy, she would chat via crystal ball with her friend Candelaria Maidenhair Widget, who was of some few years less, a few dimensions less impressive, and of some (perhaps more) repute. But nevertheless a friend.

She was in the middle of one of these chats, though it must be noted that today was a *Friday*, but allowances must be made, she supposed, for her friend to have conflicting *dance parties*—the audacity! But, to the point of the plot, she was at this moment in the midst of a conversation, yelling at her friend, as she tried in vain to explain that the pointy hat movement among witches from her childhood was not a mistake of fashion, but indeed the pinnacle of fashion and practicality.

"The conical point focuses the cosmic energy. It's your generation and the wand waving that makes no sense! You're all so busy trying to *look* impressive when the magic comes from the words and the potions and the runes."

"You forgot bones, cards and naps, old lady," her friend mocked.

"I didn't forget them! Never underestimate the power of a mid-spell nap. I cannot count the number of times I've gone to sleep with a spell cooking and woken up to it done without the seven hours of stirring old broom-era spell books require."

"You know broomers. All talk."

The witches cackled, loud and long and so sonic that the crystal ball in the center of Euphemia's table cracked in three new places, letting through more light, and distorting the image of her one century younger friend. Euphemia did not mind.

"I've got some notes on that asteroid summoning spell," Candelaria said into the absence of laughter. "Siti thinks the last one worked. It just summoned too small of a space rock. You heard about what happened to Cyrus?"

Euphemia rubbed her hands together gleefully. This was it. If the doom dragons couldn't be bothered to come on their own, she would awaken them. Perhaps she was the fifth doom-dragon all along! Perhaps that was why she'd found her way here!

"She's found five more witches who are willing to join the call."

"At last. Soon we will die in a bath of chocolate and coffee."

"And burning fire from the explosion of the planet," Candelaria said dryly. She was not backing out; she just liked to point out when Euphemia turned poetic over practical.

"Eh," Euphemia waved a hand. She dug around under the tattered cloth on her table for a writing utensil. Something to write on would be provided by the cloth itself. It had been serving this purpose for many a month now. "Hold on, hold on." She shifted the cloth around and around, reading little notes. "Left eye's always blue when lying. All blue-eyed people are liars anyway."

"You need a better system."

"The chaos dragon is not a dragon. It rides upon the serpent's back." Euphemia read the statement with a question in her voice. "A dragon rider…but that could be anyone. Dragons are notorious ride sluts; all you have to be is a small child, or a woman with rage issues and they take to the sky burning anything you like."

"Hey, don't slut shame."

"Says the slut," Euphemia muttered, annoyed Candelaria had heard her. Wasn't she reading in her mind?

"You had one of your coffee induced epiphanies and scribbled that. Remember the picture you asked for?"

"No. Did you draw it?"

"I will," Candelaria sighed put upon. "I have actual clients you know. So many people need their futures drawn."

Euphemia waved an impatient hand at her friend and went back to examining her cloth. "Draw on the moon for better coffee. Hmm." Euphemia forgot what she was looking for. *That idea had potential.*

"You already tried it! Just write on the table. I don't know why you want to improve your coffee anyway; that just means more hours awake and I haven't heard you say you felt rested since we met."

"Coffee is delicious and addictive. At three years old, I had a sip and haven't stopped wanting it since. Anyway, its purpose isn't to make one feel rested, but to feel happy. And how could I feel rested with you around? You are exhau—"

The word was cut off by a giant crash and a string of expletives so foul not even Candelaria would repeat them, and she'd been privy to the other witch's mouth for centuries.

A window cracked and crashed, spilling bad luck on the floor. Some people, she knew, found a broken mirror to be bad luck, but an inability to see oneself clearly was always beneficial. Whereas an influx of dirt, bugs, and worst of all guests to one's home were the real bad luck.

Euphemia pushed creakily to her hairy feet. The sound her bones made at the forced movement was nearly as loud as the crash that created a second door to her home not four feet from the first. Impractical.

Euphemia was in for a terrible inconvenience, and she didn't mean fixing the hole in her wall. She meant the worst of all the world's terrors, the fifth...well, sixth, she supposed as she really did count the chaos dragon, even if it was just a dragon rider. So the sixth doom-dragon of the—long awaited and annoyingly late—apocalypse.

She was in for guests.

Does Fate Believe in You?

It happened all at once; Shiraz's heart never had a chance to catch up. She kissed Makoa on the cheek, offering to give up her life-long dream if only to keep him safe, and—as if the universe and fate were laughing at her—everything exploded. The snake bracelet contracted around her wrist, searingly hot and so tight it felt like it might break bone. The boat leapt in size, lurched and the boards at the front of the ship splintered, shoved inwards as they connected with something solid. A house appeared, half in the water and half on land with bony-looking legs that seemed like they might pick up and walk away and walls of sparkling stones and hardened earth that should have been impossible to miss.

But despite all of that the most dramatic thing was Makoa.

Shiraz had a hand stretched towards him but couldn't touch. She kept trying to grab him, but he was changing shape too rapidly, shifting through his myriad of forms. In the space of ten seconds he went through five different men, two women, a merman, a snake, a cat, a bear, and a few birds. Shiraz clenched her fists and bore her teeth, ready to start attacking someone. Her heart felt like it was being trampled by horses, dragged over the jagged rocks at the bottom of the river, and watching her mother's body carried away by the waves again and again and again. And it could only be worse for Makoa.

He stopped changing form suddenly. His eyes were so wide and terrified that it was clear he was no more sure than she that he wouldn't start changing again at any second. Shiraz gripped tight onto his muscular arm. He was in a form she'd seen before, his friend, Kapuni. The man was tall, muscular, beautiful really with long wavy hair, chiseled features, and easy smiles. But nothing about him looked easy at the moment. Shiraz was sure she was holding Makoa too tightly, but he gripped her arm in return, as desperate as she felt. Their eyes met briefly, full of fear and love. Then Shiraz jerked her gaze away, catching sight of the tumbled princess. She looked dusty and frightened, but uninjured. Shiraz registered that the persistent screeching was Sweetums, hopping up and down on the deck and yelling at the occupant of the house. A very good idea.

"Azongma sifvao!" Shiraz shouted at the short, elderly—nude—woman, clearly a witch, with the smoky crystal ball on the table beside her and the usual house. "What did you do to us?"

"Me, a curse bringer?" the woman shouted back, equally belligerent. "Who just put a hole in whose house?"

Shiraz's neck felt so stiff it might break, and her eyes were beginning to go cloudy with sweat, or tears; she didn't care which. Something was terribly wrong, and she couldn't calm down.

Sweetums leapt up onto the splintered end of the River Serpent to shake a fist at the witch.

"Useless threats. I'm three centuries old, baby, what makes you think I'm scared of you, or anyone connected with you?"

"Four and a half centuries," a casual disembodied voice corrected and a head swiveled into view in the crystal ball.

Kuffik, two witches! Shiraz's free hand was clenched so tight, it pulsed and was shooting pain up her arm.

"Stay out of this," the nude witch snapped, never taking her eyes off Shiraz and her crew.

Shiraz was drawing in a deep breath, in preparation for another fight, when she felt Xinyi move up along side her and slip her hand over Shiraz's clenched fist, running gentle fingers over it. Shiraz's breath escaped in a quiet shudder, and her fist unfurled hesitantly, allowing Xinyi to mesh their fingers together. She was squeezed gently on one side with Makoa gripping her tight on the other.

"Give me one reason why I shouldn't kill you all where you stand and dissolve your boat into a smattering of dust?" the witch threatened, with her hands on her hips and her large drooping breasts jiggling. All of her was jiggling really.

Shiraz heard Xinyi stifle a gasp, or a laugh; it was hard to say.

"Chocolate would be better," the vaguely familiar floating head put in. "If it is going to be there anyway, might as well have a snack. Oooh, and save me the big guy."

"As candy or man?" the witch in the room inquired, and the threatening nature of her stance shifted. She leaned a hand on the table and crossed her ankles.

"Either. No, both! I could work with both," the perhaps equally old witch in the crystal ball said suggestively.

The humor of the situation hit Shiraz all at once, seeming to hit Makoa at the same time. His hand on her arm loosened, and he snorted softly.

"He'll melt all over you," the nudist remarked.

"Sounds like she'd enjoy that," Shiraz commented dryly, just as the woman in question remarked, "That could be fun."

Makoa groaned, so it was unlikely he expected to enjoy any such thing, but the witch in the orb cracked up, as did the nudist. Makoa tried for an easy expression, winking at the women. And Xinyi grinned in thoroughly overwhelmed but excited amusement. Shiraz meanwhile still felt like she'd been pummeled and might never be the same her again. Sea Spirits! Maybe fate did have a plan for her. But if so, it was clearly to drive her insane.

"Do you remember when you were little, Euphemia, and the spring equinox fairy would leave tiny chocolate humans wrapped in candy eggs for you to find?" The floating head in the cracked magic orb, presumably another witch, asked. "And you'd eat them as you searched, your face completely covered in melting chocolate?"

"No." The nudist observed Makoa through narrowed eyes.

Makoa hoped his silent smiles and nods were polite but uncomfortable enough to get the subject dropped. He thought he was being very understanding about the jokes despite the whirlwind of feelings going on inside.

The floating head rolled her eyes. "He looks to me like a grown-up spring fairy treat! That was the point."

Kapuni, Makoa's friend whose form he was currently using, might have been more tolerant in his place. He was used to such responses to his muscular frame, wavy hair, and winsome smile. Kapuni used it to his advantage, becoming the print model for his family's adventure tours. They lived on Seifei'a, the ugliest of all the seventeen islands in the Ooloo'a chain, and home to a tiny hostile sand dragon species, yet still they got more visitors than the garden island. All because of his ads. They called him the siren king of Ooloo'a.

Makoa had never been as handsome as his friend. And now after the years of transformations, he rarely held onto a form long enough to be objectified. So he hadn't developed a sense of humor about it. And right now…he felt queasy, weak, and uncomfortable. Shiraz's hand squeezing him so tight that it ached was a relief. Helping him feel like he was here. Really here, despite the fear that at any moment he might change against his will again. Might lose the only comfort he had found in this curse, his modicum of control. He felt like he might lose himself as he had when they slammed through the magical barrier. Might come apart.

That was what it felt like transforming so fast and so out of control —Unspooling. Not knowing any part of who he was, or what he was doing. Shiraz kept asking if he was okay, if he was sure, if he needed anything. He could feel her nerves building with every nod or shake of his head, but he couldn't say this aloud. He didn't know what to do with it. What if it kept happening? What if the witch who cursed him had put a ticking clock on his spell as she had Henri's? But had neglected to tell him? What if he was coming apart? What if his failure to find a true love would mean not only losing his old self, but this self as well?

But Shiraz was gripping onto him like she would cling on even if death wanted to rip him away, and it helped. She caught his eyes, and he knew she knew that she'd have to let go to get out of here. He took in a gulp of air and nodded. She waited a few seconds longer and let go. Both of them holding still, waiting.

But Makoa didn't change again. He clung to Kapuni's form for dear life. Because…right now, he felt more like his old self, his first cursed self, his frightened and angry and unsure self more than he had in years. And Kapuni he understood; he had been a friend. Kapuni was easy with the world, even when it was not easy on him.

Shiraz's nerves made her move. She climbed over the side of the ship and hopped down to land in the witch's home, showing off brilliant confidence he knew she wasn't feeling.

"Well now, let's see how bad the damage is, shall we?" she asked, more to herself than anyone else. Her hands kept clenching and relaxing as she examined the hull of the ship stuck in a house, destabilizing both. Makoa helped the princess off of the ship and moved towards Shiraz, desperate to feel like he could fix the crumbling house which looked like he felt.

An odd thought shifted through him. What if he wasn't coming undone? What if the spell was? What if...that weird chill that had raced through him when Shiraz kissed his cheek was the spell, being broken by a kiss of true love? What if it never had a thing to do with romance at all?

The O.G. Witch

"**B**arge in and stare at me like I'm a show witch! This generation has no manners," the old, naked witch grumbled loudly as she put on a robe. Xinyi supposed it was a reaction to her own wide eyes and open mouth. And she wanted to reassure the woman, tell her to wear whatever she wanted, but she couldn't. It wasn't just the witch; it was everything!

Sweetums tried to leap off her shoulder, intent on swinging on one of the many hanging pots around the room. Xinyi supposed they looked like a great source of entertainment, but she held onto the creature, though Sweetums protested, swatting at Xinyi.

"Such prudes," her friend in the orb agreed, her tone vague and distracted as she watched Makoa and Shiraz. "But such *pretty* creatures they all are."

Xinyi had to agree. She'd yet to meet a creature on this trip—outside of Nanghi—who she did not find beautiful. Even the witches both had striking beauty about them. Euphemia's grey eyes and matching jungle of curls gave her a secretive beauty that was balanced by her curvy form and furry feet. And her friend with softly falling white hair, cheeks wrinkled from years of smiles, and nearly golden eyes had a compelling sultry appeal. And Shiraz, when she'd stepped out on the deck showing every side of her personality at once, the bold, the illegal, the soft, the tempting, Xinyi had—

"Trollop," Euphemia said dryly.

Xinyi startled, swallowing uncomfortably, unsure if the woman was referring to her friend or Xinyi. Could she read thoughts?

Xinyi's mouth lingered wide. There were likely bugs flying through, deciding if this would be a cozy place to start a family. And she couldn't bring herself to point out that the robe the woman had selected did not conceal *any* part of her anatomy, being entirely sheer.

Shiraz and Makoa braced themselves on the ground and began shoving at their vessel. The whole room rocked and creaked, tilting them all sideways. The witch levitated slightly, managing to grab hold of the crystal ball with her friend's head, before it rolled off the table. Xinyi tumbled backwards but kept her feet, her bare feet, on the slippery moss floor of the witch's home.

"Not that." Shiraz dropped back, annoyed. She ran her hand along her ship, knocking here and there, checking its integrity.

Makoa moved around the ship to where you could see the rushing river beyond the legs of the house. He lay on his stomach, examining it.

The levitating witch threw the orb with her friend's head inside into the air. Just beneath the ceiling it released a pulse of light before falling back into the witch's waiting arms. Xinyi was entirely useless, and she didn't care at all! The only thing she did to help was hold onto Sweetums so she wouldn't rob the old woman or annoy Shiraz.

Sweetums was jumping up and down on Xinyi's shoulder, trying to grab the swinging planters and bits of cloth. And it was quickly getting difficult to care about holding onto the monkey, as Xinyi tried to scribble notes about levitating witches, and Shiraz and Makoa working as though they could hear one another's thoughts. Her notes were likely entirely illegible, but she couldn't stop.

"It looks like Narissa's work. Temperamental." Euphemia settled on the ground, dropping the crystal ball into a dirty pie pan.

"Unstable," the other witch remarked, running her tongue along her lips like she could taste the crumbs in the bottom of the pan. Perhaps she could. The pan looked a little cleaner.

Xinyi had expected they were discussing the house, but both women had their eyes on Makoa. Were they discussing his spell?

"Do you think it's because she was unstable? Because he went through your spell? Or because she's dead?"

"She's dead?" Euphemia exclaimed. "When? This is terrible. Why didn't you tell me?"

Oh, the poor woman, Xinyi ought to comfort her.

"Why do the best things always happen to the worst people? I swore that nutty windbag would cry over my grave!"

In the orb, the other witch cackled. "How can anyone mourn you if we summon an asteroid to destroy the planet?"

Xinyi's hand went lax around her pencil and her mouth fell wide once more. Destroy the planet? They weren't just witches; they were mad women! She took a step back.

"One has to have a backup plan. I can't believe she's gone. Who will we blame for the witch hunts now?"

"Merl?" the other woman suggested. "Or—I hear Larissa is on a quest to let people in on the magic."

Euphemia nodded, reaching out for her cup. She tried to take a swallow but, finding it empty, glared inside. "She is bitter enough to start that sort of mess."

"What about that strapping fellow? Is your enchantment mixing with Narissa's and making the curse stronger?"

"It's possible. But," she leaned close to the orb to whisper, "my spell is certainly dancing riot around that boat. It's got a lot of magics on it. *Powerful* magics," she whispered.

Goodness, were they to have one more foe after the boat?

"Worried something will explode?" Candelaria asked in a tone that implied much doubt. "Or hoping it will?"

The nude woman cackled, and the roof shook with angry cracking vibrations. What a voice she had, harsh and brittle. Xinyi had no space left to write. None, but the interior of the cover. Straining and smirking, Xinyi wrote out a new idea.

> V rolled her eyes at the sonic boom of her sister's voice. It rumbled over the mountain, shaking loose boulders that had stood three hundred years undisturbed. She was such a showo—

"Hey," Xinyi exclaimed as her journal was yanked away.

The witch glared at Xinyi, stopping her words with the power of her stare alone. She tilted the book towards the orb now cradled between her breast and her upper arm, so her friend could see.

"What are you up to, quiet one? Are you here to steal my secrets? Is that why you barged in?"

"Secrets," her friend snorted. "You're the least *concealed* person in the world."

"Leave her alone," the captain interjected, crossing to them. "She's just a shut-in who likes to write about the world."

"Hey," Xinyi exclaimed offended.

Shiraz went on as if never interrupted. "She didn't cause this. And those who make their homes invisible should not get angry at people who bump into them! Maybe this is how you tra—"

"Aaaaaah!" the woman in the orb screamed like a full flock of parrots. "Femmy! It's her! It's the mystery author. She was writing about V and another witch. This is Jian's author."

"No!" The nudist leaned away, peering into the journal herself.

"Jian's author is in your home!"

"It is you." The nudist observed Xinyi with a raised brow as her friend gushed. The witch's hands poured over the pages of Xinyi's journal though her gaze never left Xinyi's person.

"She came for our bookclub! Oooh, this is the best day, a hole in your house, two handsome workers, and Jian's author at our bookclub! And Siti says it's dull when you host."

"The book club is next week. We don't have the new chapter yet."

"Oh, it's today now! This calls for snacks! Hey, yummy one, you smell sweet. Make us treats and I'll paint you your future."

"Stop calling me food and I'll make you your sweets," Makoa countered.

"Oooh," she pouted, her bottom lip curving out. "Fine."

Makoa shook his head but complied. Climbing back onto the ship, he collected ingredients and pans, likely relieved to get away from Candelaria's stares.

"This is too wonderful. You must come to my home next. I'm a much nicer host. Oh, or…" Her tone shifted, lowering as if it came from deeper within. "I'm having a get together soon. A dance party. You like *dancing,* don't you?" She smiled at Xinyi in a way that should be beautiful, and was, she supposed, but also felt *threatening*. Like she was being measured for an oven. "Give you some more *life* to write about."

Xinyi nodded, though she wasn't exactly sure the words she was nodding to meant what the words usually meant.

"You know what she means by dance, right?" The captain moved between Xinyi and the crystal ball, a smile building on her lips. "Dance. Bodies moving together. Sex. She throws orgies!"

Xinyi's eyes flew wide. Had she agreed to go to an orgy? No. The captain's knowing what she meant might imply she'd been to a few. And she'd seen Xinyi agree to go to one. Now Shiraz was smiling in that flirtatious, incredulous way of hers. Xinyi just didn't think she was quite that adventurous—yet.

"Ohhhh, orgy is such a judgmental word," the witch in the orb pouted. "I throw parties and invite like minded, beautiful creatures of all varieties. And we...do as nature intended."

"Nature didn't intend shit," the hairy footed witch dismissed. "She was the O.G. witch. She had some spices, had a cauldron, threw them together saying 'let's see what this does' and bam! She had a planet. Screw what nature intended; you're doing what you intend."

Shiraz spoke to the orb witch. "I knew you looked familiar. We met at the eclipse party, maybe eleven years ago. On the Isle of Night."

Oh. She *had* been to an orgy. Wow.

"Oh, yes..." The attempt to play at remembering wasn't convincing.

Shiraz smirked. "We didn't share the pleasure. I was Crysta's guest."

The witch seemed relieved. "So you were. I hardly recognize you without the leash."

"*Leash*?" Xinyi repeated, her knee-jerk repulsion unintentionally apparent in her tone. She should apologize.

But the captain didn't look embarrassed.

"It was fun—for a visit." She grinned, and it was such a smile as Xinyi had never seen. It was confident, and prideful, and *lovely.*

Xinyi would not have thought such arrogance could look flattering. But it made her eyes sparkle and showed off the dance of freckles over her right cheekbone as that side of the face lifted. It made her sharp features look inviting. Made Xinyi's heart race.

"It was my try everything period." Shiraz popped a brow enticingly.

"Umm." The orb witch hummed warmly; her eyes took on a far off remembering type expression, while her friend just shook her head. Xinyi's gaze darted everywhere to avoid the provoking captain.

"I suppose you think everyone has such a period?" Xinyi asked.

"Why?" Shiraz snorted. "You want me to dig up my leash for you?"

Xinyi couldn't move. She wasn't entirely sure she was breathing.

"Oh, settle down. It sunk with **The Island Rebel**. *You're safe,*" Shiraz whispered. "No one can leash a force of nature."

Xinyi's skin was on fire, and she suspected she might be smiling but couldn't pull her thoughts into any order with everyone staring at her. *No one can leash a force of nature.*

"What does O.G. mean?" she blurted out to change the subject. The captain grinned smugly like she knew.

"Original Gorgon," Candelaria explained. "They are incredibly beautiful goddesses with snakes for hair. One glance at them is said to turn men to stone." Her eyebrows wiggled suggestively.

Xinyi's eyes caught on the snake crown the captain wore and the prideful smile on her lips. An airy tingle raced beneath Xinyi's skin.

Prideful. How compelling it looked on this *beautiful* gorgon.

Dangerous Preoccupation

Xinyi did nothing in a small way, and Shiraz loved it. In this moment it was the blush turning her skin truly red that Shiraz was enjoying. She did so appreciate unnerving this woman.

Makoa leapt off the ship with his tools and ingredients in hand and headed towards the kitchen. "How about a pie?" he offered without his usual lightness of spirit. Shiraz was unsurprised that he'd acquiesced to the witch's demand. He loved to bake when he was caught up in a whir of emotions. He nodded at the ship as he passed Shiraz, encouraging her to shrink it, she supposed. She really should.

Their once beautiful but this trip *destroyed* ship. Alright— destroyed was a bit of a stretch. But Shiraz could feel the crunching of the hull in her gut, and the splintering of the boards in her ribs. She felt torn apart, and she knew the feeling was the same for Makoa. Their home was coming apart.

"Get number fifteen," Candelaria instructed her friend, before turning to Xinyi. "That was your best."

"Quit being so bossy," her friend grumbled.

"Number seven is her best," Shiraz commented absently. But Xinyi looked over, her eyes going warm, and were it not for the itchy feeling along the side of her face, Shiraz would have been unable to look away.

But Candelaria had a dangerous stare; it raised an actual rash along Shiraz's neck and face as the woman examined her.

"I would have bet you'd say that," she said, as if this were an insult. Shiraz *had said it.* And she meant it! "V is plenty of fun, and an excellent foil for the girl who pretends she is done with magic. But this isn't V's story. It's Jian's, and fifteen forces her to confront all of her choices. Forces her to betray her own word in order to save the life of the man she loves."

Shiraz snorted, opening her mouth to explain how fruitless Jian's efforts were, but Xinyi, barefooted, stomped on Shiraz's toe. It wasn't terribly effective at causing pain, but Shiraz got the point. No spilling secrets, no matter how annoying their hosts were. She changed the subject. "I could use a spell like the one you use to protect your home." She spoke to Euphemia.

"So someone else can crash into your ship?" the witch challenged.

"Why don't I make us all tea!" Xinyi blurted out, as if Shiraz was about to attack the witch.

"Coffee," Euphemia snapped.

"Please," Shiraz said instructively. The woman was such an uzaok. "And...I want the spell to hide my ship from a gaggle of conspirators who want to steal it."

"Goodness, a whole gaggle," Candelaria teased.

"Eh, can't be done," Euphemia dismissed. "My spell works with the soil, with the things that grow."

Things that grew indeed. Already moss was weaving itself into the missing bits of floor. And the walls were calling branches off near by trees, bending them into the structure, making a new, scraggly domed ceiling. And even the damaged leg in the river was calling up sediment from the riverbed; it rolled slowly up the leg, like an ascending mudslide headed towards the wounds in the stone. Shiraz needed to move the boat before it became a new wall in the witch's home.

"You could leave the boat *here*." The woman leaned forward, popping her brows.

Euphemia wouldn't be much of a witch if she couldn't sense all the magic the ship held, so Shiraz was unsurprised by the offer. Witches always wanted more power. But Shiraz would be a prize dupe if she fell for that offer.

Shiraz hadn't built her ship just by nicely asking for spells. Witches didn't see themselves as peddlers of one's heart's desire. They saw themselves as gods, creators. If you wanted something from them you had to prove you were worthy. Shiraz rarely bothered with that; she just found *their* desires and peddled those for what she wanted.

This home had mostly witchy things, a few skulls on shelves; one had its jaw open holding a selection of dessert sticks frosted in various sweet creams. There were necessities like pots, pans and food. But the things that caught Shiraz's eyes were the open windows, their sills lined with nuts and fruit to call animals near. Or the giant lace decorating a doorway that was in fact a spider's web, and the massive number of notes written on the cloth beneath her orb stand. And her friend still contributing to the conversation. She liked her privacy, but she was starved for entertainment. Half her shelves were packed with novels and journals.

Shiraz's eyes alighted on Xinyi wandering the room as the coffee warmed, stopping every now and again to make notes, and having to turn her journal all directions to find the space. She needed a new one.

"I recognize magic from at least three witches on that *serpent*," Euphemia pulled Shiraz's focus back. "Have none of them told you, the more magic it takes on, the more danger it attracts?"

"No. *They* haven't," Makoa responded from the kitchen, his eyes narrowing on Shiraz suspiciously. "What sort of danger?"

No. No one had told Shiraz, though Makoa clearly doubted. Honestly, his suspicion was not unfounded. Shiraz wouldn't have cared if someone had said as much. Trouble was always coming anyway.

"Well, magic attracts magic, attracts magic, attracts magic. And most magic is…"

"Volatile," the witch in the orb finished her friend's sentence.

Magic attracting magic. If she couldn't hide The River Serpent, perhaps she could use all that magic to her advantage.

"Magic is bound to the temperament of its wielder," Euphemia continued. "Now I'm a nice old lady living alone in the jungle and leaving the rest of the world alone—"

"Except for summoning an asteroid to destroy it."

"Do you want to run this conversation? In my house. About my magic!" the woman yelled at her friend. "I'll throw a cloth over you."

"I'll crawl through and shove it off."

Euphemia cracked up. "Better hope you don't get stuck again, big hips! You should have seen it!" she addressed the room at large. "Skinny little thing got bored because of the inter-realm travel ban on account of the witch hunts. She was determined she could fit through a hole in the net, only her hips couldn't make the journey," the woman snorted. "She was stuck there, just a head torso and arms sticking out of a crystal ball with the rest of her stuck on the opposite side of the world. It took at least a week and summoning three witches at the other end to drag her back through! Best moment of my life! I knew I'd die happy right then."

"And yet you clung to existence," her friend said, heavily sarcastic.

"I know!" The witch jiggled with humor. "So I could tell them."

"Hilarious," Shiraz agreed. "But tell me more about the magic the ship is attracting?"

"What do you want me to tell you? You already know how *attractive* power can be." She winked. "It won't always attract bad, but it won't always attract good either. It's a bit...*chaotic.*" She grinned.

Everything the witch was saying sounded right, and all their trouble this trip could just be attracted to the ship's magic, but as the coffee began to bubble and Sweetums leaped off Xinyi's shoulder, jumping onto a pan and knocking a whole shelf of cookware onto Makoa, Shiraz sort of doubted it. It was Xinyi's presence that complicated and transformed everything. Attracting all manner of trouble, *magic attracting magic, attracting magic* as the witch said.

"I wouldn't stay in one place too long," the witch went on, unconcerned with the chaos in the room. "Someone will always be coming for it."

"What if I have a different spell than hiding my ship in mind? What would you need in exchange?"

"I want my asteroid," the woman snarked. "Can you get that?"

"You can't get it alone, can you? I know a *lot* of witches, and I bet I could find more. If you help me with a *tiny* trick that will help me Makoa and the River Serpent get far away from Loqwan." Shiraz very intentionally left Xinyi off the list. She was thinking about this woman far too much. No good could come of it. Xinyi was a creature of habit, enjoying a brief adventurous sojourn. But eventually she would resume her ordered life and think of Shiraz and Makoa only to fold them into a story. Shiraz couldn't afford to spend the next ten years pining over the princess.

"Ha!" The witch made the noise, then proceeded to laugh full bodied. Her various bits jiggled, including her adorable second and third chins. "Fine! If that's what *you* want." Her voice was heavy with double meanings and her eyes led the way to Xinyi.

Not that Shiraz's eyes had ever fully lost sight of Xinyi. But with her eyes resting fully on the princess, she felt a swell of excitement and wonder akin to what she'd once felt in pursuit of magic. Xinyi was something special.

She approached with a steaming cup of coffee, but her bare foot struck on the clawed, and from the look of it, bloodstained table leg. She stumbled forward. The cup flew out of her hand, the liquid inside it headed straight for the scantily clad Euphemia. Xinyi gasped, Makoa covered his grin, Shiraz lunged for Xinyi, and Sweetums used the chaos to steal a cursing doll off the stove (presumably the witch had planned to burn or boil it). But the woman most in danger looked bored. She merely shook her head, muttering, and the cup floated to her hand, followed shortly by the liquid. The coffee gathered its drops together to form a womanly shadow before diving into the mug.

Casually, the witch lifted the cup to her lips and sipped. "Take better care of those, bare feet."

Xinyi gasped and leapt as moss from the ground grew up over her feet, forming sweet little green slippers with solid dirt soles and white flowers wrapping around the ankle. Shiraz narrowed her eyes on the woman as she helped steady Xinyi. Her grumpy act was all show, wasn't it? She was all show. If the witch already knew how much magic the boat had, what was the point in hiding it? Shiraz stepped away from Xinyi. Moving to the River Serpent, she looped a bit of rigging around her arm so the boat wouldn't fall into the river and get washed away. That was all this day needed.

"You should stand back," Shiraz said grandly. Xinyi caught her eye, and Shiraz winked. It was a nothing moment, or it should have been, but Xinyi's lips lifted in a brief conspiratorial grin before she schooled her features, and Shiraz's heart fell all over itself again, sending a tingling reminder into her hand of the moment when Xinyi took it after they crashed. Azakif! She needed to focus. "I'm going to remove the ship," Shiraz said, stumbling over her grand show as she forced her concentration back. "I'm safe, but—"

Before she could hit the amethyst eye, the whole house shook. It lifted both its front legs out of the river and *kicked* the River Serpent. The boat jerked away from the house and hurtled across the river.

"Uzaok!" Shiraz shouted as she was yanked after the ship, her already injured shoulder giving a jerk that would probably dislocate it.

The ship landed before she could worry about crashing. It was caught by a bundle of branches and vines, all of them shaking as if imbued with the witch's spirit. Then they set her down on the shore. On the *opposite* side of the river. The ship lay sideways, and Shiraz hung from its rigging, feeling sorry for herself. She was in immense pain, but her shoulder was still in its socket. She just had to unwrap herself, shrink her ship, and find a way across the river safely, in her best clothes and carrying a hunted ship. This trip was getting very annoying.

Her tattoo wasn't that much worse than earlier. Probably eight miles around her were visible. She better move before it was seven.

This was all Xinyi's fault. That bright smiling, brown-eyed princess was one dangerous preoccupation.

Deliciously Tricky

"If your house could do that all along, why did we ever hit it?" Makoa was yelling.

The only thing that kept Xinyi from trying to climb out of the house, or swing out on one of the vines dropping into the room was— well, a few things. Shiraz appeared to have landed safely, the river was too wide to swing across, and mostly—this wasn't a novel. If this were a novel, if Xinyi were writing it, her character wouldn't have just stood there screaming Shiraz's name as she went from grinning so full of pride that it was infectious, to getting jerked away and slammed into the side of the ship.

Sweetums was still pointing and laughing. It was very rude, but Xinyi had a feeling if it had happened to the monkey, Shiraz would be doing the very same thing.

"My house isn't in the habit of avoiding every water bug that floats by!" Euphemia snapped back equally belligerent. "Don't be so squeamish. She's fine. She is only ever her truest, strongest, happiest self *alone*."

Xinyi heard the words with her ears, but they also sounded inside of her, not in her mind, but...under her skin. Like they knew her. Like they were intended for her. Other words shuffled through her mind carried on the hairy backs of spiders, making her shudder. She would never look at a spider the same again. But just at the moment the words they carried were almost worse than the frightening creatures.

"If you shared that you author Jian's adventures, there might be moments of discomfort with people telling you how to better write the story. But I think you are more afraid that it will let people see more of who you truly are, Xinyi. There is no shame in being yourself," Mei's impatient voice advised.

As Yinuo's memory taunted, "I wonder if hiding is not what you and Jian have most in common."

"I have to go, my love!" Wei shouted. He never shouted before the day he left, not at her. He was so gentle. But it was as if she could not hear him if he wasn't so loud. "If you want to change the world you have to be willing to change yourself first. You wrote that. But all of your stories, all of your ideas are concealed from the world. I have to go, so your ideas can escape that box you hide them in, so no one knows that you—feel. Why are you so afraid to tell people when you are angry? When you are in pain? I worry that one day you will conceal even your joys."

"Check on my pie, before I turn you into candy and hand you over to the trollop." Euphemia's sharp voice startled Xinyi out of her memories.

"Turnip," her friend responded, sticking out her tongue.

"I just put the pie in." Makoa rolled his eyes.

"My oven is magic. I don't like to wait."

"She really does use her powers for the most ridiculous things," her friend remarked as Makoa returned to the oven. "It's why no one has heard of her who didn't accidentally bump into her house."

"You've heard of me," Euphemia grumbled. "I don't recall my house bumping into you."

"No," she remarked dryly. "It just sat on my third husband."

Euphemia nodded magnanimously. "You're welcome."

The pair cackled as Makoa returned with the steaming pie. He opened his mouth to speak when they all heard a crash on the ceiling.

"*Azaqif!*"

"Tried the vines again?" The witch in the orb chuckled. Xinyi spun to face her. *Again.* What did she know?

She winked at Xinyi. "So, about your books, you will sign them, won't you? Oooh! Do you have a copy of sixteen in that bag?"

"What an interesting bag," Euphemia said, and she was suddenly directly in front of Xinyi. "Celestial markings and elf myths! Where—"

The front door flew in, cutting her off. Shiraz stood there with a few twigs caught in her hair, sweat misting her body, the river serpent hung on a rope around her neck and eyes on fire. She looked fabulous!

"I don't like to kill people, but I'll make an exception for you!" she threatened Euphemia.

The witched grinned. "Promise?"

Makoa shook his head. He shoved the steaming pie at the witch and crossed to Shiraz, one arm encircling both her shoulders to pull her to his side. "Let's steal some of her magic first," Makoa suggested, his voice failing to sound as playful as he ought to mean the words.

Sweetums raced to them, climbing Shiraz's legs, and immediately started cleaning leaves from her hair. Xinyi smiled quietly, relieved and happy. They were all here, all safe. Her crew. Shiraz and Makoa, and Sweetums. *Hers.*

"A lot of magic," Shiraz snapped. "I have plans."

If you help me with a tiny trick that will help me Makoa and the River Serpent get far away from Loqwan.

Xinyi heard the words again. They'd caused such a shock when Shiraz first said them. All Xinyi's old fears of being alone rose up, though she'd only known these people two days and certainly must still plan to go…home. Where she was safe. Where she was loved. Where she belonged. Where she had her own collection of books and her routine. Where she could have her tea every morning at the same time. And tell stories to the children then steal away to write in secret. Able to be entirely herself because no one knew.

Xinyi imagined a collection of books growing around her, ones she'd written, ones she read. World upon world collected. Imagined comfortably warm, sweet tea, and her cozy space with no bugs, or threats of death, no bruises, or vomit inducing rides through the jungle, no fear, no—

Fun.

A voice in her head startled Xinyi. *"You're too adventure hungry yet to be a cottage witch. You just didn't know it until you started dining on life, chaos dragon."* It was Euphemia's voice, but when Xinyi looked, all the woman's attention was on the pie.

"Mmmm. Taste." She shoved her spoon at the orb, and its surface rippled like a bubble, stretching to let the spoon inside, though it made a clinking noise like struck glass.

And Xinyi heard a new voice in her mind. **The things that make you different become the things that make you loved.** Xinyi imagined being loved like that, not just by one person, but by a whole crew who knew the truth of her soul and loved her still. Perhaps Shiraz's Singing Hills were just a legend, but…they could make them real, couldn't they?

"Oooh, nectar fruit. Yummy." Candelaria rolled the bite around on her tongue and looked out with an odd smile. "Where did you get that fruit?" she inquired excitably. "It tastes…*deliciously tricky.*" She stretched out the word, making it sound so much more powerful than it usually would.

"What does that mean?" Makoa demanded.

"Nothing," the woman said coyly. "Unless you want it to."

It was clear from Makoa's expression both that he did not want the words to mean anything at all and that he did not believe that was the case. He narrowed his eyes. And Euphemia cackled, seeming to confirm his suspicions.

"You're a good cook." Euphemia's smile stretched out similar to how her friend's had looked at Xinyi when she invited her to a dance party. "That is the first thing anyone needs to be a *witch.* A skill with mixing and baking — *creating.* Your curse gave you the second thing, *magic.* It's yours now. And you're drawing in more and more of it, aren't you? You aren't coming undone. You're *growing.*"

"Since you don't want me painting your future, you'll have to find the third thing you need by yourself," Candelaria taunted. "If you want to truly claim that power. That is...if you haven't found it already."

As cryptic comments went, that one was quite provoking. The shouting match that followed was enough to make Xinyi want to hide. Or it would have been, in the past. But as Shiraz and Makoa yelled at their hostess and the witches ate, Xinyi was actually thinking about something else. She was thinking all about herself.

The River Serpent crew departed in the early evening, with some more magic but no more answers. Shiraz and Makoa were annoyed, Sweetums was loaded down with stolen goods and Xinyi was...plotting. What if this was a story? What if everything was?

What would she have to do to become a witch, not a cottage witch, but a ship witch, an adventure witch, a writing witch? A *life thief!* How could she write herself into this crew?

A Most Uncomfortable Situation

They made their way through the jungle in the late evening. It was generally pointless to get to the grotto before the sun went down. No real, self respecting criminal went to a club in the daylight. Makoa found Candelaria's parting comments so provoking that he took a bite of another nectar fruit. It was deeply sweet, and juicy, and as he chewed, he felt emotions shifting through him that he rarely experienced. Unease. And fear.

He'd attributed the strangeness under his skins to the princess yesterday, but it might have come from the fruit. He tossed it away unfinished. Sweetums, greatly offended by the waste, hopped off Xinyi's neck to retrieve it. She stood on the ground trying awkwardly to fit the fruit into her hands despite all the treasure she'd been *allowed* to steal: a pinky bone carved into a tiny spoon, four pebbles, and a doll with pins stuck all over its body with an M sewn into his chest.

Giggling, Xinyi held out her bag. "Put some of it in here, sweet. I'll keep it safe."

The monkey observed her with a look of suspicion she might have pulled right off of Shiraz's face. Xinyi kissed the monkey's head reassuringly, and it not only complied, it blushed. Something Makoa was entirely unaware creatures with fur could do, but her blue face turned a strange sort of purple and she looked away, giggling.

Makoa hated the feeling in his gut. Hated the feeling that right at this moment this wasn't his gut at all. That he hadn't been feeling his own gut for years. He hated that the sweet tangy juices of the nectar fruit still coated his tongue though he'd spit it out. He hated that he still clung to Kapuni's form in fear. The women stood together, flirting, all the time flirting, while he searched the forest for threats: pixies, dragons, griffins—auditors. This trip was a constant barrage of attacks. They should all be on the lookout.

"She's going to drip that all over your clothes," Shiraz commented. Her words weren't particularly flirtatious but her looks were, and the ones she received back were.

"Your clothes," Xinyi teased breathily.

Makoa liked Xinyi, he really did. But if she wasn't some sort of magical flare attracting all of the hungry moths of this jungle, then she really must be cursed. A bounty on the ship didn't explain everything. It didn't explain anything! Why had it come now? Why was Makoa changing now? Xinyi, her presence, her existence, it was a part of things. There was too much weirdness.

The monkey leapt onto Xinyi's shoulder and pulled her face towards her between one empty hand and one with a dripping nectar fruit, getting the woman immediately sticky, requiring all her attention.

Shiraz was unable to keep the smile off her lips, if she was even trying anymore. They were cute. Makoa wanted to tease Shiraz about it, wanted to laugh and watch as they forgot anyone else existed. But he was forced to be the prudent member of the trio. *Eeeech!* Quartet, Makoa amended in his mind, unsure how the monkey knew what he was thinking, but sure he would find out sooner or later and it wouldn't be good.

So many things were weighing down his mind. Shiraz's plan counted too strongly on Felicia being the person who was after the ship. What if it was Aiattaua? What if Felicia was merely a bounty hunter? Shiraz did not share his concern, and the princess seemed not to have heard the plan at all. Nor seen all the mini crystal balls Shiraz had been given to help the witches form a "coven squared," thirteen covens of thirteen witches all working to one purpose.

That sounded super safe.

And Shiraz had agreed to help!

"They will probably be ruined when I give them back to you," Xinyi continued to discuss the clothes. "I can't help tripping and falling constantly."

"You haven't done as much of that today," Shiraz remarked. "Loath as I am to see your tumbling end, I think you might be finding your smuggling legs."

Xinyi looked suddenly luminous, aglow from within.

She couldn't just be human. They'd been given the fruit by friends of hers. They'd been manipulated into taking her on this journey. And now…Makoa put his back to them. Clenching his fist in maddening fear, he blew out the curse that lived deep within him. He transformed into a sheep and thankfully didn't transform any further. For the second time in two days, he was a sheep, and for the same purpose.

"I do so enjoy watching you bump around—"

Makoa dredged up every molecule of nectar fruit he could from the slowly digesting stomach and vomited on the jungle floor.

"Makoa!" Shiraz interrupted herself. "What's wrong?"

"Nothing." Makoa spit out the last of the vomit. He raced away from her on four legs towards the river for a drink.

"Makoa!" Shiraz raced after him. He heard a screech, and some shuddering leaves so he supposed the mo—

"Eeeeech!"

"Ow! Damnit" Makoa cried out as the monkey landed on his back and dug its claws into his wool, yanking up like it was a horse's bridle. "Get this thing off me." He kicked out, throwing himself backwards.

"Sweetums! Please, Sweetums!" the princess called out desperately.

Shiraz wasn't so gentle. "Get off," she shouted. Diving into the scuffle, she got *accidentally* kicked in the shin as Makoa threw himself sideways. "KUFFIK!" She hopped, grabbing at her left leg.

The monkey was far too agile to get crushed. She leapt onto Makoa's side. But she did release his wool. Makoa blew out his curse angrily and leapt up in Dao's body.

Making full use of the elvish agility, Makoa grabbed the monkey by its tail. It screeched and fought wildly, clearly terrified.

"Whoa! Nice reflexes."

"Ohh. Don't...that is... be careful," Xinyi said hesitantly. She hadn't seen this side of Makoa. Few people ever did. Even he hadn't in years.

"Keep off of me, pest," Makoa hissed in the monkey's face. Sweetums screamed wildly.

"Hey." Shiraz lay a hand on Makoa's shoulder. She didn't look particularly concerned with the monkey, but she looked concerned for him. "You good? Why'd you run off?"

Makoa sighed. He didn't feel well. And the change of form wasn't making it any better. If anything, he felt worse. Now not only was there nausea, and fear, and the taste of vomit in his mouth to contend with, but there was also painful stretching feeling in his gut, stabbing in his lower back, and squeezing in his thighs. He felt exhausted and just wanted to curl up on the cool ground and cry for a few days.

Defeated, Makoa loosened his hold on the monkey. It leapt out of his arms and raced behind Xinyi, pulling up her train and wrapping it around her shoulders like a shield. Xinyi crouched, blocking the monkey with her body, and pet its head.

"I just wanted to wash out my mouth." Makoa was shocked when the words came out a sob.

Shiraz stepped even closer, closing an arm around his shoulder. "Okay. Let's get you a drink. Makoa, I...I don't know what's going on, but if I can find a witch to make our boat impervious to lava, I can find a witch to help you. Just because those uzaoka in the cottage—"

"That isn't even it." Makoa fought off tears. "Or it isn't all of it. Every skin feels different all of the sudden. I can't always control how and when I change." A few tears slipped out, frustrating Makoa all the more. What was wrong with him? He shrugged Shiraz's hand off and stepped back. "I was trying to get away from the feeling and now it's worse. Maybe I'm dying. Maybe I needed to break the curse by a certain time."

Shiraz shook her head angrily, and tears filled her eyes just as quickly as they had Makoa's.

"I had a bad feeling about this day from the first. And it just gets worse, and worse and worse."

"We'll fix it," Shiraz swore. "Maybe Aiattaua can help. Elves—"

"I took this form for that so called *elvish superiority,* and I just feel weaker. It feels like something is trying to drill through my back, my whole body is heavy, and tired, and something keeps clawing at my gut," he said, digging his hands into the fabric of Dao's uniform.

"Okay." Shiraz's eyes were wide and frightened, and her hands fisted at her sides. "Let's go back. They must have done—"

Then the princess giggled.

Giggled.

Shiraz cut herself off to look at the woman. And Makoa felt everything inside him still, the pain brushed momentarily aside by a rising tide of anger and vindication. She'd done this, hadn't she? She'd cursed him, and now she would reveal herself.

Makoa turned to face the princess fully. She was crouched, looking between Makoa and Shiraz with sheepish amusement.

"Sorry." Her hand rushed to cover her lips. "I don't mean to belittle, but..."

"What," Makoa growled the word. "Did. You. Do. To. Me?"

"Her?" Shiraz demanded.

"Me?" Xinyi asked. She still looked mostly amused, but her eyes widened and her smile faltered briefly. "Nothing. I...you...it's her." She waved at Makoa. *Her?* "Don't you see? Surely you see?" she asked Shiraz.

Shiraz shook her head. "Why do you think Xinyi's done something to you?"

"Everything that's happened to us, the fruit, the catastrophes, the bounty on the ship, meeting those witches, it all started with her. I don't know if it's intentional or..."

"Makoa," Shiraz said in such a patient tone he thought he might scream. "None of it was her fault. How the hell would she take out a bounty? she doesn't have anything to offer."

"Thank you very much," the princess said, offended.

"Not like that!" Shiraz looked exasperated.

"You only have her word to go on about that."

"I didn't do anything!" Xinyi pushed to her feet. She bobbed her head sideways. "Well, I suppose I do have a bit of a bad luck curse, so some of it might have...fallen on the pair of you." Her voice dropped to a whisper and got quieter with every word. "I might have sort of *planned* on that happening when I *went looking for you*." She said the last so low they could barely make it out, Shiraz all but pressing her face against the princess to hear better.

"You see?" Makoa shouted just as Shiraz was snorting.

"Are you saying you have 'bad luck' and wished it on people you intended to travel with? That sounded like a clever plan?" Shiraz asked.

The princess blushed.

"I don't believe in luck anymore than I do fate." Shiraz turned sideways, squeezing Makoa's shoulder. "I don't know what's happening to you, but it isn't her doing. And I don't think you'd think it was either, any other day. But a lot of shit winds have been coming at us. So I get it."

"She apologized. And she knows what's happening to me. I'm not making this up out of nothing."

"She said she was *sorry*," Shiraz argued, in an annoyingly patient voice. "She says sorry as like every fifth word."

"I don't do that! Do I?" Xinyi asked. No one answered—verbally. The monkey nodded. Clearing her throat, Xinyi tilted her head towards Makoa and spoke softly. "I...I did apologize. You aren't making it up out of nothing. But I didn't do anything to you other than be unlucky. I just think...well everything you described, all the discomfort in your body and the exhaustion and even," she whispered, "the crying. I think perhaps the woman whose body you're imitating is, or when you knew her was, menstruating."

There was a long, deadening silence in the jungle.

Shiraz broke it.

"Oh noo-oo-oo-ooo-oo-ooooo!" Shiraz shook so hard with laughter that her hand fell from Makoa's shoulder. It hung in the air, pointing at him and shaking as she continued laughing. "Oh, this is too good! This may be the best thing ever!"

Makoa couldn't move. He felt a lot of things. Too many things. Physical and emotional. And yet somehow the worst of it was the two women in front of him smiling and laughing and...*absolutely right*. Kuffik! And he'd accused Xinyi of causing his suffering. *Again*!

He wanted to change bodies. Immediately. He wanted to change bodies and have all the suffering follow him so he could be vindicated. But he didn't actually think that would happen. He hadn't felt worse as a sheep. He *couldn't* change form. They were watching him, just waiting. If he changed bodies now, it would be like saying he couldn't take this. KUFFIK! He really wanted to curl up and cry now.

"I hate you," Makoa whispered as Shiraz's laughter calmed enough to shake herself alone, instead of the entire tilt of the planet.

"Never." She smacked his shoulder, not at all gently, "welcome to the club!" She popped her brows, all but daring him to change form. "Well, since you aren't dying." She clapped her hands, moving around him. "Pick up the pace, we have places to be."

"I really am sorry." Xinyi started after Shiraz with Sweetums on her shoulder still eating the dirty fruit.

Makoa took up the rear, listening to Shiraz laugh "menstruating." Ugh. He hated his life. He watched the juices from the nectar fruit fall from the monkey's lips and felt a burning twist in his gut.

"It's past time you used what you've been given and get to know others more deeply." He'd thought nothing of the old woman's words at the market. Now...they seemed sinister. Now *she* seemed sinister.

Not The Right Moment

"**T**his probably isn't the time to ask him," Xinyi whispered, catching up to Shiraz. "But do you think his spell creates a link between him and the person he's mimicking in that moment?"

"Oh, this is the perfect time," Shiraz said. Xinyi grabbed her arm to stop her, but the captain was already yelling. "*Makoa,* do you think the spell causes an in the moment link between you and the body you're using? Have you noticed any signs of that before?"

"Shut up."

"Do you think you'd be able to use someone's body still if they'd died without you knowing?" She pressed playfully.

"You aren't being very kind," Xinyi whispered.

"Shiraz, I swear, I will kill you," he bit out.

"Hey, hey," she replied with false tenderness, ignoring Xinyi. "Why so aggressive? You know I'm your friend."

Makoa glared. "Are you going to throw every stupid thing I ever said to you back in my face?"

Oh. Xinyi shook her head. This was some aspect of their relationship she did not understand and surely shouldn't poke.

"Yep." Shiraz grinned. "I have a looooong memory."

Xinyi snorted, but instantly felt bad. This was all her fault. "Come on, stop. He's going through a lot; he needs your support."

"Oh, he'll be fine." Shiraz's body gave a little shudder; Xinyi suspected Shiraz was more worried than she was letting on.

Xinyi had been reaching into her bag, for her overfull notebook, to write down her questions for a better time. But she paused, wanting to say something comforting, because it was clear that both the captain and Makoa were worried. But more than that, she wanted to take Shiraz's hand. To touch her and let her fingers communicate where words were failing her.

"Eeeech!" Sweetums screeched, batting at Xinyi.

"Oh, behave." Xinyi gently battled the swiping monkey. "I'm getting my own things."

Shiraz reached between them, getting scratched on her bare arm, and calmly lifted the monkey away. She held the little screaming thing against her chest with both arms to keep it from swiping. Xinyi grinned watching this fearsome creature gently cradling the baby monkey.

"Oh, this is going in my notes. Must have V forced to care for a wild baby animaaaal." Xinyi dragged the word out as her hands found a new journal. She pulled it into the fading light. It had a lacy green pattern embossed on black leather. "Where did this come from?"

"Thieving monkey." Shiraz shook her head disapprovingly. Sweetums tried to take a bite out of Shiraz, but the smuggler had fast enough reflexes to save her digits. "Ha, ha. Missed me." She stuck out her tongue. Like Makoa, it seemed when it came to dealing with the monkey there was no maturity to be found from the actual adults.

Xinyi ran her fingers over the cover and her heart fluttered, not for a moment fooled by Shiraz's fib. She chewed on her lip as she opened the journal and began to make notes.

"I probably shouldn't encourage her behavior," Xinyi said as her pencil rushed across the brand new, blank page.

"It wouldn't matter," Shiraz remarked. "She's set in her ways."

"Maybe her ways aren't nearly as bad as she pretends."

Shiraz laughed, and her eyes went to Makoa. They were nearer the river here; he'd taken advantage of the stop to get that drink. He was all clenched up. Xinyi ought to suggest some things to make him more comfortable since Shiraz clearly wouldn't.

"He didn't mean it, you know?" Shiraz said after a minute. "Blaming you. None of this is your fault."

Xinyi didn't speak. Everything had happened so fast, and she was used to feeling to blame for everyone's struggles so she hadn't really considered Makoa's blaming her.

But Shiraz defending her—so quickly, and with such certainty—even without having time to think about it, that sang inside Xinyi. She watched Shiraz through her lashes.

"You didn't put the curse on him. You didn't take out the bounty on the boat. Or yourself for that matter." Shiraz chuckled softly.

"So you don't think I've been attracting all of this trouble?" Xinyi couldn't stop herself from asking. Wouldn't it be better not to know?

Shiraz stepped closer, the tiny fires of her eyes growing brighter and brighter. "Oh, I didn't sa—Aaaah!" she cried out as Sweetums took advantage of her distraction to sink her teeth into Shiraz. "You brat."

Xinyi reached out for the monkey, but Shiraz turned around.

"Take your notes, this thing is safe enough for the moment."

"Are you sure? I..."

"It's fine." Shiraz took another two steps away, heading towards Makoa. Xinyi was a bit concerned. But she didn't let it stop her. She had so many thoughts whirring through her mind, and she needed to get them down before they flew away. Her mind wanted to treat Makoa like a character she was writing. Wanted to know his limitations. It was bound to help understand and thus end his curse.

Questions/Tests for Makoa's curse:

1. How close is his connection to other bodies?
2. Can the people whose bodies he uses sense it?
3. Can it be used for communication?
4. How does he take on a form?
5. Does he have to know the person whose form he takes?
6. Why does he keep his own voice?
7. Does he affect the person whose body he inhabits?
8. If he breaks a limb, does theirs break as well?
9. Will his leg still be broken if he changes forms?
10. To what purpose was this curse laid?
11. Why true love's kiss?
12. If fate and luck do not exist, does "true love?"

Shiraz walked away from Xinyi, who was too distracted to notice the monkey in Shiraz's arms screeching to be set loose. Or that Shiraz had slipped two more objects into her bag: the shrunken steering pole to the River Serpent, on which Euphimia had altered the enchantment, and a communication orb.

If something happened to Shiraz, Xinyi and Makoa would have the means to get away—then come back and rescue her.

"Shhh," Shiraz hissed at the monkey. "We need to have a chat."

The monkey quieted, cautiously.

"I know who you work for. And you can only keep one of them," Shiraz said, hoping Felicia didn't have a direct connection to the monkey. But she knew the demigoddess could talk to animals; it was how they'd gotten word to Makoa about the prison break. And Euphemia's comment to the monkey, about not being afraid of her connections...that confirmed that the monkey wasn't with them for fun.

Sweetums looked away dismissively.

Shiraz suspected the monkey had been sent to learn about Shiraz's ship and stick with them if she could. But if she didn't miss her guess, Sweetums was growing fond of Xinyi. It was easy enough to do.

"Xinyi is offering you her love freely. Can you say the same of Felicia? Think about it, because Felicia won't hesitate to hurt Xinyi."

The monkey finally looked up, her gaze narrow with rage. Sweetums sunk her teeth into Shiraz's upper arm. Shiraz jerked away, opening her arms. The monkey leapt to the ground and raced to Xinyi, climbing into her arms. Xinyi, still writing, nuzzled the monkey absently with the side of her head.

"Quit letting that thing bite you, or I'll have to take you to a witch to cure your rabies." Makoa came up on Shiraz's shoulder, his voice low and grouchy.

"Shall I take you to one for those cramps?" she teased. Her hand was fine, and so was her shoulder. If the monkey really wanted to hurt her, she would have. "Why'd you vomit anyway?"

Makoa shook his head, changing the subject. "Your plan relies too much on it being Felicia who's after the boat. What if you're wrong?"

"Oh, she's after the boat. Sweetums all but confirmed it."

"It was Dao who nodded at the monkeys and got them to back off," Makoa pointed out.

"Um-hm. So the question is why Dao would work with Felicia. It makes no sense. She's only loyal to the elf king. Although, maybe Felicia is one of the elf king's experiment children. She's an appropriate age. And they might have had trouble getting their hands on her because her powers are so volatile."

"If we're going to let the elf king claim all the absent fathered children of the world, maybe he is your brother's father." The moment the snide words were out, Makoa covered his lips and shook his head.

Shiraz shrugged, wearing a sad smile that acknowledged the possibility. "Was," she corrected. "Do you know...I never wondered who Noam's father was? Before mother got sick, I thought Father was wonderful, if grouchy and overly committed to the rules. I didn't see it. I wonder if Noam ever wanted to know. If he ever wanted to talk to me about it, but didn't feel like he could, because I loved our father so well. I hope not."

"I'm sorry, that was..."

Shiraz interrupted. "I've been there anyway. She sort of reminds me of Noam? Well, no. She doesn't. But she reminds me of the whole situation. How he accepted blame for things that were not his fault, how badly he wanted to be accepted. *Almost begging* to be part of the community, to be loved for himself." Shiraz felt her fists clench and her jaw ache. She tore her eyes off of Xinyi, unclenched her jaw and looked at Makoa, gripping his wrist in her hand. "I like her, and I don't think she is actively causing our troubles. But if you really believe that, tell me why. Help me see it. Because...I trust you, Makoa. With my life, and with all of my heart. So...what is it?"

Makoa was quiet a long while. He watched Xinyi and the monkey. His eyes fell away, and he shook his head.

"All the strangeness I feel started when we took her from the market. But that doesn't mean it's her doing. I just keep feeling like there is more to her than meets the eye. Do you not feel that?"

"Absolutely!" Shiraz agreed without hesitation. "In the, not quite, two days since we met her, I thought she was a witch, a fairy, or a trap. Being around her feels like magic. Like coming awake after a century of sleeping. It feels like...meeting you, over and over again and feeling briefly convinced fate was real. She's going to be gone in a few days, and we are going to figure out what is happening to you, and fix the boat, and leave Loqwan, probably for good. But I'll be taking things with me that I didn't have before."

"Like what, the holes in our ship?" Makoa's tone wasn't nearly as biting as his remark. In fact, it sounded encouraging.

Shiraz grinned. "Like the memory of kissing a deity statue, and not even minding. And finding a double rainbow while drifting through an underground tunnel. And—" she chuckled hard. "The pure joy of watching you cry over period cramps. We saw Dao earlier today and she didn't seem nearly as incapacitated."

"Maybe she wasn't having one yet."

"Oh, trust me, if it's as bad as all that, she was feeling something."

"She's used to it."

"Um-hm." Shiraz let the subject drop only because they both knew she'd won. Then she grew more serious. "But if you still—"

Makoa lay a hand over Shiraz's. He shook his head. "No. Ignore me. I think maybe it's like you with Aiattaua, and I was a little jealous to see someone taking up so much of your attention."

"I am not jealous of Aiattaua!" Shiraz snapped, offended to the deepest reaches of her being. And, as she was not a quiet woman, this drew Xinyi's attention.

"Are you alright?" she asked, looking up from her work. Sweetums was petting Xinyi's soft hair and glaring at Shiraz.

Makoa laughed. "She's fine."

Shiraz stomped away from her friend. Shiraz glared right back at the monkey and waved the rest of her crew on, annoyed and eager to get the plan underway. "Come on. Night is upon us, let's get this over with."

Eager to Dine on Life

"**M**akoa! Shiraz!" Hua's voice, and her gloved (thank the sea spirits) hands grabbed Shiraz from behind. The ogre lifted Shiraz off the ground mere steps outside the nightclub. "My friends, it is so good to see you!"

"Good to see you, Hua," Makoa said with none of his usual energy.

Hua set Shiraz on the ground and spun her around. The ogre was a good two heads taller than Shiraz, her yellow green skin slick with sweat that was poisonous to the touch, and the large pustules all over her body, if broken, would excrete noxious gases. She was easily one of the most dangerous creatures in the club, but Shiraz laughed in genuine pleasure and slapped her friend on the back (where it was covered by silk).

"You're wearing it!" Shiraz exclaimed, more excited than she would have expected. Flattered. She might be blushing.

"Are you kidding?" Hua spun around, showing off the floor length gown of purple silk with pink flower accents that Shiraz had made. It had a high waist, cutting off under the bust with a long fuchsia sash. Her bald head was decorated with a strand of white flowers. "Do you know how few tailors there are for ogres? Even among ogres! Most who outfit us only work in heavy material and make it as ugly as they think we are."

"You are not ugly," Xinyi and Shiraz said at the same time, but in different tones of voice, Shiraz's flatly dismissive, Xinyi's nearly awed. Xinyi was observing the ogre with excited eyes and rapidly moving pencil, though Shiraz had told her not to take notes at the nightclub.

"Oh, I'm so rude. Good evening."

"Hua, this is my client, Xinyi. Xinyi, my friend Hua. She makes the best vegetarian jerky in the world." The monkey on Xinyi's should swiped at Shiraz, showing her teeth. "And that's Sweetums."

Makoa moved around them sharply. "I'll see you in there."

"What's wrong with him?" Hua asked.

"He isn't feeling himself," Xinyi said softly. "Do you think there is somewhere he can get a warm compress?"

Shiraz snorted. "Makoa!" she shouted after him. Makoa didn't look back but the giant door guards and a few of the patrons near the entrance did. "Xinyi suggests a hot compress. And I know a good stroke always helps me! I doubt Aiattaua is talented, but maybe one of your other bonded mates!"

He never looked back, but he did grab a bowl of something off a passing tray and threw it with great accuracy backwards. It would have hit Shiraz in the face if she hadn't seen it coming and ducked away.

Hua was staring after him open mouthed, and Xinyi looked mortified, but Shiraz laughed. Had to. He was worrying her.

"Aren't you embarrassed of anything?" Xinyi asked, shaking her head.

"Sure, just not embarrassing him. That's a pleasure."

"A stroke and—Ohhhh!" Hua said suddenly getting the joke. "Really? Has that ever happened to him before?"

"No." Shiraz shook her head, wanting the word to have come out more amused.

"Vegetarian?" Xinyi blurted a change in subject—she thought.

"Makoa shows up as an animal six tenths of the time," Shiraz shuddered. "I stopped eating meat years ago. But since meeting Hua, I eat in style."

"Oh, that reminds me." Hua loosened the wide sash at her waist and pulled out a dingy rucksack. "I've got some jerky for you. And fruit jerky drops—dipped in chocolate! You have to try it."

"Hua," Shiraz laughed. "That sounds excellent, and I can't wait. But we need to get you a pretty purse to go with that dress."

"No one will sell to ogres! I like that bag." She nodded to Xinyi. "Is that the Feiyu Comet? I was born under it."

"Me too," Xinyi said, gripping tight to the strap. "And Wei."

"Not for sale," Shiraz said before Xinyi could feel bad for the ogre and just give away her most prized possession. "And if a vendor won't sell to you, *rob them*! Or tell me who they are and I'll rob them."

Hua nudged Xinyi with an elbow covered in silk. "She's always trying to turn me into a criminal."

"But she made your gown?" Xinyi asked. She held up the train of her own outfit. "She cobbled this together for me from her clothes. Now I wonder why she doesn't have *legal* employment as a seamstress."

Hua chuckled. "Oh, she can't bare to do things legally." Hua held out a bundle of jerky for Shiraz. "She's convinced she's a bad girl and she won't let anyone say otherwise." Shiraz stuck her tongue out. "I also have something special, made it out of that meat you sent my brothers earlier this year. It's very nice," she said enticingly.

Shiraz laughed and shook her head. She didn't eat animal meat, why would she make an exception for human? "You never try my specialty. It hurts a girl's feelings."

"No, it doesn't. And none for her either," Shiraz said, wanting to keep Xinyi from knowing exactly what Hua's specialty was and how Shiraz had helped her find the meat. "It is too rich for us."

Hua laughed, then she wiggled her forehead. "Damn right it is. I'm here to deliver an order for royalty."

"Oooh. Coming up in the world, are we?"

"Or going down, when the situation warrants it." Hua winked.

"Well now, there's an invitation. Come buy me a drink, fancy lady."

"This is why I like her," Hua *whispered* to Xinyi. But her voice carried. "Most other creatures would shudder in fear if I *threatened* them with intimacy. But she just flirts and demands a drink. She's nicer than she lets on."

"I've noticed," Xinyi replied quietly, but Shiraz heard, and it drifted around inside her like a hug shrugged away, wide and desperately seeking a place to land.

"Is the grotto where she's meant to take you?"

"Not exactly," Xinyi answered. "Actually—I'm not sure exactly. She is supposed to be taking me to the thieves who stole my greatest treasure so I can get it back."

"The grotto is probably the best place to look, unless she somehow knows who and where they are." Hua laughed.

"She..." Xinyi stopped walking. She grabbed Shiraz back. "Do you know who they are, and where to find them?" she demanded as if this was the first moment in which the practicalities had occurred to her.

Shiraz grinned, biting into her bottom lip. She shook her head from side to side.

"I...How...What was your plan?" Xinyi's eyes flared with that fight Shiraz loved, and her arms crossed under her delightful chest.

"Get you here. Let you flounder. Take you back empty handed." Shiraz shrugged. Hua snorted. Xinyi tapped her foot impatiently, and the young monkey on her shoulder tapped her foot too.

Sea Spirits, Shiraz loved baiting this woman.

"And that sounded like a clever plan to you, did it?" Xinyi threw Shiraz's earlier words right back at her. "How did you plan to get paid?"

"Steal your bag," she replied, her sentences growing bare and informative as she lied.

Xinyi supposed she was meant to get angry and call her scum again. But she knew this woman better after two days. Maybe better than she knew most people. Shiraz would never have stolen Xinyi's wedding bag and dumped her back at Hi'mau with nothing to her name. But she wanted Xinyi to think she would; she maybe even wanted to believe it herself. But it wasn't true. And her beautiful, statuesque ogre friend and her love for Makoa were proof of her deep and loving heart.

How was she so...compelling? Distracting! They were standing in a nightclub, had entered between two giant guards (not an exaggeration, they were actual giants, as tall as trees). Now they stood in the wild, colorful, loud world of the Mushroom Grotto. The boom of the music shook her visual perception, leaving everything in a bouncing unfocus.

And there were so many kinds of beings just wandering in and out of her sight, giant mushrooms extruding colorful bubbles, and dancers on jungle vines and flat discs growing out of tree trunks!

This place was everything! It might actually be too much, but Xinyi couldn't look away from this comparatively ordinary gorgon.

After a moment, she shook her head and held out her hand, following nothing but her desire in the moment. "I know how you can make up for your tricks. Dance with me."

The captain eyed Xinyi's hand like it was fanged and venomous. She really didn't dance, did she? Still, Xinyi found it hard to believe she would turn her down. This woman's every look over the past two days led Xinyi to believe she very much wanted to be near her. And Xinyi was unused to encouraging or even considering that. But she wanted to now. She *wanted* and couldn't explain. It was as if she'd been hungry but had never known it until she tasted the sweet tang of adventure that was this woman's company.

If someone had told her two days ago that she would set out on a journey, be robbed by monkeys, attacked by alligator gods, go over a waterfall, be shrunken to smaller than a sparrow, meet and start to befriend smugglers and witches, and love every second of it, she would have thought they were suggesting a new story. But all of this was happening to her, all of this was reality. And none of it made sense. She ought to be scared. She ought to be missing home, missing comfort. She had spent the past days damp, bruised, airsick, dirty and aching. But she also felt alive like never before.

She'd always thought of herself as quiet, and happy, and safe. Not just that she had always been safe, but she felt like she was the sort of person to always need safety. Like the captain thought. Like Wei or her mother had apparently thought. Everyone wishing her safe, because it was what she needed. But it wasn't true. She needed *this*.

"Please," Xinyi said softly, smiling at the nervous woman before her.

Shiraz looked like a more vibrant version of the woman she'd met in the market. Bold, confident, rebellious. Wasn't it funny that the more Xinyi knew of her, the quieter this woman seemed, even done up to look intimidating? Xinyi slipped her hand into Shiraz's, trying to hold the bubbling excitement in her heart.

"This will launch a whole new series of adventures. I can feel it."

She was going to say yes. The captain's thumb rubbed slow electric circles on Xinyi's skin, sending sparks through her body. Xinyi's breath deserted her, and she startled, jerking her hand a little because of the newness and all the desires she could not voice. But the captain misunderstood.

She let go of Xinyi's hand, shaking her head and her voice dropping flat. "Oh dear, Jian won't know what hit her."

"Jian? Don't tell me you finally found your favorite author?" Hua asked, startling Xinyi.

How had she forgotten a towering ogre was standing next to her? And also...*favorite author?* Was that true?

"I'm going to get that drink. Maybe Hua will dance with you." The captain turned away before Xinyi could pull words together.

Hua looked at Xinyi awkwardly, bobbing her head. "If you like?"

Xinyi couldn't refuse. She liked the woman beside her. She just... wasn't who Xinyi wanted to dance with. She wished she'd been quicker to say what she was feeling. Louder. Wished she'd been able to express fast enough that the desire she was feeling was new and overwhelming but in every way beautiful. She wished she could pull Shiraz into some sparkling corner of this wonderland and explain that for once she hadn't been talking about her stories. She'd been talking about herself. She longed to be loud enough to say—

Take me with you. Let's have more adventures. I don't want this to end.

But she wasn't fast enough. So she watched Shiraz walk away and let herself be pulled out into a dance.

Dark Thoughts in Bright Places

Another day, kuffik, three hours ago Makoa would not have left Shiraz and Xinyi alone in the night club. Shiraz's plan was too dangerous. But he hadn't spotted either Felicia or Aiattaua anywhere and... He needed to see.

Too many of the witch's words had been floating around in his head. And Shiraz's kiss on his cheek. And the shaky feeling beneath his skin. All of it demanded attention. He would usually ignore it. That was his move. Ignore the scary feelings inside for the benefit of the team, the relationship, the family.

Perhaps not in the beginning. When he first transformed, he'd gone from one person to the next, desperately seeking his soulmate. He tricked kisses out of people in committed relationships, people who'd never been kissed, or who'd kissed dozens. In that first year alone, he went through no less than a hundred pairs of lips. And didn't care what sort of mess he left behind. The four mermaid sisters who discovered they had all kissed him, along with one sister's husband, had been a particularly messy moment. But he just left. Changed into a salmon and swam away.

And that's when he'd encountered Shiraz for a second time. And gained nothing but annoyance that she refused him a kiss.

But the third time he encountered Shiraz, when she tried to save him with a *true love's kiss*, that had felt like fate. Why else did they keep meeting? She was running with a group of thieves, the sort who aimed at robbery, but weren't opposed to beatings or even murder if it meant getting what they wanted. Not really her style, and there was no reason he should have spotted her among them, but he had. And he'd wanted to get back at her for refusing him a kiss.

He pretended to be an elf, got them to rob and beat him, all to trick her into feeling so sorry for him that she would give him a kiss to save his life. So he could lord it over her. It even worked. He still lorded it over her. But...she broke with the other thieves, stopped them from killing him. Gave him his kiss.

It all seemed like a bit of fun. Until she left the other thieves behind and seemed so—*brightened* that Makoa felt jealous. He took it as a sign that he needed to do something, anything other than questing around trying to break his spell.

Ever since then, if he felt a wholly selfish urge crawl over him, he ignored it. He found Shiraz and smuggled food to starving villagers or helped people escape dangerous situations. But right now, when he should be trying to find Xinyi's thieves. Or trying to suss out if Aiattaua was helping Felicia against his will or for his own ends. Or find someone who could truly challenge that demigoddess like...her mother, or another dragon maybe. There was plenty to do, but there were tears in his throat and his heart was racing, and he knew if he didn't try this now, he never would. Dao's affliction as well encouraged him to move. Something was changing. He'd never felt this connected to the bodies he'd taken on. And this change wasn't isolated. He'd felt Ayinde too. He needed to see if this was something good or terrible. So he slipped away to the reflecting pools.

The interior grotto was bright, colorful, and obvious. But the reflecting pools were a quiet area where birds whistled and mist filled the air. The ground was perpetually damp moss. Tiny mushrooms sprinkled the ground in clusters that swayed together hypnotically. Larger mushrooms formed the structure of the pools, each with their own style and color. Some stalks held multiple blooms, so that one sunken in mushroom-cap might hold a pool of fragrant water, while another cap bent over it like a shade, drooping tendrils to conceal anyone inside. Another stalk with an upturned cap held steaming water, and coiled around inside was a giant snake, a lake monster from the south, one of the bits of contraband entertainment Shiraz and Makoa had snuck into Loqwan for Aiattaua.

Makoa headed past the pools to a stone hill. Moss climbed its side, and a few ferns grew out of divots in the stone. At the top, he found a puddle encircled in elf ear mushrooms. Soft shades of pink and blue and purple and white formed the lily-like layered blooms of the fungi.

It was said to be the world's quietest pool. The fungi eating all sound and keeping all secrets. Makoa leaned over the water. Still in Dao's body, he gazed at the reflection he cast, something he rarely did. Pulling in a deep breath he shut his eyes, envisioning the face he had not seen in so long. Wishing. Makoa blew out the spell, hoping with all his heart.

He opened his eyes.

"Do you know the first thing I thought when I saw you today?" Felicia took up the seat next to Shiraz at the bar, already talking.

Shiraz had been waiting for her. When Xinyi asked her to dance earlier...despite knowing it was a bad idea, despite hating to dance, Shiraz had been tempted to say yes. She would have if she hadn't realized she felt so much more than Xinyi. So she sat here, watching Xinyi embrace this new experience wholeheartedly. She went from dancing with Hua to a new group on the dance floor. She was such a conundrum. Even as Shiraz was drilling off her list of rules, she had known it was pointless. Xinyi didn't follow one rule Shiraz made. She was somehow more of a rebel than Shiraz had ever been. And so politely. She encountered all manner of dangers, and they...fell in love with her, like the monkey dancing on her shoulder. Like Shiraz.

Shiraz dragged her gaze to Felicia and raised a brow.

"It is ten years since we escaped prison together and you still wear that tattered vest."

Shiraz rolled her shoulders, discomforted not to be wearing it now. What if the plan didn't work? "It was one of the only personal belongings that survived the ship you wrecked. I try to hold onto it."

"So dramatic." Felicia slammed a spiked boot onto the base of Shiraz's seat. "Things come and go; you shouldn't get so attached."

Felicia was the type to intimidate most women, men, or really any beings with burnable flesh so...everyone but dragons. And Shiraz was no exception, but there was a time when Shiraz would spit in the face of those who intimidated her, and she felt that old her come out in the face of her former cellmate.

"It was my home, and my livelihood. I think you feel bad about it."

"Is that what you think?" The demigoddess reached over the bar. She grabbed a bottle of liquor, drinking straight from it. The bartender shouted and made to yank it back, but spotting Felicia, wisely chose not to intervene. "Then I guess we're even. I saved you today."

"Not even close. So, tell me why you are after the Serpent."

"What serpent? Is it magical? Can it devour flames?"

"The River Serpent. My ship. I know you took out a bounty on it."

Felicia nearly spit out her alcohol. "I don't *pay* bounties! I collect them. And I'm not out to ruin your life. I'm still rooting for you, kid."

Shiraz didn't believe her. But she hadn't expected to brazen her into admitting this. "Alright then, maybe you can help me. I've been having this pain recently, maybe you can help me figure out why."

"You're over twelve," Felicia observed. "Expect to have pain regularly until you die."

Shiraz laughed involuntarily at the reminder. "Menstruating."

Felicia raised a brow. "It makes it *less* funny when you explain it. Not more."

"That wasn't the joke." Shiraz opened her mouth to explain but didn't really feel like it. "You had to be there."

"Clearly."

"This is what I'm talking about." Shiraz held out her arm revealing her tattoo, and the burns eating away at its edges. Letting Felicia see exactly where the River Serpent was. Here, in this room.

Shiraz had tucked the chain with the boat on it under her vest, so the boat could not be seen, but if she was the one after it, Felicia would guess; she must know some of what it could do.

The demigoddess set down her bottle and dropped her boots to the ground. She took Shiraz's hand gently in her own and ran a second hand around the burns.

"So it is a magical serpent. Oh, Speedy Hands, you've gotten interesting since breaking out of prison."

The Elf Prince, Well, one of Them

"**M**akoa?" Like his mother's people the sirens, Aiattaua's voice fell upon the ear invitingly, no matter what he said. It was such a comfort some times. Pulled one out of oneself.

But at the moment, Makoa wasn't himself. He wasn't anyone. He didn't know why he'd expected different when he blew out his curse. He'd just *felt different.* But here he was, staring down at another reflection, someone he met years ago, someone he didn't even recall by name. The bits of life story he'd shared passed through Makoa's mind. Another curse victim.

He had not been thinking of this man. So why was he the face that came out? Was the magic taunting him? Showing him another cursed man to say he would always be cursed?

A day ago, he hadn't been sure he wanted an end to his curse. Then the idea built in his head that it was breaking and it was all he wanted. Now he stared into the pool equal parts disappointed and relieved. Nothing had changed. He didn't have to know if he was happy or not, because it was more of the same. And he was always...content.

It must devour your heart sometimes... you must question whether you would even know yourself if you were to find your old form again. Must question if you, the self you once knew, even exist any longer.

Yes. Some days he did, he acknowledged as Xinyi's words drifted through his mind. Was it any wonder he kept blaming her?

"Makoa?" The prince settled on the rocks nearby. "Are you well?"

"I can't say that I know," Makoa answered. He and Aiattaua had never had any need for secrets.

"This is not a face I have ever seen before," the prince observed. "Was he special to you?"

"There is a whole world full of faces you have not seen, Aiattaua, and partners you have yet to find."

The prince laughed softly. It was an aspect of Aiattaua's personality that Makoa appreciated. He took criticism with equanimity. Only fighting it when he felt there was something wrong with your argument. His lack of rising to the fighting bait annoyed Makoa today though. He wanted a fight, which wasn't like him. This him, cursed him. He wished there weren't so many versions of him.

Makoa pulled his eyes off the pool and observed Aiattaua. He was a delight to the senses. His voice coaxed the ear, his blue-green skin had a soothing tone that was comforting to look at and was soft to the touch. He smelled of the earth kissed by dew with the slightest tang of citrus blossoms. And his appearance was unquestionably beautiful. He was not particularly muscular, nor particularly thin, but it was his face, with its intent grey eyes and beautifully engaging smile, that called one most to the prince of temptation.

He had a brow in the air now and a sweet smile encouraging Makoa to talk. That trait as well was compelling. Though the prince loved the sound of his own voice, he also loved to listen.

"The man was not special. I barely remember him. We spent a few hours in a pub commiserating over our respective and recent curses. Pondering how we might break them."

"A comrade then. That is special. Even if the relationship is not long. I am always curious when I see a new face, but...did you kiss?"

Found this face attractive, did he? Makoa refused to answer. He did not have to kiss people to take on their shape, only to see them. He knew Aiattaua had no resentment of the people Makoa kissed seeking a curse breaker; he was more likely to ask to watch. But Makoa didn't feel compelled to disabuse him of this assumption. Or anyone else.

"Why is he the face you brought to this pool?" Aiattaua pondered when Makoa did not respond.

"He isn't. I wore Dao's. I...thought something had changed. I thought I could take on my old form. I was trying to transform, and this face came out instead. A reminder I will always be cursed."

"Could it not be merely that he is further in your past? Perhaps you are growing closer to breaking it but are not there yet."

Makoa shoved to his feet. He stepped over the prone prince. Aiattaua merely stretched out more comfortably, folding his arms beneath his head. The foot length folds of Aiattaua's gown were embroidered with images of a dark and moody sea storm, high waves frothing, tentacles rising from the deep, and a ship ripped to shreds. Such a violent image in contrast to the lovely prince. His long black hair stretched out across the ground and apparently tickled some near by shrooms until they began playing with the ends, braiding little bits.

Makoa didn't want to discuss his transformation, or lack there of. He didn't want to discuss his curse. He stared at the prince's attire. Aiattaua frequently wore gowns with sea themed embroidery but rarely with such violent overtones. Was it a warning?

Many of the elf king's twenty-seven children wore clothing invoking the mothers they had been forced to leave on their twentieth birthdays. Only two among them had the same mother, as the elf king wished to "share" his fortune of "strength, intelligence, and long life," around the world. His plan had created twenty-seven stunning individuals. But it had also resulted in varying feelings of resentment for him from his children. And a certain sense among them that no one but they mattered.

"Speaking of myself and your likewise bonded spouses, when shall we all be presented to your father, my love?" Makoa asked.

"About that," Aiattaua's gaze shifted to the sky. "I am not sure any longer that...our planned presentation is a good idea. It is not the best way to force my father to confront his choices. And...I do not want to use my loves the same way he does his children."

"What inspired this change of heart?" Makoa demanded, shocked by the prince for the first time since they met. Aiattaua was constantly driven by his plan to make his father see how he hurt people by forcing what he loved to stay beside him. It ruled the prince's choices. It was a flaw, but one Makoa understood.

Aiattaua pulled a hand out from under his head and tickled the chorus of mushrooms braiding his hair. "What some of us had taken for a change in fashion, his beard is in fact growing threads of fungi."

"Oh." Makoa sat beside the prince's head. He stretched out a hand, taking Aiattaua's. The king was entering decomposition. The process could take centuries, but it certainly marked the beginning of the end for an elf. And the king had had the thready white beard for as long as Makoa had known him. How long had he been concealing his decline from his children? "I am sorry. Are *you* well?"

"I cannot say that I know," the prince returned Makoa's words. "It has had an odd effect on us all. I had, up until recently, been forming plans to enter a bubble world Halimah made to find a few more spouses. I was hoping for an odd twenty-seven."

Makoa rolled his eyes at the competitive plan. "What's a bubble world?"

"One of her experiments. She took volunteer humans, of no magic, and created them a world within one of the larger bulbs of sap formed from great great, great grandmother Bowzhai. It has been developing for merely five of our months, but within the bubble, one thousand years have passed. Guomundur and Riku went through already and claim to have been worshiped as gods." Makoa laughed, his fingers playing lightly in Aiattaua's palm. He wasn't used to the prince sharing about his family, other than his hatred of his father. But this sounded almost fond. So Makoa held back questions of how much more adulation the elf princes could possibly need than what they were already afforded.

"Halimah is furious she says they ruined the experiment. She wanted to see a world without Father's influence. Daiyu pointed out that she never could have succeeded since Halimah was influenced by Father. The whole thing made Halimah posit that there are no gods, and we are all experiments in other being's decomposition bubbles."

"Shiraz would like that."

The prince nodded. "Is she with you on this journey?" He had no skill at interrogation.

"She's around." Makoa had a feeling he was more likely to get the answers he was after by sticking to the subject of the dying elf king. "What changed your mind about going into the bubble?"

"Daiyu asked us all to stay. Asked us, *for her*, to get to know our father as a king who is very flawed, but not evil."

"Your eldest sister has always been more parent to you than anyone else here," Makoa remarked as Aiattaua drifted off.

"It has been four of the most boring months I've ever spent. I have resorted to all sorts of embarrassing pastimes to get through."

Now they were getting somewhere. "Like what, knitting?"

"I already knit! What is embarrassing about knitting?" Aiattaua glared. "You never speak of your family. Have you ever gone to them?"

"And said what?" Makoa snapped. "I'm your son—" Makoa tried to spit out his own name, his old name, the name he was born with, but all that emerged was a choking sound as his vocal cords seized up.

Makoa fought it. Gagging until tears filled his eyes and he started to feel faint. He stopped trying, shuddering under his many skins, and angered that Aiattaua had provoked him.

"I am sorry," Aiattaua said softly, his hand on Makoa's knee. "I should not have asked."

"I could not convince them. It would be torture for them." *And for me,* Makoa thought, but did not voice. "Better they think I am dead."

Aiattaua threaded his fingers through Makoa's and squeezed "Not better. I am sorry. You are loved still. I am certain they love you. Even if they think you are dead. Maybe *more* that way!"

Their eyes met, and both men laughed. A dark sense of humor was one of the first things they bonded over. But it occurred to Makoa that this disconnected feeling, being forcibly separated from family they both knew to be alive but knew as well would never understand who they were now, that was another connection they shared.

"Distract me," Makoa nudged. "What embarrassing things have you been doing?"

"All kinds," Aiattaua complied. "Most recently—you remember that book Shiraz left behind when she stormed out of the grotto and cut our bond party short?" Aiattaua said snidely pointed.

"You minded?" Makoa asked. "You always say nothing in my life ought to change. Except that I go knowing I am loved and return with love in my heart."

Aiattaua sighed heavily. "Of course I still feel that way, but...when our celebrations are dependent on other voices being happy for us, ones who are openly opposed to us, and you take her side, that hurts."

Makoa leaned down and kissed Aiattaua softly. "I am sorry. It was habit to go along with her, but...I will do better. And so will she. She is not against us. She is scared."

Aiattaua scrunched up his face. "I am trying too, that's what I was saying. I kept her story. I knew she would want it back, and I am trying to make friends with your prickly best friend."

Makoa smiled. He appreciated that Aiattaua continued trying with Shiraz. Though she didn't with him. He needed to call her on it more; it wasn't fair to his relationship.

"One evening *The Immortal King* was going on about Loqwan's king and his heartbreak over the separation from his daughter and granddaughter. Waxing poetic about feeling the man's pain, having had twenty years of each of our lives *'stolen'* from him. It was sooooo self-indulgent that I started reading the story. It wasn't my thing, but it helped drown him out, so I kept reading. By the third chapter, I was hooked. When I ran out of chapters, I sent servants to get more. But there were only three additional chapters published."

Makoa's unease grew as pieces feel into place in his mind.

"I had no idea how addictive reading could be. I am utterly enthralled. I need to know how it ends."

"And for that answer you put out a bounty on its writer and our ship?" Makoa shouted. The sound was muffled from the wider grotto by the mushrooms, but Aiattaua clearly heard it as a yell.

He took back his hand and sat up, twisting around to face Makoa in one fluid movement that was oddly threatening. "Are you accusing me of something, my love?"

The Demi~dragon and the Steadfast Girl

Dens of smugglers and thieves were always dank, quiet and threatening in stories. At least the stories Xinyi read. She wondered now, as she spun around the dance floor, if that was done intentionally. Maybe they were painted as frightening places with unhappy people so that children were afraid to wind up there. Because the Mushroom Grotto was nothing but fun!

Xinyi loved it. She spun around and around with her head back, watching the colorful lights and the trees that acted like buildings above her. Their intertwined branches and looping vines looked like curtains and the gigantic mushrooms of luminous colors around their bases or growing across their branches and right up their trunks reminded her of the glow worms in the tunnel. *Their* tunnel. She could not understand why Shiraz was leaning against the bar with a scowl on her face, slowly sipping the same drink she'd had since they got here.

Xinyi didn't think she would ever be able to think of the woman as only *the captain* or *the smuggler* again. Though she was clearly both of those things. Xinyi's perception had been changing this whole trip, and it underwent its most profound change before the boat crashed, while Shiraz adjusted Xinyi's clothes and shared bits of her past. She was not a woman easily shoved into a role, even the roles she had chosen. The more Xinyi knew of her, the more she wondered why Shiraz had chosen smuggler and thief. Why she'd been in prison? And it was not because she felt those choices were scummy any longer, it was just…because she needed to know her. She wanted to know more about the Singing Hills. Wanted to know, if she was going to be a criminal, why she didn't enjoy it? She wanted to know so much about Shiraz and three days wasn't nearly enough time to learn all she wanted to know.

"Do you know why Shiraz went to prison?" Xinyi asked one of her dance partners. The two who'd introduced themselves as friends of Shiraz and Makoa were named Miti and Hikari.

Hikari was a human woman in her later fifties with soft lavender eyes. She tilted her head aside and shook it. "When was this?"

Oops. Xinyi hadn't thought it was a secret.

"Long before she came here," the much younger Miti, a fairy with dark brown skin, a tightly curled dome of hair and luminous green wings put in. "Don't know the reason. But I take it she was somewhat wilder before."

It was in my try everything period.

"Did you know her then? And her friend…Crysta?" Xinyi had heard the name only once. It shouldn't stick out so clearly in her thoughts, but it did. And she wanted to know everything, though it was none of her business. She had begun by asking about her business, but thus far no one knew anything about the thieves. Xinyi was finding it increasingly difficult to care though.

"No," Miti laughed. "I met her and Makoa three years ago. I only know about the prison stent because her prison break is legendary. It's part of a seminar my uncle teaches at the Wilcut Academy of the Fey called *Why Imprisonment is Both Pointless and Costly: a Guide to Restorative Justice and Rehabilitation.*"

"Oh my, that sounds interesting." Xinyi leaned in. "Can anyone attend, or must they be fey?"

"Well, it is a fey academy, but they've made exceptions before."

"Really!" Xinyi filed that away, excited. But her curiosity about the other woman was far from sated. "Why is the jail break legendary?"

"It led to the rest of the prisoners rising up. The whole island is ruled by what once were inmates now."

"Wow." Xinyi glanced back. The captain was no longer alone. There was another woman with her. Was this the demigoddess? She looked dangerous. She had bright blue skin, cascades of waving purple hair, and over her neck-to-toe leather clothing, she had strapped a thin blade at her back, and tiny knives around her waist, and her boots had spikes, although perhaps it wasn't the boots that were spiked. She had spiky bones protruding from her shoulders, elbows and knuckles. She looked like the type of woman Shiraz would call friend, bold, aggressive, confident.

She looked all violence, but her hand ran softly over the captain's forearm, and her face was so near the other woman's skin, it looked like she might kiss her.

Xinyi felt something tingling beneath her skin. Something that ought to be excitement or shock, even shyness at such a public display, but felt more—*annoyed*.

No one in this crowd would notice if the woman kissed the captain. There were a number of people against trees or on the dance floor kissing and touching. None of that bothered Xinyi. So it shouldn't bother her to see the stranger kiss the captain, but it did. And she could not look away.

The blue woman shifted her head towards the dance floor. Her eyes landed on Xinyi. She winked. Xinyi jerk around. She couldn't calm her racing heart or her heating skin.

What was wrong with her, spying like that?

"Quit stalling. What do you know?" Felicia had been examining Shiraz's arm for the better part of a minute, and it was all show. Felicia loved lording things over anyone, enemy, stranger, friend, if you could call anyone her friend, with the way she treated other beings.

"You're being hunted," the demigoddess said at last. "Or more specifically," Felicia popped a smug brow, "The *River Serpent* is being hunted. Who gave you the tattoo? Anyone I know?"

Shiraz drew her hand away. If Felicia knew enough to burn the tattoo off her, she knew who made the tattoo.

"You should take out a bounty. I'm available. If the price is right."

"I don't take out bounties. I let tempers cool and memories fade."

Felicia laughed, spraying alcohol on the air **and Shiraz.**

"Given up on your mother's throne then?" Shiraz asked, trying to understand the woman's motives for stealing the ship.

"Not in the least. I just need money as I prepare. I am creating an unstoppable army of fey, witches, sorceresses, and wizards. Together we'll dethrone the goddess. Then *I* will rule over the mountain of fire." She gazed into the distance a moment. "That's why I'm in Loqwan. I'm looking for a particular sorceress. She's been mentioned across the entire continent!"

Shiraz shifted her gaze, checking on Xinyi. "What's her power?"

"I am not sure. She is something of a mystery. The Sorceress of the Sands, they call her. Some say she wakes and weaponizes the dead. Some say she buries her enemies alive. They credit her with the destruction of Cyrus."

"What happened to Cyrus?" Shiraz demanded. It was on her list of interesting world sites to visit. It was a very long list, but Cyrus had the seventh largest public library in the world. Or it had.

"You hadn't heard? A few months ago, the entire city was buried. Only a few souls made it out."

"Wow."

"I know. But I cannot confirm a single rumor. Another puts the sorceress in Faahishel freeing a bunch of orphan slaves. I know which story I prefer but…"

Shiraz laughed. "You *prefer* stories of destruction to kindness?"

"Such a steadfast girl at heart," Felicia taunted. "Refusing to kill, even if it will cost you everything."

"Not taking out bounties is practical, not religious. Rob someone, give them a year or seven and they forget, but kill someone and their whole family remembers you for decades," Shiraz argued, annoyed that Felicia would bring up her past. But she didn't argue hard. She hadn't taken many things from the place of her birth, but a distaste for murder had stuck. "Anyway," she met Felicia's eyes, warning her former cellmate, "I have killed someone. Four someones this year."

"Gathering!" Felicia shouted, jumping to her feet and spewing at tiny bit of fiery lava into her own drink. It sizzled, jerking around the liquid for a moment before settling heavy at the bottom of the bottle as a shiny black stone. The music didn't stop, but the dancers did, turning this way cautiously. "A toast! My friend Shiraz is a virgin no more."

"I was never a virgin," Shiraz muttered.

Felicia tilted her head sideways with a brow in the air.

"Here," Shiraz clarified.

"A murder virgin," Felicia specified for the gathering.

Some cheered, some laughed, none but Xinyi dared do neither in the face of the demigoddess. Shiraz couldn't bring her gaze to look at her directly. Xinyi would not approve. Shiraz didn't really approve, but...she also did.

Felicia didn't say anything for the longest time after the moment passed and festivities resumed. "It's up to you to decide how to defend yourself. But I like knowing you're alive, Speedy Hands. And when that map is a tiny little speck with only the boat visible, *someone* will know where you are. Why would you put something like that on yourself? Do you know how dangerous that is? I thought I taught you to be more savvy in prison. What do you think they'll do with you and your lover?"

"Makoa is my friend."

Felicia laughed. "I meant the shiny new friend you've brought us."

"Xinyi is my *client*." Shiraz threw back the last of her drink and stood, slapping down some coin. *Taught her to be savvy.* Rude. Shiraz looked out for herself. But she'd laid enough bait, even if she didn't understand Felicia's full motives.

Most likely she thought the River Serpent would have an easier time finding her mystery sorceress. Or perhaps it was simpler. Felicia had made the mistake of announcing she was after her mother's throne. Goddess or not, no one challenged a woman made entirely of fire without putting themself in danger. The River Serpent was good at slipping by people, and if the tattoo that tracked it was gone, it might be able to vanish, keeping Felicia hidden.

"She doesn't like me touching you," Felicia said. For a moment, Shiraz thought Felicia referred to her mother. But she saw her smirk and understood.

A tingle of excitement rushed through her. She nearly asked what made her think that. But nothing could come of this fascination with Xinyi. If her plan worked, Shiraz was leaving Loqwan. And even if Xinyi was enjoying herself, she wouldn't be coming along.

"And you watch her awfully close. You worry over her opinion," Felicia went on, pouting. This was a woman who wanted all of a person's attention. If she felt neglected (as she had been by her mother) she sought revenge, shifting shape into what could only be described as a dragon and setting things on fire.

Her dragon form was only about two feet tall and seven long. She did not have the impressive, frilled faces of Loqwan's dragons, or the horned crests and backs of Great Island's dragons. She didn't even have sharp teeth. In that form, her body and face were lizard-like, not even her spiked joints came with the form, but she was nevertheless a dragon, and one who spit lava! Not something you wanted spit at you. Shiraz had learned the hard way to give this woman plenty of attention.

"I'm attracted to her," Shiraz admitted. "She is funny, enthusiastic, intelligent, weirdly adventurous. I keep giving her instructions to keep her safe, and she doesn't listen to any of them," Shiraz laughed as she spoke. "She is never safe, but she is always—I don't know—*There are women who thrive in chaotic, unordered freedom.* And somehow, incongruously, she's one of us. She makes no sense. And it's marvelous! She's been attacked, robbed, transformed, and nearly eaten, but she hasn't asked to go back once. And she is absolutely beautiful. Who wouldn't be attracted? But that's it." Shiraz cleared her throat. "It's just a prettier, more exciting job than usual."

"Or you are still the exact same girl from prison? Always falling for people who are out of your reach. Wanting them to want you more than...anything else. You should try something new."

"Why?" Shiraz demanded. "Why should I stop loving someone just because they do not love me the same way? I have never been loved by life in the way I love it. But the love is still there. Still beautiful. Can we not...love each other in our own ways? Why isn't that as beautiful?"

"*So sweet,*" Felicia squealed in a condescending saccharin tone. "Is this one in love with your brother too?"

"Ugh." Shiraz growled in frustration. Tabby was half a life time ago. She wished she'd never told this woman about her first love. Shiraz hopped up on the bar. "Hey, a word of advice," she shouted. Kindly, some patrons turned their way once more, though they looked more annoyed this time, and there were less of them looking.

"If you are ever in prison, don't tell your cell mate one true thing about yourself. Invent a name, an age, a crime. If they ask where you were born, say the sun! Because if by some catastrophe she escapes, she will torture you, using any knowledge she has to manipulate you like a vigilante emotional guide and older sister for the rest of eternity."

"True story." Felicia raised her bottle to the crowd.

People burst into laughter and conversation. And Shiraz, now that the adrenaline had passed, started feeling embarrassed of her outburst. She twisted, trying to get down from the bar. It had been easy to get up, but now the floor seemed so far away. Felicia laughed and held out her arms, letting Shiraz lean on her to clamber down.

"Let me help you, *little sister*," Felicia teased. When Shiraz was on her feet, Felicia slid a hand up Shiraz's arm to her neck. She moved her body into Shiraz gently and pressed their lips together. Shiraz was so startled she froze. But it was a useful mode of distraction. She slipped her arms around Felicia's waist and up her back. She'd forgotten her spine was spiked too. But for a spiky thing, Felicia had soft lips. They moved over Shiraz warmly, but far from passionately. She grinned against Shiraz and took a sharp nip at her bottom lip.

Shiraz shoved out of Felicia's arms, Felicia's blade stuffed up under the back of Shiraz's vest, concealing the theft.

"Just checking." Felicia chuckled. "I have it on excellent authority that steadfast women are always true to their lovers."

Shiraz rolled her tongue around her teeth. "That is one definition of steadfast," Shiraz observed, annoyed. "Though I don't think I heard the word *lovers* until I left the steadfast island."

Felicia giggled. Not something one expected of a dragon.

Shiraz didn't see Xinyi in the crowd. It wasn't that she worried the other woman would be jealous, nor was there anything in their two day acquaintance for Shiraz to be true to. But...she didn't like having lost sight of her.

"Think about what I've said. There are people who will want you as you are, steadfast girl." Felicia grinned so invitingly Shiraz momentarily believed her and felt bad that she had never noticed Felicia's interest. She kept saying she cared about Shiraz. She even seemed sincere when she claimed to be on her side.

But...The River Serpent no longer rested at Shiraz's heart, so the kiss was definitely manipulation. Why was Shiraz such an easy target?

Shiraz growled and stomped away. She didn't want Felicia to be in love with her, because *wow*, that sounded dangerous. In particular because she wouldn't return the feelings. But...Shiraz really hated people knowing where she was from.

Naked Vengeance

What Xinyi had taken for pink mist was a cloud of spores. Thin pink tinted bubbles formed in the holes in the porous mushrooms. Once they were too big to fit any longer, they burst forth. Some floated around in the air, but most popped while leaving their chambers and sprayed over the ground. Xinyi was fascinated.

She'd turned away from the captain because she thought the woman with her was deliberately trying to provoke Xinyi and embarrass the captain by calling her a murderer. Xinyi didn't believe that. If Shiraz were willing to kill, then she would have attacked the alligator god. Or tried to kill the pixies, or the monkeys.

But she could tell Shiraz didn't want Xinyi to have heard. So she turned away to give them privacy. And very quickly Xinyi's interest was reabsorbed in this magical world. She moved into the mist of spores and let them fall around her, let them kiss her skin. Let the pulsing music move her. She looked up through the spores to one overlarge bubble that was swaying and twisting in the air. It seemed to be bumping up and down on the threads of vine where the dancers shifted and swayed to the music. The closer she looked at the bubble the more she thought she saw...herself. Her tree. Her past.

Xinyi was only seven years old, but she had been tasked with caring for a portion of the garden by the family who'd taken her in. They wanted to help her cultivate peace, something she desperately needed. She kept running away. She ran to the same place every time, the tree in the garden where she'd been found.

She had lived with them comfortably for years. But a few months ago, she saw her mother in the market. The mother who left her beneath that tree with a basket of nectar blossoms and told her to wait. The woman swore to Xinyi's new family that she had never had children. But Xinyi knew she lied.

Her mother was angry with her.

Her new family didn't want her to be sad, but they wanted her to be safe. So they gave her that tree to care for. She went every day, watered it, pulled weeds that ate around its roots, watched for any change in leaves. But because she went daily, it took barely any time to complete her task. And it was always first thing in the morning, when the time she wanted to be there was in the night when all was quiet and she could feel the chill and remember the pale blue ring around the moon from the night she was left behind.

So she took more time doing the exact same things. Stood twice as long pouring water over the roots, dug through mud for any signs of future weeds, until the ground was soppy and full of holes and clumps of mud and Xinyi was terribly dirty. So the family decided she should only be allowed at the tree once every three days. They took special care that she did not run to the tree in the night again, forcing their visiting nieces and nephews to sleep together in the home's main room, so there would be no space for her to walk. She was too clumsy to get through them without waking the whole room. She'd lain awake every night that she was kept away, envisioning the tree dying in her absence because of her neglect. When she was finally allowed near it again, she was so exhausted that she'd taken the *array of mushrooms growing out of the overly damp ground for stars. She had fallen to the ground before the tree sobbing.*

"Everything is upside down," she cried out. "Ma will never find me. I have fallen into the sky. I am not where she left me."

Wei, who was just Xinyi's age and was among the cousins visiting her adoptive family, sat beside her. They had played together before, but not spoken much. He, like Xinyi, was quiet. He sat beside her, as she cried.

"Don't worry. Stars are maps in the sky," he'd said. "She will find you. But I hope she leaves you with us for a while. No one else ever thinks to grow poison mushrooms in the garden."

Xinyi stumbled through the pink haze, bumping into a woman standing like a column before her. Oh, it was Makoa. Where had he b—

"I am so sorry." Xinyi tilted her head towards the green skinned woman before her. Once she turned around, it was clear this was not Makoa, but it was the form she'd last seen him inhabit. But the differences were clear. Her eyes did not glow teal. They had brown irises, with a constellation of greenish freckles in her right eye. Also she wore her frame much more...erect. A soldier's stance. Xinyi was fascinated by the subtle differences, and with her fascination, she felt her past tugged away like a shawl in the wind. She felt better. And yet she wanted to follow that shawl, to chase it down and wrap it around herself. She was comfortable in the shawl; it was safe.

Would you wish to be brought safely home? Would you wish to stay safely there?

She shook her head to clear it. "I...was distracted by my past and did not look where I walked. I hope you will forgive me."

"You breathed in the pink spores," the woman informed her. "It is called memory. A mundane way to spend one's time in such a place, don't you think? The purple is much more fun."

Xinyi did not know how to respond. She was fascinated that there were mushroom spores that could drag one into the past merely from breathing them in. She had questions, but not just about that. She wondered if the woman felt it when Makoa took on her form. Wondered if she was menstruating, though that felt like a very invasive question to ask a stranger. She had many questions, her fingers itched to take out her journal, but she didn't realize they had actually flicked her wedding bag until the woman shifted her gaze that way.

From that angle, Xinyi realized there were freckles in both the stranger's eyes, but the ones on the left were above her iris, so they'd been hidden by her eyelid.

"Where did you come by that bag?" the elf asked intensely.

"I...My husband," Xinyi answered hesitantly.

The elf lifted her gaze once more to Xinyi, and then over her shoulder. Xinyi wondered what caught her attention. *Oh.* Shiraz and that woman who'd been examining her arm were in a passionate embrace. She was *kissing* the woman who was after her boat!

"You are Princess Xinyi, yes?" The elf pulled Xinyi's attention back. "Prince Aiattaua and Makoa sent me to retrieve you. I am Commander Dao, of the elf guard."

"Oh. That must have been awkward." Xinyi giggled nervously, but also in amusement imagining herself confronted with Makoa in her body. What would she do? Would she be amused? Unnerved? Offended?

The woman said nothing, nor did her expression really. So apparently Xinyi wasn't to know how that exchange went. Although, it was strange that Makoa hadn't come for her himself. He and Shiraz trusted no one they didn't already know. But they knew Xinyi trusted people she had never met, and she had seen him take on this form.

The elf nodded down a path lit only by tiny floating lights that looked no larger than bugs. "They have found what you are seeking."

Xinyi felt the captain yelling in her mind not to trust this woman. Even Sweetums was tugging at her, wanting her to go back to dancing. But Xinyi did not feel right stopping a servant from completing a task. And more then that...she didn't need to be coddled. An urge rolled under her skin, not just to do things her own way, but to defy the captain's rules specifically. Xinyi was always doing what other people asked, and it never made her any safer, just quieter and smaller. The sheer nerve of Shiraz annoyed her.

She flirted and flirted and flirted with Xinyi, but when Xinyi asked her to dance, she refused, all to go kiss the woman trying to rob her. Why should Xinyi feel bad for ignoring her advice? She didn't. She wouldn't. She would do what she felt like and forget Shiraz's rules.

"Lead the way," Xinyi said brightly.

Sweetums hopped off Xinyi's shoulder. She flung her body at the elf. The elf moved aside quickly, but Sweetums managed to catch her uniform as she slid to the ground. She stood between the women screeching militantly.

"What's wrong?" Xinyi coaxed. "Don't you want to come?"

Sweetums hissed, showing off her teeth, then fled towards the dancing.

"Do you need to follow?" Dao asked considerately.

"I...Don't think so. She is not my monkey. She stays with me when she likes to and leaves when she does not."

"An intelligent arrangement." The woman waited.

Xinyi tried to trace the monkey's path, but the dance floor was much more crowded than when she walked into the pink mist. She was vaguely unnerved by Sweetums's departure. Perhaps she should be following her to safety.

But she smiled at the elf, noting the long sword that hung from her belt. A potential threat! Xinyi followed her into the dim. It was probably not dangerous at all. She would walk right to Makoa, meet the elf prince.

But perhaps...there was danger down the dim path. She felt wildly hungry for danger just at the moment. "What is the purple mist called?" she asked, hopeful for something threatening.

The woman responded indifferently. "Naked Vengeance."

Xinyi giggled, releasing the last of her caution, and walked into the darkness.

The Universal Dynamics of Sibling Hierarchy

Sweetums climbed Shiraz, intentionally using claw when she could have made due with paw. Shiraz nearly ripped the pain in the ngok off and threw her, but the monkey hadn't come to her for no reason. When she got to Shiraz's arm, she hung off the outside of her shoulder and held out a fist.

The monkey deposited a pendant shaped like a silver ear mushroom into Shiraz's palm. The symbol of the royal elf guard.

"Dao." Shiraz sighed.

The monkey nodded. "Great! Just great. Looks like we're going to the Mushroom Palace. You don't happen to know where Makoa is, do you?"

The monkey hopped off Shiraz's shoulder and raced ahead of her towards one of the dark walks. Shiraz made her way through the crowd, shoving around any number of criminals, and because it felt like a day when she should, lifting anything at all that she could get her hands on from them. One wasn't technically meant to have weapons in the Grotto, but she was pleased to find that technicalities still meant nothing to criminals.

Very quickly, she realized they were going towards the pools. But more than that, they were heading towards Aiattaua. Her skin crawled and she clenched up her fists in reaction.

The closer she grew to Aiattaua, the more the air smelled of citrus blossoms. And every sound, the music of the club, the whistle of birds, the brush of wind through the trees, all coalesced into an inviting song. Her heart pounded in anticipation. The light softened, creating halos around each living thing, and she tasted a delicious concoction of fizzy bubbles and sweet strawberry juices. The elf prince was one of the most universally beautiful beings that existed. *Everyone* found him a delight to look on. Everyone! It was sensual. It was magical.

It was *creepy*.

Shiraz didn't trust it. Never had. But her own mistrust so annoyed her that she rarely allowed herself to avoid the prince entirely. Recently Shiraz had realized the reason she never trusted Aiattaua had everything to do with her upbringing. A steadfast child was raised to resist temptation.

The amusing and annoying thing about that was, when she was on the island, she hadn't resisted. Not one bit. Even when she first left, she hadn't resisted. But when she met the prince of temptation, all the lessons of the steadfast people reared up to make her distrustful. It was as annoying as she imagined curse lice to be. So she needed to make friends with that *xchuro*. Especially because if they were friends, it would be so much easier to protect Makoa.

She knew Makoa didn't mind about the multiple spouses. He occasionally spent time alone with various ones of them. Shiraz didn't get it, but if Makoa did, that was enough for her. So despite the fact that their number was what she brought up, what really bothered Shiraz was that everyone in Aiattaua's sphere was there to do something *for him*. Protect him, entertain him, help him get revenge against his father, smuggle in his contraband. That was fine for a working relationship but not for a loving one. Makoa deserved more. If Aiattaua loved her friend, he needed to give as much as he took.

Sweetums sped into the constantly damp, quiet area of the grotto. Shiraz watched her run up the little hill that led to the reflection pool and her stomach clenched up. There were two men there. Aiattaua held onto the hand of a man who was facing away. It was Makoa. ***It must be***. But perhaps it was merely another of Aiattaua's spouses because she couldn't get her stomach to unclench and her heart had started pounding. Some part of her recognized that person, but it didn't look like a body she'd ever seen Makoa in. It didn't look like his old body. She hadn't thought about it much in the past few years, but she remembered what he'd looked like. Shorter than this man, stockier, with thick dark hair. This man had medium brown hair, with wavy curls worn above the shoulders. It was those shoulders that felt the most familiar, the slump of them, the resignation. Always so sure he was helpless, because he would never risk breaking the rules and being ostracized.

It couldn't be.

"Ethan?" Shiraz whispered her brother's name.

He turned around. Her brother.

But—not her brother.

Not one of the brothers she was born with at least. It was Makoa, the luminous teal of his eyes, the shark tooth in his ear and even the confusion on his face made that clear. But it was also Ethan.

"I..." Shiraz shook her head. "Did...Did you invent that face?" Shiraz asked, stumbling up the hill. She tripped on the moss and rocks, then finally she was standing above him. Her hand clenched tight around the silver ear emblem.

The real mushrooms had a squishy texture, but the metal emblem bit into her skin with its wavy folds, and she welcomed the reality of the pain it caused.

Makoa stood slowly, shaking his head. "We met, once, long ago. Do you know him?"

She nodded but could not bring words to exit her lips. She'd never thought she would see her brother's face again. Any of them. She had resigned herself to that. But this trip upriver! These two days!

"How long ago?" Her hand rose to trace her brother's smooth jaw. He'd never been able to grow a beard like Father and Noam could. It always annoyed him.

"Just before we met at the river," Makoa said softly. "Shiraz, who is he?" He asked, but surely he knew. He'd heard her call out, and she'd told him about her brothers. He knew. He just needed to hear her say it. One of his hands came up to her shoulder.

Aiattaua stood, looking between them in an almost jealous way. Another time she might have been amused, but now…she was consumed.

"He is Ethan. My eldest brother. You met him," Shiraz whispered. "And so soon after I left the island. He must have left right after me." She laughed; her voice was teary and her eyes stung, but no tears fell. "He left right after me. But he wouldn't go with me."

Her hand fell to her side. "Isn't that exactly like him? It always had to be his idea, or it wasn't worth doing."

She drew in a deep breath, stopping up her anger behind a wall of control. She stepped back, nearly tumbling off the little mound of rocks and moss. Aiattaua caught her arm, holding on until she was steady. They regarded one another and something passed between them she had never thought to share: understanding. All these years and this was the first time it occurred to her to wonder if he had left behind siblings in his mother's realm.

"Eldests," Aiattaua said. "They are always the same."

"He's that way." She nodded towards Makoa. He smiled softly. With Ethan's face. It was jarring, but there wasn't time to dwell. She longed to ask him to use some other body. Even a goose. But she never did that. Makoa used what form he wanted, when he wanted. It would be wrong to ask for anything different. So she tried to speak only to the positive.

"It is good to see his face again. But we need to go. Felicia took the bait, but she also distracted me long enough that Dao took Xinyi."

"Shiraz...you must be..." Makoa shook his head. "I did not know." He did not appear convinced that this newest reminder of her past wouldn't break Shiraz into a bundle of tiny pieces and scatter her heart to the twelve winds of Niyol.

But the strange thing was—it didn't.

It was very nearly comforting. Maybe she'd been thinking of love all wrong. Maybe Aiattaua with his fifteen scattered spouses had it right, letting the things he loved come and go in their own time.

Shiraz always wanted her brothers to leave the island, and they had. They'd had lives, met people totally different from themselves. Ethan had encountered the man who became Shiraz's third brother. She and Ethan had kissed the same man. Wasn't that just like her, kissing someone who'd kissed her brother first? Noam had met someone so important to his heart that he was willing to die beside her. And as sad as that made Shiraz, it sounded exactly like Noam. And

Shiraz had traveled the world. Maybe she needed to stop trying to keep the people she loved with her. That she loved, and they loved ought to be enough. She—

"Eeeeeeh!" Sweetums jumped into the middle of them and began throwing fists full of moss at each one of them.

Aiattaua chuckled. Shiraz and Makoa exchanged nods. Now it seemed was not the time for thinking.

～✺～

"Aiattaua didn't take out the bounty on the ship," Makoa informed Shiraz as they all climbed down the hill. He knew she would have an easier time focusing on the moment at hand than the startling discovery that this face, this body belonged to one of her brothers.

What did it all mean?

"Of course not. He would never have needed to burn the map off my arm to find me."

"Burn it off, oh my." Aiattaua reached out and took her hand, so that he could examine the burns. "I shall remove the—"

"No, *tifit!*" Shiraz yanked her arm back. She raised her arm but stopped short of actually slapping him. "We need it to track Felicia. But first we get Xinyi."

"What does tifit mean?" Aiattaua asked. No one answered. "It's an insult, isn't it? Of course it is," he answered himself.

It should surprise Makoa that Shiraz suggested ignoring the boat in favor of the princess, but it did not, not even slightly.

"I am sure Dao will not harm your friend." Aiattaua shrugged.

"If she takes her to King Guo, when she clearly does not want to go, that would be harming her," Shiraz snapped.

"I am certain she will take her to *my father*. It is beneath the Immortal King to collect on bounties. And Dao works for the king alone. We will find your friend in the Mushroom Court."

"When will you marry that woman and give us all some peace?" Shiraz demanded.

Now she wanted him to have *more spouses*? Why? Was she trying to annoy Makoa?

"I thought you didn't like all my mates," Aiattaua questioned. "Why would you want me married to this princess?"

"Not Xinyi!" Shiraz screeched, highly offended. "Dao."

"Dao? Never. She loves me, I grant you, but like an aunt to her favorite nephew."

That brought Makoa to a stop, staring incredulously. But it was Shiraz who responded.

"The way she loves you is entirely inappropriate in any family relationship. For your father, she would lay down her life, but for you, she would lay down her sword."

"I would never ask her to lay down her sword. She is an excellent soldier."

"You're being deliberately obtuse, aren't you?"

"She means she would stop protecting your father at your command," Makoa explained.

"Then why didn't she say that?" Aiattaua asked.

Oh. She was right, he was doing it deliberately. Trying to lighten the mood.

"He knew that!" Shiraz growled at Makoa. "Stop humoring him. He's being a regular *middle child*. Taking everyone's side, collecting strays to give *him* love, pretending not to understand perfectly clear sentences just to annoy people."

Makoa was tempted to dive into the fight. He wasn't a *stray*. But Aiattaua was smirking at her superiorly. And though she was fighting with him, it seemed almost friendly.

"You are a youngest, aren't you?" Aiattaua asked. "The beloved baby, who can do no wrong? Just like Helima. We were discussing my youngest sister earlier and how well you would get along."

"We do. She's angry, smart, and snide. If she wanted to, she would kill you all in your sleep and rule the world. I accept this comparison," Shiraz said magnanimously.

"Exactly like her." Aiattaua grinned.

Makoa walked on in front of the group with Sweetums on his shoulder. He'd wanted Aiattaua and Shiraz to get along, but this might be worse than their usual relationship. Was he going to have to put up with this until morning? It would take nearly that long to reach the palace without their ship. But he didn't try to stop the fighting. He wasn't sure he wanted the hours to pass in thought instead.

Her brother's face. It...didn't seem possible.

You will need to find the third thing yourself. If you have not found it already.

What did any of this mean? Maybe one day they would have time enough to consider.

A Lack of Literary Symmetry

The journey thus far had taken walking for a mile and travel along a small canal by a two person boat. And another half a mile on foot. It had become apparent that Xinyi was not being led to Makoa. The elf no longer even pretended this was the case. She was to be a "guest" of The Immortal King. But Xinyi continued on without resistance. Very nearly skipping, and she hadn't skipped since she was young. She asked the soldier any question she could think of, taking in all of her answers, and storing them up.

Well, she'd yet to gather the courage to ask after the woman's bodily functions. But most questions she could think of she asked. And it was worth noting, with some amusement, that if the woman was menstruating, it didn't seem to incapacitate her as much as it had Makoa. Xinyi chuckled softly. She was terrible.

Dao was fascinating. Xinyi should write such a character, fiercely loyal, stoic, confident, with a flaw or two in the form of unquestioning obedience, and a lack of respect for the value of humans. Humans must have *some value*, but Dao didn't seem to know of any.

They made their way through the mushroom village and Xinyi was again wonderstruck. Mushrooms the size of homes and palaces grew up out of the trees. Their translucent skin glowed in varying colors, mostly purples, pinks, and deep blues. There were smaller glowing shrooms scattered among them of green and yellow and orange. Trees rose like smokestacks for the different mushrooms, decorated with bows of floating lights of a warm yellow color. Vines of green and wide leafed plants, even clusters of the brightest blossoms Xinyi had ever seen, decorated the forest floor. It was fabulous!

"Is the elf king truly immortal?" Xinyi asked. "I have heard that he was born to another *immortal* king who is now dead. How does that work?"

Dao glanced back and smiled. "You heard this from Shiraz, the faithless, the doubter, the sewer of distrust." The elf grinned. "I do appreciate that if she does not believe someone, she makes it very clearly known." The elf shook her head. "The previous Immortal King is not dead; his body was repurposed into the mushroom cottage where his sister still resides. Elves do not believe in waste. And death is wasteful, thus our bodies are repurposed to make way for new life, and we live on in new things."

Xinyi's twitchy fingers again drew the woman's eyes to her bag. It was uncomfortable. It occurred to Xinyi that the monkeys had also been drawn to her bag, and Hua, even Euphemia had examined it. Why was everyone so interested? The style was expensive and beautiful, but...that couldn't be all. "Which mushroom is the previous Immortal King? I must pay my respects."

"It would be my honor to show you," the soldier replied, facing forward. "When we reach it. This is but the local village. The Immortal King lives on in the bounds of the palace structures."

How were these not the palace grounds? All around were wonders. One long mushroom stalk curved out from the top of a tree trunk until its dome would be in the light during daylight hours. And a group of flat shroom tops grew in a spiral around another trunk, leading to the bulbous growth of a mushroom cluster halfway up another tree. Some of the mushrooms seemed topped with a slickness that provided light. And when the nearby flowers moved in the wind, they made music. Bells or chimes she might have expected, but they made music like stringed instruments brushed with fingers of wind.

"Your village is so lovely, I could not imagine better," she said to be gracious, but that the words were…slightly true. All this trip, it seemed she was learning the limits of her imagination. And the expanse of reality and hungering for more of both, because the more reality she encountered the more wildly her imagination flew, creating epic adventures and silly side quests. Perhaps she had not been limited in imagination, but merely in food to fuel it.

She hoped they didn't find her thieves tonight. Or tomorrow. She hoped—hoped the thieves had left Loqwan. Then Xinyi could extort the captain into chasing them around the world for the promise of that forty-nine percent of nothing. She could get to know her better, see how her growing interest developed, or if it changed into something else. They could meet elves, and witches, and gods, and dragons and she would never be safe, but she would always be inspired!

"Oh, how I wish never to leave." The thought, referring to her adventures, more than this particular place, slipped through her mind and unintentionally out of her lips. She tried to catch it with her left hand, but it was already racing into the world to cause who knew what catastrophe.

She looked around in horror, worried that there would be someone near to grant her unintentionally vague wish. But the only eyes she caught were Dao's. The woman raised a brow, and the left corner of her lip ticked up.

"We've no immediate plans to plant you with new fungi. Nor are there presently any djinn, fairy godparents, tricksters, or other similarly powered individuals charged with the granting of imprudent wishes within the elf nation. I keep close track of them." She winked.

Xinyi chuckled but she couldn't help a slight sense of unease. When would she learn to stop making wishes? And waiting around for the world to decide her fate? She didn't believe in fate, why wait on it? She needed to be making *choices*.

The Anti-Climax

Shiraz had stolen several knives, a nunchuck, a vial of unknown contents (it was from the pocket of an unfamiliar ogre so it was either deadly or a treatment for his infected wart). She also had Felicia's magical blade, a goddess killer, formed of star dust, volcanic ash, and silt from the deepest trench in the sea; it could not be broken and could pierce any heart. But that was less for using and more for making sure Felicia wanted to trade. Shiraz attempted to divvy up the weapons, but the boys were being resistant. It was her idea, so it must be wrong! The fact that Makoa said no with Ethan's face on annoyed her more than the pit of worry in her stomach.

She was fairly certain Xinyi was fine. Xinyi usually was fine. Every villain fell madly in love with her. But the elf king was unlikely to let her get a word in. And the man was not known for his observational skills. And anyway...Shiraz wanted to be near her, even if that meant being in the vicinity of the Immortal Elf King.

Aiattaua refused any blades pompously. "I will not need those. She is perfectly safe in the Mushroom Palace. We hate waste."

Shiraz rolled her eyes and focused on Makoa, but Sweetums was the only other practical member of the group. She took two knives, one in each hand, and twisted her head to the side, screaming threateningly. Shiraz might come to like that creature.

"Take one, we don't know what will happen," Shiraz tried to convince her brother to defend himself properly. She focused on his eyes, unwilling to look anywhere else because frankly it was too much right at the moment. Then his eyes crinkled; he was smiling. He lifted the monkey off his shoulder, settling her on Shiraz's so one of her knife wielding arms was wrapped around Shiraz's neck. *Very comfortable.*

"I'm going to fly ahead and scout. We'll get out of this, little sister. The same way we always do. With guile, deal making, and insults." He blew his broccoli breath—right in her face—and transformed into a tiny baby toucan.

"A *baby* toucan? Why? Can you even fly in that form?" Shiraz demanded pointlessly. He was clearly beating his wings in adorable flight, but too annoyed with him not to protest.

"Why do you think?" He rubbed against her face. But she wasn't about to admit aloud, next to Aiattaua, that baby toucans were her favorite animal. They made her go all gooey.

She loved Makoa, but she also hated him. She stuck out her tongue and walked on ahead of the prince.

"One is meant to walk behind royalty," he called out.

"By all means, think of me as your bodyguard."

Aiattaua laughed. "In that case, we should stop and dress you in my colors."

"Over *your* dead body and not a second sooner!" Shiraz said stomping through the tunnels.

She hated men. Why must she be doing this with men! They never listened. They were smug. They were entitled. They transformed into adorable birds to comfort you when you wanted to be angry. Angry was so much more comfortable.

Sweetums screeched. "Eeech! Oooh, ooh, ooooh."

"Exactly right." Shiraz nodded. It felt like the monkey was talking about how older brothers were the most annoying creatures in the whole universe and not worth one's time and energy to protect.

Then Shiraz turned a corner and found a group of elf servants and Dao waiting. Dao dipped her head towards the prince, her eyes climbing his body the way she wanted her body to be doing, as anyone but the man in question could see.

Looked like a nice stroke was just what she wanted.

"His Majesty, the Immortal King bids welcome to Prince Aiattaua and his esteemed friends. I was sent to welcome you in hopes that none of our guests would be induced to—*ear suicide,*" Dao said so pointedly and so dryly Shiraz's ears chaffed. "I was also instructed to tell you that Princess Xinyi is waiting for you."

Shiraz ran her tongue around her teeth. Aiattaua was going to be insufferable now. *More* insufferable. Dao's gaze shifted from the monkey at Shiraz's shoulder, down to the weapons in her arms. She stepped back and waved down the corridor unconcerned.

"Will you change before you meet the king?"

"You'll find me quite lacking in formal attire," Shiraz responded, thinking that her outfit had been perfectly suited to a royal meeting before she had sweat darkened half circles into the underarms.

"Clothes have been provided," Dao said. "It was worded as a request *merely to be polite.*"

Hmm. Dao's responses seemed a touch less measured than usual. She'd had a long day, chasing Shiraz through the jungle, dealing with monkeys, Felicia, and now Shiraz again. Some of Shiraz's annoyance at the situation eased under a wave of commiseration and amusement.

She reached into her bag and extracted some of the chocolate fruit drops Hua had given her.

"Long day? Want a candy?" She extended them to Dao.

"Ogre made?" she inquired.

"Yes," Shiraz said sharply, all prepared to defend her friends. But Dao snatched up the treats and ate, a small smile lightening her face.

"Ogres make the best candy."

"Mmm." Xinyi closed her eyes, her teeth sinking into the soft sticky dough right through to the sweet filling. It was amazing. This was her third cake. She ought to slow down, leave a few for others, but they were incredible.

If one had to be a prisoner, she strongly suggested they be a prisoner of the royal elf family. They had the best snacks! She had never had a tea without sweetener that went down so smoothly, though she had to say the tiny cakes, imprinted with the mushroom crest of the elf family, were superior and marvelously sweet.

"Umm. What is the filling for these? It isn't a nut paste." Xinyi lifted another before the sentence was even finished.

The elf princess across from her responded, covering a smile with a delicate green hand. Her appearance suggested she was at least sixty years of age and her countenance was one of tranquil joy.

Xinyi had not had much sleep. They arrived at the palace only a few hours before sunrise, and Xinyi was given a comfortable place to rest, only to be woken two hours after the sun reached the sky. But she had woken excited, ready to take on the day.

She'd been gifted another gown, the perfect size for her. Today she truly looked like a princess. It was a deep yellow color with pink and red accents. It was a more modern style, made largely of a sheer yellow fabric, with a high resting deep pink sash, and winglike arms of the original yellow. The white accents and the sleeves were embroidered with blossoms, pale green leaves and thin brown branches all in threads that were luminous. Like her bag. She had slid her wedding bag over her shoulder still, following the collar of the dress and could nearly feel the captain's hands doing the same thing the day before.

Perfect.

Xinyi loved this gown, but she felt...disappointed to no longer be wearing Shiraz's clothes. She'd made sure to fold them neatly and stuff them into her wedding bag; she didn't want to be without them.

She knew the captain would have her refuse the hospitality and the food, but she was ravenous, and the elves were very kind. Somewhere over the evening, her desire to defiantly resist the captain cooled. She still wasn't following her rules, but it was no longer done angrily. Eventually she would learn why she was here. In the meanwhile, she meant to eat and enjoy. She wished the captain and Makoa were here though. Shiraz's surly attitude and Makoa's easy one made such pleasant atmosphere.

"It is nectar fruit, with chopped pecans, some spices and a dusting of tangerine juice. I will see that the recipe leaves with you!"

"Oh, thank you!" Xinyi exclaimed. She hadn't much skill for cooking, but she was sure Makoa could make it with the recipe provided. "It's amazing! They are all amazing!"

Xinyi felt her pulse jumping as she realized that she had thought of Makoa preparing these cakes in her future, not Yinuo or one of the other women. It was surprising how quickly she had grown attached to the crew of the River Serpent, but it was a lovely feeling. Bright, and safe, and wild and free.

"I am so pleased. I hope your stay will not be too uncomfortable. I give you my word I shall do my best to explain the situation to the Immortal King."

"If it is no imposition, would you please explain the situation to me?" Xinyi asked gently.

"Explain even if it is an imposition," a rude voice demanded from across the room. The captain's voice!

Shiraz stood in the doorway behind them, looking as grouchy as ever and making Xinyi's heart dance. She rather liked that grouchy face. Sweetums sat on one of the captain's shoulders, brandishing two small knives. And a baby toucan that must be Makoa was flapping in the air next to Shiraz to stay aloft.

Shiraz appeared to have been dressed by the elves as well, wearing a dramatic version of her usual attire. Loose fitting pants of black were tucked into her dragon calf boots, topped with a dramatically high collared vest of deep blue that extended down to her hips and was held closed with a long sky colored sash tied around it at her waist. And a cape over one shoulder decorated with purple and silver (almost moonlight colored) snakes slithering through a garden of mushrooms. There were also no less than three weapons strapped to her person, a long thin blade at her waist, a knife stuck out of her boot, and another strapped to her left arm. She looked powerful and amazing. But Xinyi preferred her attire from the night before. Then she had looked smug, but now she looked stiff.

She stepped into the room boldly and gave a deep bow to the princess. "Princess Daiyu, Princess Xinyi. I hope the new day finds you both well."

"You never bow to me," a lovely voice grumbled behind Shiraz.

"You don't deserve any such attention," Shiraz muttered.

"Please." Daiyu waved into the room. "Join us. You are all safe and will be free to leave shortly. I will explain. And the Immortal King will join us to make his own apologies."

Shiraz walked forward, and Xinyi noticed the man behind her, the one who'd grumbled. He was tall and had teal skin and hooked ears. He wore long straight robes in vibrant gem colors so like a peacock that he wore several sashes layered on one another trailing the ground behind him, each in a different shade. His hair was down to the middle of his back with little braids behind each of his ears, and the front tied up in a knot on his head, and the knot was decorated with a curved twig growing the tiniest colorful cap mushrooms.

He looked like a god!

Was this not the Immortal King? He was perhaps forty, but his skin looked so smooth and unblemished. There was such youthfulness about him Xinyi could easily see him being named immortal.

Xinyi tried to move, tried to pull her gaze off of him. But she could not. She had never seen anyone so beautiful. And he knew it. He smiled gently at her.

His hand stretched out and lifted Xinyi's, raising it to his lips. "Beautiful one. Might I beg of you a name?"

"V," Shiraz said sarcastically, plopping down on the lounge beside Xinyi, making the seat jump. Xinyi tore her eyes from the man and burst out laughing.

All This Trouble and *Virtue* is My Only Reward?

Xinyi looked away from Aiattaua, right at Shiraz, her eyes alight with amusement. Pulling her eyes off the prince of temptation on their first acquaintance was quite the feat, but somehow the laughter seemed to free Xinyi from his spell entirely.

She grinned wide. "No one has ever compared me to the emperor's sorceress." Her clear joy made Shiraz proud of the tiny quip. "Or anyone in the stories. They are all so bold in comparison."

"More bold than you, *trouble?* Not possible." Shiraz shook her head slowly. "You came to the docks seeking thieves and smugglers and, having no experience with either, demanded our assistance—without ready pay! And got it! You—are *very* bold."

"As to the thieves of it all," Daiyu interrupted. Shiraz was enjoying the brief respite from being the only one who realized they were still in danger. But Daiyu's interruption was a cold reminder.

The Immortal King was many things, but frivolous was not among them. He didn't send out his commander to retrieve a princess for a different king.

Princess Daiyu reached beneath her seat and set a bulging leather satchel on the table between them. "Your property has been retrieved."

Shiraz had expected jewelry. But the treasure looked angular. She supposed it could contain a jewelry box.

Xinyi stiffened. This was her *greatest treasure,* wasn't it? She didn't even try to reach for it.

She was holding out a bite of cake, likely to offer it to Sweetums, but Shiraz dipped her head and nipped the food right out of her fingers to wake her up. She expected her to blush or look scandalized, even offended, but Xinyi's eyes filled with worry.

Shiraz shook her head, unable to taste the dessert in her mouth over the concern.

"I hope you can forgive my brother. Aiattaua was most impatient and acted rashly."

"Are we apologizing for me? Why?" Aiattaua noted the satchel and his features shifted into shock. "No?" He took both of Xinyi's hands into his own. "I heard you referred to as a princess. Are you the mysterious author? Such a startling beauty should not have a second talent."

"As you are constant proof," Shiraz muttered, rolling her eyes at the banal flattery. How was beauty a talent? And what did any of this have to do with her being an author?

"You admitted you find me beautiful!" Aiattaua grinned. "And I got you into my colors without even having to die first."

Shiraz's lips barely moved as she growled. "What?"

"The clothes, the mushroom grotto on the cape, the blue green of my emblem, I had them made for you the last time we met! And you look resplendent, but excuse me, I am talking to my favorite author."

"I don't even believe you read, much less that you have a favorite author," Shiraz said meanly. She wanted to kill this boy sometimes. How could anyone get to forty-three years old and still be this much of a child? She glared at Makoa. He flew off the back of the couch and came to her, tilting his wide eyes up at her. She nearly laughed he looked so adorable. She wanted to cuddle him. She'd always wanted a pet toucan.

But she didn't like how scared Xinyi looked. Even Sweetums seemed worried, petting Xinyi gently with the hilt of one her knives.

"What magic have you?" Aiattaua asked of Xinyi.

More than she knew, Shiraz thought but kept it to herself. She didn't know what was wrong; all she knew was that Xinyi was frightened of some discovery. Maybe she was afraid Shiraz and Makoa would realize she was not the king's daughter. But they had known that all along. Shiraz took Xinyi's hand into her own and squeezed. Xinyi squeezed back, but her gaze went to her lap and her voice emerged quietly.

"I am sorry. I have no magic. Nor…" She looked at Shiraz. "Any treasure."

Shiraz shook her head, uncomprehending.

"Do not be so humble," Aiattaua said brightly. "This is amazing!" He reached into the satchel and pulled out a handful of pages.

Pages.

Pieces of paper.

Shiraz snorted and started laughing in a way that sounded more like panting. Makoa hopped off the chair back. Landing on the floor, he poked his beak into the pile of pages that had slipped through Aiattaua's fingers.

No. It couldn't be.

"You transport one into another world though it is our own. You make it anew."

Xinyi could not have tricked them so completely.

Shiraz slid her hand out of Xinyi's though the author, the *liar*, tried to hold onto her. Shiraz opened the satchel. It was nothing but pages and pages and pages. Her story.

Her treasure was her story.

Shiraz laughed—hard. It was always the good girls who tricked you, wasn't it? She felt like she was back in Elder Trent's office, confessing to a crime she hadn't committed, for his daughter no less, as he lectured her. *"I worry about you, Shiraz. You seem to look on the doing of good as if it ought to lead to a prize. That isn't so. It is the doing of good itself that is the reward. The world owes you nothing for your virtue."*

Shiraz dropped the pages and stood. Sweetums hopped off her shoulder, making a tiny squeak. She raced to Xinyi. Aiattaua, realizing that something other than his interest was going on, fell silent. Shiraz should have known, maybe not that it was a book, but...she thought Xinyi trusted her, and she clearly did not. Who would? She was scum.

"It was the only way to get your help," Xinyi whispered.

Shiraz paced away, laughing. It was too funny.

"All that trouble, nearly dying, breaking my ship, losing it to a bounty hunter, and not caring because I had to come here and help you. *All* this trouble, and *virtue* is my only reward!" She chuckled. "Still no funds to pay for the spell I need, if I even get my ship back. Elder Trent will be so proud! I finally committed a selfless act. Not intentionally, but does that matter?" Shiraz shook her head. "You know, I was sure you weren't the king's daughter, but this is a very princess style move, pretending to have something you don't to get help. And *haggling* with me over percentages of *pages!*"

"I..." Xinyi looked bereft. She let Shiraz's words fall onto her, crushing her further into her seat. Broken down and crumbling, and Shiraz was as angry with herself as she was with Xinyi. She wanted to stop being angry with her, but—she had a right to be angry! She'd been lied to. Tricked. Called scum and treated so. Despite trying time and again to help this woman. She had a right to be angry.

But it also broke her heart to see Xinyi sinking down and giving in to the shame. "You lied to me this whole time," she whispered.

Xinyi shoved off the couch, crowding towards Shiraz. She notched up her chin. "So did you! You said you were the lowest of scum, then you kept being considerate, and helping me with things I hadn't paid for, and treating me like a friend and *flirting outrageously* with me. And probably every other woman in the vicinity." Her voice drifted off, and Shiraz was half tempted to confess that she'd only meant the flirting with her. But Xinyi's fight came roaring back with a vengeance.

"Yes, I lied. I am not the king's daughter. And while I am sorry that it has caused you trouble, you are wrong. It was not a princess style choice. It was a *scummy* choice."

Shiraz choked down a shocked laugh and killed her blooming smile with force of will.

"You are just angry because I tricked you," Xinyi continued. "You thought I was a sheltered, naive woman, but I have more inside of me. I can be as scummy as any criminal you've ever met. How do you like that?" She ended with her hands on her hips and her expression challenging, but her eyes entreating. As annoyed, even hurt, and definitely frustrated as Shiraz felt, she was also—in love.

Azaqif but she loved it when this woman fought back. A con artist, was she? That could be a fun addition to the crew. Maybe Shiraz should let her work off her debt.

Maybe virtue was its own reward. Scum, was she? Shiraz liked that very much indeed.

"Not the daughter of a king! Thank the sap," a high note of a voice sang across the air before Shiraz responded.

She sighed, heavily rolling her eyes. Of course the Immortal Pain in the Ngok would walk in just when things were getting interesting.

"That makes things easier for me at least; I pointed out to King Guo from the first that I managed to retrieve all twenty-five of my estranged children on my own, but he kept on with begging and woe over his terrible plight of separation from his daughter. I was not at all sure how I would explain, not only refusing to help my fellow royal find his child, but also knowing exactly where she was and it being my own palace. It is not that I fear a war with humans or any such nonsense. The human king is still busy trying to assert that he is a king; you know, elves have never had such issues. Our royalty, divinity and leadership are unquestioned and our people flourish, but one doesn't like an awkward conversation if one can help it."

"Conversation?" Shiraz muttered, under her breath. "When have you ever allowed someone else to speak?"

How Legends Spread

Everyone bowed at the king's entrance. When they stood again, he was directly in front of Xinyi. She wished he had waited a few more minutes. She wanted to finish fighting with Shiraz. For a moment, before the king entered, Shiraz was biting her lip and her eyes were crinkled up, and Xinyi got the most delightful flutter in her chest telling her she'd won.

But before she could find out what her prize was, if it was what she wanted, to have more adventures with Shiraz and Makoa, or merely that she'd impressed the smuggler. Before she could fight for what she wanted, the king showed up and everything refocused on him.

He stared now, not at her, but at her wedding bag, lifting it away from her body. Xinyi grabbed the strap, locking her fingers around it.

"This was a gift from your husband I am told," the king remarked. "A special thing, to be certain. My own wife gifted me with, well, with two daughters, my heir Daiyu you have met. She also has a sister."

"Pekoe!" the princess in question called out. "I am right here!"

The princess, with deep green skin, hair the color of moonlight, and freckles of the same color dotted across her skin, not to mention a very muscular build and startlingly little clothing for an elf, dressed only in a sash tied around her chest, and another covering the top of her thighs to the bottom of her belly was very hard to miss. But apparently, to her father, not difficult to ignore. Her sister Daiyu however reached out and stroked a hand down her hair lovingly.

The king went on speaking as if never interrupted. "But she gifted me with a particular robe that I would not part with for the world. I am sure the same might be said of you. But it is a lovely work of embroidery. Such care has been taken in the details like the family name carved on the gate, and the tail of the comet Feiyu visible in the sky, letting us know both that it represents a night thirty-one years ago, so not your wedding night, I presume, and that the month it is meant to depict was surely in May, in the nights between spring and summer. Such incredible detail, one would not think humans so fastidious. What is meant to represent you? And what your husband? What I wonder, does the basket of nectar blossoms by the gate signify?"

Xinyi was still. Inside and out. For a moment she had not even a pulse.

When one is found in a basket of flowers and raised by a family they were not born to, one must ask: where did I come from? To whom did I belong? Why was I left here? But with no answers forthcoming, eventually one stops asking. Aloud.

But the king's intensity woke it all. Why would he pull out such a detail? Was this where Xinyi came from? All around were elves of green skin and hooked ears, neither of which Xinyi had, but the lovely elf prince had different skin, with that teal hue. And Xinyi had seen white furred kittens born to black furred panthers. Perhaps she was like that, a colorless anomaly in a world of green. Was this where she was born? Or was he like the Soul Parrots, able to sense her questions and using them to manipulate her?

She was trapped in her mind, wishing she had the voice to speak her questions. Wishing she could run away. She wanted to know. But she didn't want to know.

What if she had been born here and was sent away because she looked different? What if she had found the family who had abandoned her, and they did not want her back? What if the woman she'd remembered as her mother was merely one of their servants? She couldn't speak, couldn't move. Didn't know what she would say or do even if she could.

Then the captain inserted herself into the conversation nonchalantly. "She loves nectar blossoms. Why? You want a bag like it? This one isn't for sale, but I could get you a bag like this. Say the word."

"Which word is that?" the elf king inquired. His gaze shifted, tracing Xinyi now, her features and her unease.

"Money, naturally. How much will you pay for such a bag?"

The king glanced to her and smirked. "Dao mentioned it," the king said. "And it was a particular bit of fancy as it reminds us of a legend. We wondered if perhaps that legend and a love for it was something we shared, though we doubt elvish legends have made their way into the human world. They—"

Shiraz's laugh cut him off. "Of course they have! Legends travel faster than ships and are louder than roars. Everyone wants to know the legends of other lands. It is how we get to know one another." Xinyi was captivated by the woman's passion. It no longer felt like she was speaking just to defend Xinyi; stories were precious to her. "They do not reach everyone, I grant you. But they who wonder *always* find them.

"You mean the legend of the star god and his child with the earth, I imagine. The little girl born on a night when the painted starlight of

Feiyu's tail fell to the earth and touched a tree. *Blossoms of vibrant pink burst to life, sprouting and blooming wide upon its limbs. They fell in a dancing spiral, descending neatly into a basket, overflowing it with fragrant flowers. Then the basket giggled and half the blossoms were kicked free to reveal a young girl, already a small child as if she had grown years in those moments. She had skin the color of moonlight and lips like the pink blossomed tree and eyes that sparkled like the stars.* That legend?" Shiraz asked.

Xinyi gaped. Wei's family used to speak of that legend, often, certain that it had been a prediction. That she was fated to have been found so. That she'd never had a mother who left her behind, but had been born in that basket, on that night. It used to anger her, because Xinyi *remembered* her mother. But what struck Xinyi now was the way Shiraz told the story. It was the love in her voice and the passion in her eyes. She knew legends by heart, collected books from all over the world, and held such passion for these stories in her heart that when she spoke of them, Xinyi who already knew the legend wanted to hear it anew. This was the same grouch who called Xinyi trouble and spoke belligerently to gods and kings.

She was a fabulous mystery, and as unsettled as she was, Xinyi felt hope fluttering inside her to solve that mystery.

"That was very articulately told," the king remarked, in shock. He would have said more, but Shiraz turned belligerent.

"How *generous* of you to say. But do not be too flattered, your legends are lovely but no more special than any other. I collect stories from across the world and memorize those I love, lest they be stolen from me as many have been before."

"I had no idea it was a passion of yours. You have never said as much in our prior chats. Why, I wasn't aware you had interests beyond your ship and your funds. Although I was pleased to discover of late, with the way you dispensed with those kidnappers earlier this year, that you are, as the elves, not disposed towards waste."

"You dispensed with kidnappers?" Xinyi asked, unintentionally drawing the king's eyes back to her.

Shiraz shrugged. "The ogres did most of the work. But the kidnappers were willing to hurt a child, so I harmed them first."

"Not only harm," the king interjected in a voice that implied she should not shy away from praise. "You led them to their deaths at the hands of those who would make use of their full bodies, turning bones into tools, hair into brooms, and flesh into food, and handing over their souls for your offering to Nanghi's servants! Inspired uses."

Xinyi was vaguely appalled. But also...Had Shiraz been a part of rescuing Qiu?

"Had you not brought them to Hi'mau?" Xinyi asked.

"I had. I was under contract to help any offer in good faith. Theirs was not in *good faith,*" she said with particular emphasis, as if to remind Xinyi that her own offer had not been in good faith. As if to threaten her. But Xinyi was unafraid. With this woman she was always safe.

"They said they were retrieving objects, not people. Makoa and I do not assist kidnappers. So we made an example of them."

"A most *efficient* example. Some, you know, are not as decisive in their examples and make one feel that there is room to negotiate. I was pleased to learn you were not one of these sorts, realizing that indeed, were I as limited as you, being merely human, and not even magical in nature, I might have done the same in your place, though indeed they were working for a king and intended only to return his daughter and granddaughter to him. He misses them dearly—"

"He misses nothing," Shiraz interjected forcefully. "He left his pregnant daughter behind when rebels attacked his palace. Now he sends for her because he has heard she is at peace in his absence. It is power that drives him, not love."

"An intriguing assertion, for one who has never met the man, but having done so myself, I might say it is not inaccurate. He is overly fond of power, and somewhat lacking in caring. You are more perceptive than I originally thought. For a human, quite wise. What would you say to a king who had lost one of his last attempts at progeny, spread as wide as they were, in an attempt to better the world, you understand, and is now seeking them out?"

Shiraz looked the king over coldly. "That he maybe shouldn't have had relations with so many beings that he could not remember them all."

Ever tranquil, Daiyu spit out her tea. Pekoe giggled. Aiattaua cheered "Here! Here!"

The king turned to observe his progeny, and a much lighter green skinned elf, with short curly red hair and both more height and girth than their siblings and no points on their ears, crashed into the room, wearing largely the same attire as Pekoe.

"Are we making fun of Father? Not without me!" The newcomer slid to a stop, bumping into Daiyu's chair, making the princess sputter and choke all the more. Her family including the king all moved to assist her in concern, and in the midst of the chaos, Shiraz threw—actually threw—Sweetums towards the table.

It was only about half a foot, and the monkey landed safely, but really! Sweetums immediately hopped at the coughing princess, hitting her with the cake she had in one hand and the butt of her knife in the other. Xinyi started towards the primate, but Shiraz yanked her back.

"Do not tell them what you told us," she hissed in Xinyi's ear, her words coming out in a great rush. "I could see your questions. Don't ask now. The elf king did not summon us to praise how I handled the kidnappers. *All of his children are trapped here,*" Shiraz whispered. "If he decides to keep you...I'd have to kill twenty elves to get you out the door. I'm a lot of things but—"

"Not a killer," Xinyi whispered. But she could see in the captain's eyes she took it for derision, not sincerity.

"Keep it to yourself for today. I will find your answers, *believe me,*" Shiraz insisted, nearly begged. "And all for the low low cost of one hundred percent of your treasure."

Xinyi's eyes burned and she nodded softly. "Deal."

"Sweetums!" Shiraz shouted. "You aren't helping. Come here."

The monkey gave Shiraz a very angry look and threw a mushed-up cake her way. But she obeyed, clearing the distance impressively to land on Shiraz's shoulder. With the monkey gone, Daiyu recovered with great speed. There were more elves in the room now. More of the king's children. And they were all so...unique.

One, though he had similar green skin to the king, had five tails as tall as he was of fluffy white fur like a fox's. Another had skin of such a deep green it was nearly black and he did not seem to walk at all; it was almost as if he was perfectly still until Xinyi blinked and suddenly he was in an entirely different place. One had skin of two different tones of green together. It looked mushroom-like, curling up in iridescent patches that floated up as if they would leave her body entirely when she walked, then settled into a lacy second skin when she was still. Every one of the king's children were exquisite. And the more variation in appearance she saw, the more Xinyi wondered. But she'd promised Shiraz and this promise she meant to keep.

"Speaking of elf legends," Shiraz redirected the conversation. "What say you to sending me away with a bundle of them? Maybe they'll impress me enough that I'll memorize a few." She popped her brows, as if this were great enticement. Xinyi didn't know if it would entice the elves, but *she* wanted to write something so beautiful this woman memorized it.

"We shall see." Daiyu stood. Her hair was in disarray, her gown was smattered with nectar fruit and cake crumbs, but she looked every inch a queen. She smiled at Xinyi with a soft, understanding, sisterly expression. Her gaze shifted to Shiraz, and she nodded once. "Shall we have tea and explanations now?"

Perhaps there was nothing more to that look than understanding of Xinyi's discomfort. Perhaps there was nothing sisterly to it. Perhaps Xinyi's imagination had built a world of other possibilities out of nothing. Perhaps her imagination was not so small after all.

But perhaps there was more here than Xinyi had ever expected to find. Would it still be here later? If she ignored it today? Part of her wished she were home with her tea and her journal and plenty of time to sort out her feelings, but if she were, she would not have such feelings to sort through. And no one would have spoken to her as Shiraz had just now.

Believe me. She'd looked so desperate, begging Xinyi for that bit of faith she so fervently needed. There was something deep in this woman that was not apparent on first acquaintances or even second or third. *Or C.* Xinyi felt her lips lift, and her eyes sting. As much as she wanted to stay with Shiraz and Makoa for adventures, she also needed to stay to learn more about the puzzle of a smuggler beside her.

You Could Tie it in a Knot, or You Could Tie it in a Bow, But Nooo, you had to Add a Dragon

Tea and explanations went as one might expect. The king spoke—at length. On many subjects, some pertaining to the matters at hand: *I had not, myself, consumed the stories my son was so fond of, but Daiyu pointed out that I ought to know something of his interests and that these were more innocuous than I might find a visit to the grotto he created for his friends.*

Some random musings that popped into his head: *I've been studying on creatures of the deep and found a great sense of jealousy for the seahorse. Had I been one, I might have seen all my children grow from small things, and they in turn would idolize me for all I had given them, carrying them as they gestated.*

It was worth noting that at no point did the king apologize, as his daughter had said he would. Nor truly explain why they were here, from within the immense volume of information he shared without interruption. Other than Pekoe's sarcastic asides. Over *three hours*, one could pick up only a few details. The theft of Xinyi's manuscript was paid for by a bored Aiattaua, wanting to finish the story he'd started. The bounty on *Princess Yinuo* had been placed by her own father. The Immortal King had now begun Jian's adventures and wanted to read more. He was very interested in learning more about his son's personal life. And that he maybe, possibly, suspected Xinyi could be his child with some human woman.

Why not? He'd mated with every other compatible species he could find; it was possible.

And it sort of made sense of some of Xinyi's more unusual qualities. Elves considered themselves a superior species, but to Makoa's way of thinking, they were merely an abundant one. Whatever talent they had, they possessed in excess. And Xinyi possessed an excess of good nature, an excess of imagination, and an excess of curiosity, which led to an unending supply of trouble.

Makoa could tell from the furtive looks passed their way by the ten children of the elf king present in the room, that most of them suspected their father was right. As Pekoe had said in one aside, Xinyi *being part elf would explain why so many of us enjoy her* human *stories.*

Makoa took all of this in from Shiraz's shoulder, still a toucan. But didn't say a word. Not one word. He made a regular habit of looking at Shiraz's tattoo. The River Serpent appeared to be headed this way. So perhaps Shiraz's gambit of making the witch reverse the spell on the steering pole, to no longer be drawn back to the ship, but to draw the ship slowly to it once they were separated by a certain distance, was working. That could present some trouble in coming days, but...one annoying problem at a time, Makoa supposed.

Aiattaua sat on Shiraz's right, knitting what appeared to be a giant baby sock with a pattern of bunnies gnawing on bones, so Makoa assumed his half-giant sister, Abeo, was pregnant. All the while, the king waxed wandering on the plight of the world without elf influence.

After about the third hour, Aiattaua leaned in and began to whisper in a way that not only fell on Makoa but Shiraz as well. She stiffened but didn't object which was about as nice a response as one could expect from a sister forced to hear someone whisper sweet nothings in their brother's ear.

"Why are you so quiet?" Aiattaua asked.

Shiraz looked at the prince incredulously; no one had been allowed a word but the king. Makoa made no response. The prince had said already he was not sure about presenting his spouses to his father. And Makoa had no intention of making life hard for Aiattaua.

A thought that, even to Makoa, sounded absurd. The prince had hired thieves to get the end of a story, complicating everyone else's lives. Not the least of which was his sister, Daiyu, who sat across the table patiently trying to hold her family together.

"I would never ask you to be anything you do not want to be. But I feel like perhaps you are trying to be inconspicuous, and...that is not you. One of the first things I loved about you was how conspicuously yourself you were."

"I do not feel like myself," Makoa whispered. "I am not even sure I know who that is at the moment."

Shiraz nuzzled him with the side of her head. And Aiattaua looked...troubled.

"Who you are is not a body, or a name," the prince whispered even lower now, his eyes intent on Makoa. "I love *you*, Makoa, Ethan, Cheryl, Zoltan, Fi, or whatever your name is." Aiattaua listed off some of the different forms Makoa had taken in front of him, with a lovely understanding smile on his lips. "You inspire me." His voice got lower and lower, and he set down his knitting, leaning closer to Makoa.

"When we first met, I admit, I liked you for the entertainment of your curse. It was so different from everything I knew, it was exciting. But...then I got to know you. You used to hurt people and care nothing about it, and you could have gone on doing so, even cursed. But you took that curse and used it to become a better version of yourself. You could never go back to only that man, even if the curse should break."

Slowly Makoa's head ticked Aiattaua's way, and everything but his love faded into mist. There was a halo of light behind him, effervescent as sea foam, fizzing and shifting, and somehow making the prince look even more beautiful.

"You've changed me. I was so angry with my father that I was competing with him, gathering spouses to show him that love could come and go but still be love. To show him that I was better than him. I would watch him, claim to be improving the world by spreading himself around in every species. Then I met you, and you have met as many species as he, been to as many places, but you learn about their strengths and their loves to better yourself. You are so beautiful—no matter what form—"

"Is there something you wish to share with the table?" the Elf King inquired with some annoyance in his tone, breaking out of his riveting speech of how humans would benefit from elf serenity and patience. Irony is perpetually lost on elves.

Makoa wanted to flap across the table and bite the man's nose. This was the most romantic, beautiful speech anyone had ever given, and it was being given to Makoa. How dare he interrupt?

"Aiattaua's whispers you hear?" Pekoe demanded snidely.

"How could there be anything he wants to share?" Shiraz interjected at the same time as the princess, ready as usual to draw ire on herself to protect someone else, "You've shared every word in existence already."

"Not every word." Shaking his head, Aiattaua leaned near to kiss Makoa on the head gently. "I love you."

Makoa soaked in the words as the room around him devolved into the sort of chaos that always happened when more than one of the royal elf children was present.

"I've been responding to you for hours, and you act like my voice is invisible," Pekoe snapped.

"Inaudible," Halima, who was busy attempting to draw a mandala on the table one grain of sugar at a time, corrected. Pekoe brushed an angry hand through the artwork. "Hey! It's him you're angry with."

One might expect the king to yell now, having been annoyed already, but he laughed, still behaving as though he did not notice his own children.

"I do find you an exceptional delight, Shiraz. So few humans look on elves with anything short of reverence. It is refreshing."

"Glad to be of service." Shiraz mock saluted.

"She's not your daughter, so naturally she's interesting!" Pekoe shook the table, shoving out of her seat.

"Grateful as I am for this—*extensive*—explanation of life, the universe and anything *other* than what we were meant to be talking about. My contract was to retrieve the princess's property and see her home. And seeing as I won't get paid for this one, I need to get going so I can make up the funds," Shiraz addressed the Elf King.

"Without a ship?" the king asked. "How will you get the princess home? And indeed I had plans to issue an invitation for her to *stay*. Here is much nicer, don't you think? She will be well taken care of."

"She doesn't need to be *taken care of*. Ours is no insipid princess to be coddled and protected and hidden from the horrid world. She is a war widow, an adventurer, and a con artist. Tough as old pond scum," Shiraz said proudly. Xinyi turned such a look of gratitude on her, she nearly shined with it, but Shiraz was busy focusing on the king. "Now, what do you know about *our ship*?" Shiraz demanded.

Makoa was surprised to hear her refer to it as *our ship*. True she had never made him feel anything less than at home and beloved, but she was always quick to call the boat *hers*. Now it was *our ship*. Why did that make him feel loved?

"It is a long story. How shall I explain i—

"In simple, declarative sentences, with no more than one clause," Shiraz instructed. Around the room, many a smile cracked wide the most patient of faces, Dao and Daiyu for two. Aiattaua grinned so broad one might think he wanted Shiraz for spouse number sixteen. But *that* was *not* going to happen.

"Let's call it a challenge," she continued belligerently. "Do it in less than seven sentences, and I will introduce you to a witch who can turn you into a seahorse."

The king's eyes went wide with excitement. He clapped his hands together. Makoa laughed. For a while now, he'd noticed Shiraz being, very rude indeed to elves and pointed out that it wasn't right to treat these creatures differently. Her response was, *"You should treat creatures how they want to be treated. And elves are a society that respect nothing so much as demands. If you demand something, they think you are in a position to do so. If you bow and accept, you are seen as insignificant."*

Maybe she was right.

"I put the bounty out on your ship," the king said carefully, pausing between each word. He held up a single finger at the end of the sentence. "I'd heard a story I wished to confirm directly from you. I also wanted to become more acquainted with Makoa, now he is bonded to my son. I had heard you disliked visiting me. Thus I issued no invitation." He popped his brows. "I did it in five, do I get an additional prize?"

Shiraz leaned back in her seat, looking so smug one might take her for the ruler in the room. "That all depends. One of those had two clauses, but I'm willing to overlook that if I'm happy with your answer to my next question. Where is our ship now?"

"The bounty hunter is on her way with it as we speak. I worried briefly, when she did not come directly, you understand, that she might be stealing it for herself, but then she did not have the magic bracelet that went with it, and she would certainly have had to fight with all my forces, as I am not in the habit of allowing employees to double cross me. But then she changed directions early this morning and is very nearly here according to last reports." The king smiled. Then his expression shifted to one of more command. "But in the intervening wait, there are questions I wish answered, and things I ought to do. I was unsure in the first moments of our acquaintance if you were the monkey or the bird today, but I have found if one merely talks long enough, all the world reveals itself to you. I have been studying on your curse, Makoa, and believe I can reverse it."

"No!" Aiattaua jumped to his feet, shaking the table.

Makoa regarded him incredulously. Did he just like that Makoa could have hundreds of different faces? Was he still an entertainment?

"You will do noting of the kind without first *asking him* if that is what he wants. The curse is his, it should be up to him when or if he is rid of it."

"Here, here!" Shiraz said, raising a mooncake like it was a glass. She shoved it whole into her mouth and chewed. "Mmm."

"I do not see why. A curse is by nature bad, and if I have a solution and do not use it, it is wast—"

"No!" Shiraz sputtered a cake on the table, continuing her habit of interrupting the king. "We are not debating morality. Some of us do not have an eternity to live. Respect your son's wishes and those of his spouse because it is *nicer*."

He regarded Shiraz reproachfully for a moment then dipped his head. "Very well. Do you want to be un-cursed, Makoa?"

All eyes turned Makoa's way. He didn't speak for a moment. "I... don't know."

"Perplexing. Are all humans so...confused?"

"Yes," Makoa, Shiraz, and Xinyi said in unison. They exchanged looks and began laughing.

"It's a trait of the species," Aiattaua's youngest sister Helima spoke up from the end of the table. "They eternally question their own existence and their place among the collective. Personal seeking within the protection of community. But, even outlier individuals, like these, seek out a sense of community. And once they have found it, they seek out a sense of self, though it is this very act of seeking a self which had cast them out of other communities. It's fascinating. They never learn."

"Hmm," the king considered. "And this sense of community, you have found this with each other? And it is enough that you do not wish to be rid of your curse?"

"I wish to only be rid of it, by my own power," Makoa said, understanding some of his own hesitance only as he spoke. "I used to go seeking a kiss of true love, bowing to the witch who cursed me, a woman who knew nothing of me but one action. I bent to the belief that she was right and I needed to be punished eternally or proven worthy of love with its breaking. But...*I am loved*. Bowing to her curse insults what I have. And letting you take it away means bowing to the idea that I am at the whims of fate."

"And we don't believe in fate," Xinyi added softly, smiling Makoa's way. They had yet to discuss her deception, but...he didn't think they needed to. He might have done the same in her place. And anyway, he wouldn't trade the last two and a half days of confusion for anyth—

The door slammed open and screams sounded as elves leapt out of the way of the lizard scuttling into the room with sulfuric steam escaping her nostrils.

Great. Felicia was all this gathering needed.

Why couldn't they have a nice tea and a happily ever after as they snuck out of the room with the king still pontificating on the elvish disgust for waste?

The Greatest Escape in the History of All Time Ever

Under her belt, Shiraz stored at minimum thirteen years of deals with untrustworthy characters, eleven specific deals with magical beings in which she was injured, nine experiences of being robbed by *friends* or *partners*, seven run-ins with the law of various lands that nearly landed her in foreign prisons, and five near death experiences. As well as one brief stint in prison, followed by a near drowning on her own vessel. And through all of this she had developed several rules by which she lived and a decent sense of when to run. That sense was dancing beneath her skin, twisting knots in her gut and curling up her muscles. Something bad was going on, and it didn't have anything to do with her, and that was making her feel so much more nervous.

Azaqif. She felt seventeen all over again. This was not good.

First the king was very clearly insinuating that Xinyi might be some elf/human experiment that he lost track of, and that he might want to keep her. Now he was threatening to take away Makoa's curse without his permission. Even if getting rid of a curse sounded like a good thing, if Makoa wasn't ready there was no way she was letting this king force it on him. But how was she supposed to prevent any of it? Elves were faster, more agile, and bigger uzaoka than anyone had a right to be.

So for once, when the door banged open and screams followed as Felicia entered in her usual dramatic fashion, Shiraz was overjoyed to see the temperamental ground dragon! She wore the river serpent around her neck and had that *I'm about to spit lava* look in her eyes.

"You know I hate waste, so..." Shiraz shoved back her seat, pulled Xinyi to her feet and nodded to their hosts. She threw the satchel with the princess's *greatest treasure* over her shoulder. "I think I'll take this opportunity to escape!"

Sweetums, clever monkey that she was, knew just what to do. She hopped off the table, raced between legs and over furniture far ahead of them. She slid between Felicia's legs, slicing the strap the River Serpent hung from, grabbing ahold and racing out the door.

"Thank you for defending me, darling. You have my love. Until I see you again." Makoa pecked Aiattaua on the cheek and flapped ahead of Shiraz.

"May the winds of Niyol keep you safe and bring us together again," Aiattaua called out. *Overly dramatic* elf. But Shiraz was willing to let that go after what she'd heard him whispering to her brother. "Shiraz," the prince stopped her. "I do believe this is yours." He held out her old, stuffed full copy of Jian's adventures.

Shiraz shoved it into the second bag on her shoulder, her own. Hunting around under her clothing from the day before, she found a mini crystal ball. "Don't be always waiting for Niyol," she instructed.

Tossing it to him, Shiraz ran. Dao and a few of her soldiers leapt forward to stop the escaping guests, but in a rare show of solidarity, the ten royal children present in the room, Daiyu, Pekoe, Aiattaua, Aegis, Halimah, Riku, Uwizeye, Vui, Zeynep, and Morag, aided their escape. Most blocked the guards' path, Aiattaua not even setting aside his knitting, while Pekoe leapt towards Felicia, eager for a fight.

"It is time for our guests to leave," Crown Princess Daiyu said firmly. Before halting their escape—again!—lifting a hand lovingly to the side of Xinyi's face. "It was a great pleasure to meet you, Xinyi. I look forward to reading more of your adventures. That recipe you wanted." Her second hand dropped something into Xinyi's wedding bag that looked a good deal more substantial than a recipe, but who knew? Maybe the Immortal Elf King wrote it, and it contained a compendium of every time he'd tasted the various ingredients and thus took half a century to read. Anyway now wasn't the time to investigate.

Xinyi seemed not to know how to respond. She nodded at the elf, perhaps her elder sister but certainly her rescuer in this moment, until Shiraz tugged her away.

For his part, the king merely sat at the table waving goodbye; his whole attitude expressing that they would be back. He always got his way eventually, so it was wasteful to fight in the moment.

Shiraz ran past the dragon in the doorway. Felicia was having difficulty turning as Pekoe had hopped onto her back and wrapped both legs around her torso like she would wrestle the lava spitter.

And indeed the calls from her red headed sibling seemed to confirm this. "Flip her," Aegis shouted. "Boa hold!"

"Thanks for keeping my ship safe. I'll return the favor some time," Shiraz called brightly to Felicia as they ran past. "Good luck with the matricide!"

"Get back here with my sword." Felicia spewed bits of lava, but unable to aim with Pekoe on her back, hit no one. "I'll follow you to the ends of the planet!"

"I'm looking out for you," Shiraz called back. "One cellmate to another, you don't want to rule anywhere. Look how miserable he is."

Shiraz would have said more, but she'd made it out the door. She and her party raced out of the Mushroom Palace and came to the bulbous shroom cliff that was likely some long distant elf relative. Shiraz stopped, but Xinyi grabbed a vine dangling off a near by tree.

"C times the charm." She popped a baiting brow.

Shiraz didn't hesitate. She grabbed onto the princess's waist with one hand and the vine with the other. She'd always wanted to be rescued by a pretty princess; it was how all the best fairy tales ended. They swung out over the cliff's edge.

To be honest, they did more sliding than swinging. But they laughed the whole way, and when they hit the ground, Shiraz was still holding Xinyi's waist so actual details didn't matter. When this author put her mind to it, she released some real fairy tale magic into the world.

And it wouldn't be a bad idea for her to invent them a grand rescue now. They ran with elves closing in all around. Shiraz drew Felicia's sword, preparing to fight, but Makoa blew out a breath, transforming into a large purple pegasus with a rainbow-colored lightning bolt tattoo on his right ass cheek and an equally colorful tail and mane.

He knelt. "Get on."

Xinyi and Shiraz climbed on, and he took off running. Sweetums screeched loudly, leaping out of a tree to land in Xinyi's lap. When he'd built enough speed, Makoa leapt into the air and beat his mighty wings. They flew up over the top of the trees.

"We've never done this before," Shiraz laughed, glancing below to look for elves in chase, but airborne, with everything she loved right here, she felt incredibly safe. "I like flying! Do you think I should get—"

"No more spells!" Makoa shouted. "The ship is fine."

"It could always be better," Shiraz defended.

Xinyi was giggling. Makoa was working his wings and his ass off, and Shiraz had to wonder if half the reason he didn't want to be rid of the curse was because of moments like this. Didn't he know that his value to her was not a quick escape or and adorable transformation when she wasn't feeling herself? It was him. Just him. Her brother. She should say so. Shiraz leaned around the pretty princess she was finally getting to hold again and loudly asked.

"No judgement but...well, actually *a lot of judgement,* because this is particularly important to me. Please promise me you never made out with a baby toucan."

Xinyi laughed even louder, Sweetums let out a scream that might have been agreement, even Makoa laughed.

"I don't have to kiss someone to take on their form," he bit out. "I never made out with your brother."

Shiraz laughed. "Do you know, my question was *all* about the toucan. You wouldn't be the first person both Ethan and I made out with."

Xinyi jerked around to stare at Shiraz incredulously.

"What? I didn't know they'd kissed when I kissed her. You couldn't think your cousin marrying was the weirdest thing to go on in our bunch, could you?"

Xinyi sighed. "He was my *adopted* cousin! There is a difference."

"Not a big one," Makoa pointed out.

"Face it, you're as weird and scummy as us, *princess trouble.* Isn't that right, Sweetums?"

The monkey screeched definitively and gripped onto Shiraz's hand at Xinyi's waist with her tiny fingers.

"When did you even meet a pegasus?" Makoa had never used this form before.

"Dashiel?" Makoa's voice turned smug. "Oh, well, I never told you because I didn't want you to be upset with yourself."

"When?" Shiraz growled.

"Right after we met at the river. There was a whole herd of them in town."

"Of course there were." Shiraz rolled her eyes. That was just her luck.

Her luck when she was alone anyway. She should probably stick with these guys.

The wind blowing against her felt so good, and her arm around Xinyi felt even better, and her brother was here, and even the monkey. Right now, life was pretty incredible. Off in the distance over the mountains, she saw a flash of light and color.

"Look," she called out. "A *triple* rainbow."

Xinyi and Makoa made awed noises, the monkey seemed unimpressed, but Shiraz waited. When Xinyi looked over her shoulder to praise Shiraz for embracing the moment, Shiraz grinned.

"Beat ya!"

No Bet

"Feels sort of like we're ending this adventure right where we started," Shiraz said a day later. The River Serpent had brought them back down the Nanghi river without incident once they took a few back roads and avoided a particular temple on foot and made some fast patch repairs in a cave. "But you were right, you were able to get your greatest treasure back. I stand corrected."

She had offered to escort Xinyi back to the palace, make sure she got inside safely, but Xinyi had yet to answer that. Yet to say anything. As they traveled, both Makoa and Shiraz had admitted to admiration for her gambit. Shiraz said if more women were willing to be double dealing scum, the whole world would be theirs for the taking, *"Not that any of us want the whole world." She rolled her shoulders. "Sounds like a lot of work."*

The trouble was, on the river, facing near certain death, being chased by one magic creature after the next, Xinyi had felt excited, adventurous, and brave. She'd felt alive as she never had before. Bold even.

But now, standing on the same ground along the river where four days ago she'd blundered around the market trying to find the lowest of scum, she felt her shoulders stiffening. She felt her fear of being a burden settle around her shoulders.

She had something to ask, but she didn't know how. Didn't know if they would want her, or if she would be a burden. And it would hurt her more to know definitively. She was making a habit of not trying to know things. She had not asked Shiraz to find out if the elves were her family, nor opened the little pouch Daiyu had dropped in her bag as they escaped. She wasn't ready.

"I think Sweetums wants to stay with you, if you don't mind." Shiraz let the monkey play nibble at her finger. "She's fallen in love with the sweet princess."

"Just her?" an old woman's voice interrupted.

Floating on the river, in the same little boat from four days ago, were the fruit traders. How she wished she knew their names. It felt rude to ask now.

"Of course not," Shiraz answered playfully. "She's left a trail of broken hearts down two rivers. And naturally I'll take my own broken heart with me when I leave."

Xinyi examined her face. Was that more of the constant flirtation this woman spewed like her former cellmate spewed lava? Or was there anything serious to it? Not that she thought Shiraz should be in love with her. Of course not, but...perhaps she felt some special interest. In knowing her more. Or in having her along on her adventures.

"Taking anything else with you?" the old man inquired.

"Anything I can get my hands on. You have an offer for me?"

The man shook his head. "If you ask me, you're taking a better attitude."

"That I can recall, no one did ask you." Shiraz stuck out her tongue.

The old man chuckled. "There she is." He winked.

"Glad you're all back safely," the woman beside him said.

Xinyi opened her mouth to thank the for their help, to beg forgiveness for having forgotten their names, but the pair smiled, and their eyes flashed with bright purple and turquoise lights.

"Thank you for the offering, author," the woman said, and they vanished. Boat and all.

Makoa was the first to break the silence. He burst out laughing. "Trickster spirits, informal gods, or river nymphs?" Makoa asked.

"Nuan and Feng," Xinyi answered in awe.

"Eh," Shiraz shrugged, smirking at Xinyi. "My bet is they were merely the author's tools. Isn't that so, *trouble*? You had to get your adventure started somehow."

It was pure flirtation, and Xinyi loved it, but it also annoyed her right out of her nerves.

"How am I trouble? I've lived here for years without causing any trouble. I lived with Wei's family and didn't cause any trouble. *Mostly.*" She hadn't meant to say that last bit aloud. Shiraz smirked. "Even if I wasn't with you, you'd be in trouble. The elf king was after you and Makoa. The elf prince is your friend. As is the dragon you kissed—"

Shiraz reached out her fingers stopping just short of Xinyi's lips. "It wasn't an insult," she said softly. "I enjoy every second of the trouble you bring. Before you came along, I was so...*bored*. Stuck in my head and forgetting why I do all of this. But the trickster was right, you woke me up, princess sweet. I thank you." She paused and her smile transformed her face, to a glorious—inspiring thing. "I may even go seeking some more trouble now."

Xinyi felt a sweet, tangy urge rush over her. *The author's tools,* Shiraz had said, *just a way to start the adventure.* As if Xinyi was not just a trouble magnet, but its creator. As if this whole adventure had been her doing. And she just hadn't known how to make it happen.

Well, that wasn't true anymore. She was done wishing and waiting on twitchy fingers.

Xinyi smiled coyly. "So take me with you, and I'll attract all the trouble you want."

Shiraz shook her head slowly.

Xinyi moved around her, talking to Makoa, in the form of a pale woman of middling years and dark hair. "I promised to help you break your curse, and we've barely even started trying," Xinyi enticed.

"You don't want to come with us," Shiraz persisted. "You think you do because it was fun, and we got away without any real harm. But it doesn't always go that way. There are disappointments. I was briefly in jail. Makoa is cursed! You're looking for fun adventures, with double rainbows and lots of inspiration."

"You don't know what I'm looking for." Xinyi stomped a foot and the young monkey on her shoulder stomped too.

"Alright," Shiraz asked softly. "What are you looking for?"

Xinyi pulled in a deep breath, staring at Shiraz. "Nothing." She let the word hang in the air between them.

Shiraz was trying to do the mature thing and not beg Xinyi to stay with her. Trying to enjoy what they had and ask nothing more. But here was the most beautiful not-princess in the world staring into her eyes with that one word hanging between them. It could mean anything.

Shiraz could barely breathe, waiting. *Wanting* and waiting. She'd never been any good at waiting. She was going to speak. Going—

"I wasn't looking for anything at all. I was happy," Xinyi explained with sparkling, tempting eyes. "I fully intended to find my treasure and resume my life just as it was, writing stories, drinking tea, never leaving this village. But...it is as if I went out for my usual evening walk and suddenly the sky was transformed to a thing of magic with colorful lights and wondrous, *adventurous* promise. You came upon me so shocking and lovely and changed my whole prospective. I wasn't looking for anything. But I found you. And now I can't imagine not searching for you for the rest of my life if I let you leave without me. Take me anywhere you're going. Into any danger you face. That's where I need to be."

This was the part where the hero kissed the princess, or it would be in the stories Shiraz read. But she wasn't moving. The princess had shattered her brain, or at the very least her tongue. Having known her for years, Makoa understood what chaotic bursts of wonder and disbelief must be going on inside of Shiraz.

She could shout out her self confidence all day every day. But inside she was always waiting to be on her own again. And here was this woman who Shiraz was already obsessed with declaring her own interests. She might even have trouble believing it.

Shiraz nodded her head; it was tiny and tight and fearful, but her voice emerged. "If you like."

Xinyi threw her arms around Shiraz and kissed her cheek. She leaped back. "I'm going to tell the others, and leave them what's written of my manuscript, and get some clothes. Maybe give them a communication orb, and…I'll be back. Wait for me. You will, won't you?"

Shiraz nodded. That seemed to be all she could do. The princess spun around and immediately tripped.

Shiraz started forward to help her, but Xinyi was already up and running, laughing as she went. "I'm fine. Wait for me!"

Makoa stepped forward, wrapping an arm around Shiraz's shoulder. She leaned her head into his. "Should we take off, leave her behind?" Makoa teased.

Shiraz shook her head, laughing hoarsely. When she spoke, it sounded teary. "Eventually it's going to annoy me that I did what Elder Trent wanted." She was clearly trying to distract from how moved she was by Xinyi's declaration. But really, enough was enough.

"Shiraz," he said with an annoyed sigh, "I don't mean to belittle your sad, traumatic childhood."

"Mm-hmm. But you're going to?"

"Yep. I think maybe Elder Trent would have disapproved of you helping Xinyi, even though it was done without compensation. And that perhaps you give him more of your thoughts than he deserves."

Shiraz stuck out her tongue. "Maybe."

Makoa smirked at her, addressing more real, pressing concerns. "How's the tattoo looking?"

Shiraz held up her arm. "Fully gone. Apparently your *darling*," she teased what Makoa had called Aiattaua as they fled, "can preform the spell at a distance."

They'd used one of the many crystal balls Shiraz took from the witch's home to contact him as they made their way back to Hi'mau. Since Felicia had managed to make good an escape, severely injuring at least ten elf guards and two elf children, it seemed prudent to remove her mode of tracking.

"Are you sure you want to leave? We haven't gotten the last spell for the ship."

Shiraz shrugged. "It's safer to get on the move. I'm sure there is another witch out there who can do it for me."

"Yes, but you have Felicia's sword. The spell is more important than ever; she will be coming after us."

Shiraz bobbed her head sideways. "She'll have to catch up to us first. And...she doesn't know the half of what our ship can do. And..." she broke off, a misty smile settling over her features. "Now, with Xinyi coming with us..." she giggled, "we've got a bad luck curse to throw at her." A few moments passed silently before Shiraz's voice emerged again, with her real, deeper thoughts. "Do you think Xinyi was talking to both of us? Or is she madly in love with me?" she whispered hopefully.

"Definitely the first one."

"She kissed me first," Shiraz pointed out.

"Eh, bet she'll kiss me eventually. And it won't be the first time we've kissed the same girl."

Shiraz slowly shook her head. "No bet."

An Epilogue in Two Touching Scenes, And a Visit from the Tax Woman

1:

"Shiraz?"

Shiraz looked up from her work, moving most of her things up on deck to give Xinyi personal space. The ship wasn't all that big. Xinyi wanted to come along, but that didn't mean she'd considered what it was to share space with both Shiraz and Makoa. There were times when they separated merely because they were getting on each other's nerves. So Shiraz was making this space more suited to Xinyi. She'd moved a few of her own things to give Xinyi room, changed the bed clothes, and was setting out a basket of her favorite fruit under a stack of books Shiraz thought she might like.

"Who's asking?" Shiraz demanded of the bird on the second step down into the lower deck, a kookaburra she thought.

It paced back and forth. "You are very suspicious. I am here for the order of Battle Born, with a gift from a loved one."

Shiraz sat on the edge of the bed, a few books hanging limply from her hand. "Noam?" she asked.

The bird shook her head. "No. Your mother. It has taken some time; it was not an immediate wish to begin with, intended for once you knew yourself. But the Battle Born who was meant to bless her wishes died."

"I am sorry," Shiraz interjected. "About your sister."

"Thank you," the kookaburra replied. "There was some strife among our people and a great deal of pain. But we are recovering." She hopped closer. "You are a difficult woman to locate."

"Mom." Shiraz smiled and lay down the books. That had been years, so many years. "She blessed me enough in life. She should not have spent her wishes on me."

The bird let out a soft coo and a puff of feathers filled the air. When they cleared, a short woman sat on the stairs in a gown of black and a matching turban concealing her hair. She settled her elbows on her knees and her chin on the backs of her hands and smiled at Shiraz.

"She did not wish you blessings because she thought your life lacking, but because she wanted you to feel her love always."

"But that is just it," Shiraz whispered. Her eyes were teary for the second time today, but it was a lovely feeling. Almost like her mother was here with her. She reached into the basket beside her and offered a fruit to the woman. "There are things I have resented or regretted. But I already do feel her love. The things she taught me, and the way she loved me, that is what sustains me when I am faced with disappointment or sorrow."

"Good. Then her gift will be like any other you had in her life. An extension of her love." The fairy popped her brows. She bit into the fruit and made a hum of enjoyment.

"I do so like your mother's children. It is a pleasure to bless her wishes."

"You...you have met *others*?"

"I have. But this visit is about her brave, outspoken, broad hearted, trouble magnet Shiraz. That is how she thought of you. Now, the complication that leads to you seeing me is this: she wished you love. But you have found that all on your own. So, if you are not in objection, I thought to give you room for your love to grow. And perhaps return one loved object that you had lost."

Shiraz nodded, overcome. She didn't know how she could be expected to refuse any gift from her mother. She wanted to ask about her brothers, ask which one the fairy had met. But the room filled with soft blue light like the spray of the sea. Shiraz shut her eyes and felt as though she was curled up in her mother's arms as she recited poetry.

> *Far away across the sea*
> *My love has gone away*
> *But in the crash of every wave*
> *Her love returns to me.*
> *Far away across the sea*
> *My love has gone to stay*
> *But every kiss she ever gave*
> *Lives in my memory.*
> *Far away across the sea*
> *Our souls will meet one day*
> *And every joy our hearts might crave*
> *Will live with us eternally.*

When Shiraz opened her eyes, the woman was gone, but her gift was all around. The room was more than double the size it had been, with room enough for her, Xinyi, Makoa and the monkey! No dividers between them, but they could give each other privacy when needed. But better than any of that, the walls had been transformed into shelves. Many had books lined up on them already, but most were empty. Room for her love to grow! She stood, spinning around and around in awe. Then she spotted it. Across the room, leaning casually against the back of a shelf as if its pages had never been ripped out and burned in front of her eyes, was the Book of Anolani. Shiraz lifted the copy reverently and pressed it to her heart.

2:

"Ooh! We should go to Ayowi and get sweetballs," Xinyi suggested as the boat moved down the Nanghi river towards the sea.

"I can see you will be a very demanding guest," Shiraz teased.

"Guest! I am a member of the crew and I vote we go try sweet balls."

"Seconded!" Makoa shouted from the stern where he was steering.

"Eeeeh!" Sweetums made both her agreement and her certainty that she too was a member of the crew known.

Shiraz was hiding her grin, pretending to be annoyed.

All of the other widows had come with Xinyi to the docks. They hadn't wanted to let her go and insisted on examining the vessel and its crew themselves to be sure she would be safe. It had surprised Xinyi to see how easily Shiraz got along with them. She even took Yinuo aside to give her suggestions to stay safe from her father and wrote a letter to Hua introducing them.

"Sure, ogres eat human, but...only bad ones, and once they're dead. Otherwise, they really are the sweetest creatures alive."

Qiu, overhearing, nodded and said, "Animals eat meat. We eat animals, big animals eat small animals. Ogres are bigger than us, so we're meat for them.

"Very clever. Here, I have something for you." Shiraz handed off the last of the candy Hua gave her.

It was sweet. But Shiraz liked to pretend she wasn't sweet. "I'll consider stopping in Ayowi, but…only for an extra percent of your next adventure story," Shiraz teased heading below deck.

"You already demanded one hundred percent." Xinyi trailed her down the stairs. She had seen the transformation already, and they had all spotted the new name on the hull: *The Chaos Dragon.* As well as the change to Shiraz's bracelet. It now had two snake heads, with two sets of gem eyes begging to be pressed, magic longing to be tested.

But Shiraz was being overly cautious and refusing to immediately push the new gems and see what the ship could do. She wanted to find a witch to examine it first. *Javajin.*

"There isn't any more," Xinyi pointed out.

"That's what you think," Shiraz said, flirtatiously. But she glanced back and her tone became concerned. "Hey, you okay?"

"You're faster than me," Xinyi blurted out, in much the same way as she'd blurted out that she wanted to go with them this morning.

"It's the pants, more range of motion. But let me experiment. I can come up with something more mobi—"

"That isn't what I mean. Be quiet. I don't want…that is I think you might have taken the wrong impression, because I flirted with you."

"Does it make you uncomfortable when I flirt?" Shiraz asked softly.

"No." Xinyi heard the words come out sharply, nearly followed up with *be quiet* again. Though she had wanted Shiraz to talk just then. "I like flirting with you. I mean sometimes it makes me uncomfortable, but not in a bad way, in a this is new way. And I am enjoying getting to know you, and feeling closer to you, *slowly*. I didn't want you to get the wrong idea about what I want...after what I said earlier."

"You're saying a lot, and I think I follow, but to be clear, are you saying you like flirting, but you worry that because you wanted to come along, I will think that, after only four days and without any specific indication of interest, you're in love with me and rush you into some sort of physical intimacy?"

Well, that was blunt. Xinyi nodded.

"Alright, glad we cleared that up. I won't. I'm not nearly as fast as you think I am."

Xinyi raised a brow tempted to point out that she'd seen Shiraz kissing the blue woman in the Grotto. But Shiraz broke into a small grin, like she could read Xinyi's thoughts.

"Well," she said playfully. "I can be. But...not when it's...important," she whispered. And she seemed to be blushing. Xinyi was afraid she would not say more. Then she smiled, slow, and smug, and sultry. "So what would *you desire*?" The words stopped Xinyi's heart. "How would you want someone to *show you* they want to, *slowly,* grow closer to you?"

Xinyi couldn't form words.

"Do you want to think about it? Or would you prefer to never consider something like that with me?" Shiraz paused.

"No...I..." Xinyi needed to say that she wouldn't have brought it up at all if it weren't something she wanted. She just didn't want to rush ahead of herself. Words piled up on her tongue, longing to be spoken, but too heavy to be voiced. But Shiraz was always surprising her with her consideration, and Xinyi needed to try to give that back. "I like you," she said carefully. "I've enjoyed our wild moments together and our flirting, and I do feel...*pulled* to you. *Constantly.* But...these past few days, I've felt like one of my characters. And my characters always fall in love. Not that I'm saying *I am.* Or not that I'm not! I just...don't know exactly what's real and what is part of the adventure."

"I suppose I would like to know that as well." Shiraz drew in a breath, her cheeks growing pinker as she battled what looked like shyness. "If you decide what you feel is friendship, I will treasure a platonic friendship with you, *Xinyi*." She said her name so delicately, as if it was precious to her. "I will back off with the flirting, even though it is *very* fun."

She said it with such gentle intensity that Xinyi felt moved and seen. It eased a great deal of her tension. "I just want time to know if it's all the excitement blending in together, or if it is something more."

"Just so you have all the information while you're making your decision, as far as my feelings go, I know what's real. And I desire *any level* of intimacy with you that you desire as well."

Xinyi drew in a deep breath, trying to be as forthright as Shiraz, though asking for what she wanted had never been her talent. "I like holding your hand. And flirting with you. And—" She broke off awkwardly. "It's silly.

"Silly can be very good," Shiraz pressed.

"This. Talking like this, alone with you sharing things. This feels very intimate."

"It does, doesn't it? Like when we were alone in the jungle, or when I helped you dress. We felt very connected, without ever touching. I don't connect like that often."

"Oh, dancing!" Xinyi exclaimed, then the very reason it had come to her head flew through her mind and she felt like a terrible person. "But you don't like dancing."

Shiraz stared at her for a long while, the two of them quiet and connected. "Maybe I should try again."

"Why? You don't like it." Xinyi shook her head.

"One, everything is different with you." The world held still. "Two, I meant it when I said I wanted *any* intimacy you desire as well. And—

"C," Xinyi provided with a lightness in her chest so lovely it made her want to rush ahead.

Shiraz's lips lifted and her eyes crinkled and she looked heart stopping beautiful. Xinyi worried she was dreaming, but Shiraz wasn't someone she could dream up.

"C," Shiraz agreed. "No one danced on Glen Harrow. When I left, I rushed out to do all the things I hadn't been allowed, but when I danced, people laughed. They made me feel like that little girl who never fit. So I stopped trying."

"You shouldn't do something that makes you feel that way," Xinyi rushed out, horrified to have even suggested it. "We were talking about things to feel close, not—"

"*Xinyi,*" Shiraz said softly, her name like poetry on the other woman's lips. "You aren't listening. That isn't like you. Are you nervous?" She stretched out a hand, palm up. "You make me nervous. Would you hold my hand?"

It took a moment, but Xinyi rested her hand against Shiraz's, their fingers knitted together, and her breath fell softer than before.

"*Everything* is different with you. Maybe all I needed was a chance to find someone I wanted to dance with. And anyway," she laughed.

"Dancing with you would have been a dream come true to that steadfast girl. She would have begged for the mockery for a chance to hold someone like you near."

The words sat between them, setting Xinyi's being on fire as though she was the sun. And she must be, as Shiraz was turning red from the intensity of Xinyi's light.

"Come on." Shiraz tugged her back towards the stairs. "We don't have to decide anything now. Read with me in the moonlight?" she asked. "I want you to hear the story that made me want to travel the world."

Xinyi followed her up the stairs, their hands still clasped together.

C:

"Look what I found!" Shiraz shouted, overly excited for Ristsynka's only port town where they were docked. There wasn't much here. Ristsynka was a mountain nation; most of its inhabitants lived on the high, snowy cliffs shadowing this dock. The market generally held little other than necessities, but they'd needed to get supplies before setting out on the open sea. The ship was mostly loaded now, and Makoa was just waiting for the women to return from some "fun" shopping. Shiraz made her way to the ship, bent forward under the weight of a crate over half the length of her body.

Makoa moved to assist her in the body of a local man who was currently tied up behind some bushes on the dock. It seemed a prudent precaution; this was one of the strictest and most militarized cities they frequented. Since Xinyi joined them, they had experienced many needs for fast get aways, but nothing so dramatic as the trip on the Nanghi river. They had all learned things there that had neither been reconciled with nor spoken about.

Shiraz had not brought up her brother Ethan. But she, like Makoa, tended to ignore things until they knew how they wanted to feel about them. Makoa helped lift the crate. It was lighter than expected but awkward. He set it under the canopy on deck and Shiraz threw back the lid with a flourish to reveal a yellow swash of fur.

"Shiraz, you're constantly hot, what do you need with fur?" he asked. She wasn't even wearing a heavy coat, her arms bare in the snow.

"Not just any fur, Shadowien Elk fur, and look," she nearly squealed with glee. Pulling up the first fur, she revealed several more, each one in a different color, all bright and dramatic. "I spent *so much money*, but it's worth it. Elder Trent will *hate* these!"

Makoa laughed. "Do you know, in regard to your commitment to getting the *pettiest* of vengeance, you really are the most steadfast woman I've ever met."

Shiraz threw her arm around the shorter man and smacked a kiss on his cheek. "Thank you." She squeezed him and immediately began putting away the furs. "Is Xinyi back?"

"You separated? Again?" he demanded.

"Eh, she'll be fine. It's the port I'm worried about. What do you think she'll do, wake an ancient snow spirit?"

Makoa shook his head. Xinyi was a fun addition to their crew. She kept them on their toes.

"Do you go by Makoa?" A woman stepped dubiously onto the deck without invitation. She took two cautious steps forward before looking around again and blowing out a frustrated breath. Having passed through the illusion spell, she stomped forward.

She did not look like a local, dressed as she was for the dead of winter when it was early spring. Also her skin was much darker than the locals who rarely saw the sun, and her neat bun, the glasses at the end of her nose, and the journal and pen in her hands made her look like a woman of work who were few and far between in Ristsynka.

"I do." Makoa answered the oddly phrased inquiry with suspicion.

"Excellent. You're my seventh. To verify, you were cursed approximately fifteen years ago, to—"

"Never hold my true form, nor speak my name until I find a true love and receive a true love's kiss," Makoa interrupted to finish the question for their very precise guest.

Shiraz moved to stand at Makoa's shoulder with a hand on the short sword she had stolen from Felicia.

"Excellent. I'll take that as a yes," the woman said brusquely. Shiraz and Makoa exchanged smirks. Of late, no one responded with much sympathy to Makoa's curse.

"I'm Larissa. My mother was Narissa, the witch who cursed you. Do you happen to know why you were cursed?"

Makoa was momentarily too flummoxed to speak. Was she here to break the spell? Was this precise, unfeeling woman meant to be his true love? Would her kiss break the spell? Was the spell just a way to marry off the woman's cranky daughter?

"He was a part of a crew running a con which led to him leaving his bride at the alter, saying he didn't think theirs was *true love*," Shiraz answered for Makoa.

"You know?" Makoa shouted, far more startled by Shiraz knowing exactly who he was than he was by the stranger in front of them.

"I was there," Shiraz replied in an equally incredulous tone. "You hired me to rob the guests, remember?"

"I wasn't cursed at the wedding."

"With the wording, it stood to reason that was why."

"You've known who I was this whole time?"

"You thought I didn't?" Shiraz demanded.

"You never said a thing!"

"I didn't think you wanted me to," Shiraz shouted back.

"If you wouldn't mind," the stranger tried fruitlessly to get their attention.

"How long have you known?"

"Since our encounter at the river. I mean I didn't know right away, but by the end of the night, I'd put two and two together and got seven."

"Four," Larissa corrected between her teeth.

"You knew then? But...I invited you to go with me and you said no. You didn't seem to trust me."

"Excuse me," Larissa interjected and was ignored.

"Of course I didn't *trust* you. You were a criminal who used my pickpocketing as a way to get away with a much bigger score. I was run out of town because of you!"

Makoa chuckled softly, more amused by the memory than apologetic.

"I beg your pardon."

He smiled sheepishly. "I didn't think you'd put that together."

"If I could say my piece." The woman wouldn't stop interjecting.

"I was young, not oblivious," Shiraz snapped.

"EXCUSE ME!" the woman yelled, finally managing to get their attention. She cleared her throat, straightened her collar, and tried again. "I've traveled some way to find you, may I address why?"

Shiraz and Makoa nodded magnanimously. She ought to learn some patience.

"My mother was a complicated woman. By the time she met you, she was…"

"A maniacal power-crazed vigilante," Makoa suggested.

"An uzaok."

"Experiencing senility."

Shiraz snorted. "Sorry."

"Yes, well. She'd been abandoned at her own wedding and related you to that man." She nodded to Makoa. "You are far from her only accidental cursing. I have been seeking out her victims to—"

"Break the curses?" Shiraz and Makoa said in unison, Shiraz sounding as concerned as Makoa felt.

"No!" Larissa snapped, annoyed. "Why does everyone think that?"

"You're her daughter and you—"

"*Witchiness* isn't hereditary! At least not when one isn't perfect Marissa!" She sucked in a deep breath, pushed the glasses up her nose, and when she spoke again it was at a level decimal. "I am chief auditor for the city of Rhyse. I've been forced to take a year off work to settle my mother's affairs, since Marissa is *busy*."

"I'm sorry for your loss." Makoa reached out. The woman took a discomforted step away, looking at him as though curses were catching. As if he'd wanted to touch her either!

"Yes, yes. Very sad. The point is, in her lucid moments, Mother made a list of victims, purposes of spells, how they were made, and even a few reversals." The woman bobbed her head sideways. "Your case is somewhat incomplete."

"Naturally," Makoa observed sarcastically, though he still wasn't sure he wanted to have his curse reversed.

"Her main goal was that you catch some sort of disease."

"I can attest to her success," Shiraz put in playfully.

"Hey, I beat it," Makoa joked, glad for the distraction.

"With a spell, I—"

"Not again!" Larissa yelled. She had a *very* short fuse. "Here." She thrust out a paper. "The spell. If you want it broken, I suggest you find a witch."

The woman turned around so sharply her long coat slapped both Makoa and Shiraz in the legs. She marched away muttering about sloppy, rude, piratic looking people who ought to stay cursed.

"Should I chase her down and ask if the perfect Marissa would take your case?" Shiraz asked. Makoa laughed. "Do you think there was an original witch named Issa that started the family line? Ooo! We should introduce her to your friend Henri. Temperament wise, they're well suited."

Makoa laughed hard, nearly cried. The paper the auditor had handed him was crumpled in his fist. He was half tempted to toss it into the bay; that way he didn't have to decide anything.

"You've known all this time, and you never said anything. You never even said my old name," Makoa whispered.

"I didn't know if I should. I thought it might hurt you to hear it. I also wasn't sure that even was your real name. You were running a con at the time, remember? I guess I thought you knew I knew, and you would tell me when you wanted to talk about it." Her arm closed around his shoulder. "Do you want me to say it now?"

Makoa didn't answer, and the moment stretched. He had wanted to hear it in the earlier years. But he began to suspect half of what held him back now was that he didn't want to go back to that man. It didn't feel like him anymore.

"Hello." Xinyi raced onto the deck with a bundle in her arms and pink cheeks. Sweetums was at her shoulder but faced backwards brandishing a knife and screeching. "So I should quickly tell you two things. One, there is a woman who needs passage to Lig're. Since we were headed that way, I negotiated a fair price for the passage."

"Fair better be far more than last time, soft touch." Shiraz still held onto Makoa's shoulders.

"Two, we may need to leave faster than expected."

"What did you do this time?" Shiraz snorted.

"Nothing. I just...didn't know how many people outside of Maltuba knew Maltuban is all."

"They were one of the first nations to trade worldwide." Makoa moved to untie moorings. He'd known the precaution was necessary. How had they wound up with a crew member so trouble prone?

"Well, we were haggling over a price of silk. The man told me I didn't want the swatch I wanted and that I was *clearly poor*. And I said I knew what I wanted, and he was overvaluing his wares." Shiraz chuckled. "Then as I was walking away, without buying anything, I might have muttered **nin oon kaagok uzomoh io ulin paretaq**. And the man apparently knew what that meant and tried to call a guard. I ran. Did you know they have a law against *females* using public profanity?"

"Shiraz has run afoul of it before." Makoa nodded.

"Is that why you were in prison?" Xinyi probed.

"It's a fine." Shiraz was making a point of never answering the whys of how she'd gotten imprisoned. It was a flirtatious game between them. "What a filthy mouth you have, princess trouble," Shiraz said, staring right at the other woman's lips. There were a few beats of silence as Xinyi returned the heated gaze.

"I want to add something to the list," Xinyi blurted out breathlessly.

"Oh?"

She nodded. "Kissing."

"An excellent addition." Shiraz stepped towards Xinyi, but a large suitcase landed between them with a crash. Shiraz looked up and sighed. "Not you."

"I am equally pleased to see you." Larissa stepped onto the ship. "I was given the impression that haste was important."

Rolling her eyes, Shiraz moved around the woman, pulling in the short plank that attached to the docks. There were guards running towards them. Makoa stepped out into the open to wave at the encroaching guard.

"I've got them. Bring my ledger," he called out. The men moved to obey long enough for the boat to move away from the dock. But having spotted the bound man identical to Makoa, they rushed towards them once more.

Shiraz threw some coin onto the dock as the boat moved away. "Thanks for the hospitality," Shiraz called out sweetly. "That should cover the fine."

"Why are you being nice to them? You're a grouch." Xinyi glared.

"When I'm a grouch, you're nice. When you're one, I'm nice. We can't both be grouches at the same time."

Xinyi had a hand on her hip and looked about ready to take kissing off her list. But Shiraz stepped forward and nipped the quickest of kisses on the other woman's lips.

"I can do better later, but...I've been wanting to do that since I first saw you at the river market."

Xinyi's eyes flared wide. "Really?"

"Oh, absolutely. And you taste even sweeter than I thought."

"Yes, yes. Your love is amazing and wildly important," Larissa interrupted. She stood not one foot from them, rolling her eyes at all the lovey dovey nonsense. "But is there a place to sit?"

Makoa laughed. Lig're was at minimum a week-long journey; this should be interesting. He'd have a few more chances to ask the woman about her mother, and her family, and think about what he wanted to do with the paper in his hand.

Sighing Shiraz looked across the deck at Makoa. Her expression said clearly *how did we get ourselves into this?* Then her eyes shifted down to his hand and she smiled softly. Whatever he wanted to do, she would understand and they would be together.

"Shouldn't someone stow my bags?" Larissa kept on. "Where will I bunk? I'd like to see my accommodations. For as much as I am paying, that seems reasonable."

"You can keep your money and swim back to shore for all I care," Shiraz replied. "This isn't a pleasure cruise—"

"Nope," Xinyi interjected, her bright tone balancing Shiraz's rudeness, a playful act of vengeance. She was developing quite the playful side. "It's the worlds only floating library and smuggling vessel."

"That last bit is meant to be a *secret*," Shiraz remarked.

Xinyi ignored her. "Welcome aboard *The Chaos Dragon!*"

The…beginning

Dalila Caryn is the author of fantasy novels in The Forgotten Sister series, the In The Shadow of a Monster trilogy, and the Merely Mortal Men Myths. She loves reading, nature, pie, coffee and a lot of alone time. She is currently attempting to summon an asteroid to destroy the planet. Any help would be welcomed.

Find out more at DalilaCaryn.com.

Cover art and interior illustrations by Yenthe Joline.